MELTING POTS AND TRIBAL ENCLAVES

TERRY MORGAN

FriesenPress
One Printers Way
Altona, MB R0G 0B0
Canada

www.friesenpress.com

First Edition — 2022

ISBN
978-1-03-913881-0 (Hardcover)
978-1-03-913880-3 (Paperback)
978-1-03-913882-7 (eBook)

1. FICTION, ROMANCE, MULTICULTURAL & INTERRACIAL

Distributed to the trade by The Ingram Book Company

MELTING POTS AND TRIBAL ENCLAVES

Acknowledgements

Getting this novel published was an adventure. I don't type and I have no computer skills. The entire novel was hand written. But when I finished writing it I wanted to get it published (ego). First, I had to find a typist. I tried a number of things without success. Then someone suggested Kijiji. I was very lucky to find a wonderful woman, Daniela Karageorgos, who lives in Oakville. I would wrap sections of the novel in brown paper and send them off in the mail from Hamilton. Daniela would send me the typed text by email. I do have a printer and I was able to print off each section. A few times the mail was late and I feared I had lost sections of the novel because I had no copies.

My mind and brain are frozen in the 1960s. I thought I would wrap my typed copy of the novel in brown paper and send it off to Friesen Press. The publisher would make some minor changes and print the novel. I had a lot to learn. The novel had to be edited. The anonymous editor had some great suggestions. But I was running out of steam. And everything would be done by computer.

That's when my son, Derek, came to rescue me and my project. He took over all the steps in communicating with Friesen Press. (He also had some strong opinions about my writing). The coordinator at Friesen Press, Leanne Janzen, kept the process going by offering encouragement and deadlines.

It took a team effort to get the scribbles of an old man turned into a book. So, at 82, I have my first published novel. Look out Margaret Atwood!

Hamilton - The Golden Age

The Golden Age for Hamilton began after World War II. When the necessary constraints that came with an all-out war were lifted, the great industrial city on the bay was ready for a new economy. Hamilton was ideally located for industry. Hamilton Bay was a beautifully sheltered body of water—deep and placid—and never had the turbulence Lake Ontario occasionally had. A channel between Lake Ontario and Hamilton Bay allowed lake freighters to enter the bay and sail to the numerous piers along the industrial waterfront. The great steel mills had their iron ore from Minnesota and their coal from Pennsylvania. The magnificent Great Lakes were the transportation system for the industries and commerce of seven American states and Ontario. The lakes also provided fresh water for growing cities, cheap transportation, abundant raw materials, extensive waterfront, and accessible fresh water. It was an industrial planner's dream.

Starting in the summer of 1945, soldiers, sailors, and airmen began returning home. There had been a huge victory parade to Civic Stadium. Red, white, and blue decorations could be seen everywhere. It was a time of almost delirious happiness now that the war in Europe was over. There was happiness for all, except for the families that had lost loved ones. Canada had made great human sacrifices again, just as in World War I. But it was a time of optimism, of looking forward.

As individual servicemen returned home, they were greeted by homes decorated with bunting and smiling families and neighbours. They were heroes home from the war. The welcoming dinners, however, were straitened. Canada was still on rations and would be for another four or five years. Children looked up to these warriors with worship in their eyes. More importantly, young ladies fell in love quickly and passionately. Some of the servicemen were tempted to take advantage of the willing young ladies, but they remembered they had wives left in the British Isles and Holland. Boatloads of war brides would be coming. The virility of Canadian troops was demonstrated by the number of children and pregnant wives. They came down the gang planks in Halifax wondering what they had gotten themselves into. Later, the children of servicemen would marvel that their fathers wouldn't talk about the war. Many of them had seen the horrors of modern weapons. They didn't want to remember the sight of corpses and body parts. They didn't want to remember the skeletal civilians. They didn't want to think about how the bestial nature of man could be unleashed. But a few wanted to conceal their sexual adventures. War and the fear of death lead to sexual promiscuity. The young men from Hamilton who volunteered to fight had been raised in the sexual strictures of churches—Protestant and Catholic. Most of the eighteen- and nineteen-year-olds who left for Europe were virgins. Not many were when they returned. They certainly didn't want their new wives to know about one-night stands, brothels, or bouts with VD. It was time to move on.

During the war, all power flowed to Ottawa. Although democratic institutions still functioned symbolically in Britain, America, and Canada, war led to totalitarianism. Citizens couldn't buy a car or tires for one they owned. Gasoline was strictly rationed. Workers couldn't leave their jobs and travel was restricted. If you were a Canadian of Japanese descent, you were moved from the West Coast to lumber camps across the country. Your property was confiscated, but you were allowed one suitcase for your possessions. To prove that these actions were not based on skin colour, the government imprisoned Canadian citizens of German and Italian descent as well. Canadians were fighting for freedom in Europe and in Asia, but losing it at home.

The government of Canada in World War I made a shambles of planning for the post-war period. Some sixty-two thousand Canadian troops were killed. Those who returned had no jobs and some had to join bread lines. The veterans with physical wounds got sympathy; those with psychological wounds got contempt. This time, the government was determined to do better. As early as 1943, bureaucrats were planning programs for veterans. There was a vast network of grants and loans. The most successful program was the free education plan. Veterans who could never have afforded a university education were enrolled with students five, ten, or more years younger. It was a very interesting mix of life experiences. From this plan, hundreds of doctors, lawyers, engineers, teachers, and businessmen were educated. These grads helped erect the social infrastructure for the following decades.

The Liberal government of Mackenzie King knew what the Liberal government of Wilfred Laurier knew: Canada must have immigrants. All signs pointed to an economic boom after the war. This growth economy could only be maintained and fueled by immigration. Europe was a wasteland. It is estimated that fifty million people had been killed and fifty million were refugees. The Minister of Immigration got the legislation and infrastructure in place to welcome newcomers. In theory, there was a quota system for European countries. As it turned out, the bulk of immigration came from the British Isles and Italy. Great Britain had fought for six years and didn't have a penny in the treasury. In fact, Britain owed billions to the United States, India, and Canada. The British had reached their breaking point. The glory of war under Churchill was replaced by the socialism of Clement Attlee. Rationing would continue indefinitely. Attlee brought in reforms that would improve the country in the long run, but in the short run, citizens suffered with little money and few consumer goods. For many, it was time to find a better place.

Immigration from Italy was another matter. If Britain suffered from rationing, Italy endured starvation. The poverty in Italy was worse than it had been after World War I. Citizens were literally starving in the streets. Canada had already taken deep breaths and accepted, actually vigorously recruited, immigrants from Poland, Galicia, and Ukraine to fill the Prairies before the Americans could take over the West. Canadians of English heritage wanted the Brits to come over, or the Dutch, but they weren't so sure about the Italians. During the next decade, Canada opened its doors to millions of immigrants and refugees. It was a mix of pragmatism and humanitarianism. Welcoming refugees might be a way to seek redemption after refusing entry to Jews fleeing Hitler. Some of those refused entry ended up in death camps.

Hamilton became a boom town. During the war, citizens had been forced to save. There was nothing to buy. Those who thought of themselves as patriots bought war bonds. Others stashed money in savings accounts. Now it was time to buy. The dam had burst—new cars, refrigerators, furnaces, and a million other things. The factories couldn't keep up. Then what some sociologists think was the most significant change in society began—the suburbs. Large tracts of land around Hamilton were being developed. Developers and farmers were feverish with plans. With their regular paychecks, workers could now buy a home on a nice lot, build fences in cooperation with their neighbours and start families. Those building roads and schools tried to keep up with demand. Those who needed jobs could walk from east to west along the industrial corridor of Burlington Street and weigh the advantages of two or three job offers. Everything was coming up roses. Hamilton was Utopia. Well, no. Civilizations don't work that way. Good things happen, bad things happen. There is progress. There is regression. There are problems that never go away.

Hamilton had people living in doorways. Salvation Army workers handed out food and blankets. Criminals remained energetic and creative. Businessmen remembered how to cheat and embezzle. Politicians could be tempted.

The war had been won by incredible sacrifices. The reward of victory was a vibrant economy. Now the New Jerusalem was here. Brothers and Sisters, arm in arm, building a better, more humane society.

The Steel Strike of 1946 revealed that progress is bought at a price. There was a great fissure between conservatives and progressives. The great question in Hamilton was whether or not industrial unions should be recognized. In the United States in the thirties, Franklin Delano Roosevelt had encouraged unions. The AFL-CIO (American Federation of Labor and Congress of Industrial Organizations) had become powerful. In Canada, union organization had been slower. The powerful American unions were prepared to help their little brothers and sisters in Canada. Corporate America supported Corporate Canada (usually their subsidiaries). With the end of the war, the Canadian government ended price controls. The Steel Company of Canada (STELCO) saw a huge windfall profit. They would raise the price of steel and continue to pay their workers war-time wages.

The great industrial battle in Hamilton began. Local 1005 of the American Steel Works had been organized for some time. But the majority of workers resisted. Many of them didn't like the idea of a closed shop. (Unions in Britain and the United States had dealt with that.) Men who hadn't worked for years during the Depression were happy just to have a job. Men who had bought a home and had one or two children could not afford to strike. When 1005 intensified its recruiting program, feelings ran high. Fist fights broke out in the plant. Houses were smeared with oil. Tires were slashed. Neighbours screamed at one another. Negotiations between the company and the union didn't last long. The union wanted a raise of nineteen cents. The company offered five cents. The union leaders knew they had to strike or pack up their tents.

The union declared a strike even though it had signed up only a minority of the workers. The strike would begin at 7 a.m. on July 15, 1946. This date would be a watershed in Canadian union history. The company knew how to deal with strikes. It had the knowledge of countless strikes in the United States and Britain. The company would keep the plant operating and break the union. The company had time to stock up on food and bedding. The workers would stay inside the plant and receive triple wages. The company even built a small airstrip on its vast lands. The company executives knew that most workers had no savings. A two-week strike would ruin most of them. The union counter-attacked. One thousand picketers blocked the main gate. They were joined by strikers from Canadian Westinghouse and Firestone. This would be a battle that would change Canadian society one way or the other. Now World War I strategies of warfare began. The company erected barbed wire fences and security guards patrolled the perimeter. The union brought in tents so that union members could picket night and day. The union set up a cafeteria and began canvassing the community for cash and food donations. These strikes would involve all the citizens of Hamilton, and lines were being drawn. The word frequently heard in Hamilton now was "scab." The workers who stayed in the plant were "scabs." The scabs kept the plant running on a limited basis. If they had wives, children, and homes, they became increasingly apprehensive. Theoretical debate about the role of unions could quickly turn to violence. A striker who, in two weeks, has run out of food for his family is a volatile individual. This was a civil war—brother against brother, neighbour against neighbour. There were real skirmishes during the strike. The pickets rushed to the railway gate when management tried to get a train loaded with steel out. Bricks flew back and forth between inside workers and the strikers. That train was stopped, as was a later train trying to get in. The train conductor, fearing for his life and perhaps seeing the justice of the workers' cause, put the train into reverse and headed home.

When the scabs began to run low on food, the company brought supplies in across the bay. The union responded by acquiring a speed boat to intercept the supply vessels. It was like a replay of the War of 1812 on the Great Lakes. For some of the strikers, these events were great adventures. Most of the time, the workers inside the plant and the strikers were bored to death. The union leaders organized baseball games, penny Bingos, dances where the admission was a food contribution. But the truth was that the strikers were suffering. In these circumstances, the union leaders had to keep the members united. As days passed, that got harder and harder. The leaders had to face a daily barrage of second-guessing. They got very little sleep. Even their wives and children were sour towards them some days.

The strike became a textbook example of ideological conflict—although textbooks don't always capture the intricacies and contradictions. If there could be a clear-cut example of conservative vs. progressive, right wing vs. left wing, capitalism vs. socialism, corporate greed vs. worker dignity, two political giants in Hamilton embodied these political differences. The conservatives were represented by Nora Frances Henderson, the progressives by Sam Lawrence. It's indicative of the importance of immigration in Canada and of the British connection that both Nora Frances Henderson and Sam Lawrence were born in England.

Nora Frances Henderson was thirteen when she came with her family to Winona, Ontario. In 1921, she became a reporter and then later a feature writer for the Hamilton Herald. Her columns were widely read and her outspoken opinions gained a wide following (especially among women). At her urging, four women were appointed to the board of directors of the Hamilton General Hospital. She herself ran for alderman in 1931 and was elected. The municipal system in Hamilton had one alderman for each ward, four controllers elected city-wide, and the mayor. In 1934, Henderson became the first female controller. She served on a multitude of boards and committees, and she had the satisfaction of seeing many more women participate in civic government. The women who supported her became the Women's Civic Club. Henderson was elected sixteen straight years to the Hamilton Council (in the days of annual elections).

When the steel union was organizing at Stelco after the war, Henderson came down strongly against it. She did not agree with the idea of the closed shop—mandatory union memberships. In Britain and the United States, the closed shop issue was one of the defining differences between conservatives and progressives. Those opposed to the closed shop stressed individual freedom. Those in favour of the closed shop cited practical applications and fairness. Why should non-union members get the same pay raises that union members had to fight for? They argued that by banding together, all members benefitted.

As the strike went on, Henderson became increasingly antagonistic to the strikers and they to her. She was a stubborn and feisty woman who wasn't always diplomatic. To show her support for the inside workers, she walked through the picket line at the main gate of Stelco. The steelworkers didn't know how to respond to an aggressive and brave five-foot, one-inch woman. The union leaders responded wisely by granting her free passage any time she wanted. Better that than making her a victim of union thuggery.

Sam Lawrence was a fabled hero of the union and socialist movement in Ontario. His life reads like a novel. He was born in Somerset, England to a family with ten children. He went to school until he was ten. His father was a "radical liberal" and a stonemason. Sam went to work at a quarry when he was twelve. He worked from 6 a.m. to 6 p.m. Later, his father became the foreman at Arundel Castle and Sam left for London at seventeen. At eighteen, he became a shop steward in the Stonemason Society. He then joined the Coldstream Guards and fought in the Boer War. At that time, a friend loaned him a copy of Edward Bellamy's *Looking Backwards*. Reading this utopian novel made Lawrence a socialist. In 1906 at the age of twenty-seven, as a trade unionist, he ran for office in Battersea. He lost.

In 1912, he followed three of his brothers and two of his sisters to Canada. He arrived one year before Nora Frances Henderson and was twenty-one years older than her. Sam got work as a stonemason in Hamilton. He immediately became involved in union activity. His ability was recognized and he was elected an alderman in 1922, supported by the Independent Labour Party. He ran for a Federal seat in parliament in 1925, but he lost. He was elected to the Hamilton Board of Control in 1929. In 1934, he was elected to the provincial parliament for Hamilton East. He was elected Ontario CCF (Co-operative Commonwealth Federation) President in 1941.

In 1944, Lawrence was elected Mayor of Hamilton. Henderson was on the Board of Control. The two greatest political talents in Hamilton were now poised to do battle.

Steel manufacturing in Hamilton was too important to remain a local issue. The Federal and Provincial governments were upset by the loss of revenue and the slowing of the economy. Those governments also regretted the belligerence of the unions. They supported unions, but they wanted more compliant unions. As things got more heated, Lawrence led a ten thousand-person march from Woodlands Park to the main gate of Stelco. Many citizens began to fear a communist revolution.

Henderson felt things had gone too far. A strike was one thing. A huge parade of lawless rabble-rousers led by the mayor was another. Didn't similar parades in St. Petersburg lead to revolution? Mayor Sam refused to send in police or militia to end the strike. The Federal Government sent troops to maintain order. Mackenzie King actually made a decision.

On August 8, 1946—Black Thursday—the city council was discussing the strike. Over a thousand strikers jammed the corridors of City Hall and surrounded the building. Cheers went up when Mayor

Sam spoke. When Henderson rose to speak, the strikers chanted, "We'll hang Nora Henderson from a sour apple tree!" During the fracas, two aldermen were roughed up. At the end of the meeting, Henderson picked up her purse and briefcase and walked through the crowd. Not a hand touched her. She went home that night and slept peacefully.

After eighty-one days, the strike ended. The company raised its offer to thirteen cents more an hour. Both sides signed the agreement, happy to end the agony. It was a struggle that had cost the strikers dearly, but they had established the rule of collective bargaining and the closed shop. All union activity in Canada after that followed those precepts.

The strikers went back to work. Now, the strikers and the inside workers had to work beside one another. There were no friendships across the line. The scabs were ignored; some never spoken to again. The two groups ate in different places, smoked in different places, and tried to avoid any incident that would lead to fist fights or worse.

In the community, families changed neighbourhoods, churches, grocery stores. Men dropped out of fishing clubs and rifle clubs. Ministers and priests gave Bible-based sermons on forgiveness.

The strike had all kinds of political results. Unions in Canada were given legislative guarantees of collective bargaining. The whip hand of corporations was restrained. Unions grew at a rapid pace and the economy was growing so quickly that the corporations were making huge profits. They, too, wanted labour peace.

The strike was so significant that there were thousands of articles about it, a successful stage play, and a respected documentary film. Historical research gained students MA's and PhD's. The archives are so vast that students can rummage around forever. The veterans of the strike told tales for decades at 1005 union halls. Children and grandchildren were taught the value of unions. The unions stood for courage, self-sacrifice, and self-respect. It is interesting that a young man could have fought in Europe and then returned home to fight at the gates of Stelco. He probably thought that defeating Hitler and Stelco was a good start to his life.

The municipal election of December 9, 1946, would be a referendum on how citizens felt politicians had acted during the strike. Samuel Lawrence was re-elected Mayor. Nora Frances Henderson ran for the four-person Board of Control again. She got the largest number of votes.

Nora Frances Henderson and Samuel Lawrence were giants. Both are worthy of the greatest admiration. They were fearless fighters for what they believed in. There was scarcely a day when they weren't verbally abused. But they were loved and respected by their supporters. Many people voted for both, seeing no contradiction. They both changed Hamilton. Henderson led the way for more women to participate in all aspects of politics. With her work on the Relief Board, she matched Sam's concern for the poor. Sam Lawrence, more than any other person, made Hamilton a union town.

Years later, the citizens of Hamilton honoured Nora Frances Henderson by naming a wing of a hospital after her. When large donors supported the hospital, their names went up and Nora Frances Henderson's came down. Her supporters looked around for another way to honour her. There is now the Nora Frances Henderson Secondary School. It is located near the southern border of Hamilton Mountain. She could never have imagined how the city would grow. It is not likely that the staff at the new high school know anything about the Strike of 1946.

Samuel Lawrence got a tribute he would have loved. He has a park named after him. It is not an ordinary park sitting in suburban Hamilton. The park sits at the top of the Jolly Cut, the road climbing the escarpment. It was once a quarry. The stonemason Sam would have loved that. No matter where you stand in the park, you can look northward to the bay and see the steel company. It has a different corporate owner now and a different name, but the workers are proud members of 1005.

Nora Frances Henderson died in 1949—age forty-nine. Samuel Lawrence died in 1959—age eighty.

Now that Hamilton had solved the problem of the closed shop and collective bargaining for all of Canada, it turned to the next challenge. Many immigrants already in the country didn't like new immigrants—especially if they were not of the same tribe. Canadian liberalism was displayed by its immigration policy after the war. Canada had been at war with Italy from 1939 to 1943. The armed forces of Italy had killed thousands of Brits in the Mediterranean and in North Africa. Canadian troops had landed on Sicily in 1943 and fought their way to Venice. Their opponents were overwhelmingly German, but there were a few pockets of die-hard Italian fascists. In town and city as the Canadians moved north, civilians came into the streets to cheer. Mussolini had been a disaster. Italians were starving. Emaciated children were begging along the roadsides. The young Canadians had never seen such poverty. Anger against the Italian government became compassion for Italian civilians.

Once the ships from Europe carried Canadian soldiers home (and ships were set aside for war brides), the Canadian Immigration Services went into full gear. Thousands of immigration officials worked diligently in Britain, Italy, and other European countries to ease passages to Canada. It was the first time Canadian bureaucrats worked to make things easier rather than harder. Over the next decade, hundreds of thousands of immigrants and refugees reached Canada.

Hamilton had to deal with this influx. The Anglo-Canadians welcomed immigrants from the British Isles, but Italians were not that welcome. The Anglos didn't like people who didn't speak English. They didn't like people who crushed grapes and made wine. They didn't like people who cooked with garlic. They didn't like people who put fresh manure on their gardens. They didn't like people who showed their emotions. The City Council knew how to deal with this. Many years earlier, they had restricted where Jews could own homes. They would show the same decisiveness with the Italians. They passed a bylaw that forbade Italians from buying homes south of Main Street, one of Hamilton's major east-west thoroughfares. Italians would live in the North—the dirty industrial area. Anglos would live in the South—the area with green lawns and pure air.

However, the Anglo establishment couldn't stop the integration of nationalities in the pulsating industries. Men of every national background (and a few ladies) worked side by side and became friends.

In this period, the Evans family and the Dubinsky family put down roots in East Hamilton.

Characters

Michael (Mike) Dubinsky
Betta Dubinsky
David Dubinsky
Alina Dubinsky
Alice Evans né Reilly
James Reilly
Jane Reilly
Peter Evans
Olwyn Evans
Greta Evans
Ivor Evans
Cecil Evans
Vivien Evans
May Evans
Roy Evans
Dorothy Riddell
William Riddell

Chapter One

Galicia 1912

Michael Dubinsky was a very excited eight-year-old. He had eaten his breakfast in great haste and started his walk down the wagon path to the dirt road. He had on his church clothes—basically an ironed white shirt and walking shoes. As usual, he would be the best-dressed student from his school. His parents doted on their only child. Now, he was waiting at the road with his lunch bag held tightly in his hands. The school was another two miles down the road. On school days, he would walk with two of his friends. In winter, a neighbouring farmer would pick up children in his covered sled. Every farm had a team of horses. It was the age of horse power—summer and winter. Things would be different today. Local officials working with regional mayors had spent months organizing this event. The eighty-two-year-old Emperor, Franz Joseph, was coming to L'vov. Local officials had hired all the buses they could, which would drive down a network of roads to bring children to L'vov. It was summer holidays for schools, but teachers had volunteered to ride on the buses. They wanted to see the Emperor too. The whole region wanted to celebrate the visit of their God-appointed Emperor. The government in Vienna had initiated these tours by the Emperor several years ago to help bind the Empire together. In this case, government policy and the Emperor's acceptance fused nicely.

As an eight-year-old farm boy in Galicia, Michael Dubinsky knew nothing of the structure of the Austro-Hungarian Empire. What he did know was that the Emperor was a figure that should be loved. His parents and his teachers taught him that the peace and prosperity of the country was due to Franz Joseph's rule. He was told to admire Franz Joseph's success in creating a multi-national army that was loyal to the Emperor. At school, Michael and his fellow students had to memorize the different nationalities within the Empire—Croats, Czechs, Italians, Poles, Serbs, Slovaks, Germans, Austrians, Hungarians, Romanians, Slovenes, and Ukrainians. The relative harmony of these groups was a triumph, and citizens of the Empire were proud of it. Older inhabitants knew of the great Ottoman Empire and its many different nationalities bound together initially by the Muslim faith but later by competent government. Today, Michael would see this great man.

Michael would later learn that Franz Joseph was born in 1830 in the Schonbrunn Palace in Vienna. Power and wealth flowed to the centre. For centuries, there had been enough stability to permit Vienna to have a functioning government. Hereditary rulers and families imposed order. Families stayed in power by having heirs groomed to ascend to greater positions. Franz Joseph's mother raised him to be a ruler, although he was not the direct heir to the Austrian throne. As a child, he was forced to study military doctrine and governmental functions. As he grew older, he thought of himself as a soldier.

In 1848, Europe was ablaze with revolution. France replaced its rulers in a bloody uprising. Other countries followed suit. Austria had revolutionaries marching down the streets of Vienna and public hangings. As the hereditary order was being challenged in Vienna, eighteen-year-old Franz Joseph was fighting a small regional war in northern Italy. Austria was trying to assert its control of the area. The chaos in Vienna was occurring at the same time. The Emperor at the time, Ferdinand, was overwhelmed. Franz Joseph was called home, and through the machinations of his mother, he was named emperor, although he was only the nephew of Ferdinand.

When the establishment puts down a revolution, ruthless military power is used. Then reprisals demand more ruthless military power. At eighteen, Franz Joseph oversaw thousands of executions and imprisonments. The democratic movements had to be crushed once and for all. Franz Joseph readily gave in to this policy, but the inhabitants of Schonbrunn Palace were the real authors. Once the monarchy was safely restored, Franz Joseph could enjoy the power and prestige of his position. He was, for example, the King of Bohemia, King of Croatia, and formal ruler of so many states that all his titles were seldom printed out in full. His predecessors had initiated the policy of integrating military recruits from every nationality into the national army. The Hapsburg Dynasty survived for hundreds of years because it could be very pragmatic. The regiments of the Empire would speak five or six different languages. There were fifteen different languages in the Empire. It is said that one regiment had so many languages, its operational language, of all things, was English. As Franz Joseph grew older, he gained confidence and asserted his authority. He was no longer ruled by his mother and the Court.

He knew, however, the one primary responsibility of a ruler—produce an heir. Blood was important. Blood was everything. Rulers and aristocrats charted their blood lines the way racehorse owners chart their mares. In his early twenties, the search for a wife began. All the eligible young ladies from aristocratic or royal families were candidates. The interlocking, almost incestuous, ruling families of Europe had ideas about a wife for Franz Joseph. His mother had been a Bavarian princess and she knew the aristocratic families of that state. She coaxed, or ordered, her son to go to Bavaria and look over a girl she had chosen. He went, but fell in love with the younger sister instead—defying his mother. His choice was a sixteen-year-old girl of dramatic beauty. Within months, a wedding was arranged. In 1854 they were wed. He was twenty-four.

These young ladies were born to great wealth and influence, but when they married, they had to become little more than brood mares. They had to produce children. They had to produce sons. Catherine, Franz Joseph's wife, accepted this responsibility. She bore daughters and one son. She lived in hell. Her mother-in-law never approved of her. Franz Joseph had fallen in love, but he was not a lover. He was a cavalry officer—quick mount, quick dismount. It was a loveless marriage. Catherine, whose more famous name was Sisi, was a brilliant woman known for her cultural aptitude. She became a favourite of the newspapers in Vienna and around the Empire. In 1858, she cemented her status with the Court by having a male heir. Having completed her child bearing responsibilities, Sisi began her own brilliant career separate from Franz Joseph. She became so popular in Hungary that the Hungarian government thought a formal alliance with Austria could be acceptable. After complex negotiations with complex political structures, Franz Joseph became King of Hungary. A dual monarchy was created.

Sadly, in 1889, the crown prince, a victim of melancholia, committed suicide with his mistress. The Court and legislature named Franz Joseph's nephew Franz Ferdinand as the heir apparent. Like most people in the Court, Franz Joseph hated his nephew and had never given his approval to Ferdinand's wife. She did not have royal blood. Not long after this, in a surprising rebellion for the time, Sisi left the Court. She was murdered in Geneva in 1898, age sixty. His daughters were living their own lives. Franz Joseph was now on his own, and he devoted all his energy to being a worthy emperor.

Franz Joseph had been trained to work hard. This he did. Each day, he got up at 4 a.m. to read bulletins and reports. Austria-Hungary was a mishmash of legislative bodies, but Franz Joseph and the military held it together. There was a policy of an iron-fist in a velvet glove. Democrats and nationalists were given some leeway until they became too aggressive. Then they might be executed or imprisoned. There was to be no 1848 again. Whether through his own wisdom or the advice of pragmatic counsellors, Franz Joseph gained the respect, and even the love, of different groups. In 1880 and 1881, he won the support of the Poles by granting them many rights. He gave significant protection to Jews, who made up ten or fifteen percent of the population in certain areas. In fact, Jews flourished in Vienna while pogroms occurred in greater Russia. Regions of his empire that felt threatened by Poland, Russia, Germany, or Serbia looked to Vienna for protection. The rising nationalism of different regions could never be quelled, but regions realized the need for a central government that enabled trade and commerce to function successfully.

The centripetal energy of the Empire was helped by the growth of Vienna as a great cultural and intellectual centre. Helped by Franz Joseph's liberal administration, all the arts and sciences flourished. Perhaps the importance of a centre of energy for a country should not be underestimated. London and Paris were good examples of cities drawing countries together. With more railroads and better roads, these centres played an increasingly important role. People in the provinces dreamed of going to London, Paris, or Vienna. Poles, Ruthenians, Serbs, Germans, Slovenes, and Czechs in the empire saw Vienna as their city. By 1900, Vienna had over two million inhabitants. Franz Joseph encouraged this growth and facilitated the boundaries of the city being enlarged. During this time, the city attracted intellectuals and artists from across Europe. Much of western thought in the twentieth century began in fin-de-siècle Vienna. For example, there was the Modernistic movement in art and architecture, the work of Sigmund Freud, the twelve-tone system of music, the philosophy of Ludwig Wittgenstein, the Austrian school of economics, and the high-modernistic style of literature. The melting pot facilitated and encouraged independent thought to flourish.

The liberal movements in Vienna must have had a profound influence on Franz Joseph. After all, he had to be proud of the achievements of his Viennese citizens—although he couldn't understand or agree with much of the new thought. In many ways, this was a great progressive age, Europeans were very optimistic. The Paris Exposition in 1900 put on display the new ideas in the arts and sciences. Over forty-eight million people visited the Exposition. Thinkers were so optimistic about the future that the phrase "Humans are getting better in every way every day" was often quoted. Franz Joseph decided that his contribution to the future would be to hold the Austro-Hungarian Empire together. He would become the avuncular figure for all its citizens. He would encourage the growth of progressive thought (within limits), facilitate industrial innovation, and support military preparedness. He would protect the Empire by clever diplomacy. He had been bested by Bismarck who had successfully amalgamated the German states and excluded Austria from a central role. But as agreements developed among England, France, and Russia, Franz Joseph had little choice but to turn to Germany and re-assert the Germanic bonds (Even though Germany had beaten Austria in a territorial war).

To maintain unity in the Empire, Franz Joseph had a vast propaganda program. His portrait was hung in post offices, schools, churches, and military barracks. His Ministry of Information made sure all his public appearances were photographed and made the newspapers. The governments in Vienna and Budapest had taxing powers that kept troops and federal officials in the provinces to discourage revolutionary ideas. Like the Ottoman Empire, the Hapsburg Empire combined subtle persuasion with military power.

* * *

The bus arrived at 7:45. Michael had never seen a bus before. He had seen many trucks on the road to Grabek but never a bus. His school books had drawings of buses so he was not shocked. Several students were waving to him from inside the bus. He held the bag with his lunch a little tighter, took a deep breath, and climbed the steps. Once inside the bus, he stood frozen in awe. Row after row of seats, windows along each side, and leather straps hanging down from steel tubes. The bus started to move and Michael was jolted down the aisle. A classmate, Eugene, waved him down. Michael sat beside him with his lunch on his lap. He was still speechless. The children were all very quiet. The noise of the bus and the constant swaying had them cowed. They wanted the adventure of the day, but they were overwhelmed by the assault on their senses. The bus moved relatively slowly as it travelled down the road looking for passengers. The children could see a girl about Michael's age up ahead holding her father's hand, waiting for the bus. She looked freshly scrubbed and had on her church frock. When the bus stopped and the door opened, she started to howl. The sight of the steps and the bus driver in his seat completely unnerved her. She had tears running down her cheeks and her little body was shaking. Her father and the bus driver tried to comfort and reassure her, but she pulled away from her father and started running down the lane to her house. The father, who would have loved to see the Emperor, apologized to the bus driver, picked up the girl's lunch and walked away.

Michael's teacher was waiting for them all at the school. Michael and Eugene were so happy that it was their teacher. The children on the bus were now more comfortable. The tension in the bus suddenly dropped. Their teacher mounted the steps to the bus, smiled warmly at the bus driver, and said she was so grateful for the good weather. She had obviously been on a bus before. She was relaxed and happy. As the bus moved forward, she walked down the aisle saying hello to her students and introducing herself to the other children. Michael now had a smile on his face. She returned to a seat at the front of the bus and began to talk to the bus driver about the day's event. She took two sheets of folded paper from her purse, and Michael could see that they had type-written information. Miss Senchuk, his teacher, studied the information carefully. She and the bus driver had to follow a carefully planned routine. The administrators in Vienna knew how to run this kind of event. They ran scores of them each year.

By the time the bus reached Grabek, all the seats were occupied, with some double seats having three occupants, but that was fine for children. It was just after eleven o'clock. The bus driver pulled up beside the village well. The children could get a drink of water and there was a public lavatory right there. Miss Senchuk and the bus driver had to use the same lavatory as the children, but they seemed unconcerned.

They climbed back on the bus and were off to L'vov. The children began to act like children. They kept changing seats to talk to other friends. They pulled the hair of children in front of them. They demanded to know what other children had for lunch. They established a hierarchy (Michael was near the top because of his intelligence and confidence). Groups began to sing songs they had learned in school or at Church. The school-taught songs were in Austrian. The church songs were in Ukrainian. Some children had been punched too hard or thrown roughly across a seat and they began to cry loudly. Miss Senchuk had to comfort them and threaten the assailants. Just like a work day for her. The bus driver practiced deafness. He was not new to this job, but it was his first long trip. Luckily, the children were getting worn out. Those who weren't falling asleep were increasingly passive. The many miles to L'vov wouldn't be too bad. At 2:30, their bus approached L'vov. The children became excited. They had never seen a city before. They were amazed by all the buildings and all the smoke. They had never seen buildings more than two stories tall before. The bus driver graciously drove down the street where the magnificent church stood. The children looked in awe with their mouths open.

The street to the city hall where the Emperor would be greeted was blocked off. The bus driver and Miss Senchuk checked the pages of instructions. There was a place where the bus should park. The bus driver had been to L'vov many times so he knew where to go. As he approached the area, policemen in dress uniforms pointed the way. The parking area was a farmer's field that had had a crop of barley—now harvested. The bus joined scores of other buses. The Viennese bureaucrats had done themselves proud. The vast treasury of the federal government had bought huge amounts of bread, cheese, and sausage for the children. There were picnic tables piled with food. The children from earlier buses had already eaten and some groups had started walking towards the city centre. The Court of Franz Joseph knew how to win children's hearts. Before Michael's bus load was allowed to eat, Miss Senchuk and the bus driver held them captive. They had to memorize the number of the bus and find a designated partner to stay with at all times, holding their entwined hands up in the air so Miss Senchuk knew everyone had a partner. Then the organization became more complex. Miss Senchuk went down the aisle and designated the oldest students as "pack leaders," each responsible for three of these pairs, including their own. They must remain very close together during the afternoon. Miss Senchuk told them they must return to the bus once the emperor had paraded past them a second time as he left the city. Miss Senchuk was pleased with her careful instructions.

Nothing can go wrong, she thought.

Something will go wrong, the worldly bus driver thought.

Michael was now in his pack. Eugene was his partner. Ivan, who was twelve, was his pack leader. Ivan was already becoming officious and bossy. But it didn't matter. They were walking towards the city's downtown. Michael was struck by the height of the buildings. He wondered how they built them and if people were afraid to live and work so high off the ground. Once they reached the main street, there were wide wooden sidewalks. The children jumped up and down on them, fascinated by the noise. As they walked along, they passed store after store. Many of these stores had huge glass windows with displays inside. The children had never seen women's and men's formal clothing. They had never seen row after row of boots and shoes. They had never seen a bakery with its incredible smells and displays of bread, buns, cakes, and tarts. Then they stopped. There was a candy store; a store with nothing but chocolates and hard candy. Several of the more self-assured children whose parents had given them a few pennies bought candy. Michael was amazed. He had two pennies in his pocket but lacked the courage to enter the store. By the time he had mustered enough courage, his group leader was shouting at him to move along. They could see the massive clock tower of city hall in the distance and that was their goal. Then they saw Miss Senchuk. She was on the sidewalk with her hand upraised.

"This is our place on the sidewalk," she said. She had each pack line up and form a uniform line. She told them to sit on the edge of the sidewalk and rest. She pointed out water barrels that were available for drinks. She then opened the large bag she was carrying and began to distribute small flags on wooden sticks; another item that amazed Michael and the other students. How could these little flags have been made by the thousands. Each school had a large flag of the Hapsburg double-eagle. The double-eagle flag was beautiful. The students had been taught how the Hapsburgs were the reason for their prosperity and peace. The Hapsburgs had ruled for hundreds of years and loyalty to that dynasty was well-deserved. Michael practiced waving the flag as the other children did too. The crowds were all ready. Now the Emperor had to come.

The security department of Austria-Hungary was on high alert whenever Franz Joseph made a public appearance. Many different groups were anxious to kill heads of state for various reasons. In Europe, there was an attempted assassination almost every week. This was partly due to the invention of the revolver in the nineteenth century. An assassin could now fire several shots and kill a person at thirty feet. The revolver could be carried undetected in a coat. The most famous assassination was Abraham Lincoln in 1865. At the beginning of the twentieth century, there were a number of infamous assassinations; Emile Zola the novelist in 1902; Petkor the prime minister of Bulgarian in 1905; Umberto the King of Italy in 1900.

So, the security department followed its usual procedure for Franz Joseph's visit to L'vov. The local police and paid informers for the government gave the names of known security risks. It was a mixed bag of political reformers and petty criminals. A week before the Emperor's visit to L'vov, these people were rounded up and put in prison. In L'vov, the number was close to a hundred. Once in prison, individuals had to make a good case for being released. Thousands of possible security risks rotted in jails throughout the empire.

The emperor and his entourage were getting organized in a railroad marshaling yard. There were twenty railway cars. The emperor's two personal railway cars had his sleeping quarters with a large bed, toilet, and wardrobes. His man servant had a large bedroom next door. His other rail car had a kitchen, a large dining table also used as a conference table, and four normal seats together. The seats allowed Franz Joseph to look out the window as he talked to his companions. Franz Joseph loved his train trips. He had been born to great luxury in the Schonbrunn Castle, but he had also felt the physical misery of military campaigns. He knew the pain of riding a horse in the cold and rain, for example. As a young man, he had been proud of his Spartan resilience. In his old age, he preferred comfort, although he never stopped working extremely hard.

For this trip, his advisors wanted him to use his royal automobiles. He had four huge luxury open-topped vehicles. He had two Rolls-Royce Ghosts and two Neue Automobil-Gesellschaft Darlings. But Franz Joseph was a cavalry man—he loved horses and he thought a horse-drawn carriage was more impressive than an automobile. He would rather smell manure than gasoline. The railway cars carried two ornate carriages, sixteen horses, and a supply of hay. There were twelve members of the royal cavalry. Two ordinary passenger cars carried the cavalry men in full uniform and all the functionaries for the event. Once the train pulled into the siding, there was a well-organized rush to get the procession in order. The local officials were ready for their day of fame. The mayor and his wife stood by the lead carriage. The commanding general of the local army base was perspiring in his elaborate dress uniform. Franz Joseph emerged from his railway car and strode to his carriage, waving and shaking hands when necessary. He always combined punctuality with good manners. The seat in the royal carriage was elevated for the emperor so that he sat up high and was quite visible. As soon as he was seated, the procession began its way to city hall. There were throngs of people even in the railway yard and Franz Joseph occasionally waved to them. The mayor and his wife followed his lead.

The general and Franz Joseph's aide-de-camp sat in the first carriage with military rigidity. The household cavalry at the front and the six at the back kept a significant distance from the two carriages. After the rear cavalry, four cars containing police officers and bodyguards followed. Then, quite far back, there were two cars of approved reporters and photographers. Everything was a well-planned show of public relations. The Emperor was shown as an effective amalgam of power, continuity, ceremony, and friendliness. Before each royal visit, Franz Joseph's courtiers prepared a detailed description of each city. Franz Joseph assiduously read this summary. Now, as he rode along with the mayor of L'vov, he chatted amicably about local issues and events—nothing too serious.

The procession was now entering the centre of the city. A marching band that had been waiting patiently on the road was told to begin. The martial music began—music by Austrians. The children heard the music and stood up, getting ready to wave their flags. The boredom that had taken over everyone turned to excitement again. The emperor really was coming. Michael and Eugene stood shoulder to shoulder on the edge of the sidewalk. People were now crowding in behind them and they feared being pushed onto the road. They didn't think that would be good. There were soldiers with rifles every ten yards or so. People applauded the band as it marched by. The band gave concerts around the district and every two weeks they played in the town square. Members in the crowd had friends and family in the band and they shouted loudly at them.

There was a large gap, then the first six cavalry guards trotted into view. They were magnificent. The horses were a uniform black with lovely arching necks. As their coats gleamed, Michael thought of his strong but drab farm horses. Of course, they never had their coats groomed. The horses in front of him were not only beautiful, but they were groomed and trained for cavalry charges—the most romantic and mythological aspect of war. Horses and war. European history was a catalogue of the triumph of horses in battle. Most little boys dreamed of being a cavalry officer, of owning a magnificent horse and a shining sword. Many of these boys had soft metal toys resembling these military gods. They always triumphed over the mundane foot soldiers. The little boys knew, of course, that the cavalry was limited to the nobility. The army did not give out horses to the bravest or best of recruits. Money and family were rewarded with officer commissions. The officers always had the horses. The peasants and lower classes trudged along in their locally made boots. But the nobility were not without courage. They too were brought up with tales of military exploits. They too were prepared to risk their lives for glory. Some even wished they could have been in the Charge of the Light Brigade. Young men go to war because war is glorified.

The uniforms of the cavalry officers were designed by the best tailors in Vienna. The tradition of glorious uniforms went back hundreds of years. The cavalry regiments inherited a dress code from their forefathers. Every so often, the regimental colonel and his subalterns would agree on a dress uniform change. Most of the changes were designed to make the uniforms even more spectacular. Additional gold braid was always popular, as were bright red cuffs or stripes. Sometimes changes were made for comfort or the advantage of new fabrics or dyes. The uniforms cost almost as much as maintaining a thoroughbred horse. No wonder the cavalry officers had a high opinion of themselves. Now, as they trotted by the children, they created a sense of awe and childlike worship.

Then there was another large gap and the Emperor's carriage came into view. The onlookers became almost delirious. The children began to wave their flags with unrestrained energy. They started an ear-splitting shout. Michael wasn't sure if he should be quietly reverent or burst with loud enthusiasm. He decided to shout as loudly as he could. That was more fun, and he was tired of being restrained for hours. The carriage slowed down right in front of Michael's group. This alarmed the plain-clothes bodyguards, and they ran from their car and formed a guard of six—three on each side of the carriage. There was no serious problem. One of the carriage's horses had stumbled slightly over a loose harness strap. The driver's aid quickly fixed the problem. But while the carriage stood still, Michael was only fifteen or twenty feet away from the Emperor. Michael was so overwhelmed he could hardly breathe. As he regained some equilibrium, Michael looked more closely at his Emperor. He was an old man, but he had the vigor and posture of a soldier. He had bushy white whiskers shaved into a shape Michael had never seen. (Later, an older student told Michael that they were lamb chop whiskers; a fashion in the Court fifty years ago.) He had a stiff white military jacket emblazed with gold braid and his numerous medals glistened in the sun. His helmet was cylindrical, perhaps seven or eight inches high in a bright red. The visor was shiny and black with gold embellishments. Then, for a heart-stopping moment, the Emperor looked directly at Michael's group of students and, Michael thought, at him. Michael began to shake. He couldn't stop himself. He was hardly aware as the second carriage went by, then the next six cavalry officers and the procession of cars. Michael had never seen cars, let alone these magnificent touring cars. Normally, the sight of a car would have Michael and his classmates talking for days. But now it was all too much. Michael's senses were overworked and his brain wanted a rest. Until the day he died, Michael would always recall the day when the Emperor looked at him.

The children wouldn't remain on the street for the Emperor's ride back to the railway yard. The adults who had come by wagon wanted to get home before dark. The locals went to local biergartens or, if close enough, went home for some food. The Emperor had to go through all the formalities of a city greeting at city hall. Franz Joseph was quite genial at these gatherings. Perhaps he enjoyed being away from all the intrigues at Court. His nephew and heir, Franz Ferdinand, had so many radical ideas that Franz Joseph thought all his hard work for the Empire might be undone.

The children followed the mad rush back to the buses. Surprisingly, there was still some food left on the tables, but it soon disappeared. The older boys found a row of spruce trees and that became the lavatory for all the boys. The female teachers directed the girls to a path into the woods and there they found places to pee. One by one, the buses filled up, attendance was taken, and motors were started. The children in Michael's bus had to pound on the door to wake up the bus driver. He had to choose between seeing his emperor or having a nap. Wisely, he had a nap. It had been a very long day. The children couldn't stop chattering for the first few miles. They exchanged different observations of the day excitedly. But within an hour, they were all asleep. Miss Senchuk thought it polite to talk to the bus driver, but soon, she too put her head back and fell asleep. The bus driver was content to drive in silence. It was a long way back past Grabek. Parents were waiting in roadways for their children. Miss Senchuk awoke to direct the bus driver and awake the children. After the first few stops, the children were awake again and shouted for their stop. Michael's father was waiting for him and took his hand—something he seldom did. Michael walked directly into the house and straight to his bedroom. He slept for the next twelve hours in his clothes. He woke to pee and eat some oat cereal, then went back to bed. It took him two days to get back to a normal routine. Miss Senchuk slept almost as long. The bus driver slept at the side of the road and got his bus back by noon the next day.

The Emperor's ride back from city hall to his railway cars still had people shouting and waving flags. Some of the men were pleasantly drunk. Loading the carriages and horses on the train went with the usual competence. Once everyone was on board, beer casks were rolled out for the entourage. Franz Joseph and his man servant returned to their quarters and drank Schnapps in almost complete silence. The Emperor was pleased with his day's work. A man committed to duty had a sense of satisfaction. As the train pulled out for the trip back to Vienna, there was silence and darkness in the Emperor's quarters, and the soldiers began a riotous beer fest.

Chapter Two

Galicia 1916

Week after week, Michael Dubinsky watched the marching troops stream past on the roads to Grabek. Night and day, there was a loud rumble of artillery barrages. The dust of horse-drawn wagons settled on crops for miles. Michael and his friends walked for hours just to see the show. The soldiers in the Austro-Hungarian army marching by were not much older than Michael. They were in good spirits and confident they could stop the Russians. They told Michael and his friends that the Russians had something called the Brusilov offensive. They explained that that was the name of the Russian commander. He had amazing success over a very broad front. The Austrian recruits were told that Brusilov might have five hundred thousand troops (or a million or two million, depending who told the story). They had overwhelmed the fewer Austrians. The Russians had somehow recovered from their huge losses in 1914 at Tannenberg. Now Austria-Hungary was shifting its forces to the northeast. A decision had been made in Berlin to send German troops to help their ally. If Russia knocked Austria-Hungary out of the war, Russia could resume its attack on Prussia. The German commander in the west, Erich Von Falkenhayn, opposed the decision because he was engaged in a war of attrition with the French at Verdun. He argued that if he could kill another hundred thousand German troops and 125,000 French troops, France would drop out of the war. Then he could easily mop up the British. He was overruled by Hindenburg and Ludendorff.

At twelve years old, Michael and his friends had just thrown away their toy rifles. Every boy wanted to be old enough to join the army and fight. Every week, the papers that came to Grabek from L'vov had stories of the war. Most Ruthenians were loyal to Austria-Hungary and Germany. But that was not an easy loyalty because Ukrainians were part of that vast Russian army. The propaganda ministry in Vienna, however, convinced the Ukrainians and Poles in Galicia that the Russians were sub-human, and they would plunder, rape, and destroy. At the same time, the Austro-Hungarian and German armies paid the farmers of Galicia well for their produce. The Austro-Hungarian army included Ruthenians, Poles, Czechs, Hungarians, and Jews. They all felt a loyalty to Emperor Franz Joseph. As the recruits marched east, they knew that the Austro-Hungarian army had suffered terrible losses by the Russians. They also knew that Franz Joseph had had to ask the Kaiser for help. They didn't know about the machination of Germany, England, France, and Russia. They were determined to defend their homeland. For many of the new recruits, their training lasted only two or three weeks. Times were desperate. They learned how to fire a rifle, operate an artillery piece, cook large quantities of food, or communicate over a field telephone. For many of them, they learned as they moved continuously eastward. Somehow, this poorly trained army had to have enough courage to become soldiers. Those who didn't learn quickly enough died quickly. Poorly trained and hastily promoted officers caused the deaths of hundreds. Luckily for the Austro-Hungarians and the Germans, the great Russian steamroller was running out of steam. Huge casualties, a shortage of artillery shells, fewer and fewer horses, and an overwhelming weariness ended the Brusilov offensive. It was the most successful attack during World War I, but finally defense won over offence. The Russians had taken hundreds of thousands of prisoners and Brusilov was a great hero.

During summer holidays, Michael had a long working day as the only child on the farm. His father had two farm workers who lived in their own shed. The various crops were becoming ripe and had to be harvested. The warm, dry August meant the wheat and oats could be scythed and tied into bundles. The bundles would be hauled in the wagon to the barn. Michael enjoyed driving the wagon and helping his father unload the hay and stack it. He was above average in height and weight. He was not averse to working hard. The person who worked from morning to night was his mother. She began the day by milking the two cows, then feeding the chickens and pigs. She then prepared breakfast for the three men and Michael, which was usually an oat gruel and perhaps an egg each. If Michael's father decided to kill a pig, the breakfast included a slice of pork. After breakfast, Michael walked to the creek and brought back two pails of water. The pigs got a diet of water, milk, and oats. At the end of the work day, Michael led the horses to the creek and then pegged them out in a rock-filled field to graze.

After a day and night of rain, the field was too wet to do any work. Michael asked if he could walk to Grabek with his friend Boris and see the army in motion. The two boys were released from their farm obligations for a day. The road to Grabek was muddy, but the sun was out and Michael and Boris enjoyed the freedom. They talked incessantly about the war. Various reports and rumours swept across the countryside. The interesting thing about battles is that the officers never know exactly what is happening in the field, the soldiers never know what the officers' plans are, the newspaper reporters are lied to and their movements are restricted, the civilians in the area cannot be told the truth, the generals lie to the politicians, and the politicians lie to the people. Only the broadest outline of events ever emerges. Hiding the truth is so important. Victories must be exaggerated and defeats must be minimized. Careers and reputations depend upon an acceptable truth. But Michael, who was Ukrainian, wanted to believe that all the Ukrainian soldiers were brave and fearless; Boris, who was Polish, wanted to believe the same of the Polish troops. They agreed that the Austrian and Hungarian troops could never succeed without the Ukrainians and Poles. Michael's father, on a market visit to Grabek (where they sold eggs) had bought a newspaper in May 1916. That was one of the few newspapers the family had ever seen. Michael's father knew that decisions made by the Great Powers could affect even the people who lived in the backwaters of the empire. Railways and trucks were improving all the time, and that meant the more rapid deployment of troops. For Michael, it was exciting; for his father, it was dreadful. Michael cut out photographs of soldiers and cavalry officers from the newspaper. He posted them on the walls of his bedroom. He actually had his own bedroom—the advantage of being the only child of a landowner. Now Michael's father bought a paper every week.

Michael's father knew that war was not good for the common people. Kings and kaisers, monarchs and tsars cared little for the millions of poor people they ruled. The poor would be cannon fodder. Hereditary rulers and aristocratic officers didn't worry about the casualties of war. They cared for military success and a reputable place in history—even a praiseworthy footnote. In many cases, perhaps the majority of cases, officers knew more about how uniforms were tailored than they knew about battle tactics. When they travelled, they had an entourage of servants and lived in luxury as their troops suffered outdoors. Often, advantageous positions for a battle could not be seized because a general or a colonel could not move his possessions quickly enough.

As Michael and Boris walked towards Grabek, they caught up with a large convoy. Their trucks and wagons were carving deeper and deeper ruts in the soft road. The troops were moving slowly as their boots sank in the mud. After several miles, Michael and Boris saw the incident that had stopped the convoy. A very heavy gun carriage that was pulled by six horses had veered into the soft shoulder and its right side was up to its axles in mud. The six horses didn't have the strength to move the carriage and heavy artillery pieces, although the driver whipped the horses mercilessly. Now the teamsters were unhitching six horses from another gun carriage and trying to link two sets of six horses. The horses were working themselves into a froth. As the additional team was backed into place, several horses began to kick. One of the horses on the stuck team began to buck. Teamsters and drivers from other wagons came to help. The teamsters had to use huge leather straps to join the two wooden yokes. Now there were twelve men holding the bridles of the panicked horses. Two horses on the right side of the stuck carriage were almost up to their haunches in mud. Their eyes were wide and they had startlingly white lather running down their sides. The loud braying of the horses and the swearing of the soldiers created a scene of utter bedlam. But the indomitable teamsters got between the two teams and managed to buckle the leather straps of the two yokes. Additional straps were wrapped around the lead horses.

When the teamster who had taken charge thought the teams were attached securely enough, he gave the order for the horses to be whipped. The soldiers screamed as loudly as they could. After three pulls, there was a loud sucking sound and the wagon wheels rolled forward. The wagon was moving. In two or three minutes, the gun carriage was back on the road. There were loud cheers from the twenty or thirty soldiers who had gathered to watch this spectacle. Luckily, there was a bypass lane just forty or fifty yards ahead. The teamster who had appointed himself in charge had the horses and wagon pull over. The front team was hitched up to its original wagon again and was allowed to rest. The other horses and gun carriage stayed in the bypass. The horses were spent. They could do no more work this day.

Michael and Boris were shocked and saddened by this misuse of horses. They had their own teams of horses on their farms. Those horses were treated very well. Most farmers, in fact, loved their horses, had names for them, and considered them part of the family.

When farm children were young, they rode these stocky work horses and imagined them to be the finest-boned riding horses of aristocrats. Every army had to scour the country for horses. Hundreds of thousands of horses were necessary to keep the armies moving. The logistics of feeding and watering all these animals demanded complicated planning. Requisitioning hay, one way or another, was a constant preoccupation of army planners. Blacksmiths and veterinarians played a crucial role in keeping horses fit. But horses often dropped and they were shot on the spot. Of course, the same artillery shells that killed soldiers killed horses. After a battle, fields were littered with dead troops and dead horses. Armies with more horses and more artillery shells stood a good chance of winning. The noncombative countries had horse brokers who sold thousands of horses to the warring nations. The farms of Western and Eastern Europe had to share horses to get work done.

Michael and Boris continued to trudge along. Walking on the muddy road and even muddier shoulders made them weary. But the sight of the marching soldiers, the cursing wagon drivers, the occasional songs from dry throats, the different languages were exciting for two young boys.

Sometime later, they were passed by a wagon pulled by four thoroughbreds. The beautiful horses with their narrow backs, long necks, and regal bearing were a sight to see. They had been bred to carry riders and be fast. Somehow, the horses of wealthy owners had ended up as drudge horses. They were beautiful and yet they had the strength to pull a heavy goods wagon at a brisk pace. Michael and Boris speculated about how those horses ended up as dray animals. Michael thought they had been in a cavalry battalion and their riders had been shot off. Teamsters captured them and put them to work. There were never enough horses to pull supply wagons. Scores of wagons were abandoned because there were no horses available. Michael thought that if cavalry officers saw these horses, there would be a holy row and the horses would go back to the cavalry.

Michael and Boris realized they could not walk all the way to Grabek. Their progress was too slow and they were dead tired. Luckily, a soldier had given them half a loaf of bread and a drink from his canteen or they would have turned back sooner. They wanted to see what Grabek looked like now. School friends said the town was full of soldiers. Wagons passed through constantly. The townspeople had never seen so many trucks. There were large supply depots, blacksmith shops, truck repair sheds, a large field hospital, and a command post in the school. There were tents in all the fields adjoining the town and more tents arrived each day to be erected immediately. Merchants made a great deal of money and were happy. The other residents felt threatened by the loud and vulgar field soldiers. A number of residents had fled west or south weeks ago when it looked as if the Russians could not be stopped. Now the possessions they had left behind became the loot of war.

Michael and Boris wondered about the brothels. Older school friends said there were two in Grabek now—one for the officers and one for the common soldiers. Michael and Boris didn't know what brothels were and they didn't want to ask. They knew these establishments had something to do with sex. As farm boys, they knew about the mating of their animals, but they couldn't visualize this mating between humans. Their schoolmates said that women travelled with armies and soldiers paid them to have sex. They wondered what "have sex" meant. They were told that there was always a line-up for the soldiers' brothel. The soldiers entered and came out shortly afterwards. What happened inside the house? What would they be doing?

Anyway, Michael and Boris would not see any of this. They turned for home. They planned to try again if they could. Good weather would mean they would be working hard on their farms. As they walked along against the flow of traffic, they recounted the amazing things they had seen. War was an interesting show. Just as they were walking silently, there was a huge roar. Soldiers dropped to the ground and horses bucked. Michael and Boris were flat on the ground when they looked up. It was a plane. It had flown low over the column. Now the roar was over and the plane was rapidly growing smaller. Michael recognized the insignia on the body of the plane from his newspaper clippings. It was a German plane. The Germans had shifted two squadrons of fighter planes to the Eastern Front. They were there to bolster the morale of the Austro-Hungarian troops. They were able to provide information about Russian troop movements. Forward soldiers sometimes saw dog fights between Russian and German planes. By the time the German fighters were at the front, the great Brusilov Offensive was at a near standstill. The Austro-Hungarian Empire had given up miles and miles of territory. It had also suffered huge casualties. The swift movement of the Russian army and the low morale in the Austro-Hungarian army led to hundreds of thousands of prisoners of war. With German help, the empire had held on. But that was the end of its offensive capabilities.

Two weeks later, Michael and Boris were given another day off by their fathers. Having both sons on school holidays meant extra work could be completed, and the boys were good workers. In truth, their fathers wished they could see what was happening in the great battles. Occasionally, troops wandered down their dirt roads and the local farmers asked for news. The soldiers never knew exactly what was happening, but they knew there were many, many deaths. When Michael and Boris reached the road from Grabek, they were stunned by the sight. There were miles after miles of wagons and trucks moving south with soldiers walking slowly beside them. Wagon after wagon had wounded men lying shoulder to shoulder. There were bandages and blood everywhere. Soldiers had bandages covering their whole heads. Michael and Boris wondered what wounds lay beneath those blood-soaked bandages. There were soldiers with arms missing and some had bloody stumps for legs. These amputees had been saved by fellow soldiers who had stopped the bleeding by tying belts or twine around the wounds. Their uniforms were soaked in blood and most of them were unconscious. Their mates had worked bravely, sometimes under artillery and machine gun fire, to save their friends. It was the act of brotherhood. The daring first aid workers would be brokenhearted to know that only a third of their friends would survive the trips back to field hospitals. The hospitals functioned as mortuaries as dead men were taken from the wagons and trucks. Large burial details continuously dug graves. During a large battle, there was no time for formal burial ceremonies.

Michael turned away twice to vomit. Boris had a stronger stomach. Many of the soldiers who were walking had wounds. Some were being helped along by willing comrades. There was very little noise. The wagons and horses seemed silent. The pall of death and dying silenced everything. The soldiers hardly lifted their feet as they moved along. Occasionally, there was the crying of men in pain, but the forward medics and stretcher-bearers were generous in their doses of morphine. Because the Russians had advanced so quickly and pushed the Austro-Hungarians back for miles, the medical officers didn't know where to establish their field hospitals. The last thing they wanted was to have their hospitals overrun by enemy soldiers. But if the hospitals were too far from the front, many soldiers would bleed to death before they could receive surgery. Michael and Boris saw several soldiers in the wagons who were grey-white. They had bled to death because nothing could be done for them. The wagons were supposed to be carrying the wounded for treatment. Often, they were transporting corpses.

When Michael and Boris walked up a rise beside the road, they saw retreating soldiers, wagons, and trucks all the way to Grabek. They decided to cut through fields to avoid the convoy. They were determined to reach Grabek this time. The horror could not diminish their curiosity. They reached the town within an hour. It was intact. It was out of range of the Russian heavy artillery, and it was never in the line of advance. Now the streets were congested, but there was no panic. The Austrian command was confident that the

Russian advance had lost its momentum. The very long front had only sporadic exchanges. It was a case of both sides having no more shells to fire and no more troops to kill. The armies were two boxers who had given everything they had for nine rounds and couldn't lift their arms to come out for the tenth. Now was the time to re-organize regiments and divisions—to bring new recruits to the front. There would be time to cook hot meals and to bury the dead.

When Michael and Boris made their way to the centre of the village, they saw that everything had changed. All the village stores were closed. There were no goods to sell, no food, and no liquor. The church had tents on its front lawn and back gardens. Its doors were open. Michael and Boris climbed the front steps and entered the cool and dark interior. There were soldiers in the pews; some sleeping, some praying. Michael knocked on the door of Father Michalsky's study. Their priest came to the door immediately and welcomed them warmly. He looked very tired and very thin. He offered them water and moved very slowly to get the pitcher. His housekeeper was still at the residence to cook and clean. Villagers still brought food for their priest, but the army was consuming most of the local produce. The church's caretaker and gardener had left three weeks ago when the Russians seemed poised to take the village. Father Michalsky, Michael, and Boris didn't say anything for five or six minutes as they sipped the glasses of water.

Finally, Michael asked what had happened. Father Michalsky wanted to talk. He was weary, but he needed to talk about the calamity. He needed to talk about himself. His soul had been shaken from its tethers. He could not reconcile God's love and the evil of war. Two twelve-year-old boys had to hear his confession and his agony. In the frenetic demands of war, he was too busy to think. He spent every day administering last rites and comforting the living. Now with a pause, he tried to understand this demented universe and his place in it. He had read the newspapers from L'vov and heard the Austrian and German officers' discussions. He thought that perhaps an analysis of the battles would turn madness into logic. Perhaps there was some plan behind all the chaos, death, and suffering. Could man really kill with no purpose? Could men give up their lives without really knowing why? Father Michalsky wanted to tell them about the Brusilov Offensive. That appeared to be a logical plan. Understanding the demonic strength of armies perhaps explained how nations functioned. Could there be some final order in the wars among nation states? Could battlefields littered with rotting corpses lead to a greater good? Were there righteous wars? Were there Christian soldiers? Was man improving? Could he control his bestiality? Would man ever slither out of the sea of despair? As the boys sat with their heads down, Father Michalsky recounted all the horrors he had seen.

"Well," Father Michalsky began, "you must understand that we live in Austria-Hungary. We are the allies of Germany. We fight for our freedom against Russia, France, England, Italy, and Serbia. We cannot give up our land to godless invaders. We have an advanced culture centred in Vienna but spread throughout our empire. Vienna is the centre of learning for all of Europe. We are the envy of nations. The Russians are a vulgar and primitive people, a country of peasants. When the war began, the Russians thought they could invade Prussia and through sheer numbers destroy the Prussian-German armies. We didn't want war, but the Serbians assassinated our beloved Franz Ferdinand. We faced enemies who envied our superior civilization. We were wronged. We had no choice but to fight. France had given Russia huge amounts of money to build railways to carry troops to our borders. England has always looked out for itself. But," Father Michalsky said, and a slight smile appeared on his wan face, "our generals, Hindenburg and Ludendorff destroyed the Russian armies at Tannenberg. And so, this battle is just a temporary setback. The bravery of the soldiers of the empire will drive the Russians back and destroy them."

Father Michalsky paused and asked the boys if they wanted some bread. He seemed exhausted from his vituperation. The boys said they were hungry. Father Michalsky rose slowly from his chair and rang the bell for his housekeeper. She came immediately. She was a woman in her seventies. Like Father Michalsky, she was very thin. He asked her to bring some bread and she nodded. Within minutes, she brought a tray with a loaf of bread and a knife, then retreated noiselessly. Father Michalsky cut thick slices for the boys but took none himself. He was anxious to tell the story.

He sipped his water and resumed his narrative. "We thought the Russians were finished after Tannenberg, but we were mistaken. They still had the will to fight. The Tsar wanted the war to continue out of loyalty to France and the generals wanted to create reputations. The Russians were more than peasants. They had created industries based on the models of German, France, and England. In a little over a year, they equipped another army. In 1916, the Tsar and his military command promoted General Alexei Brusilov to head the Eastern Command. Huge resources were put at his disposal. He had an army that approached five hundred thousand men. That was an incredible recovery. Brusilov felt that Austria-Hungary was just a hodge-podge country of warring factions. If this so-called country was assaulted by the full strength of troops, all fighting for Mother Russia and the Tsar, Austria-Hungary would shatter like a teapot dropped on the floor. He had a plan. He thought that attacking on narrow fronts after a long barrage just allowed the enemy to rush reinforcements to that narrow corridor. He had the advantage of a battlefield that was large and relatively flat. His divisions would not be funneled into narrow columns by mountains or marshes. He would attack on a three-hundred-mile front. He would use planes to reveal enemy strong points. He would prepare set assaults meticulously using heavy artillery. He would change his point of attack as the enemy responded. His quick advances using surprise led to situations where the Austro-Hungarian army had to retreat or have its flanks turned.

Success led to more success. The Russian soldiers were triumphant. The Austro-Hungarian soldiers retreated in despair. Some of the Slavic elements in the army deserted and joined the Russians.

"Finally, the Austro-Hungarian troops had retreated so far that their defensive line was short enough to defend. The officers knew they must hold L'vov or the gateway to Vienna was open. The Supreme Command and Franz Joseph rushed troops to the northern front."

Father Michalsky sighed and remained silent for many minutes as Michael and Boris sat stiff with apprehension. Then he said in a whisper, "It's time for the butcher's bill to be added up. War is wonderful when it is a chess game with ivory pieces, when artillery barrages are theoretical, when casualty lists are simply mathematical calculations. But wars are an accumulation of bodies and body parts. This is what we know about the Brusilov Offensive. The Russians took almost two hundred thousand prisoners and killed the same number. The Austro-Hungarian army killed thousands and thousands of Russians. Bodies and parts of bodies were buried where they lay. The stench of rotting flesh hung in the air for weeks. Townspeople and farmers couldn't open their windows. Some cattle became sick. Dogs would howl when darkness came. Hundreds of thousands of young men were either dead, wounded, or prisoners."

Father Michalsky paused again. This narrative had exhausted him. The Brusilov Offensive was the most successful operation in World War I. General Brusilov became a hero in Russia. The German and Austro-Hungarian troops who finally stopped the Russian advance were celebrated as heroes. Bodies rotted in the fields and heroes were declared. "Perhaps," Father Michalsky said, "it is time for you young boys to go home."

Michael and Boris didn't speak as they walked home. When they reached the Grabek road, they saw that troops were marching north now. The number of soldiers and wagons moving south was smaller. The fresh troops looked at the shattered remnants of an army. They became fearful and apprehensive. There was no longer any youthful illusion. Michael and Boris were hailed by a wagon driver. He was a member of a battalion whose job it was to recover useful equipment from the battlefields. His goods wagon was full of rifles and boots. He asked the young boys if they would like a pair of boots and a rifle each. He stopped the wagon and told them to jump up, take a look, and make their choices. Michael saw a beautiful pair of boots, but they were covered in blood. He chose a nice pair covered in mud. He took a rifle with some hesitation. Boris chose his boots and rifle. They thanked the driver and started on their way again. They knew that corpses on the battlefield were stripped of their money, rings, and watches. Many ghouls had a wallet of cash, five or six watches, and two or three rings. They thought that if they didn't take them, the enemy would.

Within two hours, Michael and Boris were back home. They remained silent when their parents asked them questions. They picked at their suppers and went to bed early. For the next few days, they thought about what they had seen and what Father Michalsky had said. For the rest of their lives, the horror of war remained with them.

Franz Joseph died in November 1916, at Schonbrunn Palace. Mercifully, he did not live to see his empire dismantled.

* * *

After millions of bodies had been buried and millions of refugees found tentative homes, the victorious powers met in Paris in 1919. The first order of business was to humiliate and punish the Germans. That was easy. The new gods of destiny, Woodrow Wilson, Georges Clemenceau, Vittorio Orando, and David Lloyd George met to put the world back in order. From January to July, the fates of millions of people and scores of states were decided. Paris was inundated with delegations from every inhabited piece of land. Every hotel, every ballroom, every conference room buzzed with earnest and emotional arguments. History once again tried to put round pegs into square holes. The Big Four, with their omniscient arrogance, thought they could place maps on tables, listen to delegations, and draw new boundaries that would satisfy the national aspirations of every group that claimed a unique homogeneous identity. But nationalism and geography don't always mix well. The gods were a blend of brittle, self-righteous idealism, ruthless self-interest and vindictiveness, cold realpolitik, and ignorance. Sometimes the fate of people was decided between lunch and dinner. Sometimes delegations representing many thousands or even millions of people were granted thirty or forty minutes to make their case.

Into this great cauldron came the Ruthenians—Ukrainian Catholics in Galicia. They made up the majority in Eastern Galicia. But the area also included Poles, Jews, Czechs—every ethnic group in Eastern Europe. The delegation displayed the two loyalties of the Ruthenians—the western pull of the old Austrian Empire, its culture and administrative structure; and the eastern pull towards their kinfolk in Ukraine. More than anything else, the Ruthenians wanted the Great Powers to know they existed.

The gods laid out their maps and made a decision. Poland must have Krakow and Teschen. That seemed obvious to them. L'vov was not so obvious. L'vov was a Polish city in a sea of Ukrainians. Nevertheless, L'vov went to Poland and fighting broke out between Poles and Ukrainians around L'vov. The fighting wound down and, as it turned out, it was better for the Ruthenians that they were not part of Ukraine.

The inhabitants around Grabek were far enough from L'vov not to be infected by the new virulent virus of nationalism, racial identity, new nations, and new nationalism. For farmers around Grabek, the rule of the Poles was no different than the rule of the Austrians. The weather was far more important than any ineffectual and indifferent rule from a distant capital. Would bureaucrats in Warsaw be any different from bureaucrats in Vienna? Mike Dubinsky, his parents, and neighbours debated their fate constantly, but in the end, not much changed. The local governments stayed the same. The railroads ran. The roads were repaired. Schools functioned.

Mike, the Ruthenian, and Boris, the Pole, had been friends since childhood. The wisdom of friendship overcame the insanity of chauvinism.

Chapter Three

Saskatchewan 1920

Thrashing teams came every fall. They were a combination of capitalist entrepreneurs, hired workers, and volunteers. The owner of three or four thrashers would arrive in the area with his workers. They had worked their way north from the United States. The farmers would act as a co-op and negotiate a contract. The price was based on the number of thrashers and the number of paid workers. The farmers' wives would do all the cooking—huge mounds of food. During the summer, the grain farmers would discuss the thrashing companies. Once the morning chores were done, they had lots of time on their hands. Usually, the farmers received letters from the thrashing companies setting out dates and rates. It was always a bit of a cat and mouse game. The farmers needed the thrashing gangs and there were usually competitors. But if the farmers were too difficult, they could be bypassed and then they would have to organize their own crews. The thrashers, on the other hand, liked to work a small area and not spend all their time travelling. The thrashing machines couldn't move very fast so adjoining farms were ideal. Contracts ten miles apart were not good. So usually things worked out and the same contractors came to the same area year after year. The thrashing crew was always different though. Many were young men from Ontario, Quebec, or the Maritimes on their school holidays. Most of them stuck it out for the whole summer and fall, although some left within a few days. Getting up at five and working until seven or eight, or even later, is not easy. Since they had paid for their railway tickets west, however, they didn't want to go home in disgrace. They generally knew what they were getting into and most were used to physical labour. There were the usual horrific sunburns, blistered hands and feet, various digestive disorders, and so forth, but the contractors took precautions to keep their crews healthy. Once the first week or so was over, the young men who had dropped into bed at eight o'clock and slept without moving, began to play catch with a baseball after supper, or tell stories around campfires, or flirt with the farm girls.

Alice Reilly's father had been an itinerant blacksmith and farmer. He had been a homesteader near Estevan and met his wife Grace because her family had a homestead a few miles away. It was the turn of the century and two intercontinental railroads, the CNR and the CPR, were opening up the west. Settlers were lured by a quarter section of free land. Alice's father couldn't stay in one place. He moved from farm to farm always heading north. The land was always better further north. He was one of those hardworking men who never accumulated anything because they were always on the move before their hard work could pay dividends. Starting in 1904, it seemed as if Grace had a child every year or every second year.

As the oldest daughter, Alice had been very close to her mother. For as long as she could remember, she had been by her mother's side, always helping with the chores. As a child she helped her mother gather eggs and feed the hens, brush flies from her mother and the two cows as her mother did the morning milking, and scour the woodpile for kindling to light the wood stove. For her mother, it was a life of endless work, pregnancy, child-rearing, and the inevitable move to a different farm, a new beginning just like all the other new beginnings. Yet when Alice and her older brother James were joined by a succession of siblings, the workload diminished for each child. During their five years near Weyburn, the family had a sense of stability, even financial security. Reilly's blacksmith business was doing well and their quarter section provided table food and a small cash crop of wheat. The children went to school when they reached five, and by 1916, there were five Reilly children in the Weyburn Elementary School—a big institution of four classrooms.

Brothers, sisters, and schoolmates generated a social network—rivalries, projects, conspiracies, games, plans, squabbles, and loves. For now, the Reilly children had a sense of well-being. Their father always had angry outbursts, but for now, there were no continuous rages. Now the children could think about having a hockey stick, a friend for recess, a fort by the creek, dolls' clothes, a puppy from a nearby farm. When their father ran into financial difficulty, he ranted and raved. He threw objects around the house. The children all felt guilty for being alive.

Alice was fourteen when she met her first love. Her father had rented a farm just west of Hanley. The owner had been killed in France in 1918. His widow had struggled for two more years with a hired man, but he was a bout drinker who became sentimentally amorous. She picked up her two children and returned to Ontario. A lawyer in Hanley listed her farm for sale or rent. Alice's father periodically bought a copy of the local newspaper. In a special edition, farms in the whole area were advertised. The ad for the widow's farm read: "Farm for sale or rent. Two quarters. Wheat. Horse and barn. Easy terms." The Reilly family moved again, leaving behind some good friends and some bad debts. Now there were nine children—two still in diapers. The family always sold what couldn't be taken on the train. As usual, Reilly took a loss on the horses, the plough, the harrow, and odds and ends of farm equipment. He just abandoned his primitive blacksmith tools. He arrived at the new farm at the beginning of April. Grace organized the children and waited until the next tenants pushed them out. Grace occupied the last two rows of the passenger train. She had paid for three adults. Grace and her nine children were surrounded by a chaotic miscellany of trunks, suitcases, wooden boxes, and bulging flour and potato sacks. The older children took care of the younger ones, changing diapers, reading and playing games. The other passengers crowded to vacant seats at the front of the car. Grace retired to the ladies' washroom when it was time to breastfeed her two infants. Lunch and supper was bread and butter, preserved jams, cold beef, and bottled chicken. Grace had to plan the food carefully because whatever animals or poultry could not be eaten immediately had to be sold off. Farmers were constantly moving off and farm sales were a form of entertainment. Reilly always left Grace to make the final arrangements and then ranted at her shortcomings. He was waiting at the train station with a borrowed wagon. Luckily, the train trip was only five hours and the children were all awake. They piled into the wagon with their possessions. The family arrived at the farm to the usual disappointment. The house was no bigger than the previous house.

The barn was simply a large lean-to. The winter snow still held more than half the land. The visible earth looked light and sandy—soil that would blow in the wind if there wasn't enough rain. Self-pity had to be put aside while endless chores were begun. The children found useful things to do both out of boredom and to avoid their father's bad temper. The four oldest children, James, Alice, Jane, and Susan were organizers and disciplinarians. They had been through moves before. Reilly was never in a good mood when the responsibilities of his large family dropped on him like a barn beam after he had enjoyed being alone for a time. The crises his children faced when coming to a new farm always exacerbated his sense of failure. He knew before any of them that this new start would only emphasize his perennial shortcomings.

As usual, there wasn't enough sleeping room for such a large family. The younger children would have to sleep in the kitchen-dining room with their parents. The older children shared two bedrooms upstairs. The house had no attic for the older boys to sleep in. There were two wood beds and one couch for two adults and nine children. The wooden frame house whistled with the wind so that the last of the winter gusts were accompanied by sounds that reiterated the precarious situation of farmers clinging to a slice of land juxtaposed between vast prairie and vast sky. Grace looked around and wondered how they could survive the prairie winter in this ramshackle house.

Three weeks later, the family was settled in and waiting impatiently for planting. Every member of the family waited on the weather. Even the infants seemed aware that the family's survival depended on dry, sunny days—certainly they knew that bad weather meant bad tempers. Reilly had restored the usual rural menagerie—a team of horses, two milk cows, laying hens, and a pregnant sow. Reilly had very little money left. He was a prodigious worker, however, and found various labouring jobs to earn cash. They had inherited the barn cats and a young farm dog from the widow. Farmers came and went on the prairies. It was a hard life on isolated homesteads; the winters were long and punishing; crop prices were speculative.

Farmers were always moving on to that better soil, the land of more bushels per acre. Hard work and careful planning could be destroyed in days by the weather. Goods and animals were always up for sale at discounted prices, yet manufactured goods kept pouring in from eastern manufacturers. In the long winters, farm families dreamed of Ford trucks, John Deere tractors, and a myriad of temptations from Eaton's catalogue. Of course, for the Reilly family, these would always remain dreams. Most of the children's clothing and toys had been inherited from other families. Neighbours were always willing to help one another and accepting used articles had no social stigma. Every family did it. Of course, the Reilly family usually received items and seldom had anything to give. Every now and then, however, Reilly got a good blacksmithing or construction job and the family would be treated to a shopping spree at the local general store. Reilly's mercurial moods included periods of great generosity and in some ways, he was an easy touch when neighbours begged for his help. Like many men, his blackest moods were reserved for his wife and children.

Within days of their arrival at the new farm, the Reilly's felt the effect of social organization. The local Baptist minister made a call. Grace was able to offer a cup of tea, but he declined. One of the local teachers also dropped by to give information about the school. Several of the neighbouring farm ladies came over with fresh bread or cookies. When they realized there were nine children in the house, they went away shaking their heads. The older children enrolled themselves in school. School was always better than staying around the farm, caught between chores and boredom. They had found neighbouring children within days and had joined the local transportation network, a combination of walking and haphazard wagon rides. So, one day in April, the school mistress looked up from her desk at 8:15 to find six new children lined up at the door.

Alice's older brother, James introduced himself and his siblings. He had thought about attending school himself to finish off Grade 8, but when he looked around, he decided that a fifteen-year-old boy would not fit in. There were no pupils there older than twelve or thirteen. And so Alice became the oldest pupil in the school at fourteen. She was joined by Jane (thirteen), Mary (eleven), Fred (ten), and William (nine). Her younger brother John (six) could have come, but he was both shy and rebellious (and he had no shoes that fit). His enrollment could wait until the fall. When the school mistress told Alice she would be the oldest in the school, Alice once again acknowledged to herself the passing of her childhood. Last year, she had accepted the mystery and terror of menstruation. Last fall, she had stopped playing games at recess and lunch with children a year or two younger than her. Instead, she had volunteered to supervise the play of the younger children. At home and at school now, she was an apprentice, a nascent adult—that contradictory time of life of both establishing and defying discipline. As the oldest daughter, she had become her mother's ally at an early age. Surrogate motherhood involved disciplining the younger children, or at least reporting their misdemeanors to her mother. (She wouldn't tell on her siblings to her father because that might mean a beating.) Often, she was her mother's confidante and, most difficult of all, her defender. Now the school mistress, Abigail Thompson, who was only twenty-six, recognized Alice as more of a colleague and friend than a pupil. Alice had taken more steps towards adulthood without consciously willing it. In fact, she would have preferred rushing to the playground with her brothers and sisters instead of sitting with Miss Thompson relating her family's history and sharing a cup of tea.

For James, the long walk back to the farm was the definitive journey from childhood to adulthood. The end of schooling forced him to make a decision about his life that he wasn't prepared to make. At fifteen, he had to decide if he would become a blacksmith and farmer like his father or whether he would leave home to become a lumberjack, or a railway worker, or whatever the world would offer. As he walked, he became overcome by fear and grief. He had no one to talk to or confide in. For miles, he walked down the muddy road oblivious of the changing weather, tears running down his cheeks. By the time he reached home, he had put away as much of the vulnerability of childhood as he could. He had begun the process of creating an impervious shell—the necessary armour of adulthood.

Now James and Alice had only tenuous links to childhood. They were both still chastised by their parents, but the authority was more habitual and ritualistic than real. James and Alice were simply biding their time, waiting on the edge of metamorphosis for an event to move them to a final change. Alice went to school only occasionally now. Miss Thompson kept her name on the roll only because she wanted Alice to be there. She really needed Alice's company to fortify her own resolve as the tedium and stress of being a teacher in a one-room school on the prairies weighed on her. She had stayed one more year because there was a young man who she thought might ask her to marry him. He couldn't decide whether or not he could leave his mother and father and live in a different home. If the young man didn't propose during this school year, she would try to find a teaching job in a larger school in a bigger town. The farms and small towns of Saskatchewan always carried the virus of move on, move on. Move on to more fertile soil; move on to a larger centre; move on to a better job. Move on, move on, or be left behind like the detritus of a prairie windstorm, dry and desiccated.

Chapter Four

Galicia 1920-1923

Betta wanted to be a nurse or a teacher. But those were foolish dreams for a peasant girl. Her family owned no land. They lived on the large farm accumulated by Kronas Denzo. He was called a kulak, a man with enough land to have tenants. He was a kind man. Betta's family had a comfortable one-room home. They were allowed to have their own vegetable garden, a cow, and some chickens. Farm life could be very pleasant with the animals, the change of seasons, the joy of the outdoors and nature. All that could be lost, however, if crops failed or irrational conflicts broke out. But for now, Betta's family ate well. Denzo had six families on his estate, each of them comfortable and none of them expecting more from life. They never even thought of being able to get their own land. They had their faith, the church festivals, and celebrations when all the crops were planted and when they were harvested. Their children could go to the estate school until they were ten or twelve.

Betta had been allowed to stay in school until she had finished Grade 5. She had been the smartest pupil in the one-room school. Her teacher, Miss Kovalenko, had hoped she might be able to continue, but her family needed her on the farm. Miss Kovalenko had to watch bright and hardworking children fall far short of their potential. Poverty stripped children of hope and ambition. They fell into a kind of pervasive dullness. Miss Kovalenko came from a lower-middle class family in Grabek.

Her father owned the general store. He wanted his two daughters educated well enough to run the store when he went on trips to purchase goods. His wife had no aptitude as a store clerk. The girls were both very good students and the store was doing well, so he indulged them. They were allowed to walk to the senior school. Both girls graduated with diplomas from the Education Ministry of Austria-Hungary. Their graduation class had five students. Miss Kovalenko had always dreamed of being a teacher. She applied for the vacancy in a tiny rural school. She was eighteen, with no teacher training. Her father didn't like the idea, but gave in to his persuasive daughter. Her sister stayed home to help run the store. Miss Kovalenko's family considered themselves Polish, whereas Betta's father was a proud Ukrainian, a member of the western Catholic Church. He had wondered how Galicia would be affected by the Great War and the Russian Revolution. Galicia was a mixture of Poles, Ukrainians, Jews, Germans, and Czechs. It was made up of small farms. In some areas, however, hardworking entrepreneurs had bought up a number of farms and created large estates.

Denzo sold his grain to grain merchants in L'vov. The railroads would take his grain as far away as Vienna. His vegetables, pigs, and chickens were purchased by the citizens of L'vov. Since 1920, Galicia had been part of Poland. After the chaos and fighting, the area was at peace. Now, in 1922, the future looked bright for Denzo. Some of the young men from his estate had been killed in the Great War, but since there was no fighting in his area, there was no destruction. Life was similar to that before the war. Denzo knew, however, that the revolution and civil war in Russia could affect all of Eastern Europe.

Betta's family thought she was lucky when the son of Fedir Dubinsky, a small land owner, showed some interest in her during the church service. Betta was beautiful. She had lovely blue eyes and a fair complexion. She had the athletic frame of a farm girl, formed by hard physical work and a good diet. During the summer, the church often hosted a lunch after the service. This was how the local people caught up on the news—international, national, and local.

Now their source of international news was from Krakow instead of Vienna. They knew from the tragedy of the Great War that events far from them could bring disaster. In this time of peace, young girls were thinking of marriage and children. Young men always dream of being heroes, but love, sex, and marriage could be a consolation.

Mike fell in love with Betta. He was eighteen and she was sixteen. He expected her to fall in love too. After all, he was good-looking, strong, and intelligent. He was also a young man with vibrant energy and ambition. Moreover, his family owned land. Owning land was a step up the ladder. Owning a great deal of land meant wealth and power. Betta had no thoughts of love, but she knew she was attractive. She knew because the young men at church functions began staring at her as she grew older. She began to worry over her clothes and she took great care with her hair. She thought about the women in novels she had read during her brief school years and wished that she, like them, had many dresses to choose from.

Luckily for Betta and Mike, the region around Grabek was a backwater of history, for now. The railroad that ran through L'vov often had refugees from the revolution. People who had been part of the Tsarist regime and supported the White Russians were now fleeing for their lives. Large landowners who had hundreds of peasants to work their estates now had only what they could carry. Russian aristocratic titles were a burden now. These people had spent their winters in the glittering wealth and culture of St. Petersburg. The city rivalled London, Paris, and Vienna for indulgence and decadence. While the vast population of the city suffered in the cold and thousands died each winter of starvation, the elaborate soirees and balls went on. The Tsar and Tsarina could not grasp the significance of the suffering that their people endured. They justified their criminal rule by believing they were appointed by God. The revolution and civil war were a blood bath. Now emigres fled towards France with jewels and gold coins sewn into their clothing. Their servants travelled with them because they, too, feared for their lives.

In Galicia, the remnants of the Austro-Hungarian administration withdrew to Vienna to try to comprehend the chaos of an empire spinning into disparate parts. The empire's central government had been held together by Franz Joseph and the military. Now, revolutionary forces had won every region and every ethnic group worked to establish rule. Instead of large ineffectual bureaucracies in Vienna and Budapest, regions began pragmatic efforts to create local governments—some succeeded; some failed.

Life on the farms around Grabek continued as always; good years, bad years. Hay, potatoes, turnips, cabbage, and carrots could withstand unfavourable weather. Taxes could be raised for teachers, a constable, and road and bridge construction.

There was an inevitable fruition in the relationship between Betta and Mike. They looked forward to seeing each other in church—they were both very regular church-goers now. The priest was pleased. In the summer, Grabek had concerts, fairs, and dances. With the permission of her father, Mike escorted Betta to some of these. Both families approved of a marriage. Without parental approval, marriages couldn't occur. The nexus of family, church, economics, and love worked. So, Betta and Mike were married in 1923. Mike was nineteen and Betta was seventeen—the perfect ages for farm couples.

The wedding had all the ceremony of church and farm. The best time for a wedding was after the spring plantings, so many marriages occurred in June. The priest approved of Betta and Mike (although he wished Mike wasn't quite so aggressive). There was an elaborate Catholic ceremony (with a little Greek Orthodox ritual slipped in) and the priest was progressive enough to use some Ukrainian in the liturgy. Betta and Mike's school friends were there, some of them looking at the possibility of marriage themselves. Marriages meant children and children meant farm workers—it was worth the risks associated with childbirth and the high child mortality rates. Betta and Mike moved in with the Dubinskys and their life together began.

Chapter Five

Saskatchewan 1925-1929

Grace Reilly had made breakfast for her children and husband that morning. After breakfast, she put some of her clothing and the clothing of her two youngest children into two flour sacks. When her neighbour arrived with his wagon, she got in with the youngest child on her lap and put the older one in the back. Her neighbour, Frank Gruse, knew the situation. As the wagon moved down the drive, Grace sat ramrod straight, as if frozen solid. The three middle sons ran after the wagon to say goodbye. She didn't turn around. These sons would carry that wound until the day they died.

Grace was going to stay with a friend ten miles away. She had left after many years of hardship. She had borne eleven children over twenty years. Val was twelve and Jake was ten. Now they had no mother. They sobbed until they faced the reality of their situation. Their father would return from his blacksmithing job at a neighbour's farm at any time. They had to tell their oldest sister Alice. Alice would know what to do. She had helped raise them.

They told the other children they were going to get Alice. They got Gus, the old farm horse, out of the shed and put a bridle and bit on him. They had no saddle. They mounted Gus from the garden fence. They kept their seats on Gus by squeezing their legs and feet into his side. Gus trotted along amiably at a pace slightly faster than a normal adult's walk. The farm where Alice worked was only five or six miles away. Val and Jake found Alice churning butter in the cool sod shed attached to the barn. When she saw their red eyes and the rivulets carved into their dusty faces with tears, she knew there was bad news.

When her brothers told her what had happened and began to sob again, Alice assured them that everything would be fine. She would take her mother's place. But she knew things wouldn't be fine. The world had just tilted and every fixed object was askew. She sent her brothers to get a drink at the water barrel and as she vigorously churned the butter, her body and brain hummed with frantic, desperate energy.

She had never heard of a wife leaving her husband and children. Women suffered abuse, beatings, poverty, loneliness—harsh husbands in a harsh country. But they never left. There was no place to go. More than anything else, Alice wanted to weep. But she couldn't. She couldn't make things worse for her brothers and sisters by weeping. She willed herself to be strong. She never told her siblings that she hated her father with a white-hot passion that would never be fully extinguished.

Alice's maternal grandmother was contacted and she came to help. Neighbours and church members did all they could. Reilly was in an uncontrollable rage. He took his anger out on the children. Some of his blows opened cuts and the younger boys all had large bruises. Alice's grandmother and the Methodist minister took charge. The younger children were parceled out. Parceled out! Several went to relatives who wanted farm help and genuinely felt compassion for the children. The younger ones became wards of the child welfare system in Saskatchewan. Luckily, the system found homes for these orphans. The family would not be re-united for over twenty years.

The three older children worked on nearby farms. Then James decided he wanted to do something else. He moved to Moose Jaw. Alice and Jane were close to their brother and decided to follow him. They got a wagon ride to their grandmother's where they had a tearful goodbye. They didn't say goodbye to their father. He spent his time raging around the house by himself.

James found a job in an auto repair shop in Moose Jaw. Everything was on-the-job training. He was intelligent and a hard worker so things went well. He had even found a boarding house that he liked. When Alice and Jane arrived, they stayed one night in a hotel. That was the first time either had been in a hotel, and they were delighted by what was, for them, unusual luxury. Both of them stayed in the hot bath until their skin shriveled. The white sheets and white pillowcases seemed out of a book. As children, they had slept three or four to a room—sometimes three or four to a bed. James had asked the owner of the boarding house some weeks before if his sisters could move in as well. The owner moved one boarder to the attic and reduced his weekly rent. He was happy with the new arrangement. Alice and Jane shared the room. There was a toilet down the hall and a bathroom next to them. No more than half an hour in the bath. No more than a bath every two days. Meals also had rules; breakfast between seven and eight, supper at 6 p.m. sharp.

This was a great arrangement for James and his two sisters. At least the three oldest children could be together. They discussed endlessly where their mother and brothers and sisters could be. Alice was the letter writer. She sent letters to her grandmother frequently making inquiries. She found out that two of her brothers were with uncles. She managed to get addresses and reconnect with these brothers. Her grandmother wasn't sure where her daughter was. Alice forgave her mother because she understood her plight. Alice had sheltered Jane from some of their father's violence so Jane was slower to forgive their mother.

Alice and Jane began looking for jobs just as Moose Jaw was going through a growth spurt. The town was an agricultural hub. For the last few years, crops had been good and prices above average, so farmers had been spending. Now there was a second restaurant and a theatre for films. The boarding house had a copy of the *Moose*

Jaw Enquirer delivered every morning. There were many jobs being advertised. Jane was loud, rambunctious, rude, and fun-loving, and was determined to have a good time. She needed a job that would suit her personality. She decided she wanted to be a waitress. She hoped to meet people and even get invitations out. Alice, who was shyer and more reserved, like James, wanted a more sedate job. She didn't like the idea of brash and flirtatious men annoying her. Both found jobs within two days.

Jane accepted the offer of a restaurant only blocks away. The owners were a warm Greek family—mother, father, and two daughters, twelve and eight. They liked Jane's outgoing personality. Alice applied for a job as a domestic helper. The ad in the paper said an elderly couple needed help around the house. Alice used the boarding house phone and called the couple, who described where they lived. Alice took a bus to their neighbourhood the next day. The bus stop was only eight or ten homes away from where the job was. Alice was very impressed, actually intimidated, by the beautiful homes and the lovely lawns. The farms she was raised on didn't have lawns.

She went to the front door and tapped the knocker several times rather timidly. Nobody came. She realized she would have to strike the knocker harder. She struck harder, hoping she wasn't being rude. Within a minute, a grey-haired woman opened the door. She was smiling, and she welcomed Alice inside. She led Alice to a large living room, asked her to sit down, then left to get her husband, Alice thought about how the woman didn't look elderly at all.

Alice was struck by how beautiful the furniture was. There was also an upright piano and a radio and phonograph in a large cabinet. Alice realized the couple was comfortably well-off. The woman returned with her husband. Alice guessed they were in their sixties. Their names were Dorothy and William Riddell. Dorothy offered Alice tea. Alice accepted, although she feared spilling it. While Dorothy was in the kitchen making tea, William asked Alice some friendly questions—where she was from, how she ended up in

Moose Jaw, did she have brothers and sisters? Sort of harmless male questions. Once Dorothy returned with the tea, the probing female questions began. How old was she? Had she been raised on a farm? Did she know how to cook? Did she know how to bake? Had she ever used a Hoover? What were her previous jobs? What church had she attended? (That was the crucial question. She had to be a church girl, but she couldn't be a Catholic.) When Alice said she had been raised a Baptist, she passed the test.

Alice was obviously such a quiet and dutiful girl. Mrs. Riddell was pleased that Alice hadn't asked about her pay or time off. In the past, other girls had been aggressive, almost rude, in asking about the job. The Riddells, after a hushed meeting in the kitchen, offered Alice the job right away. Without knowing all the details, Alice accepted. Then Mrs. Riddell told Alice all the conditions of her employment as she walked her around the house.

The Riddell home was large, with three bedrooms on the first floor, a very large dining room, and a laundry room. There was a single bathroom with a toilet, sink, and an over-sized bathtub. The Riddells were very progressive: they allowed Alice two days off a week—on their schedule. Alice thought the pay was generous since they provided all the food. Basically, Alice was to be Mrs. Riddell's ever-present servant. As Mrs. Riddell walked Alice around the house, asking questions and imparting information at the same time, they began to like each other. Mrs. Riddell's questions became less probing and more conversational.

"What kind of farm did your parents have?" she asked.

"We raised wheat, but we also had chickens and pigs and a large vegetable garden. My mother always planted potatoes, carrots, and usually turnips," replied Alice.

Mrs. Riddell thought that a family garden was a good measure of character. After about fifteen minutes, Mrs. Riddell asked Alice if she wanted a ride back to her boarding house. She could start the next day. Did she need to use the toilet? Alice was so comfortable she said yes. Mr. Riddell started the car on the first try and fiddled with the choke.

As Mrs. Riddell and Alice walked to the car, Mrs. Riddell whispered, "Do you have a boyfriend?" Alice said no. Mrs. Riddell looked speculative—did she plan to be a matchmaker or prohibit all courting?

Jane thought Alice was foolish to be a live-in domestic—not enough freedom. But Alice wanted stability. The heartbreaking event of her mother's leaving and the dispersal of the children left her with a desire for tranquility. As time passed, the arrangement worked out. The three siblings often met in the evenings to walk around Moose Jaw and discuss events. Moose Jaw attracted many sons and daughters from farms. To nearby farmers, Moose Jaw was a big metropolis, a city of excitement. The city had a movie theatre whereas nearby towns had none. Well-off farmers could drive to the city for a matinee and return home in time for bed. Poorer farmers would come during the summer in their horse-drawn wagons. Seeing a show was a big event, but it was also a time to shop. Moose Jaw had a good-sized Eaton's Store. If they didn't buy anything there, they picked up a free catalogue. The catalogue was the book of dreams—and it served a practical purpose in outhouses. The farm families would sleep on their wagons and head home the next day. The nice thing about the summer was that gardens could be neglected for a day or two. Arrangements were made for a neighbour to milk the cows and store the milk in the cold cellar. They might even feed the pigs, chickens, and horses. Jane was having a wonderful time flirting with the boarders and the restaurant customers.

* * *

Before Alice had arrived, Dorothy and William had been quite lonely. They had one son who was now in Vancouver working for a real estate company. They wrote letters, and once a month or so they telephoned him. He was talking of marriage to a Vancouver girl. The couple were devoted Baptists who attended church two or three times a week. Yet there was something missing in their lives. William was a successful insurance broker with his name on an office downtown and a secretary and three associate brokers. He was doing well financially. He could have become a charter member of the new Moose Jaw Golf and Country Club, but he found the businessmen who started the club too loud and pushy, and they drank. William was a reserved man who valued solitude. His great joy was driving his 1925 Ford roadster. He liked to tell people that the Ford Company had been in Canada since 1904 and that Canada was now the second largest manufacturer of cars in the world. He was a Ford man. He liked the story of the Canadian automobile industry founded in Oshawa, Ontario. The McLaughlin family switched from carriages and built the McLaughlin automobile in 1907. In 1915, Sam McLaughlin bought the Chevrolet Car Company of Canada and General Motors of Canada was founded in 1918. All that was very good, William thought. He appreciated the genius of Sam McLaughlin. The tradition had begun, however, of Ford owners hating Chevys, and Chevrolet owners hating Fords.

Dorothy and William Riddell had been born into the lower middle class. Their fathers were labourers who worked in the grain facilities in Moose Jaw. Their fathers knew each other quite well. Both families were stable and both emphasized Christian faith. Dorothy left school after Grade 6 to work at a dressmaker. William was allowed to finish Grade 8. He went to work at the grain depot in 1883. During years of good crops, the facility hired more men. In years of bad crops in the area, workers might be moved to another city or laid off. William didn't like his life being tied to the vagaries of Saskatchewan weather.

After five years, he started buying the daily paper and looking for another job. Most jobs didn't appeal to him, but one morning he saw an ad for an insurance salesman. William thought wearing a suit would be a grand idea. He had come to realize that he was intelligent—more intelligent than his Grade 8 education. He wondered if he could apply for the job even if he didn't own a suit. *Might as well try,* he thought.

The next morning, he opened the door of the Guardian Insurance Company. The middle-aged secretary greeted him warmly and asked him to take a seat. Mr. Melon would be out shortly. She tapped on the opaque glass of Mr. Melon's office and opened the door. Mr. Melon finished his phone call and came out to greet William. He was an effusive man with elaborate hand gestures. He asked William to come into his office. Mr. Melon needed a salesman, but William was only eighteen. He asked William a series of questions. Mr. Melon realized William was intelligent even if he didn't know much. William was quite articulate. His vocabulary and speech patterns indicated a person who could express himself. He asked William if he would be prepared to start learning the insurance business. There were no tests to pass or societies with mandatory memberships, but insurance salesmen had to know what they were talking about. William was a good reader. At International Grains, he had done all kinds of office work when outside work was scarce. He might start the day by sweeping the office floor. Then he might walk to the post office to pick up the daily mail before sorting it. He was allowed to open mail to read notices. He double-checked payroll entries. He was an errand boy to different work sites. He managed to read the morning paper before the manager came in. He even read teletype bulletins on the domestic and international price of commodities.

William agreed to a starting job. He would walk around Moose Jaw delivering pamphlets about home and auto insurance. After lunch, he would come to the office and read books about insurance generally and study manuals designed by Guardian Insurance. Guardian was a big company. It had thousands of agents and scores of offices across Canada. The company liked to train its own people. The founding members of the company believed in the divine amalgamation of capitalism and Christianity. Its agents had to be believers. A good salary can help people believe in anything. That was how William began. He was born in 1870 and by 1920, he owned the Guardian Insurance office.

Dorothy and William fell in love because proximity works. Dorothy was two years younger than William. They had attended the same eight-room elementary school. They went to the same Baptist Church. One church picnic in 1886 set the flame. The courtship was appropriate. The parents knew one another. Dorothy and William had never dated another person. In 1892, they had a lovely church wedding with bridesmaids, a best man, and ushers. All their friends and family were in attendance. The minister acted as the master of ceremonies at the wedding dinner in the church hall, where he attested to the fine character of the bride and groom in his introductory speech and even attempted a few bits of humour. The best man was so nervous he stuttered his speech to a quick end before spilling his glass of lemonade while offering a toast. William had a carefully written speech, and he didn't lift his head from the page. He praised his parents, Dorothy's parents, and Dorothy. Then he lifted his head, thanked everyone for coming, and sat down without ever smiling. Dorothy was proud of her man. The honeymoon was a three-day visit to Regina. Three years later, their son was born.

* * *

Alice was very happy with the Riddells, and Dorothy soon became like a mother to her. They peeled potatoes together, chopped carrots, made apple pies, and baked bread. Alice was becoming a middle-class person. She went shopping with Dorothy, and although Dorothy was frugal, Alice realized the joy of being able to shop without counting every penny. Dorothy never walked away from a purchase because she didn't have enough money. They also worked hard in the garden together. Dorothy wasn't going to give up the lower-middle-class necessity of having a vegetable garden. The neighbours on both sides grew flowers and shrubs. Dorothy thought people who grew flowers and shrubs and had gardeners were uppity. Baptists were not allowed to be uppity. Dorothy wasn't intimidated. Dorothy taught Alice how to sew; after all, she had trained as a seamstress when she was only twelve. Now Dorothy had an expensive Singer sewing machine, and she sewed for fun. She could buy patterns at Eaton's and make clothes for Alice. William was bemused and happy with Dorothy's devotion to Alice.

William Riddell began to accumulate some of the signs of a successful businessman. He accepted appointments to various boards—the Y.M.C.A., the Downtown Businessmen Association, The City Planning Committee. He was quiet, serious, thoughtful, and conservative. He was so well established, he could leave the office to his secretary and his employees. Many of the businessmen in town would take time off to play golf, but William never did. He and Dorothy began to curl though. Once their son was older, they joined the Mayfair Curling Club. The Saskatchewan winter meant there had to be an activity that was indoors. Snowshoeing or skiing in thirty degrees below zero wasn't possible. Dorothy and William loved the game and became quite good. They went to a number of bonspiels every winter. As Baptists, they didn't like the post-game drinking that many curlers indulged in, but they curled with an older crowd and many of them were teetotaling churchgoers.

In May 1924, the Mayfair Curling Club organized a Christian fellowship mixed bonspiel. William helped organize it. Curlers came from across the province. Roads were now plowed and cars were more reliable. Car owners had car blankets—heavy double-folded wool blankets. The local curlers would host the out-of-town people and there would be a common church service on Sunday. Of course, there could be no curling on Sunday. The bonspiel was completed on Saturday with each team playing three games. At 7 p.m., there was an informal dinner. Prizes were presented to loud applause. Dorothy and William had a couple from their church as partners. William told Dorothy they could have done better if the Partridges weren't such lazy sweepers. One team had come all the way from Prince Albert. The team included a man of about thirty with very curly hair and a magisterial, almost pompous, bearing. People said he was John Diefenbaker, a lawyer and determined politician who kept running for office and never winning.

The next day, there was a church service before the curlers left for home. It was an ecumenical service to be followed by sandwiches and soup. At the church service, Mr. Diefenbaker rose from his pew to thank the organizers and hosts of the bonspiel. He was an articulate and dynamic speaker. But after fifteen minutes, the congregation was both bored and restless. They wanted to get on the road. The minister—with a certain amount of brusqueness—interrupted Mr. Diefenbaker to say that lunch was ready. He wished them a safe drive home. Mr. Diefenbaker was annoyed. He hadn't completed his prepared notes. William couldn't comprehend his analogy of sweeping on the ice and sweeping up sinners.

* * *

In 1929, Guardian Insurance rewarded William for his success. The company sent him notice that he was invited to the annual meeting in Toronto. All expenses would be paid for him and his wife. Dorothy was delighted. She enjoyed new experiences. In July 1929, they boarded a train in Moose Jaw. William had left explicit and detailed instructions for his employees. All would be well in the office. Of course, they trusted Alice to take care of the house.

The first stop was Regina. Even people from Saskatchewan were struck by the endless fields of grain running to the horizon in every direction. The trip to Winnipeg was a repeat of Saskatchewan. William began to wonder how Canada could sell so much wheat and barley. The west, on the other hand, was all about the railways.

William appreciated the locomotives—giant engines with the ear-shattering sound of steam. The engines were examples of the genius of the Industrial Age. William wondered how the factories could cast such large wheels and drive-shafts. He speculated on the weight of that benign monster. The steel rails themselves took eight men to lift. Every town they passed through had two or three grain elevators. At Winnipeg, there was a huge railway marshalling yard and row after row of grain silos.

When Dorothy and William changed trains, they looked for their sleeping compartments on the new train. A conductor showed them where they would be sleeping. The numbers on the dividers were clear. They then found seats on the coach behind the sleeping car. The coach had units of two seats facing another two seats. The couple opposite them was going to visit their daughter in Port Arthur. She had taken a job as a teacher there. The two couples decided to have dinner together.

The restaurant was impressive. It represented the residual luxury from the age when only the wealthy could travel either by ship or train. The waiters had white jackets and black pants with razor-sharp seams. The tables had white tablecloths. Each table setting had two dinner forks, one dessert fork, a soup spoon, one serrated knife, one butter knife, a large dish, a soup bowl, a bread and butter plate, a heavy white napkin in ring, a wine glass, a water glass, and a coffee or tea cup. Both couples were a little taken aback. Neither couple had this kind of luxury at home. The waiter brought the four menus. There was soup, smoked salmon as an appetizer, and a choice of chicken, beef, or pork entrees with roasted potatoes and peas. Later there would be a dessert menu. It was an elaborate table setting with Canadian style home-cooked entrees. The four people made their choices and the waiter retreated. He returned with bread in a basket and a plate of butter. He left and returned to ask if they would like wine. All said no. He took the wine glasses away. He returned with four small plates of smoked salmon and crackers. He left and returned with a pitcher of water and asked each person if he or she wanted water. They each said yes. He poured the water and retreated again. William was getting annoyed with all this coming and going and oily obsequies. William guessed it was all to gain a substantial tip. But if he didn't disappear soon, he wouldn't get a tip at all. When the entrees were about to be served, the waiter returned. He took each napkin and placed it on the lap of each diner. Dorothy and William didn't like this intimacy from a stranger.

Despite the rocky start, they all enjoyed their meals and began a warm and friendly conversation. The Riddells wanted to brag about their son's accomplishments. The Drummonds wanted to talk about their daughter's accomplishments.

"Our son went to university," William said quietly. He didn't want to reveal that he was still somewhat surprised and very, very proud of this. He and Dorothy had never aspired to more education because nobody they knew went to university. They valued hard work and education nevertheless. They gave a great deal of respect for the educated in their community—teachers, ministers, lawyers, and doctors. They all lamented the absence of their child. They assumed each child would marry and they expressed hope that they would choose a suitable mate. The waiter offered them coffee or tea. They all declined. It was late for Saskatchewan people. The men each left a tip making sure the other person didn't see the amount.

The porter had put their suitcases in the sleeping compartments. William got the upper bed and Dorothy the lower. They weren't exactly sure about the procedure. Dorothy walked down the aisle to the lavatory and when she returned, William went. When he returned, the drapes had been pulled and Dorothy was on the lower bunk. William went the three-step ladder with the porter's help. William said goodnight and climbed into his bunk. Dorothy and William went through all the contortions of undressing and dressing while lying flat. They weren't that young and both had put on some middle-age weight. Both of them thought this was an adventure, but they didn't need to repeat this adventure too often.

They slept well. Their sleep was disturbed only twice by the train going around bends and their rolling against the side of the train. Undressing and dressing in the morning wasn't any easier than the night before. They were still happy, though, to be having this adventure. They both emerged in good spirits and very hungry. They walked to the dining car immediately and were happy to see a different waiter. The tables still had white linen tablecloths, but the table setting only had one knife, one fork, and one spoon. The napkin was folded under the fork. The breakfast menu was cereal or eggs (cooked in any way) with bacon or sausage. The Riddells ordered a breakfast similar to what they had at home—two fried eggs over easy with bacon and toast. The waiter took their orders and left. No comings and goings. The breakfast was served quickly and the Riddells could linger over coffee because they had been the first passengers in the room.

The train stopped at Port Arthur. The Riddells said goodbye to their new friends, wishing them a nice visit with their daughter. The conductor had to wait for some rail switches. As they passed through and picked up speed, Dorothy and William could see the huge grain elevators and the lake ships being loaded. Canada's grain was on its way around the world. The train was now beginning its sweep around the magnificent Lake Superior. Soon, the landscape was all rock and forest. William marveled at the passage through overhanging rocks. He thought the railroad builders must have had tons and tons of dynamite. Some rock faces showed the drill holes for dynamite. Every now and then, they saw the magnificent lake. They had been told it was the largest body of fresh water in the world. At noon, a porter came around selling sandwiches and apples. They could have coffee or tea and an apple tart for dessert. They were thoroughly enjoying this. The landscape was magnificent, and they enjoyed watching the people walking up and down the aisle. By 1 p.m., they had both fallen asleep.

The train chugged on. At reasonably large towns, it took on and let off passengers and freight. This was the country of lumber camps and mining communities. Freight trains carried lumber and minerals to larger centres for processing. Canada was a large country full of vast natural resources. Farmers, lumbermen, miners—they all knew how to work hard. The Riddells slept through the wide expanse of Ontario. On the third day, when having breakfast, the waiter told them they were only hours away from Toronto. On the final stretch of the journey, they saw the many small towns of Southern Ontario. The landscape was certainly different from Saskatchewan. Finally, the train was slowing down, and they could see the skyline of Toronto.

There were large marshalling yards on Front Street that sorted out passenger trains from freight trains. From their window, Dorothy and William could see most of the wide expanse of Toronto Harbour. There were scores of grain silos and warehouses. There was a large passenger train depot, and the porter directed them to the correct entrance. Perhaps a hundred yards away, there was a huge building. It was to be the new railway station. The final finishing touches just had to be completed. But the inevitable delays occurred. Union Station would open with eight rail lines to serve the passengers from east and west. Toronto could hardly build rail lines, roads, and bridges fast enough to serve Canada's fastest growing city. Just as William had been told by letter, a Guardian Insurance employee was waiting for them. He was a smiling young man who held up a cardboard sign with Guardian Insurance written on it. His name was Jim Rogers. He welcomed them warmly and took their suitcases. He explained that their hotel was just across the road on Front Street. It was called the Queen's Hotel. The Riddells were amazed at how large the structure was. Jim Rogers took them through the main door that had gaudy uniformed doormen on each side. Each doorman tipped his hat as they passed through. There were porters waiting inside but

Jim carried their bags directly to the reservation desk. He explained to the clerk who the Riddells were and he got two keys for their room. Jim took them to a soft sofa, sat them down, pulled up a chair, and outlined their agenda. After lunch, there was a bus tour of Toronto. There would be a reception in the main hall at 8 p.m. after dinner. The next day would be the general meeting, followed by a dinner and dance. The next day would be an open day with their train scheduled for 6 p.m.

Jim said they should go to their room, get organized, grab some lunch, and meet in the foyer at 1 p.m. They were impressed with their room. William said, "All my hard work has paid off. We don't have to pay for anything. The Company knows how to organize an event. Certainly, it appreciates its employees."

William could have gone on for quite a while. But Dorothy said, "I'm going to have a bath."

After finding some pleasant music, William opened his suitcase and put his clothes neatly away. He thought he could get the hotel to iron his suit. After Dorothy finished her bath, he went for his. At noon, they were ready to go downstairs for lunch. After lunch, they waited in the lobby, and they were joined by ten or fifteen other people who worked for Guardian Insurance. Jim Rogers appeared at ten to one and greeted everyone. There were perfunctory handshakes and smiles among the Guardian employees. The bus was waiting outside the front door. Jim introduced the bus driver and they pulled away. Most of the men came to the convention alone so that their enjoyment of Toronto would not be constrained by their wives. There were only two other wives besides Dorothy.

Jim was the tour guide, using a formula the bus company had. Most of the employees were from small towns and the drive along the waterfront impressed them. Toronto in 1929 was an industrial city with factories and manufacturer warehouses. It now had a population of half a million. The bus turned up Bay Street and the great tower of city hall rose above the nearby buildings. Jim continued his narrative until they reached Casa Loma. He told the story of its construction by Henry Pellatt, a Toronto financier. World War I stopped its completion. It had ninety-eight rooms and was the largest private home in Canada.

Dorothy whispered, "Imagine having to clean it!"

Pellatt ran into financial difficulties after the war. As they drove by, it was empty. The City of Toronto owned a beautiful empty Gothic Revival castle. Next stop was the Sunnyside Swimming Pool. They couldn't see inside from the bus, but they could see the hundreds lined up outside in their bathing outfits. It was the largest swimming pool in Canada.

William whispered to Dorothy, "Sounds as if Toronto has the biggest of everything. I'm getting sick of hearing it."

The tour continued with a look at the Coliseum, the Cyclorama, and the new cenotaph to commemorate Canadians killed in World War I. The tour included a great number of detours because rails were being laid throughout the city for the trolley cars. The battle between streetcars and cars was just warming up.

The tour ended at about four and Jim reminded them that there would be an informal reception in the main conference room at 8 p.m. Dorothy and William decided to walk down Front Street and then up Yonge Street. There were stores with goods of all description, but the dominant product was clothing. Toronto was the clothing manufacturing centre for Ontario and the western provinces. Dorothy and William noted the impressive bank buildings and insurance company buildings. The solid stone and brick buildings indicated the success and permanence of these financial institutions. It was a beautiful evening for a walk even though the street was jammed with streetcars, cars, and pedestrians making their way home. Dorothy chose a nice-looking Italian restaurant for dinner. There were no Italian restaurants in Moose Jaw yet. They loved the food. The owner/waiter couldn't believe they had dinner without wine.

It was another pleasant walk back to the hotel. They bathed and dressed formally for the reception. The reception was a matter of mingling around, greeting a few people. The president and executive officers tried to greet as many employees as possible, and they did a pretty good job. Dorothy was bored and William felt no need to kowtow to any executives, so they left early. All the new experiences were wearing them out.

The next day, William attended the workshops for employees. Dorothy decided to try riding a streetcar. She wasn't afraid to ask the driver the procedure and she had a pleasant trip up Yonge Street and then Bay Street to city hall. She walked around the hall and then sat on a bench. A street vendor was selling food and she bought a sandwich and a bottle of pop. She was having a wonderful time. After her bench lunch, Dorothy walked down Queen Street. There sat Canada's two great department stores—Eaton's and Simpson's. Shoppers could walk from one to the other across Queen Street and compare prices. The crosswalk was the busiest in Canada. Eaton's had been founded in Toronto in 1869 by Timothy Eaton, an immigrant from Ireland. Before Eaton's, small shops sold various goods in different areas of Toronto. The tradition was to haggle. Timothy Eaton changed all that. His department store was very large and had a very wide assortment of goods. There was no haggling. There were salesclerks, not owners. The price on the label was the price. People enjoyed going to one store to get several items. Many people didn't have the time or inclination to haggle. Eaton's was a huge success. The Eaton's Catalogue was impatiently waited for across Canada. Catalogue shopping was founded on the efficiency of the railroads. Eaton's could ship goods all the way across Canada and still make a profit. Eventually, Eaton's employed over seventy thousand people.

Eaton's competitor was Simpson's. It was started in 1858 by Robert Simpson. Its operation was basically the same as Eaton's. It had some different items. Different suppliers of clothing made its fashion different from Eaton's. Its furniture was a little more British than Eaton's. Perhaps the most noticeable difference was at the cosmetic counter. Each store had its unique cosmetic suppliers. Women would either buy their cosmetics at Eaton's or Simpson's. There the greatest loyalty lay.

Dorothy had time to look in both stores, although she had no plans to buy anything. She had heard about the escalator at Eaton's and she wanted to try it. When she approached the escalator, there was a short line-up. Dorothy joined the line. Some people were very excited. Some were apprehensive. Dorothy had a moment when she thought about leaving the line. The sound of the escalator and the relentless movement of the conveyor suggested a powerful machine not easy to control. She got on the device after some hesitation when she felt the impatience of people behind her. She immediately grabbed the hand rail. The vibration of the steps was unnerving. She wondered how she would get off. At the top, as she saw the steps disappear, she had a moment of panic, but the passengers in front of her seemed safe. As her step neared the top, she jumped for safety, almost losing her balance. A gentleman steadied her, and after a few seconds, they began to laugh. He, too, had leapt to safety. She thought about how her friends in Moose Jaw would be anxious to hear about her adventures in Eaton's and Simpson's. It was certainly a day well-spent.

William's time wasn't so wonderful. The workshops stressed statistics and mathematical formulae for insurance rates. William didn't need to do any calculations. He just followed the guidelines distributed by the company. The sales workshops demonstrated the difference between the traditional British sales techniques and the American techniques. For the longest time, Canada had a split personality. Some salesmen retained the traditional, reserved, stiff, dignified, understated approach of the English. Some salesmen adopted the exuberant, loud, backslapping, aggressive approach of the Americans. William had always used the English approach. That was his nature.

At seven, the Riddells showed up for the formal dinner and dance. The president, sales manager, and senior actuaries all made appropriately boring speeches. It didn't matter. Guardian Insurance Corp. was doing extremely well. Dorothy and William were their usual polite selves and chatted amicably with their table companions.

After dinner, they said some polite good evenings and left. They weren't going to witness the wild movements of the new dances. Baptists stuck to country dancing. The next morning, they carried their bags across the street and got on the train for the trip home. Dorothy had bought only one dress and some underwear. The trip home was just as pleasant as the trip down. Ontario had some wonderfully lush farmland; the trip around Superior was just as breathtaking; the return to the Prairies aroused a regional pride. Three days later, they were home. For the rest of their lives, they would reminisce about their rail voyage and the wonders of the big city.

Chapter Six

Saskatchewan 1930

After his visit to Toronto, William felt a new sense of worldliness. He thought he should be more aware of what was going on in Canada and around the world. He read the *Inquirer* assiduously, but it was concentrated on Moose Jaw. Now he wanted to know about the broader world. He wouldn't use the phrase, "intellectually stifled," but he had come to the conclusion that he was smarter than the limitations of his daily routine. Many people in the organizations that he belonged to had shown they respected his thoughtful ideas. He began to think of running for political office. Then he thought that at fifty-six, he was too old for that.

When he heard about a request for delegates at the Baptist Convention in Regina, he saw his opportunity to make a change. The convention was designed to clarify Baptist doctrine and to advance new ideas about church organization. The doctrine of adult baptism, for example, had to be explained and defended at each convention. There were new ideas about how to use elders for home visits and discussions about new books for Sunday school classes. The convention's program ranged from the very esoteric to the very practical. William had been an active member in his church, but he had never delved into theological issues. He thought the convention would be interesting, however.

He persuaded Richard MacRae to go with him. Richard owned the only hardware store in Moose Jaw. Most of his customers were farmers and his inventory included repair parts for farm implements. He had a monopoly on binder twine and that brought him a good income. His wife and daughter frequently worked in the store, especially on Saturdays. He was constantly increasing his inventory and was deluged with flyers in the mail advertising new products. Perhaps more than any other merchant in town, he extended credit to farmers. Like them, he always believed next year's crop would make them well off. William and Richard would spend two nights in a hotel and go to sessions at the Trinity Baptist Church in the downtown area of Regina. William would drive his new Ford Model T Sedan—a lovely all-black vehicle. At 7 a.m., he picked up Richard.

Both men brought lunches. It was a habit from thirty or more years ago when they had little money. William wanted to talk about the specifications of his new car. Richard wanted to talk about his new best-selling products. They were both polite men and they listened—although they didn't want to. The new car performed well and got quite a few envious glances. Roads were better now, William said, and Richard agreed. New roads and new railway lines—the distances in Saskatchewan were shortening. They arrived early enough to get settled in their hotel room. They would have to sleep in a double bed. That made them both embarrassed. But hotel rooms with double beds was the norm. Travelling salesmen and circuit lawyers often had to sleep in the same bed. The custom didn't raise any eyebrows. They went for supper in the hotel and decided to go to a movie. The new big budget film had arrived in Regina—*Ben Hur*. They had heard about this spectacular film. It was a nice combination of historical drama, action scenes, and the triumph of good. They thoroughly enjoyed it. They said they couldn't wait to tell their wives about it.

The next day, the session began with a long prayer. William was sure he'd heard some snoring. Then there was the presentation of the financial statement for the Canadian Baptist Congress. As usual at any general meeting, nobody understood the financial statement, but they voted unanimously to accept it. The delegates now went to the workshops they had signed up for. William had signed up for "Sunday School Texts and Curriculum." He did so as a favour for Fred Barnes, the Sunday school superintendent at the church. William would bring back material for him. After lunch, his second session would be "Christianity and Social Reform." William liked the idea of the Christianity of good deeds, and his time with the YMCA showed the benefit of helping poorer children.

When he went into the large meeting room, there were about twenty delegates seated around the room. At the front was a lectern. Before everyone arrived, a few delegates were talking to others about the films they had seen last night. Several had seen *Ben Hur* and really enjoyed it. A few went to see Charlie Chaplin in *Gold Rush*. They said they couldn't stop laughing. The conversation ended when a very slight young man walked to the lectern. He had rimless glasses that reflected light. He said his name was Tommy Douglas. He was twenty-one years old. He began speaking very slowly and quietly in deference to his elders. As he spoke, he cited examples of the effects of poverty on families he knew in Winnipeg. He talked about the children who were hungry every day, the women dying in childbirth because they had no medical help, the fathers working twelve hours a day for a pittance, lodgings that were always cold in the winter, how schooling was impossible because the children had few clothes and were often barefoot. As he talked, he became increasingly animated. He cajoled and he challenged. He began to pace. He blended logic with passion. He used emotion to make points. He looked men in the eye. By the end of his half hour presentation, his audience was worn out. If the spirit of Christ could make men look to help others, the spirit was in that room.

William was very moved. He thought this young Baptist would help the poor wherever he went and whatever he did.

* * *

In August 1930, James, Alice, Jane, and Bill Matthews were walking and window shopping in downtown Moose Jaw. Bill Matthews was Jane's latest boyfriend. Jane considered herself relatively virtuous. She had fallen from grace only two or three times. Bill Matthews was an easygoing Englishman. As they walked along, Bill was telling them a funny story about tunnels underneath Moose Jaw.

Bill had picked up the story of the tunnels in Moose Jaw at work. He began to recount the information. "The tunnels were built in 1908 to carry steam heat across the small city. The brilliant innovation didn't work."

"Why didn't the idea work?" James asked.

Bill replied that he didn't know. "But here is the interesting thing. Chinese immigrants began to live in the tunnels to avoid the head count tax."

Jane rolled her eyes with exasperation. "Do you really think we farm people are going to believe this nonsense? Chinese living beneath our feet? Nonsense! And what does an Englishman know about Moose Jaw?"

Bill was not deterred. He continued his story. "Now the tunnels are used to store liquor to smuggle to the United States because Prohibition forbids the sale of liquor. So much money is made from smuggling liquor to the United States that Al Capone himself once visited Moose Jaw to buy liquor for Chicago."

Jane was becoming increasingly annoyed by what she thought was Bill's attempt to hoodwink them. "That's enough of that nonsense. Let's go get something to eat."

Over their snacks, Bill suggested they go to see a show. "I understand that Hollywood is putting sound into films now."

Jane replied, "Nothing could be better than Charlie Chaplin and Buster Keaton. Sound is a fad that won't last."

They wandered into a drug store with no purchases in mind. Bill saw Peter Evans. They knew one another from working at the train depot.

Bill said, "Peter, would you like to go to the show with us?"

Peter was very pleased with the invitation. "Yes, of course I would."

Alice whispered to Jane, "What kind of strange accent is that?"

Jane noticed that Alice was looking closely at Peter and there was some blush at her throat.

Peter was a good-looking man and Alice found him attractive. His accent somehow made him even more attractive. Jane had had several suitors and now she had Bill. Alice was beginning to think that she too should have a suitor. That, she thought, was the normal thing, and she remembered the desperation of her teacher. She did not want to be an old maid.

Jane whispered to Bill, "What kind of accent does Peter have?"

"Welsh."

Jane accepted the answer without comment, but she had no idea where Wales was.

Peter asked Alice, "Were you born in Moose Jaw?"

"No. I lived on a farm south of here," she replied.

"What brought you to Moose Jaw?" Peter probed some more.

"Jane and I wanted to see our brother James and we needed jobs."

"Oh, what do you do for work?" He seemed genuinely interested.

"I'm a housekeeper for an older couple." Alice blushed. She was enjoying the attention.

Peter didn't seem to notice. "Do you like it?"

"Yes. They're very nice to me."

Alice thought Peter had a real interest in her and this endeared him to her. She began to blush again.

They would have talked longer, but the film, *While the City Sleeps* with Lon Chaney, was beginning. After the film, there was some talk of going to a restaurant, but Alice always tried to get home by eleven.

The Riddells weren't strict about hours—in fact, they wanted Alice to have some fun. But Alice wanted to be polite and not disturb their sleep by coming in too late.

"Oh well," Jane said. "That's too bad. Peter, will you walk Alice home?"

Peter was a little taken aback. These Canadians could be unnervingly blunt. But he liked the idea, and he actually offered Alice his arm. He had seen chaps in films do that and members of his church often left arm in arm. Jane, Bill, and James headed in the other direction. Jane was extremely pleased with her matchmaking maneuvers.

Alice had never had her arm held by a man. She blushed again, but she liked this new intimacy.

Peter wanted to know more about Alice, and Alice wanted to know more about him.

"How many brothers and sisters do you have?" Peter began.

"There are eleven children in our family."

"Do you know all of their names?"

Alice laughed at the impertinent question. She enjoyed his sense of humour.

"And how many children in your family?" Alice responded once she had stopped laughing.

"Seven."

"And do you know all of their names?"

They both started to laugh. Peter wrapped his arms around her and gave her a hug. Alice enjoyed it.

And so it went. The young couple fell in love. They walked together endlessly. Occasionally, they joined Jane and Bill for rides in Bill's car.

A few weeks later, Alice went to the restaurant where Jane worked. They had arranged for a walk.

Jane bustled up to the booth where Alice was sitting.

"I'm going to marry Bill!" Jane exclaimed excitedly, unable to even mutter a hello before spilling her news.

"What?" Alice was shocked. "You said just last week that you weren't going to see him again."

"I've changed my mind." Jane shrugged.

"But you said he was too dull for you."

"I know. But he's very hardworking and decent. He has a good job, and we can buy a house. We've both had enough of poverty."

Alice was unsure about this but kept her reservations to herself. "Well, I really like Bill. Should I warn him about you?"

Jane glared back at her sister. "That's not funny. Bill knows all he needs to know about me."

James liked both Bill and Peter. But he felt a sense of family separation again. He loved the time he had with his sisters. Now, he would be alone in Moose Jaw, and he still didn't know where his other siblings were.

After several months, Alice brought Peter to the Baptist church the Riddells went to every Sunday where she introduced him to Dorothy and William. That went well. On the way home from church, Dorothy asked what kind of English Peter spoke. William thought he knew but didn't hazard a guess. His assumption of Welsh was correct. He was also pleased that Peter mentioned he was raised a Baptist. People who had adult baptisms were special in God's eyes.

The news that Bill was going to marry Jane may have spurred Peter on, as he proposed to Alice shortly after and she agreed. They had talked and talked during their courtship and Alice understood that they would settle in Wales. Peter had painted such a beautiful picture of Wales and he had promised her their own house on a small farm.

Peter had sought Bill's advice about how to propose. Bill told him the most important thing was to have a ring. Bill took Peter to the jewellery store on the main street. Peter allowed himself to be led by the jeweller and ended up spending more than he had planned. But the ring and the box were beautiful. Once he had the ring, he kept opening and closing the box to admire his purchase. Peter knew that some men went down on one knee and extended the ring with an ingratiating puppy-dog smile. His proposal wasn't that theatrical. He simply extended his hand with the ring. Alice accepted the ring and proposal. They kissed almost chastely and became betrothed.

They set the date for October 14. The Riddells had taken Alice and Peter for a few Sunday drives and had Peter for dinner. The housekeeper and her new fiancé sat at the same dinner table as the Riddells. Dorothy was very protective of Alice. She knew that Alice was very innocent and naïve. Dorothy had heard about young men from various European countries who sought adventure in Canada. "Sowing their wild oats" was a phrase she knew. Yet, Peter was very polite. Surely nobody raised as a Baptist could be evil.

Since she approved of Peter and loved Alice, Dorothy went into action. She would arrange the wedding for the daughter she never had.

One day, William winked at Alice and said, "I'm getting out of her way and you better too." Alice laughed for almost two minutes—a beautiful cleansing laugh that banished all the worries of her unhappy childhood.

Dorothy talked to the minister indicating what Bible passages she wanted and what hymns should be sung. He knew better than to ask if Alice had any say in this. Next, Dorothy phoned the president of the Ladies Auxiliary. She chose the menu for the evening dinner and listed the table arrangements. She phoned the one florist shop in Moose Jaw and ordered all the arrangements for the day. She went to Eaton's mail order store and ordered patterns for the bridal dress and the bridesmaids' dresses. She phoned her niece in Regina to tell her she would be a bridesmaid—she would introduce her to Alice later.

If Alice had had a life that engendered some self-confidence, she might have intervened in some of the decisions. But she was years away from asserting her own views on things. In any case, she agreed with all the arrangements (when Dorothy felt she should know some). She felt a sense of importance she had never felt before. She was somebody.

* * *

SASKATCHEWAN 1925-1930

Grace and her two youngest children moved in with an old friend and her husband. But the arrangement couldn't last. Her friend had four children of her own. Grace was having trouble making decisions. Even taking care of her two infants pushed her failing intellectual capacity to the limit. There would be psychological explanations for her condition, but the simple truth was that she was completely worn out—physically and mentally. She was still a young woman, but she was like a ninety-year-old—weak and helpless.

Grace again turned to a local minister for help. The minister knew of a widower on a nearby farm who wanted a housekeeper. He drove Grace out there to meet him. He was all business. He said she could become his housekeeper, but he didn't want the children. Grace sat with her friend for hours discussing what to do. Finally, in desperation, Grace knew she had to give her children up. The minister arranged for a children's agency to take the children away. Grace had no hope now. She had no money, no children. She would be on an isolated farm with a man she had met once. She knew she had little chance of seeing her eleven children again or her own mother.

Grace lived with this man and his three children. She was a hard-working housekeeper and was very kind to his children. For three years, she heard from nobody. Unfortunately, starting her fourth year there, bad weather ruined the crop. The man had few savings. He found a labourer's job in the nearby town, but it didn't pay much. They could survive with the vegetable garden, a few chickens, and two or three pigs. It was a miserable winter and the man's mood turned dark. He began to yell at Grace for no reason. He hit her several times. Then one night, he raped her. She survived the winter, trapped by the cold. The children went to school. The man did chores. Grace worked hard but never spoke to the man and seldom to his children.

In April, the man found her in her own excrement in the hen house. She was clucking at the hens occasionally as if she were still scattering grain. His shouts, screams, fulminations, slaps, and punches could not bring her back. Eventually, he rode to a neighbour for help. The neighbour's wife came in a buggy and found Grace still in the hen house covered in excrement and blood. She washed her and dressed her with the scattering of clothes strewn around her bedroom. She tried to talk to Grace. She asked her how she got the cuts and bruises. Grace remained silent; she may not have understood anything said to her. She got Grace to eat some bread and drink some tea, then put Grace to bed as if she were a child, waiting by the bed until her eyes closed. The man would have to do Grace's chores this day.

The woman got in her buggy and drove directly to Roleau. She did this with grim determination, knowing that her husband wouldn't approve. In Roleau, she went directly to the Methodist minister and asked for his help. The minister came to the farm with the town nurse. They removed Grace without the man protesting. Grace had become a burden to him and he no longer wanted her—let others take care of her. And so, in 1928, Grace left off caring for herself and others and fell under the care of society. The minister took her to the four-bed hospital in Roleau. The next day, the minister phoned the provincial parliament and was put in touch with the minister of social services.

A doctor working for the government drove down from Moose Jaw to examine Grace. He decided she should go to the asylum in North Battleford. He found that Grace was so lethargic she had trouble answering his simple questions. Obviously, she could no longer take care of herself or her children. He thought a long rest might help, and perhaps the asylum had new treatments. Two days later, an off-duty RCMP officer and a retired nurse undertook the long drive to North Battleford. They would receive a flat two days' pay and an expense account for meals and a hotel. Grace sat silently in the backseat as they drove for hours. When they made periodic stops, she was able to go to the bathroom by herself and she ate well. She seemed in a state of semi-consciousness. At the end of a long day, they drove into the grounds of the asylum. An orderly came to the front door and Grace was handed over with very little ceremony and no paperwork. The asylum knew only her name. And so, the woman who had spent her whole life working from dawn to dusk, had scraped together meals from vegetable gardens, had borne and cared for eleven children was now a mute and an insentient resident in an asylum.

In August 1930, two months before Alice's wedding, a long-distance phone call came to the Riddell household. It was a person-to-person call for Alice. The Riddells received long-distance calls from their son in Vancouver, but Alice had never received one. She began to shake as soon as Dorothy called her and told her what it was. Alice had a terrible foreboding. Telegrams and long-distance calls were always bad news. It was her indomitable grandmother.

"How are you, Alice?" Her grandmother shouted into the phone because it was long-distance.

"I'm fine. I have a wonderful position here as a housekeeper. The Riddells are wonderful people. James, Jane, and I are like the three musketeers. We go out together frequently and Moose Jaw is a very nice town."

Her grandmother still spoke loudly, but she lowered her voice.

"I have news about my daughter. The RCMP tracked me down as the next of kin. They also contacted your father. Your mother became very, very ill. She couldn't do anything but sit. A government doctor said she had to go to an institution in North Battleford.

Earlier, the children had been taken by Child Services to be put up for adoption."

Alice didn't even say goodbye to her grandmother. She simply hung up the phone and ran to her bedroom without saying a word to Dorothy, who heard the young girl sobbing behind her closed door. She was torn between her curiosity, which she could hardly restrain, and her concern for Alice. After about fifteen minutes, Dorothy knocked on the bedroom door with tea and cookies. Alice opened the door. Her eyes were red-rimmed. Her nose was red from the numerous times she had had to wipe it. Alice looked so sorrowful that Dorothy closed the door and left.

Alice didn't want Dorothy to know her mother had been put in an insane asylum. She didn't want anybody to know. She would tell her brothers and sisters, but this would remain a deep, dark family secret. There was too much shame. Alice had learned from an early age the social mores of her time. People had to be ashamed if they were poor. They had to be ashamed if they accepted charity. They had to be ashamed if an unmarried girl in the family became pregnant. They had to be ashamed if a member of the family had psychological problems. Alice had even seen a veteran of World War I who behaved strangely being made fun of in downtown Moose Jaw. As Alice gained more control of her emotions, she realized her new life would begin with two lies. She didn't reveal her marriage to her grandmother whom she loved. And she would never tell Dorothy, whom she loved, what had happened to her mother.

Alice put on a brave face. Finally, Alice confided in Dorothy that her grandmother had been diagnosed with cancer. That lie satisfied Dorothy. It was logical enough. Three days later, Alice asked the Riddells if she could have some time off to visit her grandmother. Of course, the Riddells agreed.

Alice phoned James and Jane and asked if they could meet. They agreed to meet at Jane's restaurant. During Jane's break, they could talk. From the tone of Alice's voice, James knew something serious had occurred. He assumed it had something to do with the wedding. They sat in a booth and Alice talked very softly.

"Grandmother phoned me. The RCMP contacted her about Mother. She became very, very sick. She's been sent to the hospital in North Battleford. Our little brother and sister have been put up for adoption."

Jane and James worked hard to contain their tears.

"I want to go visit Mother in the hospital. Will you come with me?"

There was a long silence. James spoke first. He was bright red. "I can't get any time off work."

Jane looked very uncomfortable. "I'm not good with sick people. You're very good, Alice. You go first and let us know how Mother is. Maybe later, James and I can go together."

Alice knew they wouldn't.

William drove Alice to the train station very early in the morning. She kept her destination secret, and he was not the type to pry. She carried a lunch and a small suitcase. She had to bring some flannel cloths because she was having her period. Jane had laughed earlier about not having a period on a honeymoon. She blushed when she thought of travelling on a train seated next to strangers while she was in that state. Alice had a long train ride ahead of her. From Moose Jaw to Regina, where she would change trains, then through Saskatoon and on to North Battlefield. After Regina, she ate her lunch. She was pleased that she had a seat by herself. As the train moved along, stopping frequently for cargo and passengers, she began to think about her life. She had that sense of wonder and surprise that people have when they realize suddenly where they are and what they have become. One minute they are children sitting at desks in a classroom and the next they are married, have children, have jobs they never expected, live in places they had never heard of, and love and hate people they never knew. Sometimes in revelry, they suddenly start, and with some incomprehensible fear, try to understand these strangers who are themselves. So, it was now with Alice. How did she end up working for the Riddells in Moose Jaw? Who was this man, Peter Evans, whom she would marry in October? Where was this strange country called Wales and what would she do there? Her life had many jolts and sudden changes. Through all of them, she had never felt in control. She felt as if she had always made decisions, or people made decisions for her, without ever thinking of the long-term consequences. It was as if she started out walking, knowing that she must walk somewhere, making choices at crossroads but ending up in a place she didn't know and didn't want to be. Yet the ineffable sadness of life is that no one can start again. Decisions made by you or for you remain. Time plods forward, never retracing steps. The lucky ones end up happy at their destination. If she could understand her past, Alice thought, she might have more control of her future.

As the train chugged along, Alice saw farmers plowing fallow fields. Now it was all tractors. Near Pense, she saw a team of oxen, and several passengers changed sides to watch them. *Change*, thought Alice, *change*.

Alice woke up with a start. She had nodded off during her reminisces. The train was making its way through Saskatoon. Alice looked around. There were few passengers. She went to the lavatory and got a drink from the fountain. She opened her lunch bag and ate a sandwich and apple. Once the train was through Saskatoon, it picked up speed. Alice looked through the window, and the farm girl assessed the crops. It was a good year. August was "hold your breath" time for farmers. They couldn't exhale until all the crops were in. Then they would think about the international price for wheat and oats. Without being too malicious, they would hope for crop failures in Manitoba or the United States. Shortages drove up the prices they would get. The perfect thing was high prices and the granary companies buying. In a year of bumper crops, there were not enough railway cars. The farmers had their own small granaries for storage as they waited for sales. With the insecurity of crops, the instability of prices, the shortage of railway capacity, and the manufacturing of tractors and cars in the east, westerners liked the expression, "exploitation of the west." They didn't like it being called the hinterland.

Alice didn't have to worry about the farm economy now. She just enjoyed the landscape. She saw large farm horses, large barns, and large sheds. These farmers had had good years. Now they had large tractors and new cars. They could withstand a bad year or two. The original quarter section had become a section or two. Sometimes on these successful farms, Alice could see the original sod homes that their parents from Galicia, Poland, or Ukraine had lived in. Alice thought that one day, sod homes would be preserved in museums. Alice remembered how her father had ranted against the Ukrainians. So many Ukrainians were doing well and he was a failure. He enjoyed ridiculing the dress and speech of the Ukrainians (or any other group that struggled with English). He didn't know it, but one Saskatchewan paper constantly attacked the Ukrainians and the government that had recruited them in the early part of the century. Many old-timers still cursed the name of Laurier because his settlement plan would dilute the superior blood of the English. One particularly vicious person wrote for this paper. He compared the Ukrainians to dumb beasts of burden unworthy to live in refined society. He was a Baptist minister so what he said had God's approval.

The conductor came along and told Alice that North Battleford was only thirty minutes away. He had been particularly solicitous of Alice during the trip. Her beautiful blue eyes had captured him. But Alice hadn't noticed. Her mind had been on her mother and her own childhood. She had always worked so hard that she had no time for introspection, but a few days without work forced her to evaluate her life. She quickly ate another sandwich and jammed the remainder of her lunch into her suitcase. She had worn a coat for the trip but had hung it over the seat next to her. That was the advantage of so few people being on the train. Now she had her coat over her suitcase and was ready to go. Her light cotton dress was perfect for the weather. The train slowly came to a stop with the screeching of wheels and an explosion of steam. The smiling conductor was at the door to help her down the high steel steps. She smelled the stench of hot oil. She looked at the signs above the station entrance, "North Battleford." So far, so good. She went inside the station. The four long benches had only three people sitting on them. The interior was painted Canadian National Railway dark; dark paint for everything. Alice walked to the women's restroom. She had to replace her cloths. Luckily, she was not a heavy bleeder. After that chore, she washed her hands, combed her hair, and straightened her dress. She decided not to put on lipstick for this visit. She took a deep breath and walked to the ticket counter.

An older man waited, smiling, for her request. He noticed she was blushing with her shyness. She told him she was going to visit the institution the next day and she needed a hotel for the night. He recommended a hotel and told her there was a taxi outside that would take her there. There was a bus to the institution that left from downtown at 7 a.m. She could pay the bus driver. Alice thanked him politely and started walking to the door. He had answered the same questions many times. Friends coming to visit patients in the institution were matter-of-fact. Relatives coming to visit were very hesitant, embarrassed, secretive, and ashamed.

A taxi cab. Another new experience for Alice. This would be the first time she hired a taxi by herself. The driver was sitting outside on a bench, but when he saw Alice, he immediately jumped up and helped her with her suitcase. Alice sat silently as he touted the virtues of North Battlefield. She wondered about a tip. He knew the recommended hotel and they got there in ten minutes. He helped her with her suitcase, then she handed him a crumpled bill, a little moist with her nervous perspiration. She went to the counter in the lobby and asked for a room. Luckily, she and Jane had stayed in a hotel in Moose Jaw so she was not completely intimidated. This was a nice hotel, not like the hotel down the street that catered to seasonal workers. They could be a little rough. Alice had saved her money for this trip and Mrs. Riddell had given her a ten-dollar bill. She walked up one flight of stairs to her room and made sure the door was locked and that she had her own bathroom—she did. She then sat on the bed to restore her equilibrium. Buying a train ticket, travelling on a train by herself, asking a ticket agent for information, riding in a taxi, booking a hotel room—she had never attempted any of these things before. She sat for a full fifteen minutes before she felt restored. Then she had the great pleasure of a bath. She didn't have the courage to go downstairs to the restaurant. She had used up her supply. She had a squished-up half sandwich and a bruised apple. Then she went to bed.

The next morning, Alice was up early. She hadn't slept well. Her anxiety about her new life was increasing each day. Today, she would cut the main link to her childhood. She would say goodbye to her mother for the last time. She remembered the good times with her—the cooking, the baking, the egg gathering, and the cow milking. Her mother had had a very hard life, but every now and again, Alice and her mother had moments of giggles and laughter. It was usually when the other children did something humorous. Alice wondered how any woman could smile with eleven children to take care of. Alice sat in her room and thought about this before packing her suitcase and walking downstairs. Since she had eaten in a restaurant in Moose Jaw and felt comfortable doing so, she went to the hotel restaurant and ordered breakfast. The registration clerk came in and asked Alice if she would like to leave her suitcase in storage while she was away. Alice wondered if everyone knew where she was going. She wanted everything to be a secret. Then she realized that many people made pilgrimages to the institution. It was a big facility and North Battleford was a small town. People knew.

At 7 a.m., she boarded the bus. There were quite a few people on it. She guessed they were hospital workers and visitors like herself.

The bus stopped frequently to let passengers on and off. Then it left town and picked up speed. After about forty minutes, the bus passed a sign and turned into the grounds. The asylum had acres of gardens, a milk shed, a pig barn, and a horse barn. It was a farm that was almost self-sustaining. Alice was quite surprised. The bus pulled up at the main door. The workers headed to their departments while the visitors followed the arrow that pointed to the right. Just down the hall, there was a pleasant waiting room with comfortable chairs and several coffee tables. The visitors avoided one another's eyes. They all felt uncomfortable. They were facing a hard reality they had fought against. Alice was ashamed to have her mother as a patient.

A pleasant nurse in a starched white uniform entered the room. She went from person to person, writing down their names on a clipboard. She told each person that he or she could visit shortly. One by one, groups or individuals were led away. Alice waited patiently, the box of chocolates she had brought from Moose Jaw on her lap. The nurse approached her and asked her to follow. Alice was led to a small room with six chairs. Almost as soon as she was seated, a male orderly in a spotless white uniform led her mother in.

Alice was struck by how young her mother looked. She was almost plump. She looked so placid. Alice felt as though she were greeting a stranger. She was happy to see her mother look so good, but it reminded her of the hard life her mother had had. Then there was a flush of anger as she felt all the injustices her mother had suffered. Alice walked over tentatively and hugged her mother, but her mother was confused. Alice led her to a chair and sat beside her. She introduced herself and her mother smiled, her eyes finally focusing.

Alice could think of nothing to say but recount the names of all her brothers and sisters. Her mother seemed to remember the names and repeated some of them. Alice talked about the weather and the crops this year. She talked about Moose Jaw. Her mother listened, but her eyes were dull. Finally, Alice told her about her marriage and her trip to Wales. Alice's mother had reached the limit of her attention. Her eyes closed and her chin fell onto her chest several times. Alice remembered the box of chocolates and offered them to her mother. Her mother reached out to take them. Alice was struck by how large her mother's hands were. Her knuckles were very large and gnarled—the hands of a woman who had worked hard all her life. Her mother held the box of chocolates. Alice then realized that her mother had never seen a box of chocolates. She took them back, opened the package, and held out a chocolate. Her mother took it and put it in her mouth. After a few seconds, a tiny smile appeared on her face. Then she closed her eyes and appeared to sleep. Alice walked over to the buzzer and rang for the orderly. He came promptly. Alice hugged her mother until her mother squirmed with irritation. Alice let go and her mother walked to the door holding the box of chocolates. The orderly led her away, and as an act of kindness, he told Alice that her mother was a wonderful person and never caused any trouble. Alice sat and wept until a knock on the door informed her that the room would have to be used by others.

As Alice walked out of the hospital and made her way to the bus stop, her mind was full of memories of her mother.

She had worked so hard, endured so much poverty, but she and Alice had often laughed together. Alice thought about her brothers and sisters and wished fervently that their lives would be better.

Chapter Seven

Saskatchewan 1930

October 14, 1930, was very pleasant. It was called a farmers' weather day. Winter wheat could be sown and the seed potatoes and root crops could be dug up and put in root cellars. Peter and Bill had walked to the church. Even though it was a busy day at the railroad depot, the manager had given them the day off. They both looked very good in their newly dry-cleaned suits. Bill had married Jane two weeks ago in a small ceremony—Jane, Bill, Alice, James, Peter, and a Justice of the Peace. The wedding dinner was in a private room in Moose Jaw's better restaurant. They even had wine. Peter would have preferred a small ceremony like that. But he was intimidated by Dorothy.

They walked to the front of the church and were greeted by the minister and organist. They both went individually to the lavatory and then sat in the front pew. The organist, Mrs. Cartwright, came over to chat and question these foreigners as thoroughly as she could. The minister slipped away to his study. Guests, whom neither Peter nor Bill knew, began to sit in pews. Dorothy had sent out many invitations and the recipients knew it was a command performance. Most of them didn't know the bride or groom, but Dorothy and William had many friends through the church. Ten minutes before the ceremony, Dorothy came in. William would drive Alice to the church. Her brother James would give her away. Dorothy inspected the floral arrangements and gave a warm hello to all the guests. She greeted Peter and Bill warmly and was pleased with their suits and shining shoes. She took her place in the front pew and gave nods to the minister and organist. The nods meant, "You better get this right."

There wasn't a long delay. William walked down the aisle and joined Dorothy. The minister gave the organist a slight hand wave and "Here Comes the Bride" began. Peter and Bill took their places. Jane and Beverly (Dorothy's niece) started down the aisle. Beverly had met Alice when they dressed for the ceremony at the Riddells. Alice and Jane weren't sure she wanted to be there. It ruined her day off. As Alice walked down the aisle, her situation became stark in her mind. She knew very few people in the church. She was new to Moose Jaw. She had no school friends, church friends, or work friends. Only James and Jane were there from her family.

The ceremony with prayers and hymns went well. Dorothy sobbed for most of it. Alice got her ring and the ceremonial kiss. They were husband and wife. There was rice at the front door and the photographer Dorothy hired completed the formal photographs. After half an hour, the guests went down the stairs to the Sunday school room turned banquet hall. There were white tablecloths and the tables were put together for eight guests at each table. There was a head table for the wedding party and the minister. Dorothy gave a few sharp glances at members of the Ladies' Auxiliary who didn't seem to be moving quickly enough. On the whole though, Dorothy was basking in the pleasure of a job well done.

The minister said an appropriate prayer. Bill made a very short speech. Peter thanked the Riddells and praised Alice. None of the speeches lasted more than a few minutes. The older guests couldn't understand Bill's English accent or Peter's Welsh accent, but they assumed they said the appropriate things. The dinner was a wonderful "down home" spread—roasted chicken, boiled potatoes, turnips, and peas followed by large portions of apple pie. Between the ceremony and the dinner, William had driven Alice home to change into her travel clothing. After the dinner, Alice threw her bouquet towards five or six young ladies. This women's event was not like those held for people who had grown up in Moose Jaw. Alice had no circle of friends and, of course, Peter had not been in the country long enough to make friends.

William and Dorothy drove Alice, Peter, and their small travel suitcases to Moose Jaw's best hotel where they all hugged. The wedding night had come. Dorothy had had a mother-daughter talk about sex with Alice. She said that some things about marriage could be unpleasant, but a wife had a duty to her husband. She suggested that if things became difficult, she could close her eyes and think about vast fields of wheat. Jane's advice was more explicit. When she was quite young, she had obtained a medical brochure about sex for married people. Alice blushed a bright-red as Jane went through the brochure page by page, adding comments about her own experiences. Alice had never known Jane had had these kinds of relationships. Jane followed her clinical lesson with the fervent wish that Alice have a lot of fun many times over.

Chapter Eight

Saskatchewan to Wales 1930-1933

Dorothy and William drove the honeymooners to the train station on Monday. Each of them had a large leather suitcase and a travel bag. Alice had all the possessions of her life in one suitcase. Jane, Bill, and James were working so they couldn't be there to say goodbye. Perhaps that was for the better. Alice was already trying to fight off her melancholy. Saying goodbye to her sister and brother at the train station would suggest they would never see one another again. By the time they boarded the train, Dorothy was almost inconsolable. She wept copious tears and her shoulders shook. For Alice, it meant losing a second mother.

The excitement of the train ride, however, lifted Alice's spirits. She and her new husband sat back and enjoyed the wonderful fall landscape of Saskatchewan. She had more money in her purse than she had ever had. The wedding gift from the Riddells had shocked Alice. At first, she thought it was a mistake. Dorothy had expected her son to come for the wedding. When he made excuses for not returning to Moose Jaw. Dorothy was furious. She went to the bank when she got the letter from her son and withdrew an unusually large sum of money. The teller looked a little uncertain—in the past, women hadn't been allowed access to their husband's accounts. The teller, a woman of perhaps thirty, wasn't going to hesitate when she saw the set of Dorothy's jaw. Dorothy thought her son deserved less of an inheritance. In her black mood, she even thought that if William died first, she would change her will and include Alice. So, Alice felt a sense of financial security for the first time.

For the last two years, the Riddells had talked endlessly about their trip to Toronto. Alice knew most of the details about the train trip and the wonders of Toronto. Now, Alice and Peter, a housekeeper and a day labourer, could experience it themselves. They were sitting in the same seats as wealthier people. They could buy the same sandwiches that the porter brought about. They could even eat in the same railroad dining car. While living with the Riddells, Alice often ate at the table with Dorothy and William. None of them thought it strange that a domestic, a housekeeper, sat with them like a member of the family. When Dorothy and William had friends for dinner, Alice stayed in the kitchen and served the food. The friends of the Riddells liked Alice and probably wouldn't be upset if Alice had dinner with them, but Dorothy wanted to preserve some sense of appropriateness. Canada was so British; there was a lingering sense of class. But Canada's sense of democracy was changing things. Canadians were beginning to judge people by what they were, not what they had been born to. The lower classes had developed a sense of self-worth and a confidence that irritated the old order.

Alice and Peter liked the luxury of sleeping compartments. Dorothy had insisted upon it. Alice didn't mind sleeping in a separate bed. As a matter of fact, she preferred it. They couldn't afford to visit Toronto so they just saw the skyline and vast port as they changed trains for Halifax three nights away from Moose Jaw. Like the Riddells, Alice was amazed by Lake Superior, the vast coniferous forests, and the farmlands of Ontario. She also saw the St. Lawrence River and the long perpendicular farms of Quebec. Peter had seen all this when he had travelled west as an adventurer, but the size of the country and the different landscape was still amazing.

Alice and Peter missed much of the vast country because as they slept, the train kept moving along. The trans Canada railroad was Canada and Canada was the cross-country railroad. Basically, Canada's history could be summed up with "no railroad, no country." Sir John A. MacDonald understood that. Without the railroad to tie Canada's west coast to the eastern half of the country, the idea of nationhood was finished. The Americans coveted Canada. The thought of one massive country stretching from the Mexican border to the North Pole excited imagination. It was a Manifest Destiny, but the American Civil War meant that all concern must be to end the war and unite the country. Canada would have to wait. But the citizens of the northern land mass who would eventually call themselves Canadians decided that they would put their differences aside and form a country that would be independent. The American Civil War was a bloodbath and the reconstruction of the South would take American eyes off Canada for decades. Meanwhile, Canada would try to fill its vast spaces by inviting the world to come.

Of course, Alice and Peter weren't thinking of that. They had to check all the details of travel—tickets, passports, British money. They arrived at Halifax in the morning, booked a hotel for the night, and went to a bank to change Canadian dollars into British pounds. They had some time to walk around Halifax and they took a tour to see the harbour and the remains of the explosion of 1917. The tour guide explained how two ships collided in the harbour—one of them carrying high explosives. The explosion flattened a square mile of Halifax. There were almost two thousand deaths and another nine thousand injured. In 1930, Alice and Peter could still see evidence of the destruction.

Alice and Peter had dinner in their hotel. Alice wasn't so nervous around waiters any more. She actually asked their waiter for more water—after some hesitation. They got to sleep in the same bed again. In the morning, they took a taxi to the harbour where the liner *Athenia* was tied up. They were early, but they had their boarding passes and cabin number so they lugged their suitcases up the gangplank. A young porter took Alice's suitcase, looked at their cabin number, and asked them to follow him. They went down one flight of stairs and then another until they reached a hallway. Then they went down a gentle ramp. Their cabin was in a long passageway. The porter handed Peter the key, and Peter tipped him. (Peter had learned the tradition of tipping in Moose Jaw. He had never done it before.) Peter opened the door and was surprised how small the cabin was. It had a narrow bed, a lavatory with a toilet and wash basin, and an open closet. It had no window. They were below the water line. On the back of the door was a schedule of meals for their section of the ship. Two life preservers were hung in the closet along with the procedures if there was an alarm. The sheet also advised them that there would be an emergency drill before they left port. They hung up some of their clothes and put their toiletries in the lavatory. Alice was still getting used to the idea of a man's shaving gear, a man's hair brush, a man's sleep wear. Living with a man was certainly different. They had a different smell.

Peter suggested they go for a walk. They put on their warm coats and started the demanding trip to the boarding deck. Other passengers were coming in and the hallways were crowded. Peter wondered what would happen if a genuine accident occurred. He thought of the *Titanic* and a little claustrophobia passed across his brain. By the time they got to the deck, they were quite hungry. Luckily, the cafeteria had few people and there didn't seem to be any restrictions. They luxuriated in a big pot of tea and a steak and kidney pie each with french fries on the side. They paid in Canadian money. Neither had ever eaten such a full lunch.

After lunch, they walked around the boarding deck. They needed their warm coats because the wind off the ocean was quite cold in October. More and more passengers were walking around the deck and there were few restricted areas. At one place, Alice and Peter could look down and see the cargo being loaded. There were a lot of mail bags. Some crates looked as if they held parts for automobiles. The cargo hold for commodities was quite small, as the primary cargo on this ship were the passengers, the food to feed them, and the staff to serve them.

Alice and Peter were getting cold so they made the long voyage back to their cabin. The rocking on the ship was increasing as the wind grew stronger. A couple of times, they lost their balance and bounced off the walls. When they got to their cabin, Peter checked the dinner time for their group. They would eat at 5 p.m. The first-class passengers would eat at 8 p.m. and that would be followed by a musical presentation. They decided to lie down for a nap. They did sleep briefly. Then they washed. They kept their daytime clothes on.

Their designated group filled the dining room. There were scores of waiters. Alice and Peter joined six other people at their table. Everyone was quite polite and jovial. Half of them had gone to the bar for a drink. Alice was the only Canadian. The rest were British returning after a holiday, visiting family members, or giving up on Canada. Alice didn't want to hear about anyone giving up on Canada.

There was no choice in the menu. It would be soup, ham, potatoes, and squash. Dessert would be pudding. The following night they would have something different. Alice and Peter didn't drink or smoke so they felt a little conspicuous. They did have a good time, however. Their table acquaintances had some wonderful anecdotes about Canada. Alice found it strange that what she considered ordinary events, they found almost shocking. The one thing they all talked about was the flat land of the Prairies. None of them wanted to live in such a place. Most of them satisfied their desire to see Native Americans. One couple had gone to a small town to see a rodeo and was amazed to see so many of them. They were surprised that most of them had cars or trucks. They couldn't stay to talk because the next designated group would be coming. The waiters and kitchen staff almost ran as they cleared the tables.

Alice and Peter went to their cabin to get their coats and returned to the boarding deck. They walked to the side of the ship where they could see Halifax at night. Halifax was not a big city, but it curled nicely around the harbour and its lights were quite attractive. It had expanded dramatically during World War I. New wharfs and warehouses had to be built to handle all the cargo being shipped to Britain and France. The United States had shipped cargo through Halifax before they ended symbolic neutrality and entered the war in 1917. Peter knew that by 1918, the Americans had almost two million men in France. The Atlantic Ocean was awash with ships.

Alice and Peter were in their cabin by eight o'clock. Later, they heard the music from the dining room. It sounded like dance music. In fact, tables were moved and cleared. By 10:30 p.m. or so there was room for a dance floor, but Alice and Peter were asleep by 11 p.m. At about 2 a.m., Alice bolted straight up, covered her mouth, and ran to the toilet. The large lunch and pleasant dinner were floating in the toilet. Alice flushed the toilet several times and vomited several times. She stayed seated beside the toilet for about half an hour. She struggled up, rinsed her face, and then sat on the floor with the bed as a backrest. Peter offered to get her a glass of water, but she shook her head. She vomited into the toilet two more times. At about 5 a.m., she climbed back into bed. She fell asleep shortly after. At 6 a.m., Peter got up, dressed, and went to the cafeteria. He was cautious. He had only tea and toast, although he was quite hungry. Unfortunately, he had the smell of vomit in his nostrils. He also remembered his own bout with seasickness on his way to Canada. He asked the cafeteria staff if it was possible to take tea and toast to his cabin. They said that would be fine. The crew of the ship was both amused by and compassionate for the seasick passengers. Most of them had been through this themselves, but they couldn't help smiling when they saw ten or twelve passengers hanging over the rails—trying to vomit with the wind and not defile the ship. They went out of their way to give special services to the sick.

Peter stayed in the cafeteria for another two hours reading a current Halifax newspaper and a seven-day-old Liverpool newspaper. After eight o'clock, he brought some lukewarm tea and cold toast to Alice. She sat in the single chair and Peter sat on the bed. Alice was able to sip the tea and nibble on the bread, but the ship was rocking in the Atlantic swells, and Alice couldn't decide if her head did less spinning in bed or sitting in the chair. She had several false vomit attacks, bolting to the toilet where she only spat up saliva—a foul, acidic saliva. She kept a glass of water close. Alice told Peter to leave. She wanted solitude in her misery. She didn't want her misery to change to anger for Peter. Best if he got out of her sight.

Peter returned to the cafeteria for lunch. The number of people there was a lot fewer than the day before. Passengers picked at their food carefully and sipped their tea or coffee slowly. They feared a sudden stomach eruption. After lunch, Peter returned to reading the Liverpool newspaper, even though it was out of date. He enjoyed the ads for clothes, cars, and homes. He had to re-acquaint himself with the British way of life. He was gratified to see that the want ads offered many jobs. He had been promised a job with the county road maintenance department when he returned home. His old friend Walter Price was a superintendent now and had volunteered to pick Alice and Peter up at the train station when the train arrived at Brecon.

On the feature page, the Liverpool newspaper had a story from a foreign correspondent. He talked about the violent street fighting between the Communists and the right-wing parties in Berlin and other large German cities. Germany had been severely punished by the Western Allies because they said Germany started World War I. The result was large numbers of unemployed men and widespread starvation. The correspondent did not think the Weimar Republic could last—the middle could not hold. As an example of the intemperate civil war, he mentioned a military-style fringe group led by a charismatic man called Adolf Hitler. The correspondent thought Hitler's movement was interesting, but insignificant.

By the time Alice and Peter disembarked in Liverpool, Alice was feeling better. Now they boarded a train that would take them to Brecon after a few changes. Peter was hoping the weather would be sunny, but it was October drizzle. Their train compartment was unheated, so they both kept their coats on. They were travelling third class. Alice saw better-dressed people go into the first-class compartments. She thought that they probably had heat. It was a slow run south through every small town to pick up or let off passengers. After about two hours, Alice saw a sign that said CYMRV with what Peter said was a painting of a red dragon. In smaller letters, there was the word, "Wales." Alice was having trouble understanding the English accent. She wondered about the Welsh accent. Peter had told her some people even spoke Welsh. The train's final destination was Cardiff, the capital of Wales. In Europe, the cities came first and then the railroads. In Saskatchewan, the railroads came first, followed by the towns. The railroads in Europe had to find their ways through the cities and they had some circuitous routes. In Saskatchewan, the railroads ran in perfectly straight lines.

Alice thought the towns they passed through would be quite beautiful if the sun were out. From what she did see, there were some beautiful stone structures and also large swaths of row housing. Things were different, but Alice was prepared for new things. By the time the train stopped in Brecon, it was quite dark and the rain pelted down. Walter was waiting for them. He was very warm and gracious. Their destination was about ten miles away. Walter and Peter talked about the changes that had occurred in the country while Peter was away. Walter was a good storyteller, and he was a good gossip. Peter was happy to be home. Alice was wet and cold.

They were heading for Peter's family home, Ty Crwyor. Alice thought it interesting that homes had names. They didn't name homes in Saskatchewan. She wondered how Walter could see the narrow road ahead with hedges on both sides. How could cars or wagons pass each other? Finally, they climbed a dramatically steep hill and turned into a farmyard. Walter grabbed Alice's suitcase and they ran for the house. The door was opened, and there was a great deal of loud and excited talk. Peter's mother, two brothers, and one sister all lived here. His father had died in 1925. They all came to embrace Peter and tell him they were happy to see his return.

"Welcome home!"

"Did you see any Indians?"

"How cold is Canada?"

"Is Western Canada absolutely flat?"

There was a cacophony of excited voices, but Alice really couldn't understand many of the questions as she stood in the doorway soaking wet, cold, and ignored. Finally, Walter had the grace to wrap his arms around her shoulders and draw her into the family circle. The Evanses were polite but not effusive. They found Alice different looking because of her clothes, and the rain had not helped her appearance. She was placed in a chair near the fireplace. Peter's brother Ivor realized her discomfort.

"You'll be warm and dry in a short time," he whispered. "Our family can be cool to strangers." Alice realized with a cold stab that Peter's family was unhappy he had married a foreigner.

Peter's mother put the kettle on (a large kettle on a large wood stove) and went to a large cabinet. She got quite a few Welsh cakes out and put them on a platter. Peter's sister, Greta, distributed small plates. They would eat off their laps. Alice welcomed the tea. She was so cold. She ate two Welsh cakes and praised the cook profusely. Because it was late, the family excused themselves one by one. Peter's mother led them to a small room upstairs. There was a small coal fire in the fireplace. This was a luxury. Peter's mother embraced him and said goodnight. Alice got a perfunctory nod. So here was beautiful Wales—a cold and rainy day, and a cold and distant reception.

The next morning, Alice was introduced to the practices of her new family. Luckily, Alice was raised as a farm girl. She knew all about milking cows, collecting eggs, and feeding the chickens and pigs. They got up at about 6 a.m. every morning—the same as in Saskatchewan. The big advantage of living on a farm was the hearty breakfast—eggs, ham, potatoes, and bread. Alice had never seen all these items fried before, however. She didn't have her own Wellingtons, but she was able to borrow her mother-in-law's. With the slightly large boots, Alice sloshed her way around the farmyard. She made friends with the farm dog immediately.

After chores and breakfast, Ivor drove Alice and Peter down the hill to their new home, Ty Twyn. Peter's parents owned the home and the land around it. Because Peter was given the home rent-free until he got his old job back, there was sibling resentment. It was an old stone home with the barn attached in the European style. In the medieval period, cows, pigs, and humans shared the same one-room shelters. The animals provided heat. Of course, sleeping with animals led to animal-to-human diseases. Luckily, perhaps, Alice had suffered through poverty and biting cold Saskatchewan winters—one winter the Reilly family ate nothing but turnips for months. Unfortunately, Alice had become used to the lovely home the Riddells had with central heating. Alice now thought fondly of the heat coming up through the grill in her bedroom. The Riddell's coal furnace with its elaborate duct work kept the home nice and cozy all winter. Her new home had one fireplace, small windows, and a stone floor in the kitchen/living room. There was a wood stove for cooking and water was fifty yards away at the well. Alice felt she had taken one huge step backwards. But she was a worker, almost a compulsive worker. She used an old broom to sweep the floor, heated water, and found some cloths to clean the table. She cleaned out the ashes from the fireplace and the wood stove. All this activity warmed Alice, although she couldn't take her coat off. Peter checked the upstairs bedrooms. All the bed linens were lying in neat piles. He made up one bed in the larger bedroom. Even he missed the centrally heated rooms in Moose Jaw.

For the next week, Alice and Peter ate their meals at Ty Crwyn and helped with the chores. After a few days, Ivor drove them into Brecon to buy food. Alice had a supply of British pounds. The weather was cool, but it wasn't raining, so Alice could try to complete her long shopping list. She found the stores in Brecon specialized in meat, bread, and vegetables. She had shopped for the Riddells so she knew what she wanted. The proprietors had trouble understanding her accent at times, but she made herself clear. She noticed people had quite an interest in her. Peter had married a Canadian and the town gossips wanted to see what she looked like. Alice was quite a novelty in the small Welsh town. Mothers who perhaps had had plans for their daughters and Peter were particularly curious.

Alice went to a general supply store to buy Wellingtons. When she called them rubber boots, the sales lady was confused. Anyways, she got her Wellingtons and a number of cleaning supplies—soap, shopping bags, brushes, and a dish pan. She left these in the store for Peter and Ivor to pick up. With her shopping complete for one day, she walked over to the Welsh Poet to retrieve Peter and Ivor. She opened the door and waved. Women were not welcome in the pub. Peter and Ivor were surprised at all the purchases. The Canadian girl was a little different. That night, Alice was able to cook a meal in her new house. Ivor agreed to stay. Alice was used to wood stoves and the inevitable smoke didn't bother her. She was able to produce a good meal of roast beef, roast potatoes, and boiled carrots. The quantities were large, but the variety was limited. Alice was pleased with her success.

Ivor was always warm and friendly. The two men benefitted from their visit to the Welsh Poet. They both talked freely and told wonderful anecdotes. Alice joined in the conversation and felt relaxed, warm, and dry for the first time in a week.

Peter had a steady job with the road department. Living in a home ruled by his mother and his assertive sister wasn't always pleasant. Every morning, Alice and Peter walked up to Ty Crwyn to help with the chores and have breakfast. Each day, Alice's mother-in-law and sister-in-law found fault with her. Usually, they ridiculed her Canadian accent. They made fun of her Canadian clothes. They found fault with the way she did chores (even though she outworked both of them). They demanded to know what she bought in Brecon and gave her a tongue lashing for her extravagance. Peter's sister Greta was so nasty, she went into a rage because Alice used the expression "rubber boots" instead of "wellies."

Peter didn't intervene on his wife's behalf. Because the family had given Peter money to return home, he may have felt he could not speak. The other possibilities do not reflect well on Peter. One evening, Alice said to Peter, "My mother was beaten down by my father's endless petty cruelties. I may cry. But I'll never be beaten down." Peter didn't say anything.

* * *

Peter realized he had to get his farm functioning. Ivor drove Peter into Brecon to get the local paper, *The Brecon Beacon,* which had international news, local news, and farm notices. Peter wanted a milk cow, some pigs, and laying hens. Peter and Ivor knew all the farms and farmers in the Brecon area. They scanned the livestock columns. They had to find a farmer who would deliver the animals, but they couldn't find a good fit, so Peter decided to pay extra and get the services of a livestock agent. He was able to use the phone at the Welsh Poet. He talked to Ceri James for a long time about what he needed. Ceri agreed to deliver a young milk cow, a pregnant sow, and ten laying hens over the next five or six days. He would range over the county to get these animals. Peter and Ivor were happy with their work and decided to have lunch and a pint. Peter also had to go to the coal yard to order a load of coal. And he had promised Alice a puppy. An ad in the paper made that purchase easy. Peter returned to Ty Twyn a successful man—like a hunter home.

When Alice saw the border collie puppy, she was delighted. The puppy could start its life in the house and then it would sleep in the barn. For now, Alice and Peter were using milk, potatoes, turnips, and preserved meat from Ty Crwyn. As the weeks passed, they would buy all their food in Brecon. Ivor was always happy to drive them into town. Peter had never learned how to drive. Alice was happy that her Canadian savings and gifts were going so far. Peter was back at work on the county roads.

Winter set in and Alice realized she had never been so cold in her life. As a child, she lived through Saskatchewan winters in ramshackle homes, but the cold here was different. There was a dampness that penetrated everything. Their home sat in a depression. The dampness and fog settled around them. Alice sometimes thought she could wring out her clothes. She and Peter slept under three heavy wool blankets, but even their body heat never dried out the sheets. In the morning, more coal was put on the fireplace. The wood stove was lit so that they could have tea and cook their breakfast. Even with the fireplace and the stove, they had to stay in a small circle of heat. After cups of tea, Peter would feed the sow and piglets and give the cow fresh hay. Alice would milk the cow and scatter grain for the chickens. She would let her dog, Moose Jaw, a male, into the house. The work would heat both of them up. They had the warm clothes necessary for the climate and rain on the hooks by the door. Alice had learned how to prepare the Welsh "fry everything" breakfast. She was even beginning to like the fried bread. The bacon they bought at the butcher store in Brecon provided all the grease they needed.

After breakfast, Walter Price would pick Peter up for work. The road crews were supposed to start work at eight but most employees had subsistence farms like Peter, so usually the work day started later. It was before the days of punch clocks, and if necessary, the crews would stay late and work on Saturday. In a dire emergency, they would even work on a Sunday—but that was against the teachings of the reformed churches in the area and many workers refused to come in. All the scheduling for the road crews was done in Brecon. The scheduler had a broad pattern of seasonal work. In winter, most work involved dealing with flooded roads. New ditches might have to be dug or culverts enlarged. Somewhere in history, perhaps when the Romans built their magnificent roads in Britain, the tradition of one man working and three watching developed. No, not in Roman times. The Romans used slaves and the foremen had whips.

While Peter worked on the roads, Alice worked in the home. She had to bake every day on that wooden stove. She knew how to bake bread and make pies. She even learned how to make Welsh cakes. She had a lot of burnt or undercooked items because the wood stove could be balky. With time, she learned the personality of her stove. On Mondays, she would take the warm water from the stove reservoir and wash out their socks and underwear. She would hang the clothes near the fireplace. Sometimes she would complete the drying by putting the damp clothes in the oven. That could be tricky.

About every three days, her mother-in-law and sister-in-law would walk down the hill to inspect things. Alice would offer them cups of tea and slices of bread. They would find fault with both—and with everything else Alice did. Once Alice was sobbing, they walked back up the hill. Most days, Alice was in despair and cried herself to sleep.

Peter was working with friends and he often went to the Welsh Poet in the evening. He thought they had a good life. Peter chose to remain ignorant of the situation. Like a little boy, he feared confrontations with his mother and sister. Sitting in a cold, damp home by herself made Alice wonder about her life. Maybe it wasn't a good life.

Alice was saved by her own resolution and by friendship. It was the age of letter writing, and although Alice hadn't had much schooling, she wrote good letters. She wrote letters to the Riddells on a regular basis. When she felt depressed, she wrote even more letters. These were not confessional letters. It was not the age when self-pity was acceptable. So many people had hard lives that everyone was expected to work diligently, carry on, and not complain. Even at that time, the expression, "stiff upper lip" might have been used. Alice told the Riddells about her farm, the different customs of the Welsh, the rainy weather, and her baking successes and failures. When she told them she named her dog Moose Jaw, Dorothy said in her return letter that she would be flattered if Alice named her cow Dorothy. She added that if the barn had a large tom-cat, she could name him William.

The most important thing for Alice was keeping in touch with her brothers and sisters. She had the addresses for Jane, James, Eva, and William. She wrote them and told them about her life in Wales. She didn't want to tell them how homesick she was, so she told them about the good things in her life. Mail and return mail took months. Eventually she learned from James the addresses of three more siblings. That left the three youngest Reilly children out of touch with their family. They were orphans somewhere in Saskatchewan, or perhaps they were in good homes. She learned from James that Jane's marriage to Bill Matthews had ended. James didn't lay blame and stayed friends with Bill until he returned to England. Jane resumed her flirtatious ways—she introduced James to two or three of her boyfriends. James remained a bachelor, perhaps too shy to even approach a woman.

A letter from Canada made Alice absolutely joyous. When Alice, Peter, and Ivor went to the Saturday market, they had to stop at the post office. Alice knew all the stall holders at the market now and had her favourites for cheese and meat. Root vegetables were plentiful. Apples were the only fruit. Ivor promised he wouldn't tell his mother and sister what they bought—he would be questioned thoroughly when he got home. Alice knew how important Ivor was to them and she always released her men to go to the Welsh Poet. She didn't mind wandering around the market by herself. Sometimes she would even have a cup of tea and a scone at the outside stall. Alice was finding her footing.

The mandatory outing for the Evans family was chapel on Sunday. The family had a long tradition with the Baptist faith. Those obnoxious overlords, the English, had the Church of England, which they tried to impose on the Welsh. Stories were told of the Baptists and Methodists holding secret services away from English landlords. The chapel was quite small. It was presided over by Reverend Llewellyn Prince. He was a very intelligent man, a hard-working man, and a kind man. He knew all the parishioners very well. He established a strict code of Christian behaviour, but he was compassionate to human frailties. After church, the Evans family would gather at Ty Crwyn for a large dinner. That would be six adults. They had a tradition of roast of lamb from their own flock. Dessert would be pie with large amounts of cream. Every farm had a separator that could make cream and butter. Usually the youngest son Vivien had that chore. Turning the crank handle for a long, long time took perseverance and muscle.

After the Christmas service at the chapel, there was a little tea. Reverend Prince took Alice aside and asked if she had been baptized. She hadn't been asked that question at the Moose Jaw Baptist Church. She admitted that she had not. Although not trembling with fear for Alice's immortal soul, he suggested she should be. Two weeks later, on a cold January day, Reverend Prince and Alice entered the creek below the church. Reverend Prince had done this many times, perhaps his faith keeping him warm, but Alice was absolutely freezing and she felt that God and Reverend Prince had asked too much of her. Once she had bundled up in sweaters and blankets, however, she felt good. Mrs. Prince had an elaborate tea waiting for her. She good-humouredly teased her husband about forcing the baptism on Alice. Reverend Prince smiled, but adult baptism was central to his religious beliefs. The two women were not concerned with doctrinaire theology. They believed in love and kindness.

Over the months that followed, the reverend and Mrs. Prince agreed that Alice was having a difficult time. They would often drive over and visit Alice. Later, Alice confessed to Reverend Prince all her difficulties.

When the Reverend told his wife about this, she remarked in a very un-Baptist way, "Well, her mother-in-law and sister-in-law are both bitches. So what can you expect?"

The Reverend blanched. His wife was the perfect minister's wife—gentle, polite, and non-committal. He knew though that she had a very long and passionate dislike of the Evans women. She herself had suffered from their sharp tongues. So as the years passed, Reverend Prince was always Alice's refuge.

Alice was also lucky with her neighbour, Catharine Guest. Catharine had come over a few days after Alice and Peter had moved in. She brought with her an apple pie. That was the beginning of a very close friendship. Catharine took Alice under her wing and taught her some of the intricacies of life in rural Wales. She taught her the daily routine with meals. There was no elaborate cooking just as there wasn't on a Saskatchewan farm. Alice learned the different types of bread, the recipe for pastry, and the baking methods for Welsh cakes and scones. Catharine taught her the different words in Wales for the same things in Canada. Often after her morning chores were done, Alice would walk over to Catharine's farm and the two women would spend the day baking. Catharine and Jim Guest had no children. He was a real estate agent in Brecon as well as a small-holdings farmer. Catharine persuaded Alice to go to a meeting of the Women's Institute one evening. Alice had a little trouble with the Welsh accent when there were many people together, but she felt quite welcome in this group. One thing about the W.I. that made it attractive was that her mother-in-law wouldn't go. She dismissed the W.I. as a gaggle of gossiping women.

Catharine also introduced Alice to knitting. She showed her patterns and took her into Brecon to buy wool skeins. Alice found knitting a great way to pass the time and Peter was gracious enough to wear the somewhat irregular socks. Now Alice had the chapel, the

Princes, Catharine, Jim, and the Women's Institute. She was beginning to feel like less of an outsider.

Alice and Peter had now established a routine for their very simple rural life. Then in early 1933, Alice realized she was pregnant. Peter was delighted. His mother and sister were non-committal. Alice began her plans. First of all, she had to write letters to the Riddells, Jane, and James. She had bought a bicycle in the spring of 1931 so that she could ride into Brecon. Now she could start buying baby items. Once a week, she came back from Brecon with baby things in her basket. That summer, Greta got married in the chapel to the son of a nearby farmer. They had met at the Saturday market and the courtship began. At the wedding reception, Mrs. Prince whispered to Alice, "That poor man."

Alice had an easy pregnancy until the last two weeks. Then she began to throw up her food. She survived almost entirely on cold tea for two weeks. But Catharine was there every day and the Guests pitched in until all the farm work was done. Finally, Alice went into labour. Ivor got the local mid-wife from a nearby farm. She was in a grumpy mood because of a dispute with her husband, so Alice was not treated gently. Nevertheless, Alice produced a full-term baby girl. Within minutes, Alice had the baby in her arms. Peter, Catharine, and Jim came to the bedroom to see the new arrival. Alice was weary, but extremely happy. Her mother-in-law came to visit two days later with a baby bonnet. She was taciturn.

The beautiful child had constant attention from her parents. The love they had for their daughter brought Alice and Peter closer together. They would never have the love they had when they courted in Moose Jaw, but the resentments were abated.

Chapter Nine

Galicia 1934 - 1937

As usual, Betta woke while it was still dark. Necessity had become a habit. She wished she could luxuriate in the warmth of the bed. She could feel the body heat of her son David and hear the soft breathing of her mother-in-law, Kateryna, on the other side of him. The three always slept together for body heat. The weight of blankets, quilts, and coats kept them virtually immobile all night. Betta always took this time in the darkness to plan her day and to think about her life. She often lay awake wishing she could have a bath—a bath in very warm water with enough store-bought soap for a coat of bubbles. She had not been fully immersed in water since last September when she took her final bath in the creek.

The creek was the best feature of her father-in-law's farm. The creek provided their drinking water and the water for their horses, cows, pigs, and chickens. The creek was edged by elder bushes and occasional birch trees. Over the years, a path had been worn to the pool where Betta or her in-laws would dip pails and then labour home with a pail in each hand. There was no water for bathing except when David was a baby. Now that he was older, he didn't want to bathe.

Betta had to stop daydreaming and get moving. She took her coat from the bed and tucked the blanket around David's shoulders. Kateryna would rise as soon as Betta opened the door. Betta put on her boots, and wrapped a heavy shawl around her head and neck. She put on her sheepskin mitts that she was so proud of. They had been a wedding gift from Mr. Denzo. It seemed so long ago now. She wondered where he and his family were. He had become alarmed by Stalin's purges. He thought there could be a Communist revolution in Poland. In June, he had his foreman drive him and his family to L'vov. They had nothing but suitcases. Denzo gave his automobile to his foreman and they boarded the train. They had not been heard from since.

Betta made her way to the outhouse. She would try to suspend herself above the hole as she peed. The board was ice. Then she walked to the barn. Her father-in-law stayed with Alona, their cow, all night long. He was afraid that refugees might steal her. The refugees wouldn't try to overpower the cow's guard. They had some strange residual obedience to authority and ownership. Mr. Dubinsky slept beside Alona and her body kept him warm. Straw was good insulation, whether on the ground or in the walls of the home. Betta took Fedir's place beside the cow as he left to go inside the house. Kateryna would have the fireplace lit and the stove hot. Betta would wait until the sun was fully up and then she would milk Alona. A few years ago, Alona could provide almost a pail and a half of milk. Now she had only a half or three quarters. She was getting old and the hay was losing its nutritional value. But they could hardly survive without this milk. Now their breakfast was mostly boiled oats with milk. The pigs had the same meal.

Last fall, the refugees arrived. The area was warned they would come. News from central and eastern Ukraine was passed along the rail line. Stalin had merged his paranoiac murderous nature with Marxist-Leninism ideology. He planned to eliminate all private farms and make them into peoples' cooperatives. At the same time, he would snuff out a growing Ukrainian nationalism. The bloodlust of the civil war would be turned on Ukraine. Thousands and thousands of Kulaks were sent to Siberia to die. The grains and root crops were shipped to Russia. In the spring of 1932, there were no seed grains, seed potatoes, seed turnips, or seed cabbage. There was nothing to plant. People tried to travel west, but the Red Army blocked the railroads and most of the roads. Most of the refugees were turned around. The propaganda machinery in Moscow assured them they would be better off on collective farms once the new year began, but there was no food left in the country. During the summer, people survived on root vegetables hidden in cellars. The black market of desperation functioned. But by October, there was no food at all. Dogs, cats, and rats were put into soup pots with dandelion wine. Peasants began to die by the thousands. They didn't have the strength to split wood for fires. They died from either starvation or cold or both. By the spring of 1933, millions of Ukrainians were dead. The peasant shacks were charnel houses. Stalin was pleased. He would have a clean slate to establish the workers' paradise of collective farms. Ukraine would supply the grain for the new industrial cities he envisioned. Marxist Leninism would triumph and all would be well. Five or six million dead Ukrainians was not too great a price to pay.

In the spring of 1934, there was a great stench across the land—the stench of rotting bodies. Winter had preserved the emaciated and skeletal forms. Now, as the snow melted, the bodies were exposed. As the survivors themselves, paper thin, made their way from shack to shack, they were overcome with shock and despair. Along the roads, where the snow melted first, bodies were often massed together, probably in some desperate hope of warmth. In places where the snow was rapidly receding under the spring sun, arms and legs stiff with ice protruded. Then with more warmth, they became limp rags. As survivors moved across the land, they wore scarves over their noses and mouths. But the smell of putrefaction could not be shut out. Near-empty stomachs gagged and retched.

Stalin now shipped seeds back into Ukraine. The new collective farms were to plant crops. The peasants were given food so that they could work in the fields. The new political commissars, most of them Russian, ordered mass graves to be dug and stench-infested shacks to be burned. The smell of decaying bodies was replaced by the smell of burning bodies. From his new factories, Stalin shipped tractors to the collective farms. Ukraine had to produce crops in 1934. All the goals of the new five-year plan depended upon them. Russian overlords and Ukrainian officials must meet their quotas or they would join the Kulaks in Siberia. Men and women worked until they dropped so that their children could survive. They were able to plant almost half the acreage of Ukraine. Large portions of the land were now uninhabited. There were fewer tons of grains than before. Stalin regretted the loss of grain but rejoiced in the slaughter of Ukrainians. Now he could turn his attention to the execution of officers in the Red Army.

Betta had now been without a husband for four years. She didn't miss him. Mike was not an affectionate person. He had decided there was no future in Galicia. He would be limited to the farm his parents had. He was also concerned about the political situations in Poland, Russia, and Germany. The rise of Polish nationalism was not good for Ukrainians. Russia continued to threaten a world-wide revolution. Stalin could easily invade Galicia and claim it for the Soviet Union. Germany was in the throes of a battle between Communists and Fascists. Mike and his friends were certain that another war was coming. It was time to emigrate. The men would go first because few could afford the passage for a whole family. The men would make money in the new world and then send for their wives and children. The wives would survive with their parents or their in-laws. Or they might find jobs in the local area. Mike and his friends would follow the well-worn path to Canada. Since the turn of the century, five or six hundred thousand Ukrainians had emigrated to Brazil, the United States, Canada, and several other nations. The Great War had stopped this flow, but immigration was welcome in these countries again. Canada was chosen because some church members from

Grabek were already there. Their letters asserted that a better life could be found there.

Mike and his five friends found the arrangements to go to Canada easy. So many had gone before. Passports, train tickets, and ship passage—all the details of travel—were assisted by a Canadian immigration office in L'vov. Mike's parents were broken-hearted. They had hoped he would take over the farm and they could spend their last days there. David was five. He was shattered by the thought of losing his father. As days went by, he felt the loss even more.

Betta accepted the implications of Mike's departure. Her in-laws were getting older and she would have to do more work and make more decisions. Mike promised to write frequently and send postal money orders. Betta knew women in the church whose husbands left and they never heard from them again. Emigration was the dominant fact of western and eastern Europe, next to wars, of course. Millions left from Ukraine, Poland, Germany, Italy, and Ireland—every country. Parents and wives wept, but the tides continued.

Mike and his friends boarded the train in L'vov. They had a long and boring train voyage ahead of them. Their train tickets would take them through Cracow, Prague, and Frankfurt on the way to Amsterdam—weeks of rail travel. All the men carried sacks of bread, cheese, kielbasa, and tins of tea. Each meal would have the same ingredients. There was no way to cook on the train, but there was a large pot that sat on an element. This provided boiling water for their tea. The men couldn't get over this electric element. Each of them had to inspect it. Someone explained that a generator powered by the train's wheels created the heat. It didn't take long for the men to become bored and irritable. Having to sleep upright didn't help. At some stops, they could get out and walk around. One man had even brought a football to kick around. They pooled their knowledge about Canada. It was a cold country like their own. It grew grain on vast prairies. Half the country spoke French. It used dollars that were different from American dollars. The king was the head of the country, but he didn't live there. (That caused some puzzlement.)

The men talked about their dreams. Some said they were going to western Canada because they had relatives there. They pulled out letters they had received that spelled out the names "Manitoba" and "Saskatchewan." A few tried to say "Saskatchewan" as the rest laughed. The man with the letters was called Saskatchewan for the rest of the trip. Owning a large farm was the dream of most of the men. They knew that early in the century, Canada was giving land away. They knew that Canada had sent agents to eastern Europe begging people to come. They knew that all the work was done by tractors now. They knew the names John Deere and Massey Ferguson. Most of the information was correct. There were some myths. The dominant myth was that if a person worked hard, he could become wealthy.

One recurring myth that they all engaged in was the myth of Canadian and American women. Several had seen American movies in L'vov. According to them, all North American women were beautiful. They wore lovely dresses that were quite revealing. They always wore high heels. They had brassieres that pushed up lovely breasts. When they went swimming, their bathing suits hardly covered them. The men, on the other hand, always wore suits. They were puny. Any Ukrainian farm boy could knock them senseless. Canada would be sex heaven. Scantily clad, beautiful women who were easy and no worthwhile male rivals.

Some on the train had already indicated that they wouldn't bring their wives over. Why continue the same unhappy marriage? That was never part of Mike's thinking. He was determined to bring Betta and David over as soon as he could. Mike's dream was of wealth—not vast wealth, but the elimination of need. He didn't reveal it to his friends, but what he wanted most in the world was central heating. He had always dreamed of a house with central heating. He hated the winters. He hated waking up cold every morning. He had imagined a warm bed when he woke up. No more starting fires in the fireplace and stove in a freezing home.

After endless days, the train passed through Prague. Mike and his friends had never had to switch trains. At the German border, an Austrian official came into their car. He spoke an understandable Ukrainian. He said they should not get off the train as they passed through Germany. He explained that Germans hated immigrants now. Some seasonal workers from Poland had been beaten badly by militia in brown shirts. Germans wanted to keep their blood pure. The official was embarrassed, but he used the German word to describe the Slavic races "untermensch"—subhuman. Mike and his friends would certainly not leave the train. But as the train chugged along, they started calling each other "Untermensch." That was as funny as "Saskatchewan." Food was brought into the train and sold at a reasonable price. All was peaceful. Finally, they woke up in Amsterdam. They were so happy, they ran around the station and had a football game on a nearby field.

The travel agents had a barracks ready for them. They would board the ship in three days. They could do what they wanted in Amsterdam until then. Few of the emigrants had any extra money. Mike and his friends walked around Amsterdam to see the sights and discovered a public bathhouse. The fee was quite reasonable. The place also had a sauna for a slight additional charge. The facility catered to the ships' crews that arrived each day. Between the sailors and the emigrants who had been on a train for weeks, there was a lot of grime to clean off. Mike and his friends paid extra for the sauna. Men walking around in the nude was a new experience for them. They were all married men with children, but this nudity embarrassed them.

After their adventure at the bathhouse, Mike's group decided to splurge on a restaurant meal. They went to a very modest place. They loved the meal and the Dutch beer. Once they were wealthy men in Canada, they would go out to restaurants frequently. Two of the group had enough money to go to a brothel. When they came back to the barracks to tell their tale, men gathered around. They said there were drawings at the entrance displaying what services were available and the price. They had never seen most of these positions. They indicated to the madam what they wanted. She handed them condoms. They had never used them before. She led them into the inner parlour and introduced them to two ladies sitting around in lingerie. They had never seen lingerie before. The men asked one of the adventurers what the sex was like. He said it was the most exciting five minutes of his life.

The next morning, Mike and his friends had a good breakfast of eggs, ham, potatoes, and very strong coffee. They joked about the brothel. They were quite struck by the number of black and brown people in Amsterdam. The Dutch still had a vast overseas empire. Sea ports are always a great mix of races and languages. Poland and Ukraine had virtually no black people. They knew about slavery in the United States and the civil war, but they had never thought about white and black races together.

They were going to the market today. The agents for the ship had told them they must see Nieuwmarkt, the vast marketplace. They went to the currency exchange business a block away. The sales clerk gave them various denominations of Dutch money and instructions on how to ride the trolley to Nieuwmarkt. Another adventure. They had never ridden a trolley before. The market square was a vast place. It had stores for clothing, shoes, boots, hats, fabrics, and leather goods. Some stores were three stories tall. Pedestrians, cars, and trolleys intermingled with a constant hum. They had no money, but they wanted to see the farmers' market. It was row after row of booths selling vegetables, bread, cheese, meat, tea, coffee blends, elaborate pastries, and items they had never seen before or even thought of.

The customers ran the gamut from very well-dressed women to ragamuffin children slipping in and out of passageways. They had never been in such a bustle of people—it was a little overwhelming.

In one large section of the market, there were fruits from overseas—oranges, coconuts, pineapples, and bananas. They wondered how this fruit could be transported so far. Mike wanted to taste a pineapple. At one booth, he could buy a single slice. It was a new taste, but he loved it. They walked back to the centre of the market to look at the Waag, a large structure with round towers. The clerk told them it was part of the original wall of the city. They decided to eat at an outside café. They all enjoyed the Dutch beer now. Since it was a port city, they all tried the open-faced mackerel sandwiches with large onion slices. They sipped beer and watched people. They had never seen such a variety of people. They started back to the barracks but were lured by a used clothing store. They wandered around for quite a long time. They all wanted some summer clothes. Finally, two of them bought light cotton shirts. Mike didn't buy anything. Each of them was allowed only one suitcase on the ship. Mike's suitcase was full with an assortment of winter clothes. At the money exchange, they changed all their currency to Canadian dollars. They were a little surprised that the exchange had a ready supply of Canadian currency. The clerk told them that almost as many emigrants were going to Canada as the United States.

The next morning, the barracks emptied out early. There were line ups at all the nearby restaurants. The early arrivals were allowed to board the ship. At the top of the gangplank, an officer checked off names and inspected passports. The ship was a cargo ship. Its profit came from carrying squared-off pine timber from Canada for construction jobs in Holland. Carrying passengers the other way covered some of the costs. Mike and his friends were pleased with the temporary bunks, and the heavy blankets were suitable. The next day, the ship ran down the English Channel and started its journey across the Atlantic.

Most of the migrants were sick for the first two days, but they recovered. The voyage became very pleasant. There was only one day of rain and the sun was out after that. The migrants could walk around the ship and sun themselves on the deck. On the third day, Mike joined a group in making a campfire in a well of the ship near the stern. Most of the talk was about Amsterdam. The migrants talked about their plans—some were unrealistic; some were well thought out. Since most were farmers, they wanted to go to farms. They all had brochures published by the Canadian Immigration Services Department. Between the brochures and the information friends and relatives had sent them from Canada, they all felt confident they would do well. The Canadian government's brochure included a basic Ukrainian to English vocabulary. Mike and his friends practiced English words.

On day seven, they arrived in Halifax in the middle of the night. They moored at the industrial pier. Buses were waiting to take them to barracks—not unlike the ones in Amsterdam. In the morning, after a breakfast of scrambled eggs, bacon, and toast, they were bused to Pier 21 for registration. On the bus, they complained about the white bread—just mush. The immigration officials at Pier 21 were very efficient. They overlooked any errors in paperwork. As each migrant was registered, he was led into a large information hall. There were displays by the Canadian Labour Department and private companies. The majority of the migrants knew where they were going—most to Manitoba or Saskatchewan. Mike didn't want another long train ride. He didn't want to work in a fish-processing plant. The thought of going underground in a mine frightened him. Cleaning apartments in Montreal or Toronto seemed like slave labour. Mike hadn't thought about it before, but he decided to work for a lumber company. There were many lumber companies in Poland and Ukraine, and it seemed like a good outdoor job. Mike persuaded one of his friends to join him in signing up for a job at J.R. Booths Lumber Company in Algonquin Park, Ontario. They both liked the photographs of the park. The next day, they were on a train again.

Betta was becoming more and more the mistress of the farm; Kateryna and Fedir were getting older. They could no longer do the prodigious amount of work they used to do. Neither had the need to be in control. They loved and respected Betta. Betta became the bookkeeper, making many decisions about purchases by herself. The success of the farm allowed them to purchase a used car in 1932. Fedir tinkered with it endlessly. Now they took their produce to Grabek by car. They sold vegetables, eggs, live chickens, and piglets. David was a very good student, and he was rewarded with nice clothes and store-bought toys. There was a nearby neighbour who helped with heavy jobs and with the harvest. Betta was the one who paid him.

Every Sunday, the four of them went to Church. David was taught the ritual and had his Communion. Betta joined the women's group and went into Grabek once a week by wagon. The ladies exchanged recipes and learned different methods for preserving food. News was always important. Several of the ladies had either sons or husbands in Canada or the United States. There was always a sense of melancholy when the ladies talked about them, but Betta never seemed melancholy. She was enjoying her new freedom and responsibility. One of the things she enjoyed doing was making minor repairs around the farm. She frequently went into the general store to buy nails, screws, braces, rope, and paint. She was becoming a reasonable handyman.

In the fall of 1934, Father Melnyk drove out to the farm with two young children to visit the Dubinskys. Father Melnyk spoke very quietly.

"These children are orphans and refugees. The stories you've heard about Ukraine are true. Stalin stripped the country of all its grain, and hundreds of thousands of people are starving to death. The mother of these children gave all her food to them. One morning, they found her dead in bed. For two days, they just sat there. They had no energy to walk. On the third day, a neighbour came by to see how the family was doing. He took the children in his wagon to the village church. He left the body in the bed. The priest arranged for the International Red Cross to smuggle them into Galicia."

Betta and Kateryna had tears running down their cheeks. Fedir paced back and forth with agitation.

Fedir stopped his movement and said, "With God's help, we will take care of these children." Then he lost his self-control and could not hold back his tears.

The Dubinskys now had two more children who had been smuggled out of Ukraine. Their parents had starved to death giving all their food to their children. There was a clandestine aid group sponsored by the International Red Cross that arranged for children to escape. There were quite a few of these children in Galicia. Many were also placed in homes or orphanages in Austria and France. Many of these children could have gone to relatives in Canada, the United States, Brazil, or other countries, but very few had any form of identification.

The children's names were Iryna and Hedeon. Iryna was about the same age as David. Hedeon was five or six. Father Melnyk had told the Dubinskys that they had to be introduced to a regular diet carefully. Kateryna made enough chicken soup so that they had chicken broth four or five times a day. After a week, they began to eat some bread, carrots, potatoes, and cabbage in the soup. They began to talk to Kateryna in quiet voices. She became their babusya and she loved it. David was at school now and spent the rest of his time doing chores or playing with his friends. Kateryna was delighted when the children gained weight and had the energy to walk around the farm.

David should have been sulky and irritable as these new children took attention away from him. After all, he was the only son of a single mother and the only grandson of grandparents growing older. But that was not the case. David was in love with his new sister and brother. He read to them from his school books; he taught them addition and subtraction on his slate; and he offered them his clothes. As they gained strength, he played outdoors with them and took them to neighbouring farms to meet his friends. He wanted them to go to school with him. Kateryna wanted to wait until they were a little heavier. (She liked having them to herself.) When Father Melnyk made his periodic visits, he was very happy with their progress. He usually took Fedir aside to tell him of the horrors in Ukraine.

The Dubinskys received a letter from Mike about every month. Betta received a postal money order in Grebak every two months. She was able to add that to her savings at the bank. Mike described his life in the lumber camp. It was hard work, but he enjoyed it. He laughed that chopping and sawing all day had made him very strong. He had eggs, ham, and bread for breakfast. Most other meals were beans with salt pork. Beef stews from a huge cauldron were common, porridge from that same cauldron for breakfast some days. The lumber workers had complained so bitterly about the soft white bread that the camp cook had started baking nice solid rye breads. The workers could help in the kitchen some days if they wanted. Mike helped the cook a few times. He was impressed by the large-scale creations. He talked about going fishing in the evenings. The lakes and rivers were full of speckled trout and pickerel. They were allowed to cook their fish in the lodge. The lodge had about forty men with a huge iron stove in the middle. For the first time, Mike met men from Italy, Finland, England, and Scotland. He and his Ukrainian friends began to mock national characteristics. Mike said his English was improving. He was trying to talk to the few Canadians in the camp.

Algonquin Park was beautiful, but the flies were murderous—black flies, mosquitoes, horse flies, moose flies, and something the Canadians called "no-see-ums." The workers slathered on something like axle grease. It guarded against flies, but as they sweated, grease ran into their eyes. Some men tried netting, but it made breathing harder. Some men believed if you got bit enough, you would build up immunity. The hut had a large radio with strong speakers. The lumbermen heard about the Great Stock Market Crash in the

United States, but they weren't sure what that meant. They listened to music from Duke Ellington, Paul Whiteman, and Rudy Vallee. They called most of the music jazz. Four or five Englishmen would dance to the slow music. Mike thought they were fools.

The workers' pay was put into their bank accounts in Whitney every two weeks. Most of the workers just let the money accumulate, but some got rides into town to get cash for liquor or cigarettes or poker. Mike didn't drink, smoke, or play poker. He was building up a good bank balance. Every two months, he went into town to send money to Betta and mail a letter. In his letters now, he would add some English sentences like "It is cold today," or "Two of our horses died." A Canadian would proofread for him. He became very good friends with a Finn. The Finn was a compulsive fisherman. He and Mike went fishing every chance they got. They were able to borrow rods and reels from the managers in the camp office. The Finn knew about lures. They walked up a large stream several miles from the camp. They had several favourite pools. Mike became good at casting lures. Almost every time they brought back ten or twelve speckled trout. They frequently went out in a canoe that nobody seemed to own. Learning to canoe became a recreational activity of the workers. Every time the workers tipped, there would be howls of laughter. Bathing and swimming in the nearby lake was a joy for all the workers. If Mike and the Finn got to the lake before sunrise, they could take the canoe and go fishing. In the lake, they cast larger lures and wound them in slowly. They always caught several pickerel. Once they got permission to use the company's motor boat. There was a lot of noise and blue smoke, but they got the outboard motor going. They trolled for several hours and caught five pickerel. The Finn caught a fish that fought for five minutes. When he brought it close to the boat and tried to lift it into the boat, the line snapped. They didn't have a net. When they came in and talked about the fish, a Canadian said it was a muskie.

Mike's English was improving, but the accents of the Finns, Poles, Englishmen, and Scots led to some strange pronunciations. They all learned the international system of hand signals. The horses always heard Giddys! and Whoa! The bell for dinner didn't need any interpretation. After two years, Mike was put in charge of the horses. He had five two-horse teams and he could yoke them together to get a four-horse team if necessary. The logs were brought out on skiffs through the woods. Over time, the skiffs would carve a primitive road. Then trucks would venture a little closer to the cutting area. Rainy weather meant no trucks. Mike's horses had to pull a lot of trucks out of the mud.

Mike heard about the founder of the company he worked for; J.R. Booth. Mike couldn't understand English well enough to get all the details, but he learned that Booth had died only a few years ago in 1925. He lived to be ninety-eight years old. He lumbered in vast tracts of land in central and northern Ontario. Where rivers couldn't carry his lumber, he built railroads. Europe and the United States needed lumber. One of the Canadians knew that during the Napoleonic wars, Napoleon had cut off the British supply of masts from Norway and Sweden. The British found huge white pines in Ontario that could be felled and floated down rivers to Montreal and onto ships for England. Booth followed this precedent and enlarged it. He built huge lumber yards in Ottawa. His yards had thirteen band saws—the most in the world. Two million logs were trimmed annually in these yards. Algonquin Park, where Mike was working, was a provincial park where logging was carefully governed now. Yet lumber was still needed. Once in the evening, an older Canadian said that as a young boy, he had seen the large rafts of squared-off logs. The rafts were so large they had cook stoves on them. The squared-off logs were probably eighteen by eighteen inches. Once the ice broke up in the spring, the rivers had thousands of logs floating to Ottawa.

The next year, Mike was promoted to foreman. The managers recognized his intelligence and energy. His English had become quite good. When the last Ukrainians left the camp, Mike was forced to use English all the time. In the lodge, men gathered by language—Finns here, Italians in the corner, Swedes by themselves. But the largest group, who gathered around the iron stove, spoke English. With no Ukrainians in camp, Mike couldn't fully describe how he had seen Franz Joseph when he was eight or how Franz Joseph had looked at him.

Mike had been a foreman for only one year, but the isolation of the lumber camp was no longer attractive. His fishing buddy, the Finn, left, saying he wanted to live in a town or city where there were more Finns. Mike felt the same way. He wanted to be where there were countrymen. Besides, he could not bring Betta and David to a lumber camp. Like so many immigrants, Mike looked at a map and chose a city randomly. He chose Hamilton because somebody said it was warmer than Ottawa. Mike was still dreaming of central heating.

Mike handed in his notice, transferred his savings to a bank in Hamilton, and hitched a ride from Whitney to Bancroft where he got a train that took him through Peterborough to Toronto. Union Station almost overwhelmed him. The rush of people was like Amsterdam. He caught a train to Hamilton. The industrial parks, the homes, and the office buildings of Toronto amazed him. The farmland between Toronto and Hamilton was lush. Occasionally, he caught a glimpse of Lake Ontario. He knew about the Great Lakes. The train pulled into a station that was smaller than Union Station but perhaps more beautiful. There were lovely stone carvings, marble counters, scores of benches in the waiting room, and terrazzo floors.

Mike asked the porter at the front door if he knew of a boarding house where he could stay. Mike was proud of his proficiency in English. The porter pulled a copy of the *Hamilton Herald* out of his back pocket. He did this surreptitiously. He would be reprimanded if found reading at work. He turned to the "Want Ads" section.

There were quite a number of ads for boarding homes. The porter took out his pencil and circled the best sounding ones. He ripped out the page and gave it to Mike. He pointed to the corner of James and Barton and told Mike to get on the trolley and ask the driver for the street he wanted. Mike could speak English relatively well, but his reading skills were not that good. He hauled his suitcase to the corner and waited. As he waited, he heard everyone speaking Italian. Then suddenly, he heard Ukrainian.

Two ladies in babushkas were shopping. They had their bags full of vegetables. Mike was so excited he lost his normal restraint with women and blurted out, "I need a place to stay!"

The ladies' eyes went wide and their mouths opened. There was a three-second pause and then they started to laugh. They invited him to come with them. They brought him to a home where the one woman's husband was working on a hinge for a bedroom door. They explained the problem to him. The woman sat Mike down and went into the kitchen to make tea. The man puzzled over the newspaper ads. The ladies brought Mike the powerful stewed tea he drank in Galicia. They put a full plate of Khrustyays beside him. Mike drank tea and ate the cookies while the man made a decision. Once Mike was finished his tea, the man said he had made a choice. He owned a share of a car. He would drive Mike. Mike thanked the ladies profusely and followed the man to his shared car. He drove east along Barton until he turned on Kinrade Avenue. He stopped in front of the house while Mike went to the front door. A mature lady spoke in broken English. Mike recognized the accent. She was Ukrainian or Polish. She was Polish and she would take him. Mike went back to the car, got his suitcase, and thanked the man. It was 1935 and Mike was in Hamilton now.

The Great Depression had hit. When Mike was in the logging camp in Algonquin Park, nobody thought something called The Crash would affect them. Mike found out that The Crash affected virtually the whole world. Each day he set off walking north on

Sherman Avenue to the industrial area of Hamilton. He applied for a job at scores of small factories and businesses. Many of the places had 'No Help Wanted' signs out front. He walked day after day for a week until he was worn out. Now his frugality saved him. He had money in the bank. One day, he walked east on Barton Street. He saw a sign on Gage Avenue. It was a handmade sign nailed to a wooden pole—Alliance Lumber. Mike thought this could be something. He walked up Gage until he found the lumber company. He knocked on the office door and went in. A man behind a desk said gruffly that they had no jobs. Didn't he know there was a depression on? Each day, men came to ask for a job. The man felt great compassion for them and his only defense was to be loud and gruff. In the evening, he would tell his wife how difficult it was to turn men away. Mike happened to look out the window and see a skiff of logs with the names Booth and Whitney stamped on them. He told the man those logs came from the camp where he had worked. That started a conversation about logging, logs, type of trees, and band saw cuts. The man was the manager, Charles Lawson. He immediately recognized a lumber man. He offered Mike a job sweeping the floor of sawdust and loading and unloading trucks. All the wages at the yard had been cut, including Lawson's. The workers didn't get much, but it was better than being in a relief line. They had their self-respect. Mike had been a foreman. Now he was a floor sweeper.

One day, a Ukrainian who boarded two houses down approached Mike and asked him to go to church with him. Mike said he had been raised a Catholic in Galicia. He was called a Ruthenian. The man said that was all right. He could understand the service and he could meet fellow Ukrainians. Mike went to the church in an upstairs hall on James Street. The church symbols were put out every Sunday morning. All the debris from the dance the night before had to be cleared away.

Mike understood the service, and he didn't think he was betraying his Catholicism. After the service, the men sat around for hours exchanging anecdotes while the women went home to prepare dinner and the children enjoyed their Sunday freedom. One Sunday, Mike met with a man who owned a variety store on Barton Street. He made Mike an offer. He could live above the store and run the store in the evenings. The person who had this position before was moving to Toronto. Now Mike had two low-paying jobs—the lumber yard from eight to five; the variety store from six to eleven. But now he had a comfortable apartment with a kitchen, and he enjoyed being by himself.

Mike had become a member of the immigrants' network. The first immigrants to a new place had a very difficult time. They often didn't speak the local language. But once there was a foothold, the new immigrants were helped. The Irish came to Boston; Jews came to New York; Poles went to Buffalo; Germans went to Chicago, Italians came to the Bronx. Within a generation, there were doctors, teachers, lawyers, land developers, and politicians. These were communities where everyone helped everyone else. In 1926, a meeting was held to organize a Ukrainian Orthodox parish. In 1933, there was a large general meeting that decided to name the parish in honour of St. Vladimir the Great. By 1935, the Ukrainian community was well established in Hamilton. Like most Ukrainian communities, Hamilton had the pre-Great War immigrants and the post-Great War immigrants. Mike felt very comfortable now.

It was time for Betta and David to come to Canada.

The Dubinskys were doing very well. Betta and Fedir were able to do most of the jobs on the farm and the neighbour helped with any really difficult jobs. The children were all in school and everyone went to Church each Sunday. Iryna and Hedeon had been baptized in the Greek Orthodox Church, but they readily attended the Catholic Church. Fedir had an additional bedroom put on the back of the house for Hedeon and David. The children who almost starved to death were now very healthy. Iryna slept in the same bedroom with Betta. Iryna was so happy that she no longer whimpered in her sleep.

The night time prayers for both Iryna and Hedeon included prayers for their parents. At school, there were two other children who had escaped Stalin's massacre. All four children had a realistic idea of what had happened, but they wouldn't talk about it.

The money that Mike sent could be spent on the children. Betta had a bank account in Grebak that was significant. Mike wrote about his situation in Hamilton. (David looked up the city in a school atlas.) Fedir was surprised to hear that there might be more than five thousand Ukrainians there. Mike didn't mention that he was going to a Greek Orthodox Church now. Mike's letters contained more and more English. They had already received an English-Ukrainian/Ukrainian-English dictionary. While the Dubinskys had a good life, Europe was bubbling with conflict. Fedir sat around with the men after church services and discussed political events. Most thought it was just like before the Great War; powder kegs all over waiting to explode. They were particularly worried about those two autocrats—Hitler and Stalin. The Polish nationalists believed their army was strong enough to repel any invaders. After all, Polish warriors had a long, long history of bravery.

One Sunday, an older man in the church took Betta aside. He told her there was going to be another Great War. Germany was determined to seek revenge for the Treaty of Versailles. He reminded her that the Great War had engulfed all of western and eastern Europe. He said it would happen again. She must leave Galicia now. Betta went home and wrote Mike immediately. She told him he must make arrangements. Betta wanted to bring Iryna and Hedeon with them to Canada. The wheels started to move in both Hamilton and Grabek. But the wheels in Ottawa and Warsaw moved very slowly. There were too many people wanting to flee Europe. There was too much paper to process. Every month, Betta went to the government offices in Grabek. There was never any news. Their priest was trying to get many people out, but he was getting nowhere. Finally, in 1936 Betta got documents that allowed Betta and David to emigrate. The government official in Grabek said they would never get permission for Iryna and Hedeon to travel with them. The children had no identification and they were Ukrainian. They had to get Polish citizens processed first. The Polish government did not like the idea of its citizens fleeing—that suggested a government unable to protect the country. There would be no panic. No flight of currency. Calm and resolution must prevail.

The Dubinskys had to face the heart-wrenching facts. Betta and David would be leaving. Iryna and Hedeon would lose two people who loved them very much. Kateryna and Fedir had lost a son. Now they would lose their beloved daughter-in-law and their grandson. Preparations for their departure had to begin. Betta and David would have one suitcase each. So many memories would be left behind. The Dubinsky home was a very gloomy place.

Betta had the money for her train fare and her ship's passage as Mike had sent Betta a significant amount of money, so a shortage of funds would not be a problem. Betta learned at church that shipping companies did not have enough capacity to take all the migrants anxious to leave. The Dubinsky family waited and waited. Finally, eight months after their application, Betta was informed that her train reservation and ship passage could go forward. It was 1937 when Betta and David prepared to leave. The farewells were difficult. They knew they would never see each other again. Kateryna and Fedir had the consolation of having Iryna and Hedeon with them.

David had the most difficulty in accepting the situation. He yelled and screamed at Betta. He said he didn't love her anymore. He slammed doors. Once at dinner, he threw his plate onto the floor. He refused to go to school. He walked for hours along the roads. Sometimes he wept openly, not worrying about being considered a man. Finally, he became permanently sullen to Betta but warmer to the rest of the family.

The train reservation was for August. Fedir couldn't stand the heartbreak of saying goodbye at the station, so the family had a prayer with their arms around each other and final hugs and sobs at home before the neighbour drove Betta and David into Grabek. Betta's friends from church were there to say goodbye. Even a few of David's schoolmates were there. Europe was a place of final goodbyes. Most families knew the sorrow.

Betta and David would travel through Cracow, Warsaw, and through the Polish Corridor to Danzig. Betta had enough food for three days. Luckily for Betta, David found a friend. They went from car to car annoying people. They loved the swaying sections that joined cars. Betta was happy to get rid of her petulant son. She had brought a novel along to read and she studied her dictionary frequently. She hoped to know some English when she got to Canada. David knew a few English words and repeated them frequently.

On the third day, the train pulled into a siding. They would wait until dark to go down the Corridor. There had been some nasty incidents along the line. German troublemakers tried to stop rail traffic. Once they were through, the train stopped directly alongside the ship. Train passengers boarded the ship with only the occasional flashlights to guide them. The passengers were showing some apprehension. Betta and David found their room despite the dim lighting in the interior. There were two sets of bunk beds in the room. They chose the one they liked and David took the top bunk while Betta took the bottom. Fifteen minutes later, two children about twelve and ten came in and took the other set of beds. They were very shy, but Betta spoke to them gently. They were Poles but communication was easy.

Nobody had been given any orientation tours, but people found their ways to the bathrooms. This ship flew the Danish flag and the crew were almost all Danes. The four people in Betta's room all slept with their clothes on. The next morning, just as the sun was coming up, the ship left the pier with a tug boat. Once into the Baltic, the tug untied and returned to Danzig. The ship was headed to the passageway between Denmark and Sweden and then due north into the North Sea and around Scotland before heading straight west.

Those who could face food found their way to one of the three dining rooms. Betta and David weren't sick. Their two roommates were. There were lounge chairs outside on the deck and inside in several walkways. David was walking around the ship. The crew was quite affable.

On the second day out, children began to emerge from their cabins. They were extremely well-dressed. They looked as if they were going on a school outing to a museum. The outing might include dinner at an expensive restaurant afterwards. One of the crew told Betta the story. They were Jews from Warsaw. There were some hundreds of them. Several rabbis had organized the venture. Their parents wanted them safely away. Most were going to New York. About twenty were going to Montreal. Relatives and volunteer families awaited them. Now Betta felt a great sense of relief that she and David were on a ship heading to Canada. She didn't know what was going to happen, but she felt they had escaped disaster.

The North Sea was very choppy and when the ship turned into the North Atlantic, there were six-foot waves. The large passenger ship ploughed along. Passengers were a little grey, but they began to walk around the decks and climb ladders. Some of the children began to play games, and one group from a school choir began singing sessions. Betta and Mike had the novelty of a train ride and a ship voyage to keep them from boredom. One morning, the ship's loudspeaker announced there was an iceberg on the starboard side. Betta thought it interesting that the international language was English. David had made some friends among the Jewish children and they all went to see the iceberg. One of the older girls told them not to worry. They were not on the *Titanic*. By now, the Jewish children realized they were not on a holiday trip. The one rabbi travelling with them told them they might not see their parents for many months. All the adolescents who had found reasons to hate their parents now wished they could be with them. The older children were extremely kind and caring to the younger. Betta learned that most of these children came from very wealthy families in Warsaw. Their parents had been able to transfer a limited amount of money to relatives in Canada and the United States, but Poland had imposed currency exchange limitations. Families that were quite alarmed by events gave jewels, rings, brooches, necklaces, and gold watches to their children. There was a great deal of wealth in some suitcases. All the children carried a collection of family photographs.

The ship pulled into Pier 21 in Halifax on August 20, 1937. The papers for Betta and David were in order. Betta and David walked to the CNR station. She made herself understood and bought tickets for Hamilton. The twenty or so Jewish children were already waiting for the train to Montreal. Since the train would not leave for six hours, David went over to talk to his new friends. All the children went outside the station to walk or play games. There was no longer an adult guardian for the Jewish children. Within an hour, they heard the ship's horns and the ship left Halifax for New York.

Betta and David slept as the train sped through Nova Scotia and New Brunswick. It was a nighttime express train with no stops. In the morning, the train arrived in Montreal. Most of the passengers got off. Betta and David saw the large number of people waiting to greet the Jewish children. David knew his new friends were very apprehensive—most of them had never met these people before. Now they would be with new families in a new country with a new language. David had the same apprehension.

Betta and David travelled on to Toronto. They overcame the confusion of Union Station. After boarding the train for Hamilton, they had another CNR lunch—sandwiches on white bread, cookies, and pop or coffee. They weren't impressed by Canadian food. Finally, they reached the CNR station in Hamilton. Mike was waiting in the foyer. They didn't immediately recognize him. He didn't immediately recognize them. But Mike moved forward to hug Betta and David. It was awkward. Seven years of separation; three different people. The family would begin its new life in Hamilton.

Chapter Ten

Wales 1938 - 1943

By 1938, Alice's daughter May was registered in the local school. Alice walked her there every day. She met several mothers whom she enjoyed chatting with. Alice now found her life full. Once a week, Catharine would walk May home from school and Alice could bicycle to Brecon. They still had to depend on Ivor to drive them to the Saturday market. Alice was thoroughly annoyed that Peter wouldn't learn to drive. He always claimed he was too nervous to drive. Being on a farm without a car was a great annoyance, but they were not the only ones. Several of their neighbours went to town by horse and buggy. The Evanses never owned horses.

By now, the nation was consumed by war talk. The Evanses now owned a radio, and they enjoyed the entertainment and the news. There were no programs during the day, but at 6 p.m., the BBC had its news hour. The BBC was a monopoly funded by the government. It had foreign correspondents all around the world and took pride in its professionalism. Nobody wanted another war.

Britain had suffered almost one million dead in World War I. To increase the number of volunteers for the army, the British government got the idea of allowing towns to have their own battalions. The theory was that young men wanted the camaraderie of their friends. Unfortunately, when a battalion was wiped out, a village might lose scores of its young men. Several villages in Wales suffered this fate. There were very few people in Europe unaffected by the war. Perhaps forty million soldiers and civilians were killed. Unfortunately, Germany wanted revenge for all the wrongs they thought it had suffered. The charismatic Adolf Hitler was leading his nation to war. By 1938, Britain realized war was inevitable and began frantic preparations. The Munich Agreement of September bought some time. But the policy of appeasement had failed. Hitler was determined to have a war.

Peter bought a paper every Saturday now. Most of the people in Brecon had an insatiable need for news. Newspaper sales doubled. All day at work, Peter discussed the situation with his friends. Soon it would be decision time—volunteer or be drafted. The wheels of government were turning rapidly now. Restrictions on gasoline were the first step. There would be many more restrictions. Finally, Hitler invaded Poland and Britain declared war. Some were pleased; some were absolutely heartbroken. It didn't take long for children from the large cities to arrive in Brecon. The plans had been formalized years before. The bombs dropped in Britain in World War I foreshadowed air assault in World War II. Families volunteered to take in children. The Guests took on a young boy from Bristol. The Evanses weren't sure about the idea, but then Alice became pregnant again in the summer of 1939 so they couldn't take a child.

Across the land, people followed the war avidly. In the beginning, there was nothing but bad news. Dunkirk had been a great defeat turned into a miracle of British resolve. Churchill was rallying the nation. But things didn't look good. For the Evans family, things were fairly normal as the world disintegrated.

In February 1940, the second Evans child was born—a boy they named Roy. This was a hard delivery for Alice because the mid-wife showed up drunk. The baby had to be withdrawn using forceps. The mid-wife's clumsiness left permanent indents on the child. Now Alice had a baby and a school-age child. Her mother-in-law came less frequently now, but when she did come, she had a basketful of advice. Government inspectors came to the farms to tabulate livestock. Everything was rationed. Every cow and pig had to be counted. Farmers started to hide animals. Total war meant the destruction of cities and government control over every aspect of life. Alice found fewer articles for sale at the Saturday market and certain items were no longer for sale in Brecon shops. The people in Brecon felt lucky because the stories of the Blitz in London were horrific.

On November 14 and 15, there was a devastating blitz on Coventry. The Luftwaffe had been targeting Coventry because of its manufacturing plants. At night and in the morning, there were around 150 high explosive bombs and three thousand incendiary bombs. The city was on fire. The Daimler factory was destroyed. Half of the homes in the city were destroyed. The bombing of Coventry was not much different from the Blitz in London. The attacks showed the incredible destructive power of air attacks. If air attacks could destroy production facilities, the raid on Coventry was a success. The raid also showed the indiscriminate use of incendiary bombs. Homes as well as factories were destroyed. The bombs would also destroy wonderful historic buildings. In the case of Coventry, the famous Coventry Cathedral was destroyed. The fire storm also meant that bodies could not be identified and Coventry was forced to have a mass burial. Sadly, some bodies were entombed forever in the deep bomb shelter in the city centre. This was the first time the Evanses were directly affected by the casualties of war. A cousin of Peter's, Mabel Jenkins, lived in Coventry. A huge land mine, slowed by parachutes and fitted with a proximity fuse, exploded in the common garden behind the family flat. The family was composed of Mabel, her husband Henry, her young baby Gertrude, and her father-in-law, Samuel. They couldn't return to the flat and came down to Brecon for refuge. Alice and Peter were able to put them up. Unfortunately, Samuel Jenkins had suffered internal injuries from the blast. He was taken to the Brecon hospital where he died two weeks later. Henry, Peter, and Ivor drove up to Coventry a week later to see if some furniture could be salvaged from the flat. They were able to climb the staircase to the flat, but glass was embedded in all the furniture. Henry just retrieved a few items. They couldn't drive through the city, but they saw acres of burnt-out buildings. The army occupied the city and travel was very restricted. They learned more from the Brecon paper than they learned from being there.

Mabel was so traumatized by the explosion that her milk dried up. Alice, who was breast- feeding Roy, volunteered to be a wet nurse for Gertrude. Both babies were almost exactly the same age—six months. So, Alice was confined to the house for long periods of time. Mabel and Henry did the farm chores. May, who was seven, watched the feedings with great fascination. After only a few weeks, the Jenkins found a home to rent in Brecon. Henry became a farm labourer. Gertrude went from breastfeeding to bottle feeding.

Starting in 1942, there were profound changes around Brecon. The government in London decided to help farmers who had lost their farm labourers to the armed forces. The innovative idea was to ask young women from cities to work on farms. They would call the ladies the Land Army.

Brecon had an office for assigning Land Army members to farms. Farmers came in to register and request workers. The young ladies were initially given brown coveralls and they stood out. Some city girls lasted only a day or two. Sunburns and blisters were the major reasons for leaving, but girls not used to physical labour sometimes couldn't get out of bed the next day. A few girls were frightened by the farm animals. Many couldn't stand the farm day of up at 6 a.m. and bed at 9 p.m. Those who persevered through the first weeks began to thoroughly enjoy themselves. They felt healthier and stronger. They loved their new light-coloured hair, freckles, and healthy tans. Generally, the farmers treated them very well and didn't enforce strict rules.

On Saturday nights, the Land Army invaded Brecon. The local dance pavilion had triple blackout curtains and a double door entry system. It was allowed to stay open. The dances had Land Army girls, local girls, soldiers on leave, and local men. A volunteer would play an assortment of records that were primarily big band sounds with fast and slow rhythms. Near the end of the night, a jive record would be played, and the adventuresome would hit the dance floor. Closing time was 11 p.m.

One Saturday at the pavilion, Rhonda James of the Land Army was asked to dance (a slow dance) by Vivien Evans. Rhonda was from Shrewsbury. She was outgoing, vivacious, and gregarious. Vivien was a quiet farm boy. They fell in love. Never any doubt. He proposed within weeks. After haying season, they were married in Shrewsbury. The Evans family was able to be there. Of course, Mrs. Evans didn't like Rhonda because she was English. But Rhonda, unlike Alice, let her know she would not be intimidated. The farm where Rhonda worked was happy to have Vivien come as a full-time farm hand. After settling her affairs in Shrewsbury, Rhonda joined Vivien at the farm. Later they would buy their own farm.

The war was not going well for Britain. The Battle of Britain in the summer and fall of 1940 saved Britain from invasion, but it was a skin-of-its-teeth defensive battle. The Battle was a huge boost to the nation's morale, however. At this point, Britain stood alone against Germany. The German military had victory after victory. The British public, urged on by Winston Churchill, was inspired to carry on at all costs.

On March 12, 1941, Peter Evans came home from work and said he was going to sign up. It may have been the Battle of Britain, or the raid on Coventry, or the sight of seeing so many men in the area in uniform. Peter was almost thirty-seven years old. He was too old to train as a soldier. He had no unique skills. But all the services needed men and women for non-combat jobs.

Alice had had enough. Was she to be left with two children on a farm? She already couldn't even go to the Saturday market by herself—not with a one-year-old child to care for. She screamed and yelled and threatened—and Peter left for the Welsh Poet on his bicycle. That was it. Peter's registration and induction into the Royal Air Force took three weeks; three very cold weeks at home. He travelled to Cardiff for his initial training. He got the blue uniform of the RAF. He learned to march. He learned to sleep in a barracks with twenty other men. He learned to shave with cold water. He passed the four-week training session with an above average assessment. He was moved to a different barracks and was given his battalion designation. When he mustered for parade the next morning, he realized he was in a support battalion. The men in his battalion looked surprisingly like him—old. The young men went to train as pilots, navigators, bombardiers, or radar experts. Peter's battalion would have the humdrum jobs necessary to keep the planes in the air.

Peter was given a travel pass and ordered to rcport to a base outside Hereford on July 1. The rest of the time was an extended leave. When Peter arrived home, May was just ecstatic over the blue uniform. Her father looked like a war hero. She embraced him constantly and sat on his lap whenever possible. Alice was polite. After dinner, Peter was off to the Welsh Poet. His friends and the patrons at the pub were impressed. It was a time when men wanted to be in uniform. The horrors of World War I were forgotten. All the glory of war was dominant. The bombing of British cities aroused a desire for blood revenge. Hitler and the Nazis were the epitome of evil. The British Propaganda Ministry did an excellent job of describing British bravery and German evil. The BBC was the arm of government propaganda, and it was the only radio station Britain had. In Germany, Goebbels had his radio station and all the newspapers.

Peter spent his time at home doing repair jobs, finishing projects, walking the countryside with May, and visiting his mother and brothers. Every day, he got on his bike and rode into Brecon to get a newspaper. Every now and then, he splurged on a Liverpool or London paper. He tried to stay out of the way of Alice. She stayed out of his way by working in the garden. She would put the baby in his pram and take him out to the garden with her. She was weaning him off her breast and onto the bottle.

Peter reported for duty at Hereford. Again, there were the marching drills, the bed inspections, and the emphasis on neat uniforms and shiny boots. The RAF base at Hereford was a training site for maintenance jobs. The men learned the skills necessary for assembling and repairing various planes. They were even assigned their own work benches. Peter had no mechanical skills, but the jobs were easy—comparable to a job on an assembly line. On one occasion, the trainees were taken to Manchester where there was a Hurricane manufacturing plant. They saw all the components being assembled and the diligent, no-nonsense workmen.

The workers in factories knew how important their jobs were, and many companies and the government had programs to encourage and reward them. Peter's group was surprised to see women on the assembly line. There was the usual flirtation with the men in uniform. Some men at the factory resisted having women working beside them and treated them poorly. Most men, however, treated them well. After all, their wives and daughters were taking on roles normally done by men. It was a time of "All Hands on Deck!" Peter and his fellow recruits realized they were just factory workers in uniform, but they would follow the Air Force when it went.

Peter was close enough to home to visit when he had three-day leaves. He had his routine on the farm. He had his visits to the Welsh Poet. It was a pleasant experience for him. Alice was coping because she was a hard worker. She enjoyed his absence. She was the ruler of the house and farm. Her mother-in-law no longer visited. She was busy at Ty Crwyn. Ivor was Alice's rock. He came every week to drive her to the Saturday Market. He had even figured out a way to tie the baby's pram to the roof of his car. At the Market, Ivor and May would go off together and Alice would have Roy in the pram. Ivor always bought May some candy or a sweet roll. It was a fun day out. For a special treat, they would have lunch at the outside cafeteria. Alice had a portion of Peter's pay, and in the summer, the garden provided all the fruit and vegetables they needed. There was a black market for beef and pork among the farmers and Alice occasionally bought some meat. But milk, eggs, and cheese were a big part of their diet.

Alice now had a life that she controlled. She never missed a Sunday church service at the chapel. Religion was more important to her now because she linked religion with the compassion of Reverend Prince and Mrs. Prince. She had made friends with other parishioners who offered help if she needed it. In fact, one of the men in the church had done several heavy jobs that Alice couldn't do. Another man in the church arranged for one of her pigs to be butchered and the meat stored. Alice was even closer to Catharine now. They visited each other frequently. The boy the Guests had taken in was a delight. He was twelve now and he frequently came to Ty Twyn to help out. He and May would take hikes together and Alice's dog Moose Jaw would go along.

Alice and Catharine never missed a meeting of the Women's Institute. Now, rationing made cooking a challenge for the women living in Brecon. New recipes were devised, for example, because sugar was rationed. Alice overcame her shyness and showed the ladies of the Women's Institute how they preserved fruit in Canada. They started to use the same method. The ladies even had an informal clothing exchange because there was a strict limit on new clothes. In the evenings, Alice would often write letters to Canada. The foremost thing on her mind was the location of all her brothers and sisters. James and Jane had tracked down all but the two youngest children—Frederick and Thelma. They had been placed with families, but nobody in the family knew where. Mail was so irregular that Alice got few letters. She thought many of the letters addressed to her were at the bottom of the Atlantic. The fate of their mother was never mentioned. Their father had contacted the older boys, and there was reconciliation. Alice had confessed to Reverend

Prince and Catharine that she would never forgive her father or her mother-in-law or sister-in-law. Reverend Prince made a half-effort at counselling Christian forgiveness. Catharine supported and complimented her.

Chapter Eleven

Ontario 1937 - 1943

In October 1937, Betta, David, and Mike went to a used clothing store on James Street North. They had to have appropriate clothes for the canonical visitation to their parish. The parish executive rented the Palace Theatre for the visitation by the Archbishop from Toronto on October 17. The parish members were following all the steps to get ready to build their own church. Mike and David needed dark suits for the visit, and Betta needed a dress in the Canadian fashion. David was already an inch taller than his father. Like many young people, he didn't approve of his parents' dress. In particular, he was angry because Betta wore a babushka. He said it made her look like a peasant. He was becoming Canadianized.

One of Mike's friends had told him how to enroll David in school. David walked up Barton to Lottridge Street and then to the Prince of Wales School. David spoke little English but because of his age and height, he was put into Grade 8. Normally, a newcomer who didn't speak English would be bullied. But David was tall for his age and had the muscles of a farm boy. Besides, the bullies had a small kid with glasses they could beat up every day. David listened and watched. He was ahead of the class in arithmetic. He loved the stories the teacher read out loud. He was befriended by a group in his class who always stuck together. With David's addition, the group had one Ukrainian, one Croatian, one Pole, and three English who called themselves Canadian. David was submerged in English and he was learning fast. In the evening, he even listened to radio shows. His friends were really amused when he recited the introduction to the *Lone Ranger* show with his Ukrainian accent.

"In the early days of the western United States, a masked man and an Indian rode the plains . . ." When he yelled, "Hi! Oh! Silver away!" his friends doubled-over with laughter. The next fall, David started high school. Mike thought he should go to the tech school, but David knew what he wanted already. He was going to go to Delta and he was going to go to university. He didn't reveal his plans to anyone because they were so outrageous. For five years, he caught the Beltline on Barton Street up Kenilworth down Main to the west door of Delta. During those years, his only activity was church basketball. Somehow, he found out about a team out of New Westminster Presbyterian Church on King Street. The coach welcomed him because of his height and strength. No questions were asked about his religion. David got to know Hamilton because he travelled with his team from church to church. But not to the Catholic churches. They had their own league.

Betta slowly learned English as she helped Mike run the variety store. The store stocked two daily papers in English and weekly newspapers in Ukrainian, Polish, and Italian. People helped one another with English expressions. Betta was cheered by Ukrainian visitors. Within a short time, two ladies from Ukraine visited Betta frequently. They gave her tips about living in Canada.

In 1940, Mike heard Dominion Glass was hiring. He decided to leave the lumber yard because he had to work six days a week there. Shift work meant days off during the week. He could do other work. Mike started in the packing house. Bottles came down a conveyor belt, were inspected by women, and put into boxes. Men piled the boxes on pallets to be lifted up and taken away by forklifts. Then he volunteered to work in the front end where bottles were formed. Mike had to schedule work hours at the store to deal with his shift work.

In 1941, Alina Dubinsky arrived. She was the reunion child of Betta and Mike. David was sixteen years older than his sister. He was embarrassed by the whole affair. Having a new baby complicated the lives of the Dubinskys. Mike solved the problem of the store by hiring a young Ukrainian woman whose husband had volunteered for the army. Betta spent much of her time walking the baby carriage around the neighbourhood.

In June 1943, David wrote his departmental exams. In Ontario, high school was five years. At the end of Grade 13, students wrote province-wide exams. The exams came in sealed packages from Toronto. Each school put them in school vaults until the days of the exams. Exams were written in school gyms. They were held over almost three weeks. Once the exams were written, they were shipped to Toronto. Teachers from across the province came to mark the exams in July. David got very high marks. He was admitted to the University of Toronto in a general arts course. That same summer, he got a summer job at the steel company, Stelco. He would be able to pay for his tuition by himself.

Chapter Twelve

North Africa 1941-1943

The attack on Pearl Harbour on December 7, 1941, changed the lives of everyone in Britain. They didn't know it at the time but America was now at war in Europe. Hitler had declared war on America when his Japanese ally attacked. The Japanese inflicted swift and humiliating defeats on the British in Singapore and Hong Kong. The British public didn't know the full horror of these defeats. The news was strictly controlled. Even Churchill had trouble remaining confident and his leadership came under review in the House of Commons. But now the huge industrial might of America began to play a significant role. The brilliance of German General Erwin Rommel could not overcome the new resources of the British in North Africa. In a pitched battle at El Alanein in October and November 1942, the British, with their new Sherman tanks, overwhelmed Rommel's depleted Africa Corps. Churchill had the church bells in Britain rung. It was Britain's first major victory in the war.

Roosevelt agreed to make the defeat of Hitler a higher priority than the defeat of Japan. American troops would work with the British. In November 1942, the new military allies launched Operation Torch. The Americans landed in Morocco and headed east towards the last remnants of the Africa Corps.

War is a vast complex of production, transportation, and human resources. The logistics of war range from the front-line fighters to the support structure. Usually, for every fighter, there are nine people necessary to maintain him. When the planners in London mobilized British troops for Operation Torch, they responded to the needs of fighting a war overseas. Peter Evans became one of those tiny cogs in the vast machine.

There is a great secrecy around any military operation, but rumours fly. Peter's unit got the accurate information that they were going to Africa. But that seemed so unlikely that the airmen laughed it off. There was no place in Africa to go unless they went all the way around the Cape, through the Suez Canal, and tried to catch up with the Eighth Army. The answer came when the unit was told to pack its gear and get ready to move. Everyone had to put compulsory items and a few personal things into one duffel bag. They carried their gas masks from shoulder straps, had no rifles, and were trucked to Liverpool. After one night in barracks, they boarded a troop transit ship. On November 10, they left habour. Two days later, the mystery was over—they were issued a tropical kit—short pants, short-sleeved shirts, knee high socks; all these in a light-coloured khaki. The beautiful blue uniforms were handed in. Peter wondered what happened to all these uniforms. Were they thrown away? Were they dry-cleaned for other airmen? Peter thought that with the scarcity of cloth, the uniforms would find new owners; more ill-fitting uniforms for service men.

Peter bragged that he had crossed the Atlantic twice and a sea voyage wouldn't affect him. That was true until he went on deck and it was awash with vomit. Then he had to run for the railings. Once he was feeling better, he went onto the main deck. The airmen could be on deck if there was no emergency siren. If there was, they had to get below immediately. But on a quiet day, the airmen enjoyed the sun. Two days later, they could see a land mass and scores of ships. They were told they were off the port of Casablanca. But the nice trip out was ruined because they couldn't dock. The piers couldn't handle this huge crush of men and material. Peter's ship sat idle in the harbour for two days. The swells made the airmen sick again. Finally, on the third day, they disembarked.

They all marched directly to trucks that made their way through the overcrowded streets of the city. They decided that Casablanca stank worse than Liverpool. Perhaps the warmer temperatures made it worse. Once they got out of the city, the trucks moved quickly. In an hour or so, they were directed down a dusty road by a military policeman. They could see the ocean in the distance. Their new home was a date farm with row after row of date trees. For the next few hours, they assembled the tents that had come in separate trucks, which caused a great deal of chaos. But Peter's crew got their tent up and cots arranged. Peter now had three tent mates.

At eight that night, the wing commander called roll. The airmen marched to an open kitchen and joined the queues for their dinner, where they were introduced to the flies of Africa. They would make the airmen's life miserable when they ate and when they tried to sleep. The netting on the tents was not particularly effective. So now the Brits from Hereford were sleeping in tents outside of Casablanca, Morocco. The expedition was a logistical success—tents, cots, blankets, kitchen food, and waiting trucks. All the centuries of overseas wars and colonial stations made the British armed forces very good at setting up bases. Like a good cook who has scores of no-fail recipes, the armed forces had their tried and true procedures. Now that the base was set up, Peter's group needed a job, but there was no immediate job for Peter's battalion. The unit was supposed to assemble parts for Hurricanes. The high command, however, wanted to wait to see if they could land ships in Algiers. That would be closer to the final battles. There were tense negotiations between the Americans, British, and Vichy French. Meanwhile, the airmen in Casablanca had to be kept busy. Idle troops meant trouble. One solution was to have two kit and tent inspections a day. Then a modified program of exercise and marching began—modified because of the heat. There were also buses made available for groups on a rotating basis to take tours of Casablanca. The airmen also had day passes to visit Casablanca using the available trucks. Curfew was 11 p.m. at the security gate. Groups began to schedule trucks for trips to the ocean. Between airmen trying the food in Casablanca and airmen spending hours in the sun, the medical team was dealing with diarrhea and painful sun blisters.

Peter became good friends with the three other men in his tent. They were all from different backgrounds—although they all came from London. But they'd each had different jobs. One had worked on the docks, one had been a bylaw officer, and one had worked in a jewellery store until it was bombed out. Peter was the only farmer. They stuck together whenever they could. They walked around Casablanca together. They went to the beach together. There was a pleasant mix of military routine and individual freedom. Peter and his new friends had endless hours to talk. After three days, the whole camp received a supply of folding chairs. The air force knew they had time on their hands.

Peter was a great favourite because of his trip to Canada. He told them about the negative-forty degree Saskatchewan winter. His descriptions of winter wear fascinated them. Of course, they wanted to know about the Native Americans. Europeans had been reading novels about them for scores of years. Peter described his trip to the rodeo. Every event interested them—the bronco busting, the calf tying, the wild bull dodging, the chuck wagon races. They thought the idea of a chuck wagon following moving herds of cattle and cowboys was brilliant. Peter tried to limit his narratives so each story could be fully explained. He thoroughly enjoyed his storytelling role. One of the things Peter realized was that if a person thought they had a mundane job, it wasn't mundane to others. Each job had interesting details and funny incidents. Peter's friends—the dock worker, the bylaw officer, and the jeweller—all had stories to tell. For these four men, and probably all the others in the camp, it was a holiday. Some described it as a Cook's tour without the fee. After three weeks, Peter's battalion were told they would be moving out, this time by train. The Allies had arranged a truce with the Vichy French in Algiers. American and British troops had poured into Algeria. The German and Italian armies had retreated to Tripoli and were going to make their final stand in Tunis. They were caught between Allied armies advancing from the east and west. They were vastly outnumbered in every way. The hope was to evacuate troops across the narrow strait to Sicily. Allied ships and planes were set up to stop that.

In February 1943, the Americans advanced towards Tunis with all kinds of confidence. Unfortunately, the tank commanders were inexperienced. The Desert Fox, Rommel, was waiting for them at the Kasserine Pass. He inflicted a huge loss on the Americans. The American command was stunned. They relieved certain commanders and paused their offence to retrain and refit. At almost the same time, Peter's battalion arrived outside of Algiers. The planners, thinking of morale, found farmland near the ocean. Once again, the airmen would be able to bathe and swim in the Mediterranean. This time, though, there was work waiting for Peter's group. The logistics people had taken over several warehouses on the outskirts of Tangiers and brought in machinery.

The workplace they set up had the same machines and tools that Peter's battalion had in England. Once again, they would be assembling and repairing Hurricanes. After inspection each morning, the men would board buses and report to the warehouses. They would put in a day's work, finishing at about five. Then they were on the buses again for a ride back to the camp. They had a long dining hall under canvas that could accommodate about eighty men. The logistics people were now able to buy some food locally. The men began to eat dates for the first time in their lives. They had fresh oranges and grapefruit, but still ate the usual powdered eggs and canned corned beef. Every now and then, the Americans would donate slabs of beef brought in by refrigerated ships. Tea and biscuits was a staple.

Within a mile of them was a prisoner-of-war camp for Italians. During the Desert War, the Germans had captured thousands of Brits. They were usually transferred to Italy. In the final retreat towards Tripoli, around 150,000 Italian troops had surrendered. They had no armaments and few supplies. The Germans had used their trucks to transport their troops west. The Italians were left behind. The people in Peter's battalion sometimes walked over to the Italian prisoner-of-war camp. Many of the Italians spoke very good English. There were wonderful stories about friends and relatives working in restaurants in London and other British cities. Many of the Italians dreamed of going to the United States. Many had relatives in New York. Some had relatives in Toronto or Hamilton. The Italians and Brits exchanged views on Hollywood films. They both loved the gangster films with James Cagney and Edward G. Robinson. A few of the Italians claimed they knew members of the Mafia. That impressed the Brits. Some Italians thought Al Capone had been treated unfairly by the American government. Mussolini was no longer worshipped. In fact, Mussolini was cursed. Most of the spokesmen said their comrades loved the Americans and British and hated the Germans. They said the Germans treated them with contempt and accused them of cowardice. They said anybody could be brave with superior tanks and anti-tank guns. The Germans rode to battle in trucks; the Italians walked. But they admired Rommel. They said he was a genius. They particularly liked him when they heard that he had said the Italian troops were very brave but their officers were incompetent. The only serious arguments occurred over the most beautiful actress—Myrna Loy, Fay Wray, Jean Arthur, or Ann Dvorak. The Italians and Brits watched all the same films—the Italians with subtitles. The prisoners of war were fed by the Americans. The Americans had the most of everything. The Brits complained with good humour that the Italians were eating better than they. The Italians responding by saying that American food was awful—no pasta. The Italian officers frequently ate in the British officers' mess.

Films were a very important part of each army's recreation. They were considered essential for morale. Films were constantly coming in by ship, train, truck, or plane. Perhaps the nation that had the best use of film was Germany. Germany had a long history of technological excellence in photography. German cameras and binoculars were the best in the world. The technological advances in film were matched by the artistic excellence of directors and actors. That great genius, Joseph Goebbels, recognized the value of film for propaganda. His Propaganda Ministry produced important radio shows and print publications. Propaganda agencies in the west had to catch up. Britain got into war films before the United States, of course. But after Pearl Harbour, Hollywood went into action. Troops all around the world were watching films two or three times a week. The screens were sheets, flat walls in buildings, even the canvas sides of trucks. Where Peter was stationed in Tangiers, there were three rotating audiences. The Brits would watch their films and pass them on to the Americans, who would give them to the Italian prisoners. The Americans would give their films to the Brits and they, in turn, would give them to the Italians. Some films were straightforward propaganda produced by the military. The troops preferred propaganda with a plot and beautiful actors.

Each country also had travelling companies of performers that went all around the world. Unfortunately, none ever showed up in Tangiers. Peter and his tentmates often went to the canteen to listen to the BBC. They thought the news was fairly accurate. That means they knew there was a discreet amount of censorship. They were particularly interested in how the BBC reported the war in North Africa. Most of the news was reported accurately because the Allies were winning. But nothing was more interesting than the rumour mill. Imagination beats fact every time.

It was during one of the dinners in the officers' mess for the Italian officers that the subject of football came up. One of the Italian officers was bragging that Italy had won the World Cup in 1934 and 1938. He had been at the game in Rome in 1934 when Italy beat Czechoslovakia in extra time. He said Rome and the whole country went crazy. There were spontaneous parades in every city in Italy. The players were national heroes. The victory in 1938 in Paris was like a rehearsal for war. The Olympic Games in Berlin in 1936 revealed how sports, politics, and war were interwoven. The hyper-nationalism that had citizens irrational about football games was a nice warm-up for military actions. Now that the war was over for this officer, he was even more confused about the purpose of war. He even questioned how Mussolini and Hitler were so effective in arousing mass hysteria. Now he proposed a friendly match between his troops and the RAF. The RAF wing commander thought that was a great idea.

There was a football pitch about a mile away. An RAF crew went out to rake it and put the lines on. There were bleachers on both sides. The RAF men thought this would be an easy victory. They were listing all the First Division and Second Division players they had. The goalie had played for Liverpool. Coaches were appointed for both teams. After several practices, each team could list its final eleven. Both teams played in their summer outfits and their military boots. The RAF had taken fifteen undershirts and dyed them a bright blue. The referees and linesmen came from the Algerian Football Association. On the day of the game, against all military convention, the airmen and prisoners marched along together to the pitch. They took up opposite sides of the field. The Italians unfurled their flag. The Brits had forgotten to bring one. The game started at 10 a.m. to avoid the heat. It was a slow affair because the players couldn't sprint in their boots. But it soon became apparent that the Italians were controlling the ball. Italy scored twice, but the players were called offside both times. The prisoners screamed and made obscene gestures. In the second half, the keeper from Liverpool was very busy. His talent kept the score down. Italy won 3 – 0. On the march back, the Italians hooted at the Brits who kept their heads down. Occasionally, a frustrated airman would remind the Italians who was winning the war.

Two weeks after this, Peter and nine others were told they were being transferred to the air field south of Tangiers. The ground crews needed more help. Peter and his friends would do all the simple labour jobs so that the engineers and technicians could concentrate on tuning the planes. Peter ended up handing tools to technicians working on planes. The heat of the desert was hard on everyone. This was the final push so that the remnants of the German and Italian armies would surrender. Their escape across the Mediterranean was now closed. Rommel was gone now, but Hitler ordered the troops to fight to the last man.

One day as Peter was working, there were a series of shouts and then sirens. A Halifax bomber was coming in for a landing. It was on fire and bouncing up and down in the air. It had no working controls. It hit the tarmac with a smack and skittered along, fragments flying everywhere. The firetruck was at the fuselage immediately, spraying foam. Peter and the ground crews ran to see if they could save any of the air crew. When Peter got there, he could see a leg protruding from a hole in the fuselage. He didn't know what to do. An officer shouted at him to pull that man out. Peter ran to the plane and pulled the leg. He staggered back with a leg in his hands.

The airfield had a perimeter fence to try to stop the Arabs from stealing things. The Arabs were desperately poor and did desperate things. If they got under or over the fence, they could steal food or items for the black market. The airfield command had guards walking the fence line. Peter was given a fifteen minutes training session on the Lee Enfield rifle. Every third or fourth night, he had to do guard duty. One night, Peter was walking along with his rifle. The darkness made all the guards tense. He heard some noise at the fence. He got three shots off, although his hands were shaking. Then there was silence. Darkness and silence. He was in a sweat. When his relief came, he went to the barracks but couldn't sleep. The next day, he went to the fence where he had fired his shots. There was some blood on the ground.

In May 1943, the war in North Africa came to an end. Once again, there were large numbers of prisoners. The row over starting a second front in France intensified. The British convinced the Americans that an invasion of France could not occur in 1943. That would have to wait until 1944. Meanwhile, the armies in North Africa could get ready to invade Sicily. The Brits and the Americans would be joined by the Canadians who were stationed in England and becoming a nuisance. Once again, Peter's battalion had little work to do. They were told to await further orders. The rumour mill began. There were two possibilities: follow the armies into Sicily or return to England for the invasion of France.

In July and August, the invasion of Sicily began. Initially, the Allies captured only one airfield. They had more planes than room for them. Some long-range bombers flew missions from Egypt. Malta changed from being on defense to offence. Peter's battalions were moved forward to Tunis. All during his time in Africa, Peter wrote letters. He wrote to Alice, May, and Roy, to his mother, his sister, and brothers, to James in Moose Jaw, and to his friends in Brecon. When Peter and his friends heard about the great Russian victory at Stalingrad in February 1943, they thought about life after the war. They had no doubt now that Germany would be defeated. The allies took Sicily in six weeks. The Italians formally surrendered in September. The surrender made Hitler determined to hold the country. The Allies began their laborious climb up the Italian peninsula. It was a perfect country for defense. The Germans always held the high ground. The RAF set up a base at Naples. Once again, there were squadrons of Hurricanes for Peter's group to service. Now Naples was the city to tour. Once again, the soldiers and airmen were told to stay in groups. Naples was a dangerous city. Peter had difficultly dealing with all the ragged children begging in the streets.

Red Cross aid had to wait for available shipping. The need to kill outweighed the need to help.

Peter never said anything to his friends, but in July, he had received a letter from Alice that would change his life forever.

* * *

Warsaw 1942 - 1943

In the Jewish Ghetto in Warsaw, people survived and people starved to death. The Germans had established a form of Jewish self-government. There was always the hope that the war would end. Live and hold on. In the summer of 1942, the Germans shipped off over a quarter of a million Jews to die at Treblinka. Now it was time to fight. The Jews smuggled in guns and explosives provided by the Polish underground. On the eve of Passover, 1943, the police and SS units moved in for the final clearance of the ghetto. The war began. The Jews had no hope, but they wanted to die on their own terms. The Germans set fire to the ghetto. Jews used Molotov cocktails and rifles to fight back. Jewish fighters hid in basements and sewers. In April 1943, the main fighting ended. Some fighters escaped by tunnel to the Michelin forest. After that, the Germans used dogs and smoke bombs to drive fugitives out. Hitler signaled the German victory by blowing up the Great Synagogue of Warsaw.

On April 10, Joseph Adler, a young man of eighteen, rushed out from a bunker and fired his last two bullets at a squad of SS troops. He didn't hit anyone. They riddled his body with their automatic weapons.

Joseph Adler was the last living relative of the Jewish children who had been on the ship with Betta and David. He didn't know it, but he had a sister and brother in New York. Now none of the over one hundred children who came to Montreal and New York had a family.

Chapter Thirteen

Wales to Ontario 1942 - 1943

Alice enjoyed being in charge of the little farm. The farm girl from Saskatchewan could handle feeding chickens and pigs, milking the cow, gathering eggs, and weeding the garden. To all outward appearances, Alice was happy enough. But she missed her family and still had not found all her siblings.

May was a happy child. She was doing very well in school. She and her cousin Gareth were the same age and inseparable. Their farms were so close together that they could visit back and forth. The Brecon area only had a few bombs dropped on it. May and Gareth were free to roam once they did their chores. Four girls with the Home Army were working on two local farms. May and Gareth used to visit them to talk, although they pretended to be working. They loved the stories the girls had to tell. Their accents were so different. May and Gareth loved listening. The girls told them about the most popular songs now and even demonstrated some of the latest dances. One of the young ladies always got Gareth up to dance. Gareth felt like quite the little gentleman. The girls told them about their homes and the food they ate at home. Whenever they came back to the farms after a visit home, they would describe to May and Gareth what was happening in the large cities. Every month that went by, people were more optimistic. Sometimes they brought sad news of neighbours killed in bombing raids. So far, the girls' families were unscathed. When the girls took butter home, their families were delighted. The rationing was very strict. They ate much better on the farms. When young men came by to visit the girls, May and Gareth wouldn't go home. They knew it really irritated the would-be suitors. May and Gareth laughed.

The other great novelty in the area was the German and Italian prisoners of war. At the prisoner-of-war camps throughout Britain, prisoners could volunteer to work on farms, as there was a shortage of farm labourers, but the army had an intensive vetting program for the volunteers. Those released to work were older and usually had a farming background. The fanatical Nazis and Fascists were in high security prisons. They were young men with fire in their eyes. The majority of volunteers spoke some English. Of course, the local constabulary knew where the volunteers were and so did the neighbours. If neighbours objected strongly, prisoners would not be placed in the area. After 1942, the Brits no longer feared invasion. Farmers who had had crops rot in the field because they didn't have the labour to harvest them welcomed help. With most food rationed, the government didn't want any crops going to waste either.

May and Gareth were very bold and mischievous when they were together. One day during school holidays, they got up early to walk to a farm that had a prisoner of war. Quite a few people had gone by that farm to look. One or two found an excuse to talk to the owner as their eyes swept the area for the prisoner. May and Gareth were lucky. As they walked down the country lane, they saw the prisoner scything hay by the roadside. Completely unafraid, full of cheek, they introduced themselves. His name was Hans. He offered them water from his flask. They were happy to have a drink. They asked where he was from in Germany. He told them where he was from and what he did before the war. He waved a friendly goodbye and returned to his scything. May and Gareth ran a good portion of the way home. Gareth's parents and Alice heard the long account from their excited children. The parents said it was all very interesting, but the children were not to go again.

By the end of the war, there were many prisoners working on farms. One group wove baskets from the roots of trees and sold them at the local market. Some prisoners actually went to town pubs with their farmer-supervisor. In a few cases, prisoners with training found jobs as auto repairmen. In any area, there were some who could never accept this plan. If a son had been killed, it was difficult to be friendly. Some families created strong bonds, and after the war, letters went back and forth from Britain to Germany.

May and Gareth felt it was their duty to be kind and protective of the two refugee children at their school. The two children were from Cardiff. When the city was bombed, they were sent to their uncle's farm in the area. The children had gone to a large school in Cardiff. They were a little condescending to the rural children in a two-room school. May and Gareth overlooked that, however, and took them on hikes over the rolling hills. The four of them would leave with lunches and have a full day. One day when May and Gareth hiked over to see their friends, the farmer told them their parents had come for them. They were returning to Cardiff. There were no goodbyes.

There was an American camp in the Brecon Beacons. It was a large national park with a thick forest and biking and walking trails. The Americans trained there. Sometimes, artillery could be heard in Brecon. The soldiers would come into Brecon on day passes. The merchants loved to see these rich Americans. One day, the village was all aflutter. Black troops came into town. They were in a segregated section of the camp. Most people in Brecon had never seen a black person. Children left the street to hide. Ladies peeked out from behind lace curtains. Gentlemen nodded politely, proud of their courage and civility. Dinners in Brecon had a great deal of animated conversation that day. After that, black men walked the streets of Brecon and nobody paid much attention.

The roads around Brecon often had convoys of American troops heading to Cardiff or Southampton. The Welsh children loved these convoys because the Americans would throw candy and gum. One day, the clever May and calculating Gareth put two-year old Roy in the middle of the road when they saw an American convoy coming. Roy just stood there. The American convoy had to stop. The driver in the lead truck lifted Roy up a little roughly and put him on the side of the road. May and Gareth put their hands up and pleaded. The Americans showered them with candy. May and Gareth were smug for a week, but they didn't try the trick again.

The winter of 1942-43 was very bleak and cold. There was snow on the highlands. Alice brought May and Roy into bed with her, but three in a bed was still cold. Every morning, Alice had to get the fireplace going and get the wood stove lit. She was thirty-six now and wondered if this was to be her life. There didn't seem to be any hope of improvement. During the winter, all three of them had heavy colds. May couldn't go to school. Alice had to get her neighbour to split more firewood. The hay in the barn was damp and turning mouldy. Their milk cow had some hoof infection and the vet had to be called. Just when Alice couldn't be any more miserable, a letter came from Peter. It contained a photograph. There was Peter and his friends swimming and sunning on the beach at Tangiers.

In April 1943, Alice's brother Henry got leave and came to visit. He was in the Canadian army stationed near Swinton. Alice's prodigious letter writing kept her brothers and sisters in touch. Strangely, the ties that kept the family informed originated in a Welsh farmhouse. The children were delighted to meet their uncle. Men in uniform always had chocolate. Henry described the huge build-up of men and equipment in England. Everyone knew the Allies were getting ready to invade the continent. The Canadian army had suffered a great disaster at Dieppe. It was described as "a raid in force." Ninety percent of the raiding party was either dead or captured. British and Canadian officers sauntered away to avoid blame. Censorship saved Churchill from criticism. Now officers and politicians had learned from the raid. The full invasion would be better for the lessons learned at Dieppe. Henry said that meant Canadian soldiers were practicing beach landings in landing crafts. They practiced getting off the beach quickly. They also had drills where commanding officers became "dead," and junior officers had to take over.

When their mother left, Henry had been taken in by an uncle. He had a farm near Weyburn. His uncle and aunt treated him well and he thought of them as his parents. It was a pleasant life after the trauma of the family disintegration. Then the Great Dust Bowl hit. For a number of years, the great American midwest had scarcely any rain. Then the light soil began to blow. Farmers planted more grain to make up for smaller crops. It was a cycle that led to disaster. Saskatchewan was at the northern end of the disaster. Henry said that dust piled up beside fences almost three feet high. The wind blew thistles across the fields. South of their farm, locusts came in clouds. Henry left to see if he could get a job in Regina. He got there by jumping into a box car on the CNR track. There were already five or six men in the car. A job in Regina was the hope. In Regina, Henry slept at the Salvation Army hostel. There were no jobs. The Saskatchewan government initiated a work relief program. Henry was put on a road crew laying more asphalt. The federal government of R.B. Bennett didn't believe in government intervention in the free market system. If enough people starved, the system would correct itself.

Henry, like Alice, didn't know where their youngest brother and sister were. Nine members of the family were re-connected. Now they had to find the two youngest. When Henry left to go back to his unit, Alice felt the pain of family separation again. Shortly after that, she made her decision to return to Canada. It may have been the miserable winter. It may have been Henry's reminder of the loss of a brother and sister. It may have been the photograph of Peter having a great time in a warm climate. Alice confided in Reverend Prince and his wife, her close friend Catherine Guest, and her brother-in-law Ivor. She got Catherine to take care of Roy while she rode her bicycle into Brecon to get passports for herself, May, and Roy. The official told her she needed only one passport. The children would travel on hers. There wasn't an emigration ministry in Brecon, but the passport office said she could write to the ministry's head office. Within two weeks, the ministry sent her a return letter saying she had been put on a waiting list for travel to Canada.

The hardest part was to break the news to May. She was inseparable from Gareth. She enjoyed school and had school friends. Every letter from her father described how happy he would be to be back on the farm with his family. May was waiting for his return now. Alice was so nervous about breaking the news to May that she spent many hours with Catherine trying to figure out a strategy. Eventually, Alice told May over dinner, excusing herself by saying she wanted to see her brothers and sisters. May was inconsolable. For her, the world was falling apart. She had a happy childhood. Now she had an uncertain future. For quite a few days, May had very red eyes.

Alice went ahead with her preparations. She bought a steamer trunk in Brecon. She sold her animals to her neighbour-friend. He would pick them up as she left. She bought travel clothes for May and Roy. She was getting a monthly family cheque from the RAF. She had always been frugal and had a reasonable bank account. Her last summer in Wales was quite nice. It was warm and sunny. May and Gareth roamed everywhere. Roy played around the yard. He had a tricycle that he rode constantly. He had taken a few falls but that didn't halt his recklessness. Within a short time, everyone in the small community knew that Alice was returning to Canada. There are few secrets in small towns. Some were offended that Alice hadn't fallen in love with Wales. Their sense of patriotism was offended. Some wondered why she would return to a country that was so primitive. Nothing but lumbermen and fur trappers in a frozen landscape.

Wasn't she afraid of the Native Americans? Some traditionalists were offended because a woman dared to make this decision on her own. They knew that Peter Evans would want to return to his farm. Some were dying to know where Alice got the money for passage.

Of course, Alice's mother-in-law was in a rage. Her sons could not calm her down. She ranted from morning to night and increased the number of inspections of Alice's stewardship. Her tongue-lashings became increasingly vituperative. She tried to enlist May as an ally by ridiculing her mother. Finally, one day, she stormed into the house, sat down at the table, and began a tirade. As usual, Alice just listened meekly. Then Mrs. Evans made a mistake. She said she had seen Alice's brother in a Canadian uniform. She snorted that that was just one more useless Canadian in the country. Alice began to shake. Her hands were trembling. She seized the dish pan and poured the whole pan of water over her mother-in-law's head. Mrs. Evans was so shocked she just sat there sputtering water. Within a minute, she recovered and tried to regain her dignity, even while looking like a wet mouse. She barged out of the house and marched up the hill taking huge steps with her head bowed. She left a trail of water.

Alice was shaking uncontrollably. She stood in the kitchen unable to move her limbs. Once she had regained control, she went to the top shelf of the cupboard. She kept a tin of biscuits there for company, out of the reach of May. She sat at the table, opened the tin of biscuits, and began to eat the reserved-for-company biscuits. After fifteen minutes and five biscuits, Alice started to laugh. She kept bursting out in laughter. Two or three times, her whole body shook with laughter. Roy was out in the yard with the dog. He came into the house and looked at his mother quizzically. He had never seen his mother like this. That afternoon when May came home from school, she found her mother smiling and occasionally laughing suddenly. She wondered why the mother who had been so unhappy was suddenly full of joy.

At the end of September, Alice got a letter from the Ministry of Emigration. During the war, no ministry liked to give out many details. Secrecy pervaded everything. But she was told she would be leaving from Liverpool within two or three weeks and to make her final preparations. Within days, Alice packed the steamer trunk and three suitcases—exactly what the ministry allowed. Alice didn't realize how much she was loved until her final months in Brecon. Reverend Prince used Alice as a model of good in his sermon one Sunday. Members of the Women's Institute had a special tea for Alice. They gave her a gorgeous Welsh linen blanket. (They worried about her being cold in the ice-covered wastes of Canada.) Neighbours trooped over with cookies and cakes for the trip. The Evans brothers (without their mother's knowledge) came to say goodbye. Alice's neighbour who always did the heavy work on the farm came over to do the chores so that Alice could concentrate on her preparations.

On September 3, 1943, a telegram came for Alice. The telegram delivery man in Brecon got in the agency's car and drove out to the farm. The man had a uniform that resembled a police officer's. Week after week during the war, this man delivered telegrams to families that informed them of the deaths of sons and husbands. He found it very difficult. He was too affected by the grief to stay at the door. He handed the telegrams over and tried to leave as quickly as he could. His behaviour seemed callous, but he was actually too sympathetic. He had tried to change jobs at the telegraph office, but nobody else would do it. As he drove down the narrow lanes to Ty Twyn, several of Alice's neighbours saw him. They shook their heads. Alice came to the door when he pulled into the yard. Her mind began to race. He handed her the telegram and said goodbye quietly. Alice rushed to the table and ripped open the envelope. The telegram from the Ministry of Emigration said she would be leaving for Canada from Liverpool on September 7—four days from now. Alice rushed up to Catherine's and left Roy there. She got on her bicycle and rode into Brecon. She booked the train tickets for Liverpool. Then she rode to her neighbour and asked him to drive her into Brecon on the departure day. He said he would be happy to do that and asked what else he could do to help. As she rode her bicycle home, she thought about a gift for him that would remind him and his wife of her. When May came home with Gareth in tow, she sent them to Reverend Prince with the news. May and Gareth felt very self-important with this mission. On the way home, though, May was overcome with unhappiness. Nothing could save her now. Her father wouldn't be appearing at the door to say they were staying. Gareth caught the mood. He wondered what he would do without his best friend.

Two days later, Alice, May, and Roy were boarding the train for Liverpool. Reverend Prince and his wife, Catherine and her husband, Gareth, and several ladies from the Women's Institute were at the station to say goodbye. It was a very tearful time. May was tearful. Roy didn't like being dressed up. Gareth kept an eye on Roy because he was likely to do anything. There were the final goodbyes and then Alice and the children found seats. May was very quiet. Roy would probably find some mischief to get into. The conductor came around to give Alice the identification cards for the ship passage. There were already a number of people with these cards. Just south of Liverpool, the train slowed down and then stopped. The ship passengers from this train would sleep and eat in a converted school. The conductor told the passengers they could leave their large trunks on the platform. There were military guards to secure them. Alice, May, and Roy got cots in a renovated science lab. They could go to the cafeteria any time they wanted.

On September 7, a train with many passenger cars began picking up people from many different places. Passengers had been housed in schools, churches, sporting clubs, and warehouses. Many of them looked a little worse for wear. After almost four years of war, the country was good at emergency arrangements. People were showing stiff upper lips daily. As the train moved closer to the city, passengers could see barrage balloons. Then they saw anti-aircraft guns.

They knew the worst was over now, however. Most of the German air force had to be transferred to the East against the Russians. The train pulled up beside a long concrete walk. Alice and the children climbed out of the train and saw the great behemoth. It was a huge ship painted all grey. There were eight double gangplanks running up to the ship. Alice double-checked her card. She was to enter using Gangplank 3.

It was controlled chaos on the dock. Every inch of the pier was covered with passengers and large baggage carts. The carts inflicted a great number of cuts and bruises. May was upset that she didn't have a gas mask like most of the other children. Roy was too overcome by the rush to cry or misbehave. Alice had to put the two suitcases down several times to rest. Everybody was becoming increasingly irritable. There were some curses and swearing. Finally, Alice and the children were at their gangplank and were able to begin climbing. May was finding her suitcase heavier and heavier. Once, she offered her hand to Roy, but he slapped it away. Mr. Independent Three-Year Old would climb by himself. The passengers behind him were not impressed by his independence. He was slowing up the traffic.

At the top of the gangplank, Alice was directed to the level where their cabin was. May had renewed energy now. She was very excited. The door to their cabin was wedged open. Swinging doors are a hazard on a ship. Inside the cabin were two sets of triple bunks. The other three passengers had put their suitcases down. Roy wanted the top bunk of their set. He started a crying-screaming fit to get his way. Alice didn't give in. May would sleep on the top bunk. Roy could have the middle bunk. Alice didn't want the adventure of a high bunk. An announcement came over the PA system. Alice had trouble understanding it, but May said the announcement said they were to stay in their cabin for an hour. With the announcement, the other three passengers returned. They were young ladies between the ages of fifteen and eighteen. They were very friendly and bubbly. They were from a suburb of Manchester and had been roaming around the ship against all instructions. They had all fallen in love with a young, cute crew member. Alice had to listen to them gushing. She thought, *I've got this to look forward to.*

As the passengers rested in their cabins, the procedures for setting sail began. The chaos of several hours ago became a calm, practiced routine of getting underway. The pier ropes were detached. The ship swung away from the dock. Four tugboats had their lines fastened. A guide for the Mersey Estuary was in the bridge. They were moving the longest passenger ship in the world. Once into the Irish Sea, the tugboats disengaged and the pilot was lowered onto one of the tugs to return home. The ship moved at half speed up the channel past the Isle of Man. Within a short time, the crew could see the skyline of Belfast. They moved in the heavy swells between Northern Ireland and Britain. They got signals from Londonderry. Once they turned due west into the Atlantic, the crew spotted two Beauforts doing surveillance. They would stay with the ship until it was twenty miles into the Atlantic and running at full speed. Then it was on its own.

Starting at 5 p.m., different decks of the ship were called for dinner. Alice still had cookies in her suitcase and she passed them around the cabin. The girls from Manchester were delighted. They left the cabin together and lined up for the dining room. The room had rows of tables bolted to the floor. In rough seas, the chairs could be fastened underneath the tables. May and Roy were becoming overwhelmed by the constant number of people. They did not have this at home, even when they were in Brecon. Now they had to join a food line. The first day out there was meat loaf, mashed potatoes, and carrots. There were rolls and butter at the end of the line. May didn't think it was a big deal to get butter, but the girls from Manchester got only two ounces a week for the family at home. May couldn't believe what she saw. Children at the next table were eating bowls of ice cream. May hadn't had ice cream for two years. There used to be an ice cream parlour in Brecon, but war-time rationing shut it down. She and Roy had their ice cream as soon as possible. It was the first time Roy had had ice cream. He wanted a second bowl. When the steward said no, he banged his spoon on the table. May said to her mother, "Why didn't we leave him at home?" Shortly after dinner, it started. The Manchester girls left the cabin in haste. The precocious May named the ship the *S.S. Puke*.

The passengers were a wide mix. Most were women and children going to Canada to stay with relatives for the duration of the war. There were a number of war orphans being met by adoption agencies sponsored by churches in Canada. There were citizens of Canada and the United States who had been trapped in Britain when the war broke out. There were Canadian Merchant Marine sailors rescued from the Atlantic. They were going home, probably not to sail again. They were very silent. Canadian businessmen were still making transatlantic journeys to sign deals. The rewards were worth the risk.

Alice had learned at dinner that they were on the *Queen Elizabeth*. It dwarfed the ship Alice and Peter had come over on. When the *Queen Elizabeth* was being transformed to carry as many troops and civilians as possible, the planners debated about keeping the three hundred-person theatre or transforming it into more sleeping quarters. They decided that all the travellers would need the theatre for their morale. Alice had seen the large number of canvas bags carrying 16mm film cans. She had seen them at the Moose Jaw theatre. The officer responsible for scheduling the theatre tried to break its use into one and a half-hour segments. Passengers would go to the theatre by deck number and age. It worked most of the time—but not always. The first show for everyone was a history of the ship. The first thing the officer told the passengers was that they had no fear of U-Boats. The *Queen Elizabeth* ran at three times the speed of a German submarine. The officer said that if you took the square miles of the North Atlantic and put a vessel in it the size of the *Queen Elizabeth*, the chances of a submarine crossing the path of the *Queen Elizabeth* at the right speed was 3,250,000 to 1. Seemed like a safe voyage. When the officer said the *Queen Elizabeth* was built at Clydebank, Scotland, the Scots let out a cheer. It was built in the mid-thirties as a luxury passenger ship. It was a little bigger and a little better than her sister *Queen Mary*. When the ship was ready to sail in 1940, she was painted a dull grey. Her first voyage was to New York with massive security precautions. She zigzagged across the Atlantic to avoid U-Boats. The United States was still neutral at this time. The *Queen Elizabeth* tied up beside the *Queen Mary* and the French *Normandie* in New York Harbour. It was the only time the three largest passenger ships in the world tied up together. The officer reiterated that they were on the largest, going at almost thirty knots. Nobody in the audiences knew what that meant but they assumed they were going pretty darn fast. He said the ship sailed halfway around the world from New York to Singapore in November 1940 to get outfitted as a troopship. The officer paused there. Singapore had been captured by the Japanese early in 1942.

"Just remember this about this great ship," the officer said. "She carried eight thousand American troops from San Francisco to Sydney, Australia. That was a 7,700-mile voyage." He paused for quite a while, then said, "So I don't want any of you to start whining on this little trip."

The audiences always laughed at that line. He said they had a crew of four hundred always ready to help. At their session, May whispered to her mother, "Three hundred and ninety are mopping up puke." May had become puke-obsessed.

The latest film updating passengers on news from around the world was shown on the second day of the voyage. The passengers were pleased because the news was good. The British were busy creating war heroes. Of course, Churchill and the royal family were always prominent in the news. Passengers were happy that the ship was named after their queen. The first film for the children was *Bambi*. They all loved the film. But when Bambi's mother was shot, many of the children cried. That didn't stop the program director from continuing to show it. He liked the idea that the film had been banned in Nazi Germany. The children also got to see *Snow White and the Seven Dwarfs*, *Pinocchio*, and *Dumbo*. May and Roy were having a great time. The adults got to see *Alibi*, *Mrs. Miniver*, and *The Balloon Goes Up*. Many of the passengers from rural Britain had seen very few films. Besides showing films, the crew took passengers on carefully planned tours of the ship. They got to see a section of the engine room, a view of the ship's progress from the bow, the anti-aircraft guns, and a carefully selected part of the crew's quarters. On the last day, the crew put on a series of skits and pantomimes. The skits and songs for the children delighted them. The skits for the adults were a little risqué. Alice didn't see them because she was with May and Roy.

On the fourth day, four small ships could be spotted. They were Corvettes of the Canadian Navy. The ships had been designed for convoy duty in the North Atlantic. Corvettes were small and could be built quickly. The sailors assigned to these ships said it was pure misery. They bounced up and down with every wave and they had nothing but hard surfaces. Sailors were black and blue after a stint. The ships carried a crew of eighty to ninety men. A number of the Flower Corvette class were built in Canada. Now the 1,025-foot *Queen Elizabeth* was looking down at the two hundred-foot Corvettes. The *Queen Elizabeth* was approaching the port of Halifax. There was a defensive network of Corvettes, barges equipped with depth charges, three or four Fairey Swordfish planes overhead, and a series of anti-submarine nets. Halifax was the busiest port for trans-Atlantic shipping until the United States entered the war. In peacetime, there would be all kinds of horns and whistles to welcome a passenger liner. Now, the *Queen Elizabeth* entered the harbour and moved to Pier 21 in silence.

Alice, May, and Roy were ready for dry land. They had a warm goodbye with the Manchester girls and wished them luck. The crew members were lined up to say goodbye to the passengers. After all the passengers were off, the crew would do a thorough cleaning.

Cleaning up after almost five thousand passengers was quite a chore. They were aided by cleaners that the Cunard Line hired in Halifax. New supplies for the next journey would be waiting in trucks and rail cars. The crew would get a few days of leave in Halifax once they had finished their jobs. After each voyage, five or six crew members would be dismissed for incompetence or improper behaviour. Often, several members of the kitchen staff would ask for different jobs. Working in the kitchens was a brutal job.

Some of the passengers got through customs and were on trains within an hour. Alice, May, and Roy would have to wait another day for a train. A bus took them to a recently constructed military base outside Halifax. Alice assured the children there would be a home waiting for them in Hamilton, Ontario. Her brother Bill and his wife had left Saskatchewan for jobs in Hamilton. Manufacturing plants in Hamilton were desperate for workers. Both Bill and Brenda had well-paying jobs. Brenda joined thousands of women working in plants in the city. The Canadian government had a Crown Corporation called Wartime Housing Limited that built twenty-six thousand homes for war workers. Bill and Brenda were renting one of these "strawberry box" homes. Alice and the children followed the route millions took—the CNR train from Halifax to Union Station in Toronto. Union Station was the train hub for passengers heading west.

Alice had a short trip west to Hamilton where Bill and Brenda waited at the CNR station for her and the children. Alice and Bill hadn't seen each other for fifteen years and Alice had never met Brenda. Bill had splurged on a taxi and everyone squeezed in. Bill asked the driver to go along Burlington street. Alice and the children were amazed by the factories. There was an awful lot of smoke. It rivalled Liverpool for that. Bill was like a great many newcomers to a place. He made a point of learning about it. He knew more about Hamilton than many life-long residents knew. He was telling Alice about steel production in Hamilton as they drove along. He promised to take them to see the bay. May was bored and Roy fell asleep. As they approached the national steel car factory, Bill became increasingly animated. He talked about the long history of the company. He pointed out that most of the freight cars and passenger cars that rolled across the Prairies had been made in his plant. His plant! Bill and Brenda had been there a year. As they passed the main gate, Bill waved to the guards to give the impression he knew everyone at the plant. They didn't wave back. Bill said the plant needed guards to protect secrets and prevent sabotage. Many people felt there were German spies under every bed. Bill said the company existed before the Great War. In 1912, the plant was making steel and wood freight cars. Soon the plant was making steel frames for trucks and streetcars. Now, Bill continued, the plant was being used for war production.

"We make the most shells, gun parts, and army truck bodies of any plant in the British Empire and North America." Alice thought she saw Bill's chest expand with pride.

As they drove up Kenilworth Avenue to Barton Street, Bill continued his narrative. The taxi driver wished he would shut up. He was getting a headache.

"Last month," Bill said proudly, "the Prime Minister visited the plant to thank us for our efforts. Mackenzie King is our Prime Minister, Alice. He's been Prime Minister three different times. His party walked all around the plant. I was within ten feet of him. The party had the mayor, the plant manager, a member of parliament, reporters, and photographers. It was quite a show. The Prime Minister had his picture taken with a female lathe operator. There were three tall men in grey suits who were bodyguards. They had conspicuous bulges where shoulder straps would be. The prime minister is a fussy-looking man, not very tall. At the end of the tour, there was a microphone waiting for him. A movie camera from the National Film Board was set up. Mackenzie King made a speech that could make a standing man fall asleep. The only interesting part was when he quoted Winston Churchill. Our prime minister pretends that Churchill and Roosevelt seek his advice constantly."

The taxi came to an abrupt stop—98 Glennie Avenue. Bill gave the cabbie a tip. The driver didn't think it was enough for the pain he had suffered.

Brenda said that everything was ready for them. She had a bedroom with a cot and a double bed. She thought Roy could sleep with his mother and May could sleep on the cot. She said they could stay as long as they wanted, then offered May a bubble bath. May was a little shy and hesitant. Brenda drew the bath for her and put in bubble bath. She had a bar of soap and a bottle of shampoo by the side of the bath. This was something new for May. Alice came into the bathroom to help May. Once in the water, May felt very happy and contented. Alice had to knock on the door and enter the bathroom to get May out. Alice then had a bath. She had baths like this in Moose Jaw. Roy, of course, refused to have a bath. Alice would leave it. She didn't want Roy screaming the first night with Bill and Brenda.

Over dinner, Brenda explained how difficult it had been to get used to shift work. They were used to early up, early to bed. Farm time. They were on the same shift. The plant never shut down. Four shifts, seven days a week. One week the hours were seven to three; the next they were three to eleven; and the third week they were eleven to seven. It was better now, but in July and August, after the eleven to seven shifts, they couldn't sleep in the daylight heat. After dinner, Bill insisted they listen to the CBC news. The Canadians were fighting in Italy. The Allies had Americans, Brits, Canadians, Poles, Indians, and volunteers from around the world. The Germans were fighting a slow retreat up the peninsula. In Canada, the old rift between Canadian Brits and French Canadians was getting wider every day. The British Canadians wanted conscription and the majority of French Canadians were against it. It was a replay of the conscription battle in the Great War. It was apparent to the generals and the politicians that depending on volunteers wouldn't raise enough troops for the battles ahead. Mackenzie King had the famous line, "not necessarily conscription, but conscription if necessary." Bill was furious with the French Canadians, but he was on shaky ground because he had a medical exemption. Yet he could work in a factory. Alice was never told what Bill's ailment was.

When they were going to bed that night, May whispered to her mother, "Do you think they'll let me take a bath every day?"

In the morning, Alice and the children were introduced to North American breakfast cereals. They had Kellogg's Corn Flakes—real wartime nutrition. Roy had his nose pressed to the window when he saw the milkman come. The horse knew all the stops and didn't have to be told anything. The milkman had a nice white uniform with a military cap. When his Aunt Brenda brought the bottles of milk in, Roy followed her to the kitchen. His three-year old mind was trying to digest all the new things it was seeing. Alice didn't say anything, but she was so happy to wake up in a warm bedroom. Sleeping with only one blanket was quite a novelty now. May was also quite pleased. She went to the hot air ducts several times a day. After breakfast, Alice went to the bedroom to check in her purse for anything she needed now. She had sixty dollars. The officials at Pier 21 had given her ration coupons for two months. Alice was pleased to be able to contribute something to Bill and Brenda's food budget. Alice went through all the documents she had accumulated. Reverend Prince had helped her fill in all the forms accurately. Alice thought again of what a wonderful man he was. She had her passport and birth certificates for all of them. Now that she was in Hamilton, she could throw out a stack of documents. She did keep her boarding pass for the *Queen Elizabeth*, however.

Alice asked Brenda what she could do to help around the house. Brenda suggested she do laundry and hang all the clothes out on the line. Brenda and Bill had a washing machine with a wringer. Another marvel for May and Roy. They watched the machine agitate, fascinated. The wringer seemed like a miracle. Alice was able to hang out all her family's clothes on a double line. It was a warm fall day with a breeze. The children were a little intimidated by the homes on both sides and at the back of the yard. Their closest neighbour in Wales was about a mile away. Brenda suggested that Alice take the children for a walk. Alice said she would check yesterday's paper for a job. Going through the paper looking for a position reminded Alice of how she and Jane had done that in Moose Jaw. Alice shook her head. That was more than fifteen years ago. Now she had two children. There were no suitable jobs in yesterday's paper. Alice thought she could work as a cleaner when the children were asleep or when Brenda and Bill would look after them. But she knew they couldn't stay with Brenda and Bill for too long. Alice took the children for a walk in their new city. The children found many things to surprise them—the concrete sidewalks, the asphalt roads, the manicured front lawns, picket fences on some properties. When they reached Parkdale Avenue, they saw all the construction crews building homes. The homes were fairly close together and they were exactly the same—lumber and clapboard. That was so different from the brick and stone homes in Brecon. There were a few cars on the road, but wartime gas rations limited drivers.

When they returned, Brenda had lunch for them. She had Campbell's vegetable soup and salmon sandwiches on white bread. Canned soup, canned salmon, white bread. Alice thought, *welcome back to Canada*. Hamilton in 1943 was very different from Moose Jaw in 1929. In 1928, the Riddells had a great choice of food. Now, the war restricted everything. Canada was exporting tons and tons of food to Britain. Alice had even heard of powdered eggs. She wondered about that.

After Bill and Brenda left for their three-to-eleven shifts, Alice steeled herself to bathe Roy. There would be running to escape, screaming, and fighting. Alice grabbed him by the shirt and dragged him to the bathroom. Her ally, May, had the water and soap. May was proud of herself for learning how the taps worked. Roy struggled, fought, kicked, but Alice was a strong farm girl. Roy was subdued, but he was crying and his sobs racked his body. Alice had no sympathy for him. May enjoyed seeing the little pest get his comeuppance. Once Roy was passive, Alice gave him a good shampoo. This was the cleanest Roy had been in his young life. While Alice dried Roy, May asked if she could go into the tub. The greatest thing in Canada for May was a hot bath.

The *Hamilton Spectator* was delivered by a boy on a bicycle at about 5 p.m. Another marvel! Alice went to the ads immediately. There were many job offers. Hamilton was short of labour. But there were no jobs Alice could take. May read the first section of the paper. Her reading skills were very good. Everything about the war was overshadowed by the speculations about the invasion of France in 1944. There was no secrecy about what was going to happen. May wondered how her father would fit into these great plans. He was in Italy now as that front wore on. May was interested to note that Canadians were also fighting in Italy. She wondered if her father had seen Canadians. After reading the newspaper, May turned to her novel, *Ivanhoe*. Alice thought her daughter must be very bright to be reading that book. She overlooked the book stamp from the school.

On the third day of looking at ads in the paper, Alice saw an advertisement that looked promising. A widower with an eighteen-year-old son wanted a housekeeper. Alice phoned the man and arranged an interview. Brenda and Bill took care of the children. Alice followed Bill's instructions. She got on a bus at the corner of Barton and Kenilworth. Then she got on a streetcar—the Beltline. She found Lottridge Street and the man's house. She explained the situation.

He said, "My son and I have been lonely in this big house. We would love to have two children to play with. The truth of the matter is that my son and I have been eating terrible meals and we are on each other's nerves constantly. This would be like having a real family. Not only that, our neighbours will think we're making a sacrifice for the war effort." He smiled at his tart joke.

He offered her the job and her children would be welcome. Once again, people took to Alice immediately. Just as with the Riddells and other people, Alice always made a good impression. She was serious, but always very warm.

This agreement would be serendipitous. Mr. Hughes was not in good health and he worried about his son being on his own. Alice was desperate for a job. In fact, the five members of this new arrangement became family and loved one another.

Alice went back to being a housekeeper. She was thirty-seven years old and only owned the contents of a steamer trunk and three suitcases. But she still had almost fifty dollars in her purse.

Chapter Fourteen

Naples to Wales 1945 - 1946

Peter Evans was still in a camp near Naples when the war finally ended in May 1945. The celebrations in camp were muted because the end had been coming for months. RAF servicemen were reluctant to go into Naples because they might be assaulted. There had been some bad incidents. The Allies did some indiscriminate bombing of the city that killed over twenty thousand civilians and damaged some culturally important structures. There were some people in Naples who still felt some loyalty to Mussolini. Some were still upset by Mussolini's murder and the desecration of his body.

On July 5, the serviceman lined up to vote in the general election. Their votes would count in their home ridings. These ballots had to be flown back to Britain and then distributed to the various areas. It was an example of the painstaking exactitude of British democracy. Ten days later, Peter's wing was boarding a ship in the Naples harbour. As the ship sailed past Morocco, some of the original airmen revived stories of their days in Casablanca and Tangiers. The ship landed in Southampton on July 20. The port was lined with abandoned anti-aircraft guns. There were two half-sunk ships in the harbour. Certain sections of the city near the harbour had been bombed flat. Heavy machinery could be seen all over, rebuilding the city. The servicemen joked that there would be lots of jobs in construction for the next five years.

They were off to the barracks again for one final day and night of military discipline. The next day, there was a long line to get civilian clothes. Their military passbooks were updated and stamped with their day of release. Their duffle bags were checked with indifference for any dangerous armaments. Peter had several camel hide wallets and a covering for a hassock made of camel hide. Peter said goodbye to his friends. They were scattering all over Britain. Only three were returning to Wales from this wing.

On the train ride to Brecon, Peter had to clarify his feelings. Sometimes he felt that Alice had betrayed him and there was a simmering rage. He wondered if Alice had acted out of spite, if she had acted impetuously without thinking things through, or if she had hidden her feelings while making cold calculations. Peter even admitted to himself that his mother and sister had treated Alice horribly. Peter knew one thing for certain. He did not want to go to Canada. He wanted things to be as they were before the war. He wanted his little farm. He wanted his job on the county road construction team. He wanted his trips to the pub. He wanted his children. In foolish moments, he even thought his wife and mother could become friends.

At the train station in Brecon, Peter was met by Ivor and their mother. His mother had decided to hold her tongue on Peter's first day home. Tomorrow would be soon enough to excoriate Alice. Peter was greeted warmly by everyone he saw in Brecon. Most made a comment about his African tan. Many of the men said they would buy him a beer when he went to the pub. People were so happy that the war was over. Peter's mother embraced him a tentative way. He knew she would not wait long to uncork her rage. For now, she would withhold her wrath.

Ivor embraced his brother and whispered in his ear, "You're in for a skin flailing. Try to remain silent and take long walks."

Peter's mother had prepared a nice dinner for him, and Greta, Cecil, and Vivien were there as well. It was the old Evans family with no spouses. Peter didn't like the look of that. It was conspiratorial. Peter suspected they met like this when he had been given money for his return to Wales.

Everybody avoided the subject of Alice and the children. Peter talked about his time in Africa. There were many anecdotes to recount. Then everyone wanted to talk about the war. There would be no other subject for months. Peter's mother caught him up on all the local news, then on all the local gossip—she was her usual acerbic self. Ivor remained silent. He realized he could have a daily, unrelenting war or find peace in solitude. The barn was his refuge. Mrs. Evans had subdued all the men in the family with her strident aggressiveness. His mother wanted Peter to remain at Ty Crwyn. Peter was content to remain there for now. He was a man who could scarcely boil water. From mother, to wife, to the RAF, Peter had been well taken care of.

The next morning, Peter rode into Brecon on a bicycle. He was greeted by many people. Veterans would be treated very well until the goodwill wore off. Returning to normal meant that being a veteran didn't gain special privileges. Peter went to the Brecon Travel Agency where Mr. Williams greeted him warmly. Peter explained that he needed a passage to Canada and Mr. Williams explained that there would be a long wait for a ticket. Millions of troops were returning to Canada and the United States. There wasn't enough shipping to get people to North America quickly. Mr. Williams told Peter that since he was a veteran, he would get some priority, but he shouldn't expect passage in the near future. He would register him using his service number. The government in London still controlled everything. Shipping businesses would not return to private control for quite a while. Peter looked so unhappy that Mr. Williams didn't say more. Peter wasn't upset by the delay. He was upset because he had to go back to Canada.

The next day, Peter persuaded Ivor to help him clean up Ty Twyn. It had sat idle for two years. When they went there, the house smelled of mould and almost dripped with dampness. They spent the whole day feeding firewood into the fireplace and stove. The bedding had been stored in cupboards and Peter was able to hang sheets and blankets on the clothesline. As he did these chores, Peter realized how cold and damp the house was. Sitting in a depression meant that the house always had pools of water nearby. Peter's stay in Africa and Italy made him appreciate warm and dry countries. As soon as they saw the smoke, Peter's neighbours came over. This is the couple that had been so nice to Alice. They had bought the animals from Alice. They also took over the garden and the grazing fields. Peter's mother had them pay rent, of course. It was good for the neighbours because it doubled their vegetable garden produce, and they had many raspberry bushes. Peter had to face the fact that he did not own the farm. His mother did. He would get his job back on the roads, but he would have a long climb uphill to be well set financially. Forty years old, a low-paying job, and his wife and children in Canada.

On July 27, a bomb was dropped that shook Britain almost as much as the Blitz. The election results were announced by the BBC. Sir Winston Churchill, the nation's hero, was kicked out of office. Clement Attlee, the Labour leader, was the new Prime Minister. The election wasn't close. Labour won in a landslide. The people had pulled off a stunner. Historians rubbed their hands. This would be the subject of study for decades. Churchill was deeply hurt. Stalin was incredulous. For him, it proved that dictatorships work better than democracies. The post-war conference at Potsdam, Germany, was taking place as the British election went on. The conduct of the war in the west had been planned and executed by the Big Three—Churchill, Roosevelt, and Stalin. Only Stalin remained in July 1945.

Peter wasn't that surprised by the results. He said the servicemen in Italy turned against Churchill when he said Britain must continue to maintain its armed forces to fight against Japan. The men in uniform had had enough. The Americans were late to the war and had made huge profits from Britain's agony. Let them finish off Japan. The civilians didn't think the Conservative Party would ever care about the lower classes. Labour promised huge social reforms. The majority of the population was sick of stiff upper lips and make-do. Now they wanted some reward for their incredible sacrifices.

That night at The Welsh Poet, emotions were high. First the war had come to an end and now the election. History was knocking down doors. When the servicemen returned to Brecon, they didn't look favourably at young men who had received exemptions from serving. The reasons could be fair and just, but the word slacker was often used. All the servicemen claimed a warrior status, despite most having never been near a battlefield, but nobody was prepared to question them too closely.

As the pints added up, the pro-Churchill and anti-Churchill voices grew louder. Finally, the inevitable happened. A table was knocked over. Chairs began to fly. Fists hit noses and heads banged off the floor. Cooler heads prevailed after a time and the local constabulary was called. It was the usual pub brawl; a broken nose or two, a few missing teeth on the floor, broken fingers, and torn shirts. Wives would listen carefully to explanations. Grown men would be told to stop acting like little boys. Peter was a very moderate drinker and had never been in a beer-fueled brawl. He stood discretely by a wall and watched the spectacle.

People were anxious to get back to the lives they lived before the war. For many, it was a way of coping with loss. Things could never be the same, but trying to make it so was a form of therapy. In Brecon, one aspect of this was the revival of the Brecon Rugby Club. Wales is a country that loves rugby. It has a long, long history. The first recorded rugby match in Brecon was 1868. Abergavenny beat Brecon 3-0. In 1881, Brecon was one of the founding members of the Welsh Rugby Union. Eleven clubs were in this union. Travel from town to town must have been interesting. In the spring of 1945, when everyone knew the war would end any day, the executive committee of the Brecon Rugby Club began getting ready for some interclub games. Volunteers painted the inside and outside of the clubhouse, a plumbing firm repaired the water system, and the former groundskeeper was re-hired and began work on the field. The treasurer reported to the committee that the club still had a bank balance from 1940. The manager in 1939 offered his services again. He even began to draw up a preliminary team roster. Six years of war would make a difference. One of the first debates was about how to commemorate the members killed in the war. They decided on a plaque exactly like the World War I plaque, to be mounted beside it. The notable thing about the plaques was how many more members were killed in World War I than World War II. In the First World War, there had been a battalion exclusive to Brecon. All the young men of the town had joined up together. The battalion had been fed into the meat grinder of the Somme. In one day, sixty young men from the little town of Brecon were dead.

Ivor had always been a great fan of rugby, although he had only played in school. He had been born with a slightly turned-in foot that doctors couldn't correct. Ivor was taking Peter with him to watch the Brecon team practice and scrimmage as often as possible. The manager had to mould a team from the veterans and the new young players. The Welsh Union Rugby League planned to play games in October with a modified schedule. In 1946, there would be a regular schedule.

All international play had halted at the beginning of the war, but now there was news that the Victory Internationals would start up again. Around the world, athletes were starting up football, baseball, hockey, and every other sport again. Civilization cannot survive without sports. The English rugby team would play a series of games at Twickenham Stadium. This famous rugby stadium had been turned into a military depot during the war. Wales would have to select a team. There was the usual heated debate about the roster. National honour depended on the team making a good showing.

Only one player from Brecon was chosen for the national team: George Ruddick. The citizens of Brecon were outraged. Most felt there should have been at least three players from Brecon.

Once their anger subsided, the citizens of Brecon began to make plans to go to Twickenham. The English would play a New Zealand military team, then Ireland, Scotland, and Wales. The game against Wales would be on November 20. The British Railway Corporation was freed from military control in July 1945. Now it could run its own events. Special trains were scheduled for the Scots and the Welsh. Within the corporation, there was debate about how many extra security guards would have to be hired to control the rugby fans.

Ivor and Peter got their tickets. Like Ivor, Peter had played rugby at school but never enjoyed it much and never played as an adult. The Brecon Rugby Club ordered scarves and flags. Both Ivor and Peter got scarves with the Welsh Dragon embroidered on them.

On November 20, eighty fans from Brecon boarded the train at 6 a.m. The choirmaster from the chapel in Brecon sorted the fans into two groups—first string and second string—which were then organized by tenor, baritone, and bass. Ivor and Peter were politely discarded into group two. The choirmaster was choosing singers he knew for group one.

Shortly after the train left the station, the singing began. It was too early for the beer casks to be opened. Ivor and Peter sat in the second car with the disorganized and inferior singers. One in five Welshmen carry a pitch pipe in his pocket, so things got sorted out quickly. Ivor and Peter both sang off key so they cancelled each other out. The "second team" was no less enthusiastic than the first team. They were even louder, trying to annoy the beautiful singers in the first car. The choirmaster had brought with him ten or twelve hymn books from the chapel. For each hymn, he went through the same ritual to get his railroad car choir ready. He made the same hand gestures, the same rotation of his head, the same fingers on lips. Then he brought his hands down quickly and the voices began.

The choirmaster allowed a hymn in four-part harmony. He encouraged Dewi Morris to perform the solos. The first group was so well-behaved. The choirmaster disclaimed any knowledge of the louts in the next car. He knew that the worst was soon to come.

As they neared Cardiff, the miners would join the train. There wouldn't be any restrained or disciplined hymns with them on board. Perhaps in the morning they wouldn't be too bad. As the train moved down the valleys towards Cardiff, there were large tracts of land where surface mining had been done. It was grey and bleak. Then they began to pass the deep mines. There were huge spoil tips like small mountains. All the waste from the mine was carried up the mounds by conveyor belts and deposited at the top. Occasionally there were slides, but the mining companies didn't seem to mind. Hauling the waste away in trucks or rail cars was too expensive. Peter said to Ivor that he wouldn't want a house near these tips. Ivor said that year by year, the tips were getting larger and closer to homes that had been built many decades ago. The coal companies said the tips were very stable and couldn't possibly move. The tips had been part of the mining industry since the nineteenth century.

As the train got closer to the station in Cardiff, the Brecon voices hushed so they could hear the singing. It was a huge and exuberant chorus. The Brecon train passed and then backed up. The miners scrambled into the eight cars, hardly stopping their singing. A number of miners ran to the Brecon cars and yelled obscenities about sheep farmers, suggesting sexual relations with sheep. The choirmaster turned a little pale. There were ten cars of Welshmen heading to London and Twickenham.

Now the beer in all ten cars was flowing. Some of the more difficult Welsh words were getting slurred. Brecon was not a region where Welsh was spoken and Ivor and Peter knew very few words. When the train slowed or went around a bend, Ivor and Peter could hear the marvelous songs in Welsh. A few of the miners made their way up to the two lead cars to say hello and sing beery rugby chants.

Some of the Brecon Baptists were a little taken aback. Peter had been in the services for three years and wasn't shocked.

Every third song the miners sang was, "Men of Harlich." They had all seen the film *How Green Was My Valley*, released in 1941. Hollywood did a good job of depicting the events in the novel. Few of the miners had read the novel by Richard Llewellyn, published in 1939, but many of them claimed to have seen the film five or six times. It played in Cardiff for months. The story revolved around a wonderful family of Welsh coalminers. The novel and film depicted the coalmine owners as uncaring, ruthless bastards. And they were English to boot. The coalminers organized a union and went on strike. The owners put it down mercilessly. That summed up coalminers and owners. Coal strikes became a constant in Britain. The female romantic lead was Maureen O'Hara. Every miner would give up his wife or girlfriend or children for one smile from Maureen. It didn't matter that she was Irish.

"Men of Harlich" celebrated the Siege of Harlich Castle that lasted from 1461 to 1468, the longest siege in British history. As a nationalistic inspiration, it was similar to the Battle of Culloden where the English defeated the army of Charles Edward Stuart in 1746. In Ireland, there was the Battle of the Boyne in 1690. All these battles created myths for all sides. It didn't matter that they occurred hundreds of years ago. World War II provided many battles the different nations could brag about: the Battle of Britain, the Battle of Dunkirk, the sieges of St. Petersburg and Stalingrad, the battle of Iwo Jima, and so on. History enjoys celebrating victories or creating never-ending grievances.

The train stopped a mile from the stadium. The passengers had seen some of the bombed-out sections of London as they passed. The Welshmen walked along the residential streets towards the stadium. Occasionally they saw a bombed-out house from a stray bomb, but this area was not part of the Blitz. There were about thirty Bobbies at the stadium to direct them. They wouldn't have seats. They had a concrete walk sloping at twenty degrees. They would stand for the whole game. The English were on the opposite side of the field in bleacher seats. Most of the English had fedoras. Most of the Welsh had cloth caps, including Ivor and Peter. The singing never stopped. Every twenty minutes, another chorus of "Men of Harlich" would begin. The standing crowd had tents at both ends of the spectator area for meat pies and beer. The vendors were having a great time.

The game itself would have been called boring except for the passion of the spectators. The field was muddy after several games and some rain. There were no great sweeping runs, as runners could hardly lift their sodden boots. It was boring trench warfare. Advances were measured in yards like the great offences in World War I. But the great Welsh kicker, Ceri Jones, put a ball through the uprights. The Welsh defence held as the English side got closer and closer. The singing stopped. The drinking stopped. The Welsh stood silent. The English spectators cheered their hearts out. The players were covered in mud and could hardly tell who was on their team. It looked inevitable that England would win, but they couldn't force their way through the mud and the Welsh defense. The whistle went. The Welsh were almost hysterical. They had won 3-0. One inebriated but logical Welshman ran onto the field and raised his arms. The Welsh fans became silent. With a sense of drama, he quickly lowered his arms. The entire crowd of Welshmen began to sing, "Men of Harlich." The whole stadium rocked with voices. The English sat in amazement. At the end of the first chorus, they applauded. True English sportsmanship. They weren't prepared to stay for the full performance, however, because they knew it might go on for hours. And indeed, it did. The Welshmen sang all the way back to the train. The residents of nearby homes came out to watch and sometimes clap. Some choir members had to be helped along. The ride back to Cardiff was a test. Half the fans fell asleep or passed out. Half continued to drink and sing. At Cardiff, the conductors poured the miners out. Ivor and Peter didn't see the miners staggering away.

They were fast asleep. There was no singing or drinking between Cardiff and Brecon—only the melodious sound of snoring.

The *Brecon Beacon* newspaper put out a special edition with the headline, "Wales Overpowers England." The local boy on the team was praised to the skies. A few in the town thought of A.E. Housman's poem, "To An Athlete Dying Young."

Ivor and Peter had massive headaches the next day. Their mother tried to inflict as much pain as possible. Baptists weren't supposed to drink to excess (or drink at all). Ivor and Peter had even more pain when they realized they had lost their caps. When the whistle went off at the end of the game, they had thrown their caps in the air like everyone else. They were so drunk, they didn't try to recover them. In the rush out of the stadium, caps were trampled into the ground. Ivor and Peter weren't the only ones going home bareheaded. They made sure they hid that fact from their mother.

Mrs. Evans had been working on a plan long before Peter came home. She and her daughter Greta had a few planning meetings incidental to other events. They agreed they would do anything to stop Peter from going to Canada. They had no reason to despise Alice, but they did. Some people are born to hate and nothing can change them. Mrs. Evans and Greta were born to hate. Peter was now working a regular day on the Brecknock county road maintenance crew. Things were changing on the roads. There were very few military vehicles and private cars were coming out of garages because more gasoline was available. Gasoline was still rationed, but the allowances were raised. Peter still refused to learn to drive. It seemed a perverse decision to Ivor and everyone else. Luckily for Peter, Ivor was always available. Peter went to most places on his bicycle, however. Bicycles and farm wagons were the most common modes of transportation.

Peter was happy to be back with his construction friends. He led the life of a bachelor. He rode his bicycle down to the crossroads pub, The Plough and Harrow, where he discussed politics and played darts. He rode his bicycle home in the dark down the narrow, hedge-lined lanes. Ivor drove him to Brecon to see rugby games. The reconstituted Brecon side was top of the eleven-club league. After each home game, Peter and Ivor would go to the Welsh Poet to replay the game. But the most common topic was the trip to Wickenham to see Wales beat England 3-0. The anecdotes got better and bolder all the time.

Mrs. Evans took her time moving her plan along. She had to be very subtle because nobody could know she was the puppet master. In Brecon, there was an attractive widow, Phyliss Powell. She had two sons, age eight and six. Her husband had been drafted into the army in 1941. He ended up in India and then took part in the campaign in Burma. He was killed near the fabled city of Mandalay as the Japanese fought a rear-guard battle. The nature of the world war was that young men from Brecon could be stationed in Africa, India, or Burma. That was true of Canadians, Americans, and every other nationality. It would have been a great travel adventure in peace times.

Phyliss had ended her mourning. She had a job as a postal worker in Brecon and her mother had moved in with her to help take care of the children. Phyliss was not desperate to re-marry, but she would take another husband under the right circumstances. Those two manipulators, mother and daughter, decided that Phyliss would be their candidate. She was personable and attractive, and she was Welsh. Mrs. Evans knew Phyliss' mother from the Saturday market. Before the war, Phyliss' mother occasionally bought mutton from the Evanses farm. Mrs. Evans planned to turn that old relationship into a friendship. She turned up at the Powell home one afternoon with cookies. She said she worried about Ruth's grandsons with no father. Phyliss was very grateful for this act of kindness. Mrs. Evans continued these visits claiming she missed her grandchildren so much. Slowly, month after month, visit after visit, Mrs. Evans built her web of lies. Each visit had a small revelation. The final house of lies was this: Alice had returned to Canada because an old lover from Moose Jaw had written her from Hamilton. Alice had moved in with him. She planned to get an uncontested divorce in Canada. Ruth's heart went out to the children and poor Peter. Mrs. Evans didn't make any suggestions, but Ruth began to think of some solutions to this problem. Her grandsons should have a father.

Now there were two mothers determined to be matchmakers. Both thought they were doing the right thing. Although they never mentioned this in their plans—these things weren't generally talked about—there was another consideration. Peter had been celibate for over three years—at least they assumed he had been. They didn't want to speculate about other possibilities. Civilians were never told about the rate of venereal disease among servicemen. The military hid the figures from the politicians. If the politicians found out, they hid them from the public. It was important to sustain the myth that the nation's warriors were pure in body and mind. The British Military Medical Corps was not pleased by the rate of VD. They were quite worried. It re-doubled its information campaign about casual sex and made condoms available more easily. Infected servicemen were a strain on medical facilities. Mrs. Evans and Ruth believed that Peter could be tempted by sex because he was a man. They assumed that Phyliss, because she was a woman, would be indifferent. Perhaps Mrs. Evans and Ruth were projecting their own feelings onto Phyliss.

Two weeks after the last meeting between Mrs. Evans and Ruth, Ruth accidentally ran into Peter at the market. She invited him to dinner on Thursday. He accepted. When he told his mother about the invitation, she suggested he take flowers. On the day, Peter dressed up and took his mother's advice to bring flowers. One thing that always caused a certain amount of social uncertainty was the question of beer. The abstemiousness Baptists frowned on beer drinkers. But the Welsh loved beer. Hosts were never sure if they should offer a beer to a guest they didn't know. Phyliss and Ruth wondered if they should offer Peter a beer. (Both Phyliss' husband and father drank an occasional beer). Peter wondered if he should accept a beer if one were offered.

Turns out, they offered him a beer and he accepted. It was a pleasant dinner. Ruth gave credit to her daughter for all the cooking, and the two boys were well-behaved. After certain shyness, Peter opened up about his service in Africa. The boys were eager to know everything about the war. While mother and daughter cleaned up and did the dishes, Peter amused the boys with war stories. Peter became quite outgoing and warm. He enjoyed the company of the two boys. He didn't stay to see the boys put to bed. When he said goodnight, everyone felt the evening had been a great success. Ruth couldn't wait to report to Mrs. Evans.

On their next trip to Brecon, Peter mentioned that he had had dinner at Mrs. Powell's and he had met her daughter, Phyliss. Ivor said he knew her. She was Phyliss the Post. Peter started to laugh loudly. He said when he was in Africa, he told his tentmates about the custom around Brecon to identify people by their jobs. For example, the sheep broker in Brecon was called Dai the Sheep. The school teacher was Andrew the School. Mabel who worked at the shoe store was called Mabel the Shoe. Fred Davies who owned the Funeral Parlour was called Fred the Death. Perhaps the worst was Darlen Jones. He owned the green grocer store. He was Darlen the Fruit. Peter remembered the great amusement of his friends. They decided that since Peter was all thumbs when he was working, his new name would be Peter the Thumbs. Peter had very fond memories of his service and his friends. They made the mistake of not exchanging home addresses. Peter wondered where they were now.

Ruth and Mrs. Evans decided the next meeting between Phyliss and Peter would be a month hence. Arranging meetings too close together would start bells ringing. Mrs. Evans said her son was naïve. Phyliss was already taking more time with her makeup and dress. A few men who picked up their mail at the post office noticed how attractive Phyliss was. In the Great War, about eight hundred thousand Brits were killed; in World War II, about four hundred thousand. The deaths in other countries were much higher. After both wars, there were a lot of widows and spinsters. The photographs of lost husbands and lost lovers sat in prominent places in many, many homes.

On market day about a month after the dinner, Mrs. Evans stood beside the pastry tent slightly out of sight. She remained there for almost twenty minutes—silently watching. Then Phyliss and her two sons appeared. She was doing the weekly market shopping and her sons usually got a treat. Mrs. Evans moved forward as if pricing items. She feigned great surprise as she approached Phyliss. She mentioned how she and her mother were such good friends. She praised the behaviour of the sons and, to Phyliss's surprise, she offered to buy the boys pastries of their choice. While the boys ate the pastries standing up, Mrs. Evans showed great interest in them, as if overcome with affection.

She said to Phyliss, "You have such wonderful sons. Do you think they might want to come to my farm to see the animals?" Phyliss thought that would be a good experience for town boys. They agreed on a day and time. Mrs. Evans went away smiling. A few merchants were surprised to see the dour Mrs. Evans smiling.

When Peter was told that Phyliss was bringing her sons to the farm, he was delighted. He walked over to a nearby farm to borrow two cobs for the day. Ivor drove to town to bring Phyliss and the boys to the farm. Peter walked the boys around the farm. They enjoyed seeing the chickens, pigs, and cows. When Peter brought out the cobs with riding saddles, the boys were ecstatic. Peter walked them all around the farm. Twice he let go of the lead ropes and the boys had the joy of riding by themselves. Phyliss went into the house to help Mrs. Evans with dinner. They got along very well. Phyliss thought that Mrs. Evans was matchmaking for Ivor. He was a bachelor, but about five years younger than Phyliss. She didn't think her mother and Mrs. Evans had a married man in mind for her. Surely Baptist women wouldn't do that. Peter and the boys came in with ravenous appetites. The dinner was a great success again. After dinner, Phyliss had to leave early to put her sons to bed.

Ivor drove her to town. He, too, enjoyed Phyliss' company. When Ivor came home a little moonstruck, Mrs. Evans realized she would have to straighten him out. The next day, Mrs. Evans told Ivor he was not to have anything to do with a woman who was five years older than him and who had two sons. As usual, he was cowed by his mother. He would have to look elsewhere for a wife. So far, so good for Mrs. Evans and Ruth. The question was when would Phyliss be told the carefully constructed pack of lies. It had to be done in a way that would melt Phyliss' heart. She had to feel so much compassion for Peter that she would flaunt all the social norms. Of course, her mother and Peter's mother would stand by her.

Ruth was a clever conspirator. She didn't mention Peter for weeks. Once or twice in the next month, she commented as part of a general conversation that Peter was a good man. Finally, Ruth and Mrs. Evans decided that Phyliss was ready to hear their carefully constructed pack of lies. One day when Phyliss came home from the post office, she found her mother very depressed. She asked what the problem was. She had to tease and coax the answer from her mother. She didn't want to say. She protested that she was sworn to secrecy.

Finally, now that Phyliss was really curious, Ruth whispered in a quiet and subdued voice, "Alice Evans is living with a man in Canada. He's an old boyfriend and is adopting the children." Phyliss was heartbroken. Peter was such a decent person. She wished she could help in some way.

A few weeks later, Phyliss contacted Peter. She said her sons wanted to ride the cobs again. Would he meet them at the neighbours' farm? Phyliss was going to pay the farmer for the rides. On a Saturday morning, Peter rode his bicycle to the farm. Phyliss was waiting with her sons. The boys were happy to see Peter and he gave them a big hug. The cobs had saddles on so they began the ride: Peter, Phyliss and the two boys. As they walked around the farm, Phyliss was extremely warm and amicable. At one rough patch, Peter caught her as she seemed to be falling. He seemed reluctant to take his arms from around her. A little way on, she smiled and took his arm.

It didn't take long. After service at the chapel the next day, Mrs. Moore took Blodwyn Prince aside. First of all, Mrs. Moore talked briefly about the weather. Then she praised Reverend Prince's sermon. Then she complimented the performance of the choir, of which Blodwyn was a part. Then she got down to brass tacks. The brass tacks were Phyliss and Peter walking arm and arm around her farm. A student of physiognomy would have enjoyed watching Mrs. Prince's face. The first impact of the news made her eyes widen and her mouth open slightly. As Mrs. Moore gave more details, Mrs. Prince's eyes narrowed and her lips became very thin and straight.

"Thank you, Mrs. Moore. I'm sure all of this is very innocent, but you know certain people like to spread harmful gossip."

"Yes, Mrs. Prince, some people have nothing better to do. That's why I've mentioned this to nobody but you."

"We should all remember the dictum about people in glass houses," said Mrs. Prince.

Mrs. Moore nodded her head in affirmation and self-righteousness. Mrs. Moore was pleased with her mission. But she wouldn't remain silent on the matter.

Mrs. Prince didn't say anything to Reverend Prince. They had a nice drive down the lane to their home. They had the usual pleasant dinner, although the reverend thought Blodwyn was unusually quiet. In the evening, they listened, as always, to the BBC classical music program from Albert Hall. Again, the Reverend thought his wife was unusually quiet. Usually Blodwyn conveyed news from the congregation to her husband.

Monday was a typical day for Reverend Prince. He visited two people from the chapel in the Brecon hospital. He had lunch at the hospital cafeteria, and in the afternoon, he visited a shut-in. He was home for tea at the regular time. After tea, the reverend told Blodwyn that he wanted to read and work on next Sunday's sermon.

"No, you are not," Blodwyn said. She got his coat, umbrella, and hat, and thrust them at him. "You're going to see Peter Evans."

She told him why and Reverend Prince was stunned. He pleaded that he needed more time to think about what to say. He would approach Peter in a day or two.

"No," she said. "You're doing it right now. If you want a sermon, get it from your book, *The Best Sermons in the Baptist Chapel.*" The reverend thought about Hell and Brimstone when he looked into Blodwyn's eyes. He was on his way.

As Reverend Prince drove to Ty Crwyn, he formulated a plan. He reached an agreement with God about a white lie. That evening, the Evanses were doing some domestic chores. Mrs. Evans was scrubbing a roaster, Ivor was mending his socks, and Peter was polishing his boots (the RAF let him keep his service boots). They welcomed their minister and offered tea. Reverend Prince said he wanted to talk to Peter alone about a position in the chapel. He turned down the tea because he said he was curious about Ty Twyn and he asked Peter to bring his key. Once inside the home, Reverend Prince asked Peter about Phyliss. Peter was quite taken aback. He had often thought about Phyliss these last few weeks, but he thought that was his secret. He was quite stunned to find out other people noticed. His blush overtook his African tan. Reverend Prince didn't need to belabor the point or make a tedious condemnation. Peter got the point, and very well. When he returned home, he told his mother and brother that the Reverend was thinking he should become an elder.

That ended that. Peter and Phyliss never met socially again. Phyliss understood. The mothers were thwarted. They never found out how.

The next Sunday, Reverend Prince used a sermon, almost verbatim, from *The Best Sermons in the Baptist Chapel.* It was about faithfulness in marriage.

Peter was in limbo now. He had accepted the fact that he was going to Canada. He had his job, rugby games with Ivor, pub visits, and rabbit hunting to keep him busy, along with helping on his mother's farm. He had a letter from May about every month. Alice didn't write much. He wrote letters to Alice, May, and Roy, and Alice's brother, James. He was a conscientious letter writer—just like Alice. He found more excuses for never learning to drive.

In 1946, he moved out of Ty Crwyn and returned to Ty Twyn. He was tired of his mother's insistence that he stay in Brecon. Now he just had to wait for passage to Canada.

Chapter Fifteen

Ontario 1945 - 1947

Alice had settled into her new situation on Lottridge Street nicely. After a few months, the widowed father, Michael Hughes, and the son, Art Hughes, really loved Alice and her two children. Michael was in failing health and Alice took special care of his diet (within the limitations of rationing). Art was a very outgoing and friendly eighteen-year-old. Later, Alice asked Michael Hughes if she could take in two boarders to make some money. It was the age of boarders. Families often had boarders to make ends meet. There was no shame in it; it was a social convention. Strangely enough, father and son went along with this plan. It showed how much they respected Alice. Now the three-story house went from two to seven people. Luckily, the first two boarders were gentlemen, and everyone got along. Art actually became buddies with the two boarders.

Michael Hughes took a special shine to Roy. When music came on before the news broadcast, Michael and Roy would march around the living room. May was enrolled at the Prince of Wales School—the same school David Dubinsky had gone to. There she was made fun of for her Welsh accent.

Art volunteered for the army in 1944 and was shipped to the Maritimes.

To increase her income, Alice took a job cleaning a funeral home late at night. Cooking and cleaning all day at Lottridge Street and then off to another job in the evenings.

By 1945, Michael Hughes was quite ill. Roy was enrolled in kindergarten at the Prince of Wales School. At recess, Roy would leave school to be with Mr. Hughes. In June 1946, the kindergarten teacher kept Roy in after all the other children had left in happy delirium for the summer holidays. She gave Roy a stern talk about his absenteeism. She even suggested he might have to repeat kindergarten. In later years, Roy joked about failing kindergarten.

In May 1944, Alice heard the news she had always dreamed of. The two youngest Reilly children had been found. The baby of the family, Rebecca, was getting married in June and she knew she had brothers and sisters somewhere. She went to a radio station in Edam, Saskatchewan, and asked them to put out an appeal. The message was conveyed to a station in Saskatoon. Her brother Val was stationed in the army there. A fellow soldier heard the appeal. He went to Val and said there was a Rebecca Reilly in Edam getting married and she wanted to find her brothers and sisters. He asked Val if that could be his sister. That was followed by a torrent of letter writing and phone calls. The Reillys were spread out from Ontario to British Columbia. Each of the children felt a sense of completion. A sense of being whole. The fragments of their family had been glued back together. The sadness of the past could never be forgotten, but the joy of the present pushed it away. Alice was overjoyed. She had felt the loss more than anyone. She had taken it upon herself to keep her brothers and sisters connected. She had written scores and scores of letters. Every time a brother or sister moved, Alice would send out the new addresses. Finally, in 1944, all the Reilly children knew where all their brothers and sisters were.

Alice felt the need to travel back to Saskatchewan. She wanted May and Roy to know their relatives. As soon as school was out in June 1945, she was on her way. She made arrangements with

Michael Hughes to be away for two weeks. Jane joined her on the trip. She had remarried and her new husband's name was Alphonse Lafrance. How she had met him was always obscure, but she lived in Montreal for a time and somehow met him there.

Alice's brother was working on a farm in Carrot River with their father. Carrot River was at the end of the rail line in northeast Saskatchewan. In the 1940s, land was still being cleared. The rail journey for the family started in Hamilton and ended in Carrot River. Alice had an uncomfortable reunion with her father. He did seem to be a changed person now, but Alice couldn't forget that her mother was in an asylum and the children had been scattered. She remembered what Reverend Prince had said about forgiveness and she tried to forgive her father. She treated him in a polite and well-mannered way. But there was no warmth. Both remained silent about the past. Her father had mellowed, and he and his son, Jake, were very close. Jake and his wife Mid lived in an extended log cabin and, in the summer, their father lived in a shack. The family had a week's stay at the farm and then they were back on the train for Hamilton.

Art Hughes returned from the army in July 1945. He was an extremely handsome young man in his uniform. May renewed her crush on him. In September, his father died. Michael Hughes had made a will that said Alice and the children could stay in the house as long as they wanted and Alice could have boarders. When they left, Art would own the house. Art was quite happy with this arrangement. He was only twenty. He returned from the army with absolutely no money. Alice loaned him fifty dollars to buy a used car. Shortly after that, he found a job.

In the fall of 1945, Alice's brother Henry returned to Canada and became another boarder in the Hughes house. Henry quickly found a job at Harvester. Alice, May, Roy, Art, and four boarders. The house was a lively place—and there was only one bathroom.

Henry had been in the Canadian Army's campaign in the Netherlands. He returned to Canada with a pair of wooden shoes and the promise of marriage from a Dutch girl. Henry had gone through all the paperwork to bring her to Canada, but shortly after returning to Canada, he received a letter from her saying she had changed her mind. Somehow, he met a lovely Italian girl, Mary Callura, from Burlington Street. On one occasion when Mary invited the Evanses for an Italian dinner, Roy ate so much Italian bread that everyone thought he would be ill. As time progressed, Mary became Mary Reilly, and Mary and Roy became fast friends.

In September 1946, May was off to Delta. She used the same Beltline route that David Dubinsky had used.

In July 1947, Peter wrote that he expected passage to Canada soon. Alice had worked and worked, scrimped and saved, until she had over five hundred dollars in the bank. She was an independent woman now. She decided she would use the five hundred dollars as a down payment on a house. She would decide on a house without Peter's advice or approval. She studied the ads in the paper and saw a house that wasn't too far away and had enough space for her to have four boarders. She contacted the real estate agent and had a tour of the house. May didn't think much of it. The real estate agent was very persuasive. He convinced Alice it was a great buy and she shouldn't delay because other buyers were looking at the house. Alice was a very trusting person and naïve in some ways. She signed the contract. Two weeks later, the real estate agent phoned to say the owner had withdrawn the house from the market, and despite all his efforts, Alice had lost her five-hundred dollar down payment. Alice was stunned. That down payment was every penny she had. She wept for two days. Sometimes, she wept at the kitchen table so that everyone in the house symbolically wept with her. She went to her minister, Reverend Priddle, for help. He went to see the real estate agent who had the money. He refused to return it. Reverend Priddle arranged a formal meeting with the Real Estate Bureau. He had a genuine religious wrath. But nothing could be done. The swindler got away with it.

On August 21, 1947, Peter Evans arrived at Pier 21 in Halifax on the *Aquitania*. From there, he made the trip to Hamilton. Alice and the children were at the CNR station to meet him. With the crush of people, they missed one another. Alice and the children returned home by streetcar. Peter waited for a long time at the station and then hired a taxicab. The Evans family was reunited on Lottridge Street. Alice embraced Peter and said how happy she was to see him. May was beside herself with joy. She hugged and kissed her father fiercely and followed him around the house for weeks. Roy was sullen. This stranger looked as if he would impose discipline. Michael Hughes had indulged and spoiled him. Now, there was a person with authority over him. Alice and Peter both thought there could be a new start. But there would be no long discussions—no expressions of deep feelings. Their generation tried to hide deep emotions, not reveal them. The war in Europe ended in May 1945. Peter arrived in Hamilton in August 1947. Within a week, a neighbour three houses down who was a foreman at Dominion Glass got Peter a job at the plant.

Roy and his friends had a tradition of going to the Saturday matinee at the Playhouse Theatre on Sherman near Barton. Most of the parents gave them fifteen cents for the admission and a treat. Some generous parents gave their kids a quarter. Roy and his band of six- and seven-year-olds would merge with other bands of children as they neared the theatre. The children could walk from Lottridge to Sherman and not hear a word of English. It was all Ukrainian, Polish, and Italian. Some older immigrants never learned English. They could function perfectly well in their own community. Their children would be part of the larger English-speaking city. Stiff-necked Anglos hated hearing people speak their native language. They would hiss, "Learn English or go back to your own country!" Roy had one friend who was Croatian and one who was Polish. Those languages were spoken in the homes so Roy had no trouble accepting different languages. Many of the immigrant children were learning English at the Playhouse Theatre. Films were a great teaching device.

Saturday matinees at the Playhouse were absolute mayhem. The kids screamed all afternoon. The carpets in the aisles were such a luxury that children rolled up and down them. Wrappers from popcorn and candy bars were thrown back and forth. Every week, *The Bowery Boys* would be played. But even those films couldn't keep the children's attention. Things would suddenly calm down when the weekly serial came on. One week, the show would end with the hero trapped in a car that went over a cliff, or in a plane that had crashed, or he was submerged underwater with his hands tied by the villain. Yet the next week, he would emerge unscathed with a plausible explanation. Then quiet turned to chaos again when the cartoons were shown. The screen went dark and these roiling mobs of children were released into the community. Most of the boys went home to play games based on films they had seen—six shooter gun fights, sword-fighting, horse riding by galloping in a sideways fashion. The girls had few screen models to imitate. One Saturday, Roy and his friends remembered to bring extra money. The admission was going up to ten cents from six. Most of the kids were given a quarter. When Roy got to the theatre, there was a little girl weeping outside the front door. She had only six cents. The manager kept telling her that they had advertised the new price for three weeks. She just kept bawling. The manager didn't know what to do. Roy and his friends and all the other children paid their ten cents and went in. For a long time, Roy wondered what had happened to that little girl.

The Evanses were able to save enough money in a year for another down payment on a house. Peter had a stable job and Alice still had her boarders. They moved to Hope Avenue and one boarder went with them. Roy spent his first week at Queen Mary School crying because he had left all his friends behind. He used to ride his little bicycle all the way back to Lottridge Street to visit his friends. Those were the days when children weren't closely supervised. An eight-year-old riding through the city in the dark seems irresponsible now.

Chapter Sixteen

Ontario 1946 - 1950

In 1945, the Ukrainian community bought a lot for its new church on Barton near Lottridge. In 1948, they hired an architect. Shortly after, they began construction of the lower portion of the church. Members of the parish volunteered their labour, including Mike Dubinsky. There was an official opening of the half-finished church in 1949. In 1954, the upper portion of the church was finished. After that, all the functions of an active church membership followed.

David Dubinsky returned to Hamilton from Toronto in May 1946. He was given a job at Stelco again. His first day back, he discovered the tensions at the plant. The Steelworkers of America were recruiting members. The plant was divided over the issue. It wasn't a friendly divide. David remained silent. His father was very anti-union. Mike linked unions with communism, Stalin, and Holodomor. During the summer, hard lines were drawn between the union and anti-union forces. Finally, the Steelworkers called a strike for August. Stelco wisely released all its student workers. The Ukrainian community, like every other community in Hamilton, was split over the strike. David was offered a job as a labourer by a member of his church who was a home builder. Later on, David would be able to use his connections with Ukrainian construction businesses.

Once Mike was settled in Hamilton, he was able to correspond with his parents. Then with the German invasion of Russia in 1942, all correspondence ended. At the end of the war, the Soviet Ukraine encompassed L'vov and Grabek. In 1948, Mike finally got a letter from his parents. The isolation of their farm saved them from the scorched earth of the Russians retreating east and the Germans retreating west. The Germans had taken all their pigs and most of their chickens. Now, under Soviet control, their farm was part of a collective, but they were allowed one cow, chickens, and pigs. Two farm labourers were billeted with them, but they were well. There was bad news about Iryna and Hedeon. When the Germans came, many thought they would be saved from Stalin and Ukraine would be a semi-autonomous state in the Third Reich. It didn't work that way. Hitler considered the Ukrainians sub-humans and his troops were ordered to be as brutal as possible. That meant destruction, rape, and mass killings. Iryna and Hedeon were seventeen and fifteen in 1943. Although they wondered about being on Stalin's side, they were recruited by Ukrainian partisans in the area. They acted as spies and messengers, reporting on German troop movements. In 1944, they were caught by the Germans. They were shot and their bodies were thrown into a ditch. They had survived the Holodomor, but not the war. Mike decided not to tell David about this.

David Dubinsky had met a very beautiful and intelligent girl at university named Ella. She was a Ukrainian girl from Edmonton whose father was a prominent lawyer. Perhaps that reinforced David's determination to become a lawyer. He received admittance to Osgoode Hall Law School and passed the Bar in 1949. They decided to get married that same year. Ella agreed to live in Hamilton because David had a job waiting for him.

Mike was happy that David had met a Ukrainian girl at university and that Ella was a wonderful person. David now associated with many wealthy and upper-middle-class students at the University of Toronto and Osgoode Hall. David was shedding his lower-class roots as quickly as he could. He wanted to be part of the intellectual and cultural milieu of the well-to-do. In Toronto, the dominant financial and cultural class was Anglo-Canadians. He didn't brag about how his immigrant parents had become successful. He didn't talk about them at all.

* * *

In 1950, the Dubinskys sold the variety store and moved into a basement home in their apartment building on Barton Street east of Kenilworth. Betta did all the cleaning when tenants came and went. Mike was now a foreman at the front end at Dominion Glass. Alina went to her new school without complaint. Mike's energy couldn't be limited to a job and an apartment building, so he joined three other members of his church in buying a beer parlour on Wentworth Street North. They would share the management and work hours.

When the Dubinsky's moved east, they left one cultural environment and joined another. The area around Barton Avenue was a mix of Ukrainian, Polish, Italian, and British. When Alina went to school, she had many Ukrainian classmates. They used to speak Ukrainian during recess. The Poles could join in. At Alina's new school, there were only a few Ukrainians, Poles, and Italians. The whole area was predominantly British, made up of the well-established families and new immigrants. The only language heard on the streets, in the parks, and in stores was English. Alina and David were perfectly bilingual. Mike was pretty close. Betta was quite weak in English.

Now, Alina was exposed to different activities. David had fallen in love with basketball when he came to Canada, even though the most popular sport in their original neighbourhood was soccer. At the Prince of Wales School, David was introduced to basketball. Mike was dismayed and puzzled when he saw his son bouncing a ball up and down the sidewalk on Barton Street. He was even more dismayed when he found out his son was in a church basketball league. Protestant churches! Now the Dubinskys got another big cultural shock. Alina announced that she wanted to go to a dancing academy with her friend Audrey.

Betta and Mike gave Alina anything she wanted, as they hesitantly wanted their children to become Canadians. But at the same time, they didn't want them to jettison their Ukrainian heritage. Mike and Betta never could understand their son's need to constantly bounce a large ball and throw it high off the side of the building. Now Alina told them she was in a tap-dancing class. They paid for the instructor, gave her the money for the shoes, but when Alina came home with shoes with steel cleats on the toes and heels, Betta and Mike were stunned. Alina started dancing around the kitchen, giving Betta and Mike headaches. But Alina was very happy.

Alina and Audrey never missed a dance class. Alina would go over to Audrey's house because she had a basement with a concrete floor. Audrey also had a record player. They would tap dance for hours. Audrey's mother sometimes made lemonade for them. Of course, Alina had to have a record player, and she got one. Alina also bought two records—*Rag Mop* and *Chattanoogie Shoe Shine Boy*. She danced in her bare feet in her bedroom, practicing her tap-dancing steps. Mike didn't like this music. He warned Alina never to buy Negro music. Alina and Andrey sang, "The Thing," "If I knew you were coming, I'd a Baked a Cake," and "Goodnight Irene" over and over. As they walked down Barton Street to the recreational hall beside Mahony Park, they sang and other girls joined them near the hall.

Audrey's father played the guitar and Alina joined Audrey and her parents in singing sessions. It was all Western music—Hank Snow, Hank Williams, Eddy Arnold. At these times, Alina wished her parents could be more like Audrey's parents.

As the time came for the annual recital, the dance instructor was more forceful and demanded that the girls practice at home. Then their costumes arrived. They were all going to be toy soldiers tap dancing on parade. When Alina got her costume, she was delighted. She hurried home to try it on. She emerged from her bedroom in full costume with her tap dance shoes on. Betta and Mike looked on in silence. They didn't know what to make of it. They didn't come to the recital. Mike was working and Betta couldn't come by herself. Alina was ashamed of her parents. Most adolescents are ashamed of their parents, but when there is a language and cultural separation, things are worse.

Alina danced for another year, but she wasn't a natural dancer and lost interest.

* * *

Mike's investment in an apartment building turned out really well. He had inherited some very good tenants who provided a steady stream of income. Mike found an accountant at the church who took care of all the legal and tax requirements. He did some major improvements when they first moved in, but once he bought a share of the pub, he had little time. Betta took over the management of the building. Her English was good enough. As Alina got older, she helped her mother more and more. She was her mother's translator on some occasions. Betta kept the books and handed over the monthly rents to Mike. It was unthinkable that she would have her own bank account. With shift work and the pub, Mike had very irregular hours and was away most of the time. The apartment was a mother-daughter enterprise. Betta and Alina became very close. Betta told Alina about the happy times in Galicia. She did not tell Alina about the horrors that had swirled around her country. So many people had so much history to forget.

In her teens, Alina was given the job of collecting the rents. She enjoyed doing it and being entrusted with adult responsibility. The tenants liked Alina's warmth and outgoing personality. Alina liked to chat and many stay-at-home wives were pleased to have someone to talk to. Betta collected the rent from the one Ukrainian couple in the building. They had sold their home because the man had retired from

Procter and Gamble and wanted to travel and go fishing. Betta could talk to the wife in Ukrainian and feel the liberation of speaking one's own language. Her hesitancy in English made her shy. It also hid her intelligence. These two middle-aged ladies gossiped about everything. They mostly gossiped about the tenants because that was a big interest. They talked about eccentric behaviour and habits and had a prurient nosiness about the young married couple in apartment four. The wife sometimes wandered outside in very scanty sleepwear to put out the garbage. These ladies had never owned scanty clothes. The tenants in apartment five had terrible battles and their screaming could be heard through the walls. Betta's friend was scandalized by the tenant in unit three. He was a taxi driver with odd hours. He never said hello if they met. She said he always smelled of liquor. Sometimes at three or four in the morning, she would hear a female laughing and squealing inside his apartment. She thought he hired kyba, sex workers, at the end of his night. She didn't like that man at all. Betta was unaware of all these things. Her basement apartment kept her sheltered from some things.

For the most part, the tenants were very good. If they had repair problems, they would wait until Mike wasn't home and approach Betta. If Betta couldn't understand the problem, Alina would translate as well as she could. When Alina was twelve, she had gone to Ukrainian summer camp where she learned to write the Ukrainian language. It was a perfectly phonetic language and Alina had a very good oral vocabulary. When the problem was clear, Betta phoned George Bonderenko. He was the ultimate handyman. He could fix anything. The tenants were pleased with the quick repair jobs. The requests were solved within days. They always thanked Betta profusely, and in return, they were happy to pay their rent in full and on time.

One day, Alina was making her rounds at the end of the month. She had some good conversations with several of the tenants. She waited until four o'clock to call on the taxi driver because she knew he slept late. When she knocked on the door, he waved her in, just the way all the tenants did. She noticed he was a little unsteady on his feet, but she thought that was because he had just woken up. She had been in his apartment before to collect the rent, and she was always dismayed by the dirt and debris. She thought of her poor mother having to clean the stove, which was covered in food that had been spilled and burned on. There were clothes on the floor in the living room and the smell of fruit that had turned rotten. As he wandered around in a disoriented way, Alina realized he was very drunk. He couldn't find his wallet, he said. He would pay cash as usual. Would Alina please sit down on the couch as he searched for his wallet? Alina didn't want to offend him. She was hesitant, but she sat down. The TV had some afternoon soap opera on and the volume was quite loud. He approached her with the money in his hand and sat beside her. He wrapped his arm around her with unexpected strength. Alina was frozen at first. Then she tried to bolt up. He wouldn't let go and he fondled her breasts. She twisted and broke free. He was too unsteady to pursue. She ran down the steps to her own apartment and went to the bathroom directly. Betta was preparing dinner and didn't notice. Alina knelt over the toilet. She thought she was going to bring up. She didn't. She filled the bathtub and lay in the warm water in shock. As she recovered, she shampooed her hair several times and washed her body rather roughly several times. She said nothing to her mother. Betta wondered why her effervescent daughter was so quiet over dinner.

Alina and Betta were by themselves as Mike was working the four-to-twelve shift. After dinner, Alina helped her mother with the dishes then went to her bedroom and closed the door. Before she went to bed, she bathed again. Betta thought that was odd. Perhaps her sixteen-year-old daughter was having some insignificant adolescent crisis.

Alina never told anyone about this. The taxi driver moved out a day later, leaving Betta to clean up an unholy mess. She found his rent in an envelope and wondered why he had left so suddenly.

Chapter Seventeen

Ontario 1951 - 1958

May was a very successful student at Delta, as she was extremely intelligent. For some reason, she left school after Grade 11 to work at the Hamilton Cotton Company. It was 1951, and she was only sixteen. Hamilton at that time was not only a steel manufacturing city, it had vast cotton mills. Hamilton Cotton Company went all the way back to 1880. It was part of the diverse manufacturing in Hamilton. It was a city of jobs and opportunity.

After they moved to Hope Avenue, the Evanses used the Beltline to get to Trinity Baptist Church on Main Street. By 1950, photographs were becoming more common. In 1949, the ubiquitous Brownie Hawkeye Camera was designed. Film and development became cheaper. Everywhere, people were seen holding cameras at their waists to focus the pictures. Now the Reillys could send photographs along with their letters. The Reillys were all over the country, but the communication network was functioning well.

In 1951, Peter Evans received a letter from Ivor. Their mother had died several weeks earlier. When Peter told Alice, she remained silent.

Alice was determined to see her family. During the winter of 1951-1952, her brother Jake came to Hamilton to work at Harvester to make some money. Of course, he moved in with the Evanses. He had a contract with the Ford dealership in Carrot River to buy a Ford at the Oakville factory. In July, in the new car, Jake, Alice, and Roy headed west. Alice's father was dying of cancer. Alice and Roy spent a number of weeks at the farm. Jake and Mid were still in their log house. The soil around Carrot River yielded good crops. The farmers stored grain in their own small granaries and waited for phone calls saying the grain companies were buying. Then they would shovel wheat or barley into their half-ton trucks and head to town. Roy had a female cousin his own age and they wandered around the farm together. Roy got to ride the old farm horse. Alice finally found some peace with her father. When she left, she hugged him. No words were spoken. Then it was on the train back to Hamilton

In the summer of 1953, Alice took Roy west again. That summer, Alice got to meet her youngest sister for the first time since the family dispersal. Rebecca and her husband had a farm near Edam, Saskatchewan, and they had two daughters. While they were there, Alice's sister Susan drove over with her two daughters. Roy had now met six cousins, all girls. From Edam, Alice and Roy took a bus to North Battlefield. Alice had to see her mother. Alice and Roy were escorted into the psychiatric hospital. Roy was very intimidated. Alice and her mother talked quietly for half an hour. Alice gave her mother all the family news and her mother responded with a few words. Roy was struck by how much his mother looked like his grandmother. Alice and Roy didn't say a word on the bus trip back to Edam. Grace Reilly lived to be over ninety. She spent some fifty years institutionalized.

Alice continued her journey to Hanley. Her sister Kay was living there. Roy got to meet two more cousins—one girl, one boy. The highlight of that trip was a fishing trip to the South Saskatchewan River. The lines were thrown into the river, anchored to the shore, and then his uncle took a nap. He caught one fairly large fish. The final stop in this great odyssey was Moose Jaw. Mrs. Riddell was still alive, but she had been widowed for ten years. She was very anxious to see Alice. They sat for hours reminiscing about the time when Alice was a housekeeper there. Roy was allowed to wander around outside. He had spent countless hours listening to adults talk about the past. He was anxious to get back to Hamilton and his neighbourhood activities. Mrs. Riddell cooked a lovely dinner for them and had beds made up. In the morning, Alice had another sad farewell. Then back on the train to Hamilton. Alice was very happy to have seen so many brothers and sisters. The Reilly family was growing every year. The bonds between brothers and sisters were stronger than ever.

When Roy was twelve, he fell in love with soccer. He played for a team that was sponsored by his Scout Troop. There was a men's league that played their games at Civic Stadium. Roy would ride his bike to the stadium and watch the games. No admission price. A few teams were organized by work places. A very good team for years was Westinghouse. But most teams were ethnic-based—the Polish White Eagles, Abruzzi, Serbia, Croatia, and so forth. World War II could be a touchy subject. One week, Roy went to the stadium and found that the Italo-Canadians were playing the British Imperials. Roy suspected what might happen. He walked to the top row of seats so that he could see the spectators and the game. The spectators were more interesting than the game. Within minutes of the game starting, the insults began to fly back and forth. The Brits loved to insult the Italians over their war record. They had all kinds of facts and figures. After the triumph of the Battle of Britain and the heroic stand against Hitler, the Brits were triumphant and full of themselves. The Italians called the Brits barbarians—no art, no opera, no warmth. The exchanges were usually good-natured. Sometimes the men throwing insults back and forth were good friends at work. The problem occurred when the women became involved. That meant a lot of high-pitched screeching and husbands holding wives back.

For some inexplicable reason, Roy grew up with few prejudices. When he lived on Lottridge Street, he was in the middle of a multi-ethnic and multi-religious community. His two best friends were Croatian and Polish. In his last year at Queen Mary School and his first years at Delta, one of his best friends was black. Black people were so few in those days that when Roy and Frank went downtown to see a film at the Capital or Palace, people were curious. As Roy and Frank walked along Main Street near the Chicken Roost, Roy could see heads twisting in his peripheral vision.

Many Black people in Hamilton went to Stewart Memorial Church. There, Reverend John Christie Holland led his flock. His father was an escaped slave who came to Canada in 1860. He was from Maryland and the story was that he swam across the Niagara River to get to Canada, where he then married and settled in Hamilton. He fathered thirteen children and John C. Holland was the fifth born. John was very bright and hoped to go to university, but he had no money. He worked at Westinghouse Electric in menial jobs and couldn't get promoted because he was black. In 1901, he got married and got a job on the Toronto, Hamilton, and Buffalo Railway—known affectionately as the T.H. and B. He worked as a porter for over thirty years, rising to attendant for the VIP car used by the company president. Since he had four children, he couldn't go to university. He studied for the ministry by correspondence. In 1925, he was ordained as a minister by a college in Ohio. He had always been active at St. Paul's African Methodist Episcopal Church. It reformed as the non-denominational Stewart Memorial Church in 1937. Church members who could trace their ancestors to the Underground Railroad had a certain prestige. But the members of the church had a great variety of family histories. Slavery had existed in Canada. Some black families had immigrated to Canada as early as the eighteenth century. A few members traced their roots to the Caribbean and the infamous triangular trade route—slaves, sugar, cotton.

Frank's family came to Canada from Detroit in 1944 to escape the aftermath of the Great Race Riot of 1943. Like most black people in Canada, they had many relatives in the United States, scattered all over the country. The United States was a country of great internal migrations. The most impactful migrations were caused by the 1930 Dust Bowl and World War II. Reverend Holland became the pastor at Stewart Memorial Church. He retired eleven years later to dedicate himself to humanitarian causes in Hamilton. He became well known in the city for his work. He was the first Canadian of African heritage to be named Citizen of the Year. When Roy was going to Laidlaw United Church Sunday School, Reverend Holland's son, John Junior, would visit periodically to speak to the boys' class.

One day when Roy and Frank were having lunch in the Delta cafeteria, the president of the Boys' Athletic Committee came over. He was extremely genial. He asked Frank if he would like to try out for the track team. Frank politely declined. Roy was annoyed. He could run faster than Frank. The president's assumption was that since Frank was black, he could run fast, sing Gospel hymns, and play jazz on the piano. Frank couldn't do any of those things. The president probably also had some strange ideas about what Frank's family ate.

* * *

Hamilton 1952

Roy's dog Ricky was lying where he always did Monday to Friday at 4 p.m.—the corner of Kenilworth and Hope streets. He was waiting for his mistress, Alice, to get off the bus. Ricky was well known by the nearby storekeepers. They thought his intelligence and devotion were really quite marvelous. Gino, from Gino's Shoemaking across the street, would often bring leftovers for Ricky. The dog was always appreciative and wagged his tail warmly. Gino told his wife and children about this marvelous dog.

Once the last boarder had left the house, Alice was determined to get a job. The house became too small for another boarder once May and Roy became older. Each of them demanded a separate bedroom.

But Alice had to have her own money, even a small amount of money would give her a sense of independence. She wouldn't ask Peter for extra money to buy the things she wanted. Once the last boarder told Alice he was leaving, she began to look in the *Spectator* in the 'Jobs' section. The economy was booming and jobs were plentiful, but Alice had little education and she knew she would have to take some menial job. She spent a number of days trying to decide where she would apply. She phoned several places, but was told the positions were filled. Then she phoned a company called Parkdale Hardwood Floors. The man she talked to had a heavy accent and Alice had some trouble understanding him, but he said they needed one more woman to sort lumber. Alice knew she could get a bus at the corner and transfer to the Barton Street bus to Parkdale. She liked the old days when the Belt Line would take her every place she needed to go. But the city outgrew the Belt Line with its regular trolleys on fixed rails. Buses were needed for all the new subdivisions.

The next day, Alice tried out the bus route. The bus driver told her about the transfer slip she would get and how to get on the Barton bus. She found the procedure quite easy and she got off the second bus at the corner of Barton and Parkdale. From there, she walked north to the black concrete structure that had the sign 'Parkdale Hardwood Floors' hand-painted on the wall. Alice tried the bell on the front door, but nobody came. She opened the door and saw a large room with concrete-block walls and a cement floor. She immediately smelled the wonderful scent of lumber. She stood and watched what was happening. There was a large entrance door at the back and a pile of cut boards. Three men were operating machine saws and three women were standing beside a slow-moving conveyor belt. The three women noticed her and smiled. They waved to a man who was standing at the back door inspecting the pile of lumber.

The man walked up from the back, looking critically at his six workers. He stopped in front of Alice and abruptly said, "Do you want a job?"

Alice took a few seconds to decipher what he had said. She was taken aback by his brusqueness and heavy accent. Her hesitation made him bark, "Yes or no?"

Alice wanted the job. She said, "Yes."

He turned his back and walked away. Once he had passed the three women, and it was safe, the women started to laugh. They waved Alice over. One of them explained that that was Josip—the rude brother. The factory was owned by two brothers. One was hot-tempered and rude. The other brother, Ivica, was quite nice. They were Croatians. The women told her to go see Ivica in the office and pointed the way.

Alice knocked on the door and Ivica stood up from his desk and greeted her warmly. Workers were not easy to get, especially women workers! He told her what her job would be and walked her around the factory. The men on the saws smiled and nodded a welcome. Ivica introduced her to the three women and explained what they were doing. They were sorting lumber cut for hardwood flooring. There was first class, second class, and random cuts. Once the boards were sorted, they were sold to floor installers in the construction business. House building in Hamilton was almost at fever pitch with the post-war prosperity.

Alice told Ivica that she could start the next day. He pointed to the three women at the conveyor belt and suggested she wear similar clothes and bring a lunch. The working hours were seven to three. She would make sixty cents an hour and be paid for eight hours with a half-hour lunch.

The next day, Alice made her way to the factory by bus. She had gotten up at 5:30 a.m., had a breakfast of tea and toast, and arrived at 6:45 a.m. ready to work. By seven, all the women were in place to work. The most experienced worker, Anne, showed Alice how to grade the lumber. As the pieces of wood came down the belt, she showed Alice how to judge the quality of the pieces. Alice learned quickly and stayed by her side. At 11:30, work stopped for lunch. Alice had a beef sandwich, an apple, and a thermos of tea. Alice was told to keep her head down and look busy whenever Josip approached the work area. He was always angry about something.

Alice had been given a pair of cotton gloves by Anne, but she would have to buy her own gloves in the future. She had picked up several slivers before lunch and the women told her to expect that every day. At lunch, the women were very friendly and anxious to explain why they had this job. They each had different circumstances, but they all needed the money. The two Croatian women had mothers-in-law living with them who took care of the children and did the cooking. Both families had bought homes and needed two paycheques to pay the mortgage. Alice was the oldest of the women. Now in her late forties, her hair was turning from grey to white. The women didn't say anything to Alice, but among themselves, they wondered why an older woman would have to do such a hard job. The three hoped they would not be in that situation by the time they reached that age.

The first days of work were very hard for Alice. She was standing on a concrete floor, reaching across a conveyor belt, and lifting heavy pieces of lumber. Her feet, legs, and back ached. The other workers remembered younger women quitting after one day. One woman quit at lunchtime on her first day. But Alice persevered. That was the story of her life.

Over the weeks, Alice became very friendly with everyone except Josip. The women could talk as they worked unless Josip was skulking around. Each person had an immigrant story. Everyone in the factory was an immigrant from the chaos of Europe. Of course, not all stories were told. The others found Alice's trip on the *Queen Elizabeth* in 1943 fascinating. The other women loved the fact that Alice had defied her husband. The two Croatian ladies would not dare such a thing. Sometimes, Ivica would join them for lunch and he enjoyed listening to the stories. One day, for the first time, Ivica revealed their role in the war. He and Josip had joined Tito's

Communist partisans. He said they had many ups and downs before Tito finally triumphed. He didn't mention the atrocities of war. But one episode still amused him.

Winston Churchill had sent his thirty-two-year-old son Randolph to Tito's territory to pledge British aid. Randolph, like his father, was extremely brave. He had been on a mission with the long-range desert commanders behind German lines in North Africa. He had parachuted into a safe area near Tito's headquarters. Tito had assigned Josip and Ivica to act as Randolph's chauffeurs and bodyguards. Ivica said the mission had been a success for the British. Tito received the support he needed from both Churchill and Stalin to carry on the struggle. But Randolph was falling-down drunk the whole time. He was arrogant, rude, and unpredictable. He seemed to be partly insane. They were happy to see him leave in a truck convoy.

Ivica looked around and whispered to his workers, "He was much worse than Josip." The workers exploded with unrestrained laughter. For the rest of the day, the workers, whenever they saw Josip, would smile and suppress their laughter. Josip wondered what was going on and became even more agitated and miserable than usual.

At the end of each day, Alice was bone-tired. The work was exhausting. Even if they ran out of lumber deliveries some days, Josip would have them take rasps or sandpaper to upgrade the boards. He couldn't stand seeing his workers not working.

One day, Anne whispered to Alice, "He's like a fart on a hot griddle." Alice was shocked at first and then she started to giggle. The ridicule of Josip made everyone feel better.

Ricky saw the bus approaching several blocks away. He began to wag his tail slowly. He wagged his tail faster and faster as the bus drew closer. Finally, when the door of the bus opened and he saw Alice, he wagged his tail furiously and almost contorted his body into a circle. Alice's tiredness disappeared when she saw him. Ricky knew his mistress was exhausted and he did a little half leap in her direction, but he wouldn't leap up on her. Alice greeted him warmly and reached down to pat him. She dipped into her bag and gave him some scraps that had been left at the lunch table. He gulped them down. Then they started their walk home.

Alice kept up a stream of questions for Ricky. "How was your day? Did you walk Roy to school? Did May keep your water dish full? Did you play with the German Shepherd next door?" Ricky was her loving companion and he knew exactly what she was saying. Alice trudged along, tired, buoyed up by Ricky's affection. Ricky pranced along like some regal cavalry horse, imbued with his sense of duty and confident in his importance.

When they got home, Alice took off her heavy brown coat and knitted hat and brought out Ricky's dinner. Then she got a needle and removed two slivers from her fingers. Only two slivers meant it was a good day. If the lumber was very rough, she might have five or six slivers. At least once a week, a sliver would go so deep, a finger would bleed profusely. The cotton gloves she had bought at Woolworth's on Ottawa Street had blood stains. She wore two sets of gloves at work and rotated them from right to left hand to even out the wear and prolong their lives. Once a week, she would take out a needle and thread and make repairs.

It was a hard life, but she had been raised to live a hard life. Her childhood in Saskatchewan had been characterized by poverty and hard work. She had been lonely and unhappy in Wales. The happiest time of her life had been in Moose Jaw with the Riddells and her brother and sister. Now her life was full of perseverance and taking pleasure in small things. Her next goal was to buy a TV set. Some neighbours were buying them and telling her about programs. She wouldn't tell Peter because he always pooh-poohed her ideas. But one day, she would have a TV delivered. That would be a sign of her independence and a small triumph.

Peter was a good and moral person. Unlike some husbands, he never drank or treated her badly. He really had no vices. But, unfortunately, he wasn't interested in doing much. There would be no Sunday drives, no trips to the theatre to see a film, and no square dances at the Legion. Alice saw her friends and neighbours enjoying their new prosperity. She had to find solace in her own income and making improvements on the house. Most of the time, she was so weary from her job that she fell asleep before 9 p.m. listening to the radio. But she would carry on.

A life of quiet desperation.

In 1950, a Japanese family moved across the street from the Evanses on Hope Avenue. It was a tiny home for a family with three children and another child on the way. Mr. Takahashi had been a successful restauranteur in Vancouver. He had a comfortable income and was highly respected by the community. The Japanese began to immigrate to Canada in the nineteenth century. They faced the same racial prejudice that the Chinese did. There was even legislation to limit Asiatic immigration. In 1895, the British Columbia Government denied voting rights to residents of Asiatic origin. The government also restricted the number of fishing licences allotted to Japanese-Canadian fishermen.

Japanese-Canadians volunteered to fight for Canada in World War I. In 1931, these veterans were granted the right to vote. Mr. Takahashi then knew all about the persistent persecution of the Japanese. Yet despite this, the Japanese-Canadians in British Columbia made steady progress. They remembered the attack by white supremacists in 1907 on Japanese and Chinese immigrant quarters. When tensions rose between the United States and Japan in the late thirties and early forties, Canada responded in the same way. With the Japanese attack on Pearl Harbour on December 7, 1941, the lives of Japanese-Canadians changed forever. Canada had been at war since 1939. There was a military alliance among Germany, Italy, and Japan. Canadians of German and Italian ancestry were already in prison camps. Now Canadian fury turned on the

Japanese-Canadians. Even before Pearl Harbour, Japanese-Canadians over eighteen were fingerprinted and registered with the RCMP.

In January 1942, two RCMP officers came into Mr. Takahashi's restaurant. One of the officers had breakfast there frequently. Mr. Takahashi greeted him warmly. The officer did not return his greeting. The officers were stone-faced. They handed him a government letter that said he must leave British Columbia within three days. The letter gave him the time and place of the train's departure. His family would be allowed one suitcase each. A lifetime's work gone with one decree; all across British Columbia, fishing boats, businesses, and farms were confiscated. Clever white men rubbed their hands and profited. The Japanese-Canadians knew this would happen. Being model citizens was not enough. Fighting in World War I as volunteers in the Canadian army was not enough. A few white politicians and clergy protested this inhumane action, but not many.

The Takahashi family boarded the train in Vancouver with hundreds of other families. Most families would go to abandoned logging camps and deserted construction sites. The housing was inadequate and the food rations were meagre. The Takahashi family could not be housed in the interior of British Columbia so they were shipped all the way across the country to Arnprior, Ontario. They had a ten-day trip on the railway with inadequate room. Everyone slept sitting up. There was a diet of stale sandwiches and water. Sometimes, compassionate townspeople, when they knew the situation, brought food to the train. The armed soldiers were as miserable as the prisoners. A few of the soldiers played with the children. As the train travelled east, sane people began to realize that the whole program was hateful insanity. Racial prejudice. War fever. A devil's brew.

Arnprior was a nice town if you weren't a prisoner. The Japanese-Canadians had a very large tract of land for their new home. Arnprior had been a lumber town and there were huge parcels of land cleared of trees. There were tents waiting for them. The government provided lumber and the prisoners were allowed to cut trees and have them hauled into Arnprior to be milled. There was a Colonel from the Canadian Militia in charge of the camp. The Canadian government didn't want the scandal of malnutrition or freezing. There was a growing number of human rights advocates speaking out about this injustice.

The Takahashi family were released from the camp in 1945, but there was no point in going back to Vancouver. A white man bought their restaurant for one-tenth its value and his lawyer sent a cheque to Mr. Takahashi with some forms to sign giving up ownership of the restaurant. The new owner had no sense of guilt. Mr. Takahashi decided to move to Hamilton because one of his friends from the camp was going to start a home construction business there. Unfortunately, when the war ended, news of the atrocities in Japanese prisoner of war camps was revealed. A regiment of Canadian soldiers had been captured in Hong Kong in a brainless political decision to send unprepared troops to an unprepared city. Hong Kong fell within days in 1942. The Canadian troops spent the rest of the war being mistreated, beaten, and tortured. The average soldier went from 160 pounds to one hundred. Now a second wave of hatred was directed towards Japanese-Canadians.

The Takahashi's lived in two rooms in downtown Hamilton. At least they were warm in the winter, which was different from their wooden shack in Arnprior that was heated by a wood stove. Mr. Takahashi was picked up each day for work by a fellow employee. It was an all Japanese-Canadian company. The children were enrolled in school and experienced the usual bullying, punching, and spitting. The teachers did everything they could to protect them, but it would never be enough. By 1950, the Takahashi family had saved enough money to buy their home on Hope Avenue. There were no other Japanese families in the neighbourhood. There were three children now and the fourth was born in 1952—Rick, Susan, Elizabeth, and George. When Roy was fifteen, he played tennis with a group of teenagers at Laidlaw United Church. Susan was part of that group. There seemed to be some connection between Christianity and tennis. Many churches in Hamilton had tennis courts. Alice and Peter still went to Trinity Baptist Church, which had a tennis court. In 1956, Roy was sixteen and little Georgie was four. Georgie would walk across the street to talk to Roy. The sixteen-year-old and the four-year-old would sit on Roy's front steps and discuss the world.

Mrs. Takahashi would yell across the street, "Georgie, stop bothering Roy. Come home." But Roy loved Georgie's visits. He loved him like a little brother.

One day, Roy came home from school and saw that his mother had been crying. Georgie had died in his sleep that night. The neighbours never found out the cause of the sudden death. There was a lot of idle speculation. Roy was stunned. He didn't eat that night. He spent the evening in his bedroom. He didn't know what to do. The neighbours felt a genuine sense of sadness and compassion, yet the cultural chasm was so great, they didn't know how to respond. They ended up collecting money and sending flowers, but nobody knocked on the Takahashi door. They thought that might offend a Japanese tradition. Georgie had a private family funeral.

In the spring of 1958, Susan walked across the street and told Roy he was taking her to Delta's GAC-BAC awards dinner. Susan was a very assertive girl. She didn't seem to realize that as a Japanese person in Canada, she was expected to be very meek and submissive to whites, always have downcast eyes, and try to be invisible. When Roy showed up to escort Susan to the event, Mrs. Takahashi thanked him. Mr. Takahashi was becoming more and more withdrawn. When Susan and Roy showed up at the dinner, there was a bit of a buzz.

Chapter Eighteen

Ontario 1962

In 1962, a Jew persuaded a Catholic to run for Mayor of Hamilton. The WASP establishment gasped. The Jew was Ken Soble. He was a powerhouse in the broadcasting industry. He had multiple successful ventures in radio and television. Hamilton became his base when he started CHCH TV as an affiliate of CBC in 1954. In 1961, he made CHCH an independent station and it became the most profitable independent station in Canada. He bought the Barton Arena and the Hamilton Tigers hockey team. He became a governor of the Tiger Cat football team. In 1961, he worked to help the city deal with its housing crisis. He participated in the plan for urban renewal. One of his projects was a plan to have a Medical School at McMaster. He was a giant in the city.

Perhaps Soble thought the city administration was moving too slowly with his ideas. But he had an energetic and personable employee in mind for the job. Victor K. Copps came to Hamilton in 1945. He worked as a sports announcer for CHML radio—one of Soble's enterprises. He became interested in politics and ran for a controller seat in 1960 and was elected. The Ken Soble-Vic Copps partnership was ready to move forward.

The patrician who served as mayor was Lloyd Douglas Jackson. Like Soble, he was a successful businessman. He had started Jackson's Bakery in 1922 and it grew to have two hundred delivery routes in

Hamilton. He had a wonderful background. He had graduated from McMaster with a degree in chemistry while the university was still in Toronto. In 1962, he had already served as mayor for thirteen years. He had the distinguished look of an aristocrat with his white hair and regal posture. He was now seventy-four years old.

Roy Evans was in his second year at McMaster when the election occurred. He applied for a job as a polling clerk. It was good pay for one day's work. He was assigned to an office in the Durand neighbourhood. It was the centre of old wealth in Hamilton—very large homes built by successful businessmen beginning in the nineteenth century. Homes near the escarpment were very imposing and smelled of money. Roy had an assistant—a woman in her fifties who was diabetic and kept eating sandwiches. Roy was puffed up by his sense of importance. He was slow and deliberate with each voter. That showed his authority. The vote extended to 6 p.m. and as work ended, the number of voters increased. Finally, it was time to tally up the votes. Lloyd Jackson got ninety percent of the votes cast in Durand. Roy handed in the ballots and all the paraphernalia. As he drove home, he listened to the results on his radio. Victor K. Copps was the clear winner. Turns out there were different voting patterns in Hamilton.

The next morning, people listened to the news on CHML. Everyone in Hamilton woke to the voice of Paul Hanover. He'd had a morning show since 1945. Peter and Roy would listen to no one else—although Peter sometimes complained about Hanover's juvenile sense of humour. Hanover was a Hamilton boy who went to Westdale Collegiate. He was the most successful radio personality in Hamilton's history. And he was Jewish.

Two other giants in Hamilton politics were Ellen Fairclough and Lincoln Alexander. Fairclough was first elected to parliament in 1950. In 1957, John Diefenbaker appointed her to the Cabinet. She was the first woman to be a cabinet minister. Another politician rising to the top in Hamilton was Lincoln Alexander. He would eventually become the first black member of parliament and the first black cabinet minister.

A Catholic mayor, a woman in the Federal Cabinet, a Black person in the Federal Cabinet, and the most popular radio personality a Jew. Did this mean that Hamilton was progressive, tolerant, and inclusive? Maybe narrow-mindedness and bigotry die hard.

The old religious antagonism between Protestants and Catholics was aroused when Mayor Copps, as one of his first decrees, abolished the Annual Orange Parade, a tradition in Hamilton. The Loyal Orange Institution was a Protestant fraternal society based in Northern Ireland. The religious hatred of Ireland had been exported to Canada. In Canada's first years, politicians, including Sir John A. Macdonald, had to pander to this sometimes-fanatical organization. For example, they had demanded that Louis Riel be hanged. And he was. But time moves along. By 1962, a Catholic mayor could end their parade and get away with it. Victor K. Copps became arguably Hamilton's most popular mayor ever.

In 1962, another powerhouse of Hamilton politics was elected to the House of Commons for the first time. His name was John Munro. He would become a cabinet minister and even campaign for the leadership of the Liberal Party. One of his right-hand men was David Dubinsky, who had a law office on Barton Street. By the 1960s, David had two partners. He was a real estate lawyer and entrepreneur. He had scores of projects from home sales to business developments. In many ways, he was the "go to" man for the Ukrainian community. He was a devoted Liberal. He and John Munro were both graduates of Osgoode. He was a very active fundraiser for John and the Liberals. Some called him John's primary bag man. Munro had built up a political organization in East Hamilton that rivalled the Kennedy network in Massachusetts. When there was an election, two-thirds of all lawn signs were for John Munro. David and John were very good friends. They were at the centre of the Liberal society in Hamilton. Of course, it included Ken Soble, Vic Copps, and all the aspiring Liberal politicians. Sometimes the socializing and the long strategy meetings at Mary's Chinese Restaurant on Barton Street led to too much drinking. Munro, at times, seemed like a man burning the candle at both ends.

David followed the pattern of all successful immigrants in North America. They moved from modest homes in city centres to large homes in new suburbs. Ella and David had a beautiful new home on the escarpment with a swimming pool. When Betta and Mike first saw the swimming pool, they couldn't believe it. They thought there must be some construction error. Then Mike thought his son was flouting his new wealth.

Ella was the one who arranged for the Dubinskys to be involved with the Provincial and Federal Liberal Party. David was a grass-roots man, raising donations from small business people in East Hamilton. Because of her father, Ella knew there was an exciting cultural and intellectual aspect to national politics. She maintained their Liberal memberships and arranged for them to go to all the provincial and federal policy conventions. She was a member of the Provincial and National Women's Liberal Organization and held several posts in the national organization. She understood and argued political policy and ideology vigorously. She was the intellectual in the family.

A flourishing legal practice, a new home with a pool, and connections to the governing party of Canada; the little immigrant boy had done all right.

Chapter Nineteen

Ontario 1957 - 1963

McMaster University began as a Baptist college in Toronto. It was housed in McMaster Hall, named after Senator William McMaster, the first president of the Canadian Bank of Commerce. The university was sponsored by the Baptist Convention of Ontario and Quebec. It was a sectarian undergraduate institution for its clergy and adherents. Its first degrees were conferred in 1894 in arts and theology.

By the 1920s, McMaster Hall was overcrowded and a decision had to be made about its future. The proposal that won out was to move to Hamilton. Through fundraisers, the Convention raised 1.5 million dollars for the move. The citizens of Hamilton donated five hundred thousand dollars. Lands were donated by graduates of the university and lands were transferred from the Royal Botanical Gardens. The first session of the university was in 1930.

By the 1940s, there was a feeling that practical courses should be taught, but the Baptist Convention couldn't raise enough money to build science facilities. Because it was a sectarian university, it was not entitled to public grants. The solution was to break the university into two parts—one college would remain under Baptist control, the other would be public and could receive government grants.

The university grew as provincial grants were awarded. By 1950, the university had built three buildings for the sciences. Then the humanities and social sciences were given buildings. Eventually, there was a separate McMaster Divinity College. By 1957, there was a Faculty of Graduate Studies that could confer PhDs. That same year, McMaster began construction of the McMaster Nuclear Reactor. It was functioning by 1959 and was the first university-based reactor in the Commonwealth.

Roy Evans was a lazy, irresponsible jerk—with a good side to him. He was the type of student teachers would have loved to strangle or kick down a flight of stairs. He could be extremely rude and disrespectful. Yet he had been president of the boys' class at Laidlaw United Church. When he worked summers at Dominion Glass, his foremen loved him and asked for him the next summer. At Delta, he seldom did homework. He staggered from grade to grade with minimum passing marks. He took six years to cover five. His second year in Grade 13 was great because he was a successful football player. His two-year record of subjects in the provincial exams somehow gained him admittance to McMaster. When the local radio station reported that the class of '63 was being initiated that week, Peter Evans was quite surprised that only sixty-three students were going to McMaster that year.

Roy didn't have a clue about his future. The Russians had put up Sputnik in 1957. The western democracies were clamoring for more scientists. Roy thought he would do his bit. In 1959, he started a science course. He met a lovely Polish girl from Central Secondary School and fell madly in love. He then realized he had no interest in science, so he followed his usual practice of doing no homework and skipping classes. The Polish girl had ambition and realized Roy was a loser, so she dumped him. In the spring of 1960, Roy officially found out he had failed. Peter suggested it was time for him to work at Dominion Glass full time.

But Roy was a perverse character. He applied for the arts program in 1960 and was granted an interview with the Dean of Studies. He promised to change his ways. The Dean said he had scored very high on the standardized tests, so he would give Roy a second chance. Roy was now twenty. He had a Volkswagen that Alice had bought, hoping he would drive her around. She was now working at a counter restaurant on Main Street. Roy was his usual jerkish self. He didn't drive his mother much at all.

Alina was just the opposite of Roy. She was a very conscientious student at Delta. She didn't get spectacular marks, but she was always in the top half. She was very friendly, usually quiet, but every now and then, there was a burst of extrovert behaviour. She wasn't an athlete so she didn't play sports. As she reached the senior grades, her blonde hair and beautiful green eyes started attracting male attention. She went on a number of dates to school dances, but she never joined a social group. Her parents were quite protective. The lives that Betta and Mike had led made them very wary for their daughter.

Alina went to St. Vladimir's on a regular basis. All through elementary school, she had attended the church's Sunday school. David was an important member of the church. His law firm arranged countless mortgages and sales for the Ukrainian community. In high school, Alina went to church less and less. Her father wasn't really religious, although the community of St. Vladimir's was important to him. He had many friends there. Now Mike scarcely had any time for church. His shiftwork at Dominion Glass often meant working Sundays; he had the apartment maintenance; and he had to put in hours at the beer parlour. Betta and Alina were usually alone at the apartment.

Alina, in a sense, was being "Canadianized." None of her friends were Ukrainian. Her best friend was Anne Brock. They visited back and forth constantly. Sometimes they did homework together at Anne's. They were both stay-at-home girls. But both had been out on dates. Alina's three dates had all been with Anglos. She had turned down an invitation to be in the Ukrainian Dance Ensemble at the church. Her main concern was to be a good student. No matter how sick she was, she always went to school. She never missed a day of high school. At graduation, she got a special diploma.

From an early age, Alina had wanted to be a nurse. In some ways, that was odd because nobody in her family had ever been sick enough to go to a hospital. It may have had to do with her visits to see Ella when she had her two sons. Perhaps the nurses with their crisp uniforms and lovely smiles impressed Alina. She was initially going to leave Delta at the end of Grade 12 and go into nurses' training. But her brother and sister-in-law intervened strenuously. They were both university graduates and they wanted Alina to have the same prestige—it was important for second generation immigrants to achieve. The trials and tribulations of immigrants had to be justified by their children and grandchildren doing well. That is why they emigrated.

Ella knew of the nursing program at McMaster from her university ladies club and the ladies in the local Liberal party. It was just the thing for her sister-in-law. She could live at home and take the bus to McMaster. Of course, McMaster was not as prestigious as the University of Toronto, but it would do for Alina.

Alina started at McMaster in the fall of 1960. Roy started at McMaster for the second time that year.

Alina met the six young women who would be her classmates. They were in a separate college within the university. They would combine practical nursing courses with studies of nursing theory and liberal arts subjects. The results of good-paying jobs in the industries of Hamilton was almost overwhelming McMaster. The children of lower-middle class parents were beating down the doors. There was a common theme—parents wanted their children to do better than they had. "We suffered for the sake of our children" was a common sentiment. All the bright students from Cathedral Boys School, Loretta Academy, Central, Delta, and Hill Park were getting on buses or forming car pools to get to McMaster. The university couldn't build fast enough. The booming post-war economy meant that Canada needed university graduates of every discipline—doctors, lawyers, engineers, and teachers. The once relatively sedate Baptist university felt overwhelmed by the unwashed but brilliant hordes. The power of the new social mobility and the force of secularism changed the mood of McMaster from intellectual contemplation to kinetic innovation. Some of the old professors were horrified. The Baptists tried to hold on, but it was a futile rear-guard action. When Alina and Roy were undergraduates, there was a break in the morning to attend chapel. To graduate, a student had to take three courses in religious studies.

Alina and her classmates were also part of another significant change. Young ladies were coming to McMaster in large numbers. They had been held back by social norms, financial constraints, and cultural traditions. Now, more and more, the girls in the family were given the same opportunities as the boys. By the 1960s, forty percent of McMaster students were women. Initially, these very bright girls were steered into nursing and teaching. But the male domains of engineering and physics soon had female members.

In 1960, Roy was able to drive to McMaster by himself in the Volkswagen Alice had bought him.

Alina was part of a carpool. She was so personable that three boys asked her to join their pool. The owner of the car was Bob Gauley. His brother Jack and Tony Dicenzo made up the other members—two Scotsmen, one Italian, and one Ukrainian. They had been classmates all the way through high school. Jack was brilliant in science and math and Tony was brilliant in languages. Alina and Bob accepted their help. Bob had been saving money since his childhood days when he had a paper route and picked fruit in Stoney Creek. He bought the 1951 Studebaker when he got accepted into McMaster.

Studebakers were made in Hamilton from 1947 to 1966. Steel was close and the American border was close. Bob's "Stude" had a few problems. The heating system had the habit of closing down unexpectedly. One window in the rear could not be fully closed. The shocks needed replacing—it was a bumpy ride. Every now and then when starting after a stop, the engine would cough and blue smoke would fill the air. But Bob loved the car and was always tinkering with it. Bob had a short-fuse about most things, but especially about his Stude. The passengers knew enough to keep their mouths shut. They also carried bus tickets.

Classes at McMaster began at 8:30 a.m. Alina was picked up by the Guys at 7:30 a.m. Bob was usually in a bad mood in the morning. Either the Stude was misbehaving or Jack was ragging him about something. Jack was an irrepressible tease. Sometimes he crossed the line. Alina liked being teased by Jack. It was a nice way of flirting. Tony was always ready by 7:45 a.m. He lived by Delta and had decided to become an intellectual. The first step would be to become an expert in the various teas. He bored the others by talking about how he went to an international tea shop in downtown Hamilton. Then he added to the boredom by describing how he brewed the different teas. The four of them were friends. Alina was a friend who happened to be a girl. Jack escorted her once to a McMaster dance. There were no romantic sparks. There was always lots to talk about in the morning once they woke up. Each of them had stories about the classes they were taking, although they had no interest in the studies of the other three.

McMaster, like all universities, had great chasms between the pedagogies. Alina always learned in a collegial manner. She and her six classmates were always together. All their projects were group projects. Since there were only seven students in the year, they were on close terms with their instructors. Seldom did they have individual assignments or tests. Because the faculties were just being set up and because the university was still relatively small, there were also small classes in geography and engineering, for example. The lab work was always done in groups or pairs. Students usually got the same marks.

Roy's experience was just the opposite. He went to lectures where there might be two hundred students. In third or fourth year, the classroom lectures might have only twenty-five students. In his four years of taking English, history, and economics, not a single professor ever knew his name. He handed in his essays, which were graded by grad students. In his last two years, Roy never knew anyone in his classes. At the end of the year, there were three-hour exams in the gymnasium. There was no interaction among students to test their ideas. They read their novels, books, and lecture notes and took exams.

Roy was beginning to do more work now. He was taking subjects he was interested in. As a teenager, he would sit on the veranda on Hope Street and read history books. He was fascinated by World War II. He read all six volumes of Churchill's history of the war. He read Allan Brooke's two volume history. He read General Slim's account of the war in Burma, Butcher's study of Eisenhower, and studies of De Gaulle and Rommel. He also read Field Marshall Montgomery's autobiography of the war.

When Alina and Roy were at Delta, there were about two thousand students. There was the same number of students when they went to McMaster. It was a very nice campus with lots of open space. At the back, there was a forest and a marsh. First year biology students did projects based on the plants and insects there. That area was also a courtship retreat. Students took walks arm in arm along the hiking trails. If the couples spent time necking, it was referred to as "watching the submarine races" in the marsh.

Roy was happy in the fall because he could play football and soccer. There was an intramural football league with the four teams based on years. Young men in the physical education program would lay out football equipment in the field house. First year students would scramble to get equipment. They might have thirty players. Fourth year students would be lucky to get fifteen players. The pants didn't fit; the shoulder pads didn't fit; the helmets didn't fit. There were even some leather helmets as a joke. The referees were students. Sometimes there were some short-lived fights, but generally, everyone had a good time. At the end of the games, all the equipment was thrown on the floor until there was a large pile of unsorted debris. The physical education students would throw the debris into a storage room until the next game. Each year, the student newspaper would select an all-star team. Roy made the team twice. That was quite an achievement for him because when he took his glasses off, everything was a blur.

The game that was more serious for Roy was soccer. He could wear his glasses and was the only player to do so. He had to be very careful when he headed a ball. He had played soccer in an organized league for two years when he was thirteen and fourteen. He rode his bike to the game at Mahoney Park. He hadn't played after that. But the McMaster soccer team didn't have enough players and an old friend from Delta remembered Roy's playing abilities from years before. So, Roy was talked into playing. It became a joy for him. It was a genuine intercollegiate team, playing against the University of Toronto, Guelph, and Western.

In January 1962, Roy was driving home when he saw a car pulled over on Main Street. Jack Gauley waved him over. Roy didn't know the people in the car well, but he knew them from Delta. Jack explained that Bob's Stude had broken down again. Roy offered the three passengers a lift. Jack, Alina, and Tony jumped in. There were a lot of funny stories about the Stude and Bob's temper. Tony got out first, then Jack. Roy was left with Alina in the front seat.

"What classes are you taking now?" Roy asked. He already knew she was in the Nursing Program.

"We're studying anatomy and chemistry," replied Alina. "Anatomy is quite interesting. We started by dissecting frogs. We all have a thick book about human anatomy. But luckily, there are no cadavers for us to study. The book has both female and male anatomies."

Alina turned red and wished she hadn't said that. She remained silent for a few minutes. Roy found that attractive.

"Chemistry is extremely difficult," said Alina. She didn't like long silences. "We have to take the same chemistry classes as the engineers, but we don't have to take the exam. We have a summary just for us nurses."

Alina continued to talk for the rest of the ride to her apartment. Roy was smitten. That was it. He knew her first name but not her last. Luckily, McMaster had a student directory. Roy didn't think there would be another Alina. He started on page one, going down the list of names. Alina Dubinsky was on page four. There was her address and phone number. The next evening, he phoned her for a date. She accepted.

Alina was quite nervous the following Monday morning. Her class was going to be in residence at the General Hospital for two weeks for practical training. Betta had made her daughter a larger-than-usual breakfast. Betta was always up early to make Alina her breakfast. If Mike was working days, she would make his too. Betta didn't say anything, but she didn't like Alina being away for two weeks. She always felt better with Alina in the apartment. Mother and daughter had a good relationship. They often talked for hours about unimportant things. Betta spoke in Ukrainian. Alina spoke in English. It was odd, but it worked. Last week, Alina's class had been measured for their uniforms. Today they would be wearing them. Alina would travel to the hospital on the Barton Street bus. Betta asked her for the third time if she had everything. Miss Reid had given all the students a list of what to bring and Alina had a new suitcase. Now she was anxious to get to the bus stop. It was an easy trip from her apartment on Barton Street to the hospital on Barton Street. The half-asleep passengers noticed Alina because the bus driver had to get out of his seat to help her with her suitcase. She found a double seat that was empty and heaved her suitcase up. At the hospital stop, she was able to carry the suitcase down the steps.

She was tired by the time she got to the nurses' residence. Miss Reid was at the front door to welcome her. Alina was one of the early ones. Once all the students were there, Miss Reid led them up the stairs to the second floor. They were all out of breath from carrying their suitcases. Miss Reid took them to the common room where they all found comfortable chairs and caught their breath. Miss Reid listed the roommates and the schedule for the day. She sent her students off and said their uniforms would be brought to them. Alina would be in the same room as Deborah. Deborah was in residence at McMaster so this was nothing new to her. Three of the students lived in Hamilton, one lived in Burlington, and three came from other places in Ontario. Alina did what Deborah did to get comfortable and organized. All the clothes were either hung up or put in drawers. There were two single beds. Miss Reid went from room to room to see if everyone was organized. She took the students by twos to the common bathroom down the hall. There were no bathtubs. The students would take showers.

Miss Alderson brought the uniforms around with the new pin-on name badges. She told them to put on their uniforms and get ready for a tour of the hospital. When the students emerged from their rooms, they were dazzling. The bright uniforms were almost shining. When the students saw themselves in mirrors, they were shocked at how good they looked. That brought colour to their cheeks and sparkle to their eyes. It was a moment when all of them looked absolutely beautiful. Their mission to help the sick and injured was confirmed. The group had an aura. Miss Reid and Miss Alderson were pleased. They had seen this many times over, but each time the transformation was full of joy. This made their mission in life so satisfying.

The tour of the hospital couldn't be completed before lunch, so the students were taken to the nurses' cafeteria. The working nurses looked at these students with some curiosity. All of the working nurses in the hospital had gone directly from high school into nurses' training programs. None had gone to university. Nurses who had worked for ten or twenty years didn't think much of students who thought they had become experts. There was a big difference between theory and practice. After lunch, Miss Reid broke the group into pairs. Two of the instructors at the hospital joined the group as guides. Alina and Jennifer were paired up and assigned to the fracture department. The instructor led them to the X-ray machine. She explained how different bones could be X-rayed. There were drawings of how to X-ray different possible bone fractures. Alina and Jennifer were shown a child being X-rayed. They were told again—for the third or fourth time—the danger of X-rays. They went to an adjoining room while the X-rays were being taken and they looked through a window. The instructor told them this would probably be a "greenstick" break. Children's bones tended to bend rather than break. To impress Alina and Jennifer, the instructor named the eight types of fractures. The technician came out to talk about the practical techniques of X-raying people. She showed them some X-ray plates and Alina and Jennifer puzzled over these blurry images. Reading X-rays was an art and a science combined. Experience was important.

After the afternoon tours, the students returned for dinner. They had a wonderful time relating their experiences. After dinner, they wandered into the common room and met a number of nurses in the hospital nurses' training program. They chatted and compared programs and instructors. The young women, who had been at the hospital for months, had some wonderful anecdotes to tell. Miss Reid, of course, wouldn't give the students a night off. Each pair had to write a five-hundred-word report on what they had learned. Jennifer wrote it for her team. Alina wasn't a good writer.

Starting the second week, the students would be working nurses. They would go to different wards where an experienced nurse would direct them. On Sunday, Miss Reid had to give the advice that embarrassed her. After some preliminary details about their work schedules, Miss Reid paused for a full minute. She began to blush noticeably. She told the students that when they had male patients, they should expect this. Some men would grab their breasts or bums. Some men would get erections, especially when they were being bathed. Ignore this behaviour, she said, if it can be ignored. If not, just walk away calmly and with all your dignity intact.

The ward work began on Monday. The students did a variety of tasks. Some supervising nurses were kind; some were miserable fault-finders. The students were exhausted after each day. They had many stories to tell over dinner. They had no homework during this week. In the evenings, they went to the common room to watch *The Beverly Hillbillies, The Dick Van Dyke Show*, or *The Donna Reid Show.*

In the second week, the students were introduced to the peep show. The student nurses in the other program had been in the hospital for months. They had been told about this tradition and now they were passing it along. The nurses' bedrooms on the second floor faced the men's ward on the third floor of the hospital. There was a fifty-yard grass courtyard between them. Once the nurses had made their final rounds in the men's ward, the students would turn on their bedroom lights, as if in a random and unplanned way. Then they would start undressing as if going to bed. A very innocent activity. The patients in the men's ward had a tradition of coming to the windows. That tradition had been passed on. Alina was embarrassed and a little scandalized. She hadn't thought young ladies could do this. She had trouble undressing in front of her roommate. She wanted to believe that all nurses were pure and virginal. After all, they were on a sacred mission.

Once, a young man who was being treated for a shoulder injury asked his parents to bring him his binoculars. That seemed like an odd request to them, but he said there was a nest of robins in the courtyard tree. The peep show came to an end when a very brazen young lady stood at the window bare-breasted. Most of the male patients loved it. But a retired minister whose bed was next to the window didn't. The hospital administrator and the director of the nursing program called all the students into the hospital auditorium. There was a very forceful lecture and then nightly surveillance. So, a tradition came to an end.

At the end of the week on the wards, the McMaster students learned nursing wasn't all lovely uniforms and grateful patients. It was patients who never stopped complaining. It was abrasive supervisors. It was men with three sets of hands. It was blood, vomit, piss, and shit. Now reality imposed itself upon their idealism. But Alina still loved it.

Roy was showing all the signs of growing up. His marks were high enough that he was in the honours English and History program. He didn't make any friends in his classes. He and Alina's friends were from high school and Alina's class. There were four couples that did things together. Three of the boys played on the soccer team, so in the fall, social events were linked to soccer games. All four couples were headed for marriage.

The soccer team was a random mix of players. Eligibility rules were very loose. Some well-known athletes in Ontario had university sports careers of eight or nine years. Players in law, medicine, or PhD programs kept playing. The strength of the McMaster soccer team was determined by the number of MA or PhD students who showed up on campus. The coach, Bill McNaughton, had to wait around patiently for five or six practices until word got around that there was a soccer team. For some reason, McMaster was getting graduates from the new "Red Brick" universities in Britain. These universities were a creation of the post-war Socialist Party of Clement Atlee. The grad students who joined the soccer team were all rabid socialists and great beer drinkers.

The soccer team practiced by scrimmaging every right. There were no drills or strategy sessions because each game had a different line-up depending on the course schedule of players. The soccer team had a room in the field house with its name stenciled on the door, but it shared the space with archery targets, tennis nets, and any sports debris that needed a temporary home. There were no lockers for the players. There weren't even enough benches for all the players to sit down at once. Water leaked out from the shower room and made the floor perpetually damp. The players had to live out of their gym bags.

Next door, the football players all had their own lockers. There were lots of benches and tables. There even was a sauna. There were blackboards and a screen for scouting films. The team had four coaches and three trainers. The equipment for two football players cost the same as the total budget for the soccer team. The Brits on the soccer team loved it. It gave them something to rail against. They saw football as an extension of American imperialism. They refused to use the term "soccer." The game was always "football." Practices started around four with two or three players. Other players showed up at random times and joined the scrimmage. By five o'clock, there might be an eight against eight game. The practice had to end by 5:45 p.m. Coach McNaughton was very strict about that. The players had to be changed by 6 p.m. Most of the players showered. It was a good workout. The Brits never showered. They hated water. They thought North American hygiene was another example of American imperialism.

The team had to get to the off-campus pub, Paddy Greene's, before 6:30 p.m. as Ontario liquor laws closed pubs between 6:30 p.m. and 7 p.m. The theory was that forcing men to go home saved marriages and families. Coach McNaughton was always the first to get there. The waiters allowed him to move tables and order beer. The rule was one patron, one beer. Six players, for example, could not have eight glasses of beer on the table. And they weren't allowed to move from one table to another with a beer in their hands. Last call was at exactly 6:30 p.m., although patrons were allowed another ten minutes to finish their drinks. Coach McNaughton and the players drank a lot quickly. If they wanted to continue socializing and drinking, they could move into the restaurant. Ontario allowed drinking with food after 6:30 p.m. McNaughton and a few players would order the standard meal—four slices of cheese and four soda biscuits. That would satisfy the law makers.

The team was an eclectic mix of nationalities and ages. Some were first year students. Half were post-graduate students. The team captain was in his final year of a PhD in physics. Playing for eight years gave him immense authority. The team was dominated by the Brits, but there were two Germans, three Scots, one Welshman (Roy), one black Kenyan on a missionary scholarship, and two Italians. They became fast friends. The team usually won more games than it lost. The bus trips were a huge amount of fun. There was an annual game against Niagara Teachers' College. In September, the Niagara coach would send Coach McNaughton his roster. It always included state all-stars. Crossing the border was a bit of a problem. The team never had more than two players who were born in Canada. The American border guards waved the bus through. They didn't want to examine fifteen passports from five or six countries.

The newcomers on the team were amazed to see cheerleaders at the game. They watched their opponents doing precise drills to a nice musical cadence. They were fit and energetic like two-month-old puppy dogs. They expected to run up a score against the rag-tag team from Canada. Of course, the two coaches and returning players knew differently. The McMaster players had started playing soccer when they were two years old. Soccer was their passion. They had consumed tactics from the time they were five. The result in the game was that the Americans ran and ran and ran. They ran until they were exhausted. The McMaster players made the ball do all the running. Long and precise passes had the Americans chasing their tails. Sometime in the second half, one of McMaster's badly overweight players asked to be taken out. He was an older chap in a science PhD program. When he got to the sidelines, he asked Coach McNaughton for a light and lit up a cigarette. When the Niagara team's bench (some twenty players) saw this, they went berserk. They screamed and pointed. Even the cheerleaders were pointing. The McMaster players were adults. They did their own thing.

After the game, which McMaster won, they were off to the all-you-can-eat smorgasbord in Buffalo. Another new experience for most players. Then off to the Stage Door strip club. Another new experience. The player on a missionary scholarship really enjoyed it. Back to the McMaster campus at 1 a.m.

Roy lived at home during his days at McMaster so he wasn't involved in most of the hijinks and pranks that university students do. The students in residence had the time and precedents for a lot of annual shenanigans. Roy was a participant in one well-publicized event—The Bed Push. The University of British Columbia and a university in the United States helped publicized events by adding wheels to beds and pushing them across a region. So, a bed frame was rigged up with four bicycle wheels and a circuitous route was planned.

Roy was welcomed because he had his Volkswagen. Runners would sprint about fifty yards, all the while pushing the bed, and then be picked up by car when the next runner took oever. The bed was moving along at high speed. Perhaps to avoid traffic or to add some adventure, the chief navigators put the bed on railway tracks for certain sections. Whoever was in charge of publicity certainly got the word out. The local newspaper, radio stations, and TV station did a segment on the event. The reporters for the McMaster paper went along with their cameras. Then McMaster hit the big time. A reporter from *Life* magazine was sent to cover the run. To dramatize the event, the reporter had the runners in a posed picture lifting the bed over a wire fence. Then he had them pushing the bed through two feet of snow. In the next edition of the magazine, there was a two-page photo report. According to the article, the first world record for a bed push was seventy miles in eight and a half hours.

This was beaten by another group who pushed a bed 105 miles in less than twelve hours.

The *Life* reporter wrote this: "The well-drilled team of nearly one hundred students from Hamilton, Ontario's McMaster University fitted a donated bed with bicycle wheels and set a record in endurance and perseverance by completing 317 miles in forty-three hours; in spite of being ruled off the highway by police, losing their way for six hours on a frozen lake, and having their bed hijacked by a rival group. The ultimate indignity came when two members of the team strayed onto the grounds of a mental hospital and were restrained there until someone was found who would vouch for them." The article also reported that McMaster won the hockey game 12-3. The article didn't mention how the students overwhelmed pubs along the way. Roy and his friends were a little tipsy. He was stupid enough to drive that way on roads he didn't know.

Two years later, for some reason, McMaster students planned another bed push to publicize an event. This time, the organizers put a toilet bowl on the bed and called it the Great Toilet Bowl Push. This was probably a copy of a crazy event at some American college. And, for some reason, the push was planned for the Simcoe area. The bed was moving along at high speed. The problem was that the route was on a major highway. The Ontario Provincial Police would have none of that. The bed was pulled over and three students were charged under the Highway Traffic Act. Roy, in his Volkswagen, got away. One of Roy's friends knew a family in Simcoe. They drove there. Roy got on the phone to McMaster. The student president told him the police were looking for a black Volkswagen. Roy and his friends stayed in hiding for three hours and then drove the backroads.

They had to stop for beer, of course. They found a pub in a small town. Roy and his three friends found a table. By unhappy coincidence, there was a table of Western students next to them. To begin with, everything was quite friendly, but then words were spoken. And more words. And some more beer was drunk. And then some loud words. Suddenly, both groups lunged for each other. Chairs and glasses were flying. Then Roy couldn't see anything. His glasses had been knocked off. He got down on his hands and knees under the table to find them. He found a pair. They weren't his. He found another pair. They weren't his. Finally, the third pair was his. He put them on and could see again. He left the other two pairs of glasses on the floor along with a scattering of gloves and toques. Roy had his vision restored just in time to see a sucker punch. One of the Western students was looking away and one of Roy's passengers blindsided him with a fist to the side of the face. The sound shattered the air. Roy was stunned by the brutality of it. Then they ran. Later, Roy would laugh about crawling around on his hands and knees as bodies and objects flew around. Three pairs of glasses on the floor proved the stereotype of near-sighted university students, but the blindsided punch always haunted him.

Sometime in the early morning, the Dean of Men got a phone call from the Simcoe detachment of the OPP. They asked if he would be willing to vouch for the McMaster Students. If so, they would be released under his supervision. The dean was a Baptist minister. He cultivated the appearance of a naïve and otherworldly man of God. In reality, he was a tough-minded pragmatist who knew the gritty side of life and faced it honestly. Getting three students out of jail was a minor event.

In 1962, J. Robert Oppenheimer was scheduled to give the Whidden Lectures at McMaster University. Roy was beside himself with excitement. He had read so many World War II histories, he knew all about Oppenheimer. When Roy was in Grade 9 at Delta, he skipped school to watch the McCarthy hearings on TV. He watched hour after hour as McCarthy droned on in his nasal voice and Roy Cohen whispered in his ear. McCarthy had a communist under every bed and he was determined to destroy people. The fact that Roy watched this when he was only thirteen did mark him as slightly eccentric. Roy rushed to get two tickets for the first lecture for himself and Alina. She didn't know who Oppenheimer was and didn't understand Roy's excitement. Roy knew all about the Manhattan Project. Only the United States had the resources to make a bomb like that. Oppenheimer was the physicist in charge. The Project involved scientists from all the democracies, including Canada. Canada provided much of the uranium. The project cost about two billion dollars and employed a hundred thousand people at various sites and in various capacities. They tested the first bomb on July 16, 1945, in New Mexico. The new president, Harry S. Truman, who hadn't known about the project when he was vice-president, had to decide if the two atomic bombs would be dropped on Japan. They were. History changed forever. Oppenheimer opposed the further development of atomic weapons. In 1954, he was stripped of his security clearance. He had always had friends who were Communists. He was an easy target in the McCarthy period.

Now, this historical figure was coming to little, old McMaster. Hamilton and McMaster were abuzz. The first lecture would be for the general public. The second lecture would be for mathematicians and scientists. In 1959, there were a series of lectures by C.P. Snow called, "The Two Cultures." He talked about the divide between the humanities and science. Oppenheimer was not only a physicist, he was a student of literature as well. In his first lecture, Oppenheimer would discuss the difference between the humanities and science as he saw it. Roy made sure that he and Alina got to the drill hall very early. They were still three quarters of the way back. Of course, the lecture was way over their heads. Oppenheimer made so many references to arcane knowledge that Roy was baffled. At the end of the lecture, Roy thought that Oppenheimer had said this; knowledge in the humanities is an accumulation of random and individual genius; science is the logical accumulation and transmission of facts. Of course, Roy was probably wrong. The one thing that really impressed Roy was that Oppenheimer said he didn't completely understand all of Einstein's theorems.

After the lecture, Oppenheimer graciously stayed around to answer questions. Roy and Alina made for the car. As they drove along, Roy thought about Oppenheimer. Roy was beginning to think he was quite intelligent. After all, he was in an honours program. That vanity ended with a thud. Oppenheimer had more knowledge and more intelligence in his baby finger than Roy had in his whole body. Then something happened that Roy would talk about for years. As he and Alina were driving east on Main Street, a car slowly passed them on the left. There, in the passenger seat, was J. Robert Oppenheimer. Roy was so excited, his hair almost caught on fire. Then, in one of Roy's most brazen and stupid actions, he followed Oppenheimer's car. The driver was letting Oppenheimer off at the Royal Connaught Hotel. Roy quickly parked his car. He hustled a reluctant Alina into the hotel lobby. Oppenheimer was at the reservation desk picking up the key to his room. Against Alina's protests, they followed Oppenheimer down the corridor. He went into the hotel bar. Roy peaked in. Oppenheimer sat on a bar stool all by himself having a drink. Roy couldn't get over it. The man who had changed history sat like some insignificant travelling salesman after a long day. The bartender had no idea whom he had served the drink to. At least Roy was wise enough to walk away. Later, he wondered what would have happened if he and Alina had walked into the bar and congratulated Oppenheimer on the lecture. As Alina and Roy walked back to the car, Alina wondered about this madman she was dating.

Roy was walking along one of the paths of McMaster between buildings in November 1962. One of his soccer teammates was walking towards him with a worried look on his face and a transistor radio held to his ear. Roy asked him what the matter was.

Hans said, "Don't you know? We could be dead in a few days."

Roy didn't know. He hadn't been watching TV. Hans quickly explained and continued on his worried way with the transistor radio glued to his ear. As more and more people on campus realized the situation, a certain apprehension grew. It was just like August 1939 when British citizens wondered if there would be another catastrophic war. Now it was different. Thanks to science, man could wage a nuclear war that would destroy the planet. Two ideologies and two men were testing the bounds of insanity. People were watching events on live TV. The Cuban Missile Crisis was being followed minute by minute. People around the world were beginning to stock food. Cuba had Russian missiles. President Kennedy said they had to be removed. Premier Khrushcher said he would put more there, and ships carrying missiles were heading to Cuba. In the final hours, Russian ships were heading towards American warships. It was feared that if the warships boarded or sank the Russian vessels, Khrushcher would order a nuclear attack and the United States would respond. End of planet. Luckily, there was a last-minute resolution and Kennedy was hailed for his resolution and brilliance.

That was the closest the world had come to a nuclear war. Nothing had stopped at McMaster. Things went on as normal. What could people do but carry on and pray? For the most part, Alina and Roy tried to avoid the people who were very upset and following events minute by minute. When the crisis ended, Roy admitted to Alina how worried he had been.

Roy was in one of his Friday afternoon lecture classes. That was always a difficult time. People wanted to get away. But there were also Saturday classes. Long weekends could be shut down by course selections. Near the end of the lecture, Roy looked up to see two excited faces at the small window in the door. It was two girls gesticulating wildly to get the attention of a friend in the class. Nothing could happen until the professor stopped speaking. When the professor stopped, the door swung open and there was a gush of exclamations. Kennedy had been shot. Sentences could hardly stumble out fast enough. Students were literally jumping up and down. Everyone on campus who could was running to TV sets. There were very few pedestrians by 4 p.m. Kennedy had been shot at 12:30 p.m. Central

Time in Dallas. Roy rushed to his car and turned the radio on. He had only half an hour before he had to pick up Alina. They were usually travelling home together now. When he stopped for Alina, he had the radio up loud, listening to news reports. Alina asked him to turn the radio off. She wanted to tell him about a crisis in one of her classes that day. Roy was very annoyed, but he did what he was asked. Roy was without news for almost forty minutes while he drove Alina home. He had the radio on again as he drove home. At home, the TV set stayed on almost continuously for three days. Alice and Peter were also very interested. They ate all their meals with the TV on, which was very unusual. Roy saw Lee Harvey Oswald shot on live TV. Millions of people didn't sleep as events unfolded. Between no sleep and weeping, there were many red-rimmed eyes.

At school, a few of Roy's classmates approached the professor of Shakespearean studies and asked him to cancel his class on Monday, the day of Kennedy's funeral. He asked what had happened. The students had to explain to him the significance of the events. He wasn't sure they should take precedence over the study of Shakespeare. He did agree, however. Roy watched the whole moving spectacle on Monday.

Roy was annoyed that Alina had no interest in the Kennedy assassination, history, or current events. Alina was annoyed that Roy never seemed interested enough and sympathetic about her problems. Roy had some brilliant professors in English, history, and economics. Most of them asked students to ingest huge amounts of knowledge. Some offered ideas that changed prejudices and opened closed minds. The real test of learning for McMaster students was the caldron of debate at Paddy Greene's. Students had no pub on campus. The great watering hole was about two miles away at Paddy Greene's. Students knew to the second how long it took to get there by car. Paddy's was an old and dirty place. The name went all the way back to 1906 and the first owner, Paddy Greene. He had come from Ireland in 1850 and owned several pubs before. He passed the pub along to one of his sons. Graduates looked back with fond memories on this decrepit building. In those days, all the pubs in Ontario were shabby, smoke-infused dens of iniquity for men. The tables were the standard, square-shaped, Arborite-topped monstrosities, supported by the thick centre leg made of chromed metal that had turned black from foot marks. The ash trays were inevitably filled to the top and spilling over. Greasy skins of pickled kielbasa often littered tables. Sometimes the waiters would wipe the beer glass rings off the table when new customers sat down—sometimes not. The chairs were those old-fashioned chrome pipe type, with semi-padded seats and back rests. Usually the corners were worn off the pads and a pale-yellow sponge stuffing stuck out. The floor was cheap tile, black and white, probably installed in the thirties. The pattern of wear revealed the habits of beer drinkers. The tiles leading to the washrooms were worn right through. The ceilings were the Victorian type—high and fancy—extending three feet down the walls where a hardwood edging finally drew the line. The high, proud ceilings didn't have it so good though. The place was always stinking with smoke and blue cumulus clouds at the ceiling almost seemed to threaten rain while yellowing the plaster.

Paddy's was divided into six main rooms which groups used to visit on various occasions. The soccer team always tried for the smaller inner room. There was some prestige in entering from the parking lot, walking right through the large room, and sitting down with a sense of ownership. Through an arched door was the ladies room. Men could enter this room if accompanied by a woman. Women could never enter the men's room. Sometimes after a practice or game, the team could go to the ladies room because players had girlfriends with them. Alina and Roy came together because Roy was driving Alina home most days. The common gathering had ten or twelve players and two or three girlfriends. The team liked going to the ladies room because it was so much cleaner.

On most nights, Paddy's started to fill up at about seven. It was a mixture of working men and McMaster students. When the Stanley Cup was on, the place ran out of chairs. Paddy's was the debating room where Roy saw various ideas thrashed out—politics, economic systems, history, psychology, and philosophy. Information imparted in the classroom had to withstand the analysis of beer-quaffing intellectuals. For a number of years, Roy had been a liberal and a Liberal. He found himself defending capitalism and entrepreneurship against the Brit socialists. Roy was always outnumbered. But the annoying thing for him was that the Brits knew their facts. They were very intelligent and most of them were born into working-class families. Usually, Roy got skinned. The Brits also hated the Americans because they claimed to have won World War II by themselves. Roy wasn't anti-American, but he could see their point of view. Any evening Roy looked around Paddy's, he could see McMaster students at various tables talking loudly and gesticulating. Beer-fueled debates. Occasionally, Roy left Paddy's skunky drunk and drove home. In those days, there weren't as many cars on the road.

For Christmas 1963, Roy presented Alina with an engagement ring. She accepted. They were in love and they were moved along by the inevitable stream of events. The three couples that were their best friends had set wedding dates. Two of Alina's classmates had just received engagement rings. Social norms were dictating behaviour. Students graduated from university and got married. That's what they did. In another decade, these social norms were challenged and rejected by many young people.

Alina knew that her father would be very angry when she announced her engagement. Her mother would be protective. The Evanses would be delighted. They loved the warm and personable Alina. They thought she had been Roy's salvation. She came to the Evanses home for dinners and casual visits. She talked and told them the plans she and Roy had formulated. Roy never confided in them.

Roy was never invited to the Dubinsky home. He picked Alina up at the front door and they left.

ROY EVANS

Roy wanted to become a teacher. That was ironic since he had been a terrible student. His former teachers at Delta, if they heard about it, would be surprised and dismayed. Good teachers hate bad teachers. Roy's school record did not suggest a dedicated teacher. Roy graduated from McMaster at the right time. The post-war baby boom was flooding the high schools in Ontario with students. School boards had trouble building schools quickly enough. Each spring, *The Globe and Mail* had two or three full pages of ads for teachers. The starting salaries seemed very good to Roy. In fact, his salary would be more than what most workers at Dominion Glass made. Peter was quite surprised when he saw what Roy could earn. If a university graduate had basic qualifications, he or she could get a job anywhere in Ontario. School boards had polite and restrained bidding wars for teachers. Alina and Roy thought they should move out of Hamilton to get an independent start.

The Great Cattle Auction, as it became known, was held at the Royal York in Toronto. The Royal York was the great aristocrat of railway hotels. Dotted throughout Canada were luxury hotels built by the great railway companies—the CNR and CPR. The wealthy could travel by rail in great comfort. Before adequate roads were built across the country, long-distance travel had to be by train. The same railroads that catered to the rich also transported "the huddled masses" from Europe. The accommodation was quite different. The Royal York was completed in 1929. It had twenty-eight floors and for a time, was the tallest building in Toronto and even the British Empire. Its design was based on the Chateau look. It was linked by a walking route to that other great edifice of the 1920s—Union Station. If a company was successful, it booked rooms at the Royal

York for its executives and sales force. Dinners and dances in its ballrooms were special events.

Roy and his friend Bill Jenkins were going there on May 10. They had circled the jobs that looked attractive in *The Globe*. Bill wanted to go to northern Ontario. He was an avid fisherman and hunter and he and his friends sometimes drove to northern Ontario to fish and hunt. It was a long journey from Southern Ontario. Bill thought it would be fun to live in fishing and hunting country. He had no girlfriend so he could go where he pleased. There was also a theory that beginning teachers should go north, make all the mistakes of new teachers up there, and then return better qualified. There were also many anecdotes about the drinking that went on in the north. Teetotalers would feel out of place.

Alina and Roy wanted to remain in Southern Ontario. Roy thought living in Toronto for a few years and enjoying the urban amenities would be great. Since many people had that idea, Toronto school boards had many applicants and could be more selective. Northern boards offered better salaries and were more aggressive pursuing applicants. In those days, an extra two hundred dollars could persuade teachers to change boards. Some teachers changed boards almost every year. The annual auction at the York was their recreation.

Roy and Bill were able to find street parking near the hotel. Each of them had the Saturday *Globe*. The headline story was about a plot to kill the American secretary of defence, Robert S. McNamara, when he visited Vietnam. Roy and Bill agreed that the U.S. should get out of Vietnam, but apparently, Lyndon Baines Johnson didn't agree. The lobby of the York was full of tables with board representatives. It looked as if the wealthier boards could pay extra money to get a lobby position. There were placards for Scarborough, York, Peterborough, and so forth. There were three or four genial representatives behind each table with printed handouts about salaries and benefits. The representatives were principals and superintendents with the power to hire teachers. The joke was that they took the pulse of an applicant, and if he or she were alive, they were hired. Bill and Roy took the handouts from several boards and chatted briefly with the representatives. They were so happy. It was nice to feel wanted. There was almost a feeling of arrogance. Near the elevators, there was a large display board with the names of all the other boards and the hotel rooms where they were set up. Bill noted the northern boards. Roy looked at the boards in Southern Ontario. They agreed to meet for a late lunch at 1 p.m.

Roy visited a number of hotel rooms. He found it a little disconcerting to see hiring teams sitting in front of a bed. Roy wasn't sure about Bill, but he wanted to find a job today. He wanted one big decision in his life settled. After about two hours of visiting different rooms, he saw a sign for Thorold District School Board. He thought Thorold was just north of Toronto—a perfect place. The board representative was the principal and he seemed friendly enough—Roy had been terrified of his principal at Delta. By now, Roy was tired of looking. He was like a person looking at cars, or boats, or houses day after day. Then the time comes when there is an impetus to end the speculation and choose. Roy chose Thorold. The principal was delighted. Principals were judged by how well they could staff a school. The important thing was numbers not quality. Although Roy's paper qualifications were good, he was hired after a fifteen-minute chat and the principal was pleased with himself.

Bill was having a wonderful time talking to the representatives of northern boards. Once he questioned them, they all said the fishing and hunting in their areas were superb. A few touted the curling facilities, but Bill didn't know what curling was. Bill wasn't anxious to sign. He wanted to come again next week to this wonderful event. The northern representative also wanted to come again. They had all-expense paid weekends. Sometimes they brought their wives. They attended plays and musicals and went to the best restaurants Toronto had to offer. The men by themselves enjoyed the bars in the hotel. The northerners enjoyed meeting, drinking, and telling anecdotes. Often, they were helped to the elevators and their rooms. There was a rumour that during hiring season, the price of sex workers went up in Toronto.

Over lunch, Bill told Roy about all the job offers he had had. He was coming again next week and would make a decision. Roy said he had signed for Thorold and would wait for the legal signing date to be official. Bill explained to Roy that Thorold was not north of Toronto but attached to St. Catharine's. Roy was hired by a Principal who knew nothing about him, and Roy took a job for a city that he didn't know the location of.

Now with his teacher's contract, Roy could go to summer school in Toronto for his teacher's training. Six weeks would make him a highly competent teacher.

Meanwhile, Alina's nursing professors at McMaster had found her a summer job at Mount Sinai Hospital on University Avenue in Toronto. Alina and Roy would have to find a summer home in Toronto and a place near Thorold for the fall. Alina would also have to find a nursing job in the Thorold area.

Chapter Twenty

Ontario 1964

Alina had enjoyed working summers at the ladies' dress store at the Centre Mall. It was an easy bus ride from her apartment. She would start in May and finish in September. She loved interacting with the customers and staff. The wages were minimal, but she had no great need of money. Sometimes she would walk up to the Evanses house on Hope Avenue. Alice and Peter loved her. She was so much better than their monosyllabic and private son. Alina told them all the details about the wedding and the immediate plans that she and Roy had. They were delighted to have her as a daughter-in-law.

The store was very much a school of life for Alina. The regular staff were older women. The only other young salesperson was Rita. Alina and Rita became very good friends. Rita was very earthy and blunt and a good antidote to Alina's naiveté. Rita would be her maid of honour. Several times, Rita and her boyfriend had double-dated with Alina and Roy. But as the wedding grew closer, Alina became agitated. One day, Rita found her in the storeroom sobbing. At the end of the day, Rita took her to a nearby restaurant in the mall, thinking she had pre-wedding jitters. Finally, after seven years, Alina told someone about the incident with the cab driver. She was overcome with self-criticism and guilt. She told Rita that she sat on the couch because she didn't want to offend him.

Didn't want to offend him?

"Didn't want to offend him?" Rita cried. "That son of a bitch! That's how we're taken advantage of! Being nice can make you a victim. You should have scratched that bastard's eyes out! You should have kicked him in the balls!"

Rita's voice kept rising until everyone in the restaurant was looking at her. Rita was so angry, she walked over to a table where two men were eating and yelled, "What are you looking at?"

They remained silent. Alina was bright red. The manager stuck her head out of the kitchen.

Rita slowly cooled down. But occasionally, she snorted. Then she said, "That was a long time ago. Why think about it now?"

Alina looked at the table. She said she should tell Roy, but she was ashamed.

Rita almost started up again. She waited for a few minutes until she could speak calmly.

"Alina," she said, "you are so naïve. And that's good. Most women have been assaulted in some way. The worst case is rape. But many women are physically assaulted. Most have had their asses grabbed in an elevator. Some have had their breasts accidentally brushed at a party. This is my advice. Don't feel guilty because you were an innocent girl who got assaulted. Don't tell Roy. Always be nice to men because they can be useful creatures. And I like men, but kick any man in the balls that tries something funny."

Alina and Rita sat for another hour until they both felt better. The two men ate quickly and left. The waitresses relaxed. Walking to the car, Alina and Rita were so giddy, they almost seemed drunk. They began to sing in full throat, "Kick him in the balls! Kick him in the balls!"

The older ladies at the store gave Alina practical life advice. They debated the advantages of renting or owning a home and taught her about interest rates and mortgage payments. There were many debates about child raising. Should diapers be cloth or disposable? Rita was disgusted by the thought of dirty diapers. As a nurse, Alina had seen a lot of worse sights. One woman had a religious commitment to breastfeeding. She considered bottle feeding a baby irresponsible. It meant the mother thought more about herself than her baby. There was another dust-up about the use of soothers. Let the baby cry. Don't jam a rubber stopper into its mouth. There was no consensus about toilet training. Regular feedings or food on demand? Alina thought that if she had children, she would have to think about these matters.

The women tried different makeup styles on Alina. She was their pet and her affability made them embrace her. Of course, they had to instruct Alina on how to deal with men and husbands in particular. One woman was divorced. She frequently gave Alina an earful about how shitty men were. The other ladies tended to look down on stay-at-home wives. They thought that made them docile, subservient to their husbands. Working women changed the household equation. Husbands had to do more childcare and housework. Women with their own money had a sense of independence. Alina wondered about that. In the ethnic communities she knew, the husband was still the lord and master. Sons were more important than daughters. Alina realized that when her parents encouraged her to go to university, they were quite progressive. She thought about some of the girls in the church who had the equivalent of arranged marriages.

The women in the shop gave their approval to Roy. They thought he was pleasant. He was not likely to be aggressively dominant. He could certainly never be a wife-beater. Cecelia, one of the senior sales ladies, had a lot to say on the subject of wife-beating. Her friend and neighbour had to endure frequent beatings. She always lied to Cecelia about how she got the cuts and bruises. Finally, she confessed to Cecelia. One day, when the husband was working, Cecelia and her husband took her friend and her two children to Cecelia's in-law's home in Guelph. The parents were delighted to have two new grandchildren. When the wife-beating husband came storming over to Cecelia's, she feigned shock and surprise. She told him his wife was a terrible person. When the man left, Cecelia and her husband laughed so loudly, they were afraid he would hear. Cecelia, on pledges of secrecy, told the women in the immediate neighbourhood what had happened. The wife-beater became a figure of scorn and silent ridicule. But he was too stupid to know it.

On Alina's last day, the employees had a small shower for her when the store closed at 9 p.m. They bought a cake for her from a bakery at the mall and smuggled in bottles of wine. They wanted a party. Once they had their glasses of wine, they sat Alina on a chair in the middle of the floor. Then they wheeled out a cart with presents on it. They were a combination of nice gifts and joke gifts. The first box she opened had a beautiful blouse. Then there was a summer sweater. Next was a book on how to survive on five dollars a day, then a toy whip to keep Roy in line. Then a very sexy black negligee. Alina blushed. They loved making the sweet and virginal Alina blush. Then a survival cookbook. The final gift was a book covered in a brown paper wrapper. She opened the wrapping to find a book titled *The Twenty Best Sex Positions*. Alina turned bright red. When Rita said she should turn to pages ten and eleven because she knew they were the best positions, Alina was so red, she gave off heat.

* * *

Roy's final shift at Dominion Glass was on June 15, 1964. He had worked summers there for the last nine years. He was only sixteen when he worked his first summer and now he was twenty-four. He wasn't sentimental, but he felt the sadness that final goodbyes engender. He had bought wallets for the department's supervisor and his foreman. Those final handshakes revealed mutual respect. The supervisor wrote a very warm letter for Roy. Peter could never understand the affection and respect that his son had at work. At home, he could be obnoxious.

Peter and Roy had always had a difficult relationship. When Peter arrived in 1947, Roy had already had a surrogate father in Mr. Hughes. He had always indulged Roy. Now this stranger imposed some discipline. The family story was that Roy used to blubber, "Why don't you go back to the Army?" The interesting parallel was that David and Mike also had a difficult relationship. Millions of families were in similar situations after World War II, which gave psychologists a lot of case studies for better understanding the effects of sons being separated from their fathers for a long period of time and being raised by their mothers. They also had millions of case studies for families whose fathers never came home.

Roy thought of his summers at Dominion Glass as a good time. His job in the test room was easy. When he was sixteen, he could ride his bicycle to work. After work, he and his friends would ride their bikes to Van Wagner's Beach or the nearby fruit orchards to steal fruit. Roy went to every Tiger Cat game he could. He and his Delta buddies played pick-up baseball. When he was nineteen and Alice bought the Volkswagen, Roy began dating. He went to a few parties with Dominion Glass girls. He had his heart broken in his first year at McMaster. Then he met Alina and they could drive places. Shift work allowed him to go to the Downtown YMCA during the day where he played handball and jogged on the steeply banked track above the gym.

Roy thought about his days in the plant. When he first arrived there, there were two test room foremen who were World War I veterans. The one man was very distinguished. He was tall and straight and had a military moustache. The rumour was that he had been an officer—perhaps a captain. Nobody knew because he didn't talk to anyone. He was cold, even angry, always. He seemed to feel that his job was beneath him and he felt his superiors were not as good as him. The other foreman was just a tiny man. He was about five foot four and a hundred pounds. His assistant foreman was a six-foot-four redhead who had boxed recreationally for a time. They were an interesting pair. The foreman didn't eat much and always threw the orange his wife packed for him to the redhead. Because Roy was scheduled where there was an opening, he worked for both these foremen and the other two as well.

Roy read a lot of history books sitting on the veranda on Hope Street. Later on, he wished he had talked to these gentlemen about World War I. In 1956, he was young and these men seemed old. In fact, they were probably in their early sixties. Not very old at all. Roy remembered two anecdotes from the little man, whom Roy really liked. He was stationed in Belgium with the Canadian army. He said that when they entered a town, the billeting officers would walk down the streets, inspect homes, and assign troops. He didn't know if the civilians were recompensed, but they certainly couldn't say no. Of course, the Germans did exactly the same thing. He did know the Canadians shared their rations and even scrounged up extra food for their hosts. But Bill Gale (our little man) still felt guilty about this.

The other anecdote Bill told Roy was about returning to Canada. All the troops on the Western Front were infected with lice. The soldiers in the trenches said the lice were worse than the rats. Soldiers had bleeding sores where the lice bit and laid their eggs. When the war ended in November 1918, the Canadian government started bringing troops home. Bill's regiment got its notice. The whole regiment went to a de-lousing facility. Once naked, the soldiers were dusted with a white powder that had disinfecting chemicals. Bill said they dusted his hair and even his privates. He still blushed about it. The soldiers rubbed the dust out of their eyes and proceeded to tubs full of very hot water. Their uniforms were put into gyrating washing machines with soap and hot water. After their baths, the soldiers put on their damp uniforms and marched to the nearby barracks. Bill said they damn-near froze.

They sailed over to England from Antwerp. On arrival in England, they were de-loused again. It was much the same procedure. After a week in barracks, the soldiers sailed for Canada. Bill's regiment was dismissed from service in Toronto. Bill got the train back to Hamilton and moved in with his sister and her husband. On the following Sunday, his sister made a huge dinner to celebrate his return. The whole family was at the extended dinner table. He was just about to take his first bite when he got a hell of a bite on his neck. One louse had followed him from Belgium to Canada. Bill said with glee that he caught the louse, squeezed him to death with his fingers, and then stomped on him on the floor. Bill started to laugh at this point. He said some of his relatives moved away from the table and didn't finish their meals. Bill ate heartily. He was used to lice biting him.

Roy also had a foreman who was a World War II veteran. The plant had many veterans. Later on, Roy was struck by the fact that the veterans never talked about the war. Meanwhile, he was reading book after book about World War II, and the film studios in England and Hollywood churned out scores of films about the war.

One summer, Dominion Glass didn't have room for him in his regular job, so he was sent to the decorating room. Here, pop bottles were painted with their logos. There were two machines. The supervisor put solid blocks of paint into heating pots on the tops, then the paint would melt and flow down to the printing mechanism. Women sat on stools with backs, and as the bottles came down a conveyor belt, they would grab a bottle and insert it into an opening. The machine would take the bottle and spin it through the painting process. The women would then take the bottle with their left hand and put it in a box. The women were like mechanical additions to the machine with the constant repetition of right hand, left hand, right hand, left hand, from conveyor belt to box, over and over again. The women took this job because they were on a kind of piece work, bonus system. If things went smoothly, they could make good money. Roy was given the job of putting pop bottles on the conveyor belt to one machine. If the bottles were packed upside-down in the packing house, the task was easy. Roy just flipped the box of bottles over onto the conveyor belt and straightened them with his arm. If the bottles were packed right side up, Roy had to grab four bottles at a time and place them on the belt. Often, he couldn't keep up. The women would swear and curse at him. He was costing them money.

Another job in that department that Roy did was put bottles on a conveyor belt into a machine that bathed them in a corrosive mixture that gave the glass a slightly rough surface and an attractive misty look. He was doing this job with another young man one shift, and they had trouble keeping up with the belt. The young man kept yelling at Roy to speed up. Roy thought the young man was a regular employee because his technique was so good. Roy was absolutely exhausted at the end of the shift. When their eight hours were up, Roy spoke to the young man for the first time. He said he was a medical student at the University of Toronto. Roy was furious. The slave driver had been a fellow student.

The interesting thing about that for Roy was that after a week of hard labour, when he fell into bed, he got used to it. By the second week, he was back running laps and playing handball at the YMCA.

Roy thought about the continuous and endless motion in the factory. Everything began with the continuous flow of molten glass. To feed the furnaces with silica, there were railway cars loaded with fine sand. The cars moved along railway tracks, and then the sand was unloaded on conveyor belts that took the raw materials for glass above the furnace. The chemists and engineers controlled the flow into the furnace. The amount of molten glass in the furnaces had to be carefully controlled. The molten glass became bottles that moved down long conveyor belts. When Roy was in the decorating room, he fed two conveyor belts. The visual reality of men and women being chained to conveyor belts was captured perfectly by Charlie Chaplin in his film, *Modern Times*, made in 1936. Charlie's character couldn't keep up with the conveyor belt and eventually, he was sucked into huge wheels that powered the operation. Modern man. Before industrialization, there was the natural cycle of the day and the seasons. Mother nature was replaced by machines that never stopped. Nature's natural cycles were destroyed. Roy had a nightmare where he was on the decorating room conveyor belt. The woman on the paint-decorating machine picked him up by his head and placed him in the machine. The machine spun him around and the hot paint was stamped onto his chest. He was spun out of the machine, and the woman placed him in a box. He had Coca-Cola written in white paint across his chest. His chest hurt like hell. Then he failed the quality control check. Roy woke up in a nightmare sweat.

Chapter Twenty-One

Ontario 1964

As Peter Evans walked back from the packing house towards the front end, the noise and heat increased until his body felt assaulted. He had made his final inspection for the shift and now he would take a final stroll around the front end to make sure there were no problems. Peter was a lehrman. The lehrs took red hot glass down to the temperature that allowed it to be packed in boxes. The process allowed the glass to be properly annealed or cured. The test room boys would sometime put micrometers on a bottle at the front end. Often, they exploded. One of the hijinks in the test room with new employees was to sneak an unannealed bottle into the bottles being tested. The poor chap might pick up a bottle and have it explode in his hands. The lads would kill themselves laughing. The annealing process could be so carefully engineered that tricks could be demonstrated. A person could take a pop bottle and smash a potato with it. Then the person would remove the cork at the top, drop a ball-bearing in, and the bottle would explode. There was a machine in the test room that could check the annealing. That was part of Roy's job. He never worked on his father's shift so he never checked his father's work. Over a number of years, Peter had the best record of all four lehrmen. If fires went out on the lehrs or wind gusted down the lehr, a great deal of ware would have to be thrown out.

Peter was happy in his job. Most of the time, things were pretty routine. Peter never wanted to be part of the stress and frenzy of being an operator or foreman at the front end. Perhaps because he was forty-three when he started at Dominion Glass, perhaps because he had little education, perhaps because he had no initiative—perhaps, perhaps. Peter did only his job and was satisfied with that. For over a hundred years, the Industrial Revolution had taken farm boys and enticed them to work in the hell of factories. It is a test of the human animal to adapt. Peter wanted to be back on a farm in Wales. He was trapped. Yet he was cheerful. He was a pleasure to work with. He always had a smile or a joke. One of his great joys was following the lehrs into the packing house. There he flirted with the women packing bottles. Usually, they enjoyed his appearance. These poor women had to stand in front of the conveyor belt coming from the lehr and check the ware. If a bottle had a flaw, the light would reflect off it. They would take four or five bottles and spin them on their arms. With practice, they could catch the flaws. It was backbreaking work, but somehow, they got used to it. Their pay was better than most jobs for women in the community. They were unionized factory workers. With this type of back-breaking labour, many women left after a short time. Some of them didn't like wearing the mandatory grey overalls. They were very unflattering. The younger women would enhance their coveralls by rolling up the sleeves and putting darts in the bust line so that the uniforms were drawn tightly across their chests. Some romances did blossom in the packing room, but not many.

One of the interesting women in the packing house was Pat MacRae. She was a union steward—a very outspoken steward. She would bend anyone's ears about working conditions and what the union should do. The poor president of the union had to listen to her day in and day out. She always advocated strike to show the company who was boss. She was also a demented Tiger-Cat fan. Every time the Cats lost, she became volatile. One time, Peter made the mistake of teasing her the day after a loss. She picked up a gallon jug and threw it at him. The jug shattered all over the floor. Other women and floor boys who saw it gasped and then started to laugh. Peter made a diplomatic retreat. The foreman of the packing house made a new procedural dictum. Nobody was to come close to Pat after the Tiger-Cats lost.

All these workers suffered the depredation that came from shift work. Three shifts kept the factory going continuously. At Dominion Glass, the shifts were eight to four, four to twelve, and twelve to eight. The steel companies went from seven to three, three to eleven, and eleven to seven. Each company thought its system was superior. In Hamilton, in the summer heat, workers scarcely got any sleep on the twelve-to-eight shift. Very few people had air conditioning. The four to twelve shift meant no sports or social activities. Perhaps church people thought it was blasphemous to work on Sunday. But Hamilton industries didn't worry about that. Ten or twelve years after Peter started work at Dominion Glass, the union negotiated the forty-hour week from forty-eight hours. Most factories in Hamilton had introduced that improvement for the workers. That was a huge betterment for the workers without affecting company profits. Peter came from a farm, but he remembered the Welsh coal miners working from seven to seven, six days a week. Some entered the mines when they were ten. Of course, on the seventh day, they went to church.

Peter had never been interested in sports and by the time he came to Canada, he was too old. He wasn't a fisherman or a hunter. Other men on his shift arranged fishing and hunting trips, but Peter was never part of that. Two organizations helped his social life. The union organized the Dominion Glass Social Club. The members met about once a month for a dinner. Later, the group had enough money to rent a small hall. It was a good place to socialize and drink beer. The other organization was the new Royal Canadian Legion on Barton Street. Alice didn't approve of beer drinking so Peter had to be discreet. Baptists could do uninhibited square dancing, but beer drinking was forbidden. Mostly, Peter was a homebody. In the winter, he watched TV. In the summer, he sat on the steps of his veranda and watered the lawn with a garden hose.

Now Peter was being teased at work because his son was marrying Mike's daughter. Everyone knew that Mike wasn't happy. Some of Peter's co-workers suggested he should take a self-defense course. He should learn ju-jitsu for when Mike attacked him. Perhaps he should start carrying a gun or at least a knife. He should be careful walking around the front end. He might find a gob of molten glass going down his shirt. After the four-to-twelve shift, he should walk to the bus with a partner. He should learn Ukrainian and join St. Vladimir's church. One of the Ukrainians in the front end even offered to teach Peter Ukrainian. One of the Ukrainian ladies in the packing house offered to show Peter how to cook borscht, pierogies, or holubtsi. People on Peter and Mike's shift were really amused by the situation. Peter and Mike were so different. Peter tried to take all the teasing in good humour, but he was becoming increasingly irritated. Like most of this type of teasing, it went on too long, and it was no longer funny.

The red-hot glass was banging into the steel barrels with a crash that could be heard above the din of the machines. Small, misshapen caricatures of Coke bottles were wheeling out on the conveyor belt like drunken soldiers marching back to barracks after leave. Some bottles were four squat inches, some were the regular height but had no shoulders, some were a perfect half, some had twisted necks as if seized by an evil spirit. The cutting shears on the feed from the furnace had lost a restraining spring and the timing was sometimes too fast and sometimes too slow, like a watch with sand caught in it. The operator panicked when he saw the first bottles come out of the blanks. He screamed for the assistant operator to grab the bottles and throw them into the barrel. When all six heads began to send out evil little incubuses, he realized the malfunctioning was affecting the whole machine. He slid under the machine to check the forced air hoses, banging his head in the process and getting hot oil on his cap and shirt. He came back up screaming and cursing so loudly, the assistant operator ran for more barrels to get out of the area, while deformed shapes splattered on the floor and sent clouds of burnt oil into the air. The operators on adjoining machines came over to help, both pointing upwards at the feed line. They could see the blobs were falling at different speeds and sizes. There was a moment of indecision as all three operators looked at the feed line and shears. The indecision was broken by a sudden shout from behind that rose above the machines and made the operators freeze.

"Stop the fucking feed! You fucking assholes! The shears are broken!"

Mike Dubinsky's red face bulged from his shirt collar like a tomato in a press. His eyes were wide. Spittle frothed at both sides of his mouth. His right hand pointed insistently at the shears and his left-hand banged tongs rapidly against his thigh. The two helpful operators scurried back to their own machines, leaving their colleague to withstand the whirlwind. Everyone at the front end knew Mike's demonic beating of his thigh with the tongs. They knew then he had lost control. Twice in the last five years, he had gone from banging his thigh to leaping at the unfortunate workers and shaking them by the throat.

"You fucking idiot! Couldn't you see the feed line? How could you be so fucking stupid?"

The operator just kept staring at the shears. He didn't respond. He had worked with Mike for ten years. He knew that when Mike exploded, it was better to stay silent. He would gaze at some fixed point while Mike ranted; then he would do what Mike demanded. It was humiliating, but he could accept it. After all, he sometimes screamed at assistant operators or mould men. Replacing the shears would be expensive, however. The machine would lose at least two hours of ware, maybe more. So much for the production bonus this week. There was no way he could leave this problem for the next shift. Now, after the panic and the screaming, the solution was simple, if expensive. He and Mike would get a new shears kit, dismantle the old one, and replace the unit.

The operator hurried over to the area between the two furnaces where a steel ladder was stored. He grabbed the ladder and hustled back in a disjointed two-step dog-trot, banging it twice into running machines. Mike was now grabbing the misshapen Coke bottles and hurling them angrily into the barrels. Now there were three or four assistant operators filling barrels and wheeling them out to the hot ware chute. The assistants kept their caps down to avoid Mike's eyes and to give themselves the illusion of being hidden. Normally, those three were full of good humour and horseplay, but now they behaved like dogs that had just been whipped and expected another whipping at any moment. Mike's temper generated so much psychic energy. Operators on both furnaces had suddenly become circumspect and unsmiling. Their sixth senses could feel the tension in the air like the summer atmosphere before a storm. Even people in the packing house knew there was some volcanic explosion, although they didn't know where or why.

As the operator approached his machine, Mike literally leapt towards him, seized the ladder, and rammed it up thorough the support beams. He would do the fucking job himself. An assistant operator had brought the shears kit and scurried away. Mike was at the top of the ladder in an instant. He smashed the feed line closing lever with his gloved hand. The rivulet of molten glass stopped immediately. Mike's hand came away with the glove burned black and smoky. In his rage, Mike was breaking plant safety rules. After a hand signal from the operator, an assistant had stopped the machine. Now there was a small pocket of silence surrounded by the usual cacophony—a little foxhole of silent tension as the usual battle raged all around. The operator would rather have been in the noisy battle than stranded in this foxhole with his demented commanding officer. Mike banged his smoking glove against his pants to extinguish the embers, then he signaled for a wrench. The operator grabbed a wrench from his toolbox and held it at shoulder height with a quizzical expression. He himself had replaced shear kits many times. He expected Mike's acquiescent nod. Instead, Mike slid down the ladder, pushed the operator aside, grabbed two other wrenches from the toolbox, and mounted the ladder again, cursing all the while. The operator felt his oil-soaked shirt sticking to his chest where Mike had pushed him. Mike's thrust on his chest had moved him back a step. The shock and pain of the movement had stunned the operator. But before he could respond, Mike had been back up the ladder. That physical jolt had almost made the operator instinctively retaliate with a punch. Luckily, his slow response probably saved him.

Mike was rapidly removing the bolts from the broken shears kit. Sweat was pouring down his face and his shirt had a dark river flowing between his shoulder blades. Eight of the ten bolts had come away easily, falling with a clonk on the rubber mat placed on top of the steel lattice floor. But the ninth bolt was bent. The motion of the shears had torqued the bolt into a U shape. Mike would have to cut it. With large sawing motions, he signaled to the operator for a hacksaw. The operator noticed that Mike continued to curse during this whole pantomime. He had never seen Mike this angry for so long. He advanced the hacksaw like a timid child offering a horse sugar cubes. Both hope to escape with their hands unharmed. Mike grabbed the hacksaw and the motion freed the wrenches from his belt and they clanged to the floor. As he turned his back, Mike jabbed his forefinger at the wrenches. The operator knew that meant, "Get those fucking wrenches or I'll break your fucking neck!" Within seconds, the wrenches sat in the operator's belt, awaiting Mike's next order. Even the wrenches seemed a little cowed. Mike cut the bolt with a violent sawing and pushing motion. As the bolt dropped away, he threw the saw straight down. The operator watched the saw bounce twice crookedly and then lie vibrating as if in pain. Mike then twisted his wrist rapidly. The operator flew up the first four steps of the ladder with both wrenches professed like sacrifices to the angry god. Mike's mouth continued to work as he took the wrenches and turned to the last bolt. Mike supported the shears kit with his left hand as he removed the bolt. When the shears kit foolishly jammed between two steel support rods, Mike heaved the whole apparatus away with a violent tug and let it smash to the floor. The expensive kit lay scattered across the floor as if hit by an artillery shell—from precision to junk in an instant.

Mike didn't move from the ladder or look at the wreckage. He signaled for the new shears kit by moving his fists sideways across his chest, duplicating the movement of a man with hand shears. The operator carried the new unit up the ladder and handed it to Mike. Mike took the unit without a nod of thanks. He braced his thighs against the ladder, arched his back to gain position, and placed the unit in supporting brackets. He set and tightened the bolts at either end of the unit. Twice he dropped bolts and the operator had to scamper to retrieve them and carry them up the ladder. Mike's entire shirt was now soaking wet. The beads of sweat on his face were now continuously flowing rivulets. As he wiped the sweat out of his eyes, he smeared his forehead and eyelids with grey oil, which seeped into his eyes and made him blink rapidly. Then he wiped his eyes and deposited more oil. Luckily for the operator and any hapless bystander, the shears unit fit into place. Mike just had to attach the motor arm and the unit would be set. Again, all went well. Mike signaled for the glass flow to resume so he could test the timing. Once again, the lava came down the chute. The new shears cut the lava into golden-red gobs that fell into barrels manned by the assistant operator who had come out of hiding. Mike had moved several steps down the ladder to time the shears with his stopwatch. The shears should cut ninety-two times per minute. The speed and diameter of the flow and the speed of the shears were engineered to produce a blob of hot luminescent silica that would become a Coke bottle.

Mike had just stepped off the ladder to signal the start-up of the machine when there was a sharp sizzling sound like cold meat hitting a hot frying pan. At the same time, there was a sudden flare-up of yellow-red light. Mike looked up to see the shears frozen shut. The molten glass was piling up on them. Then, as Mike watched, frozen by both anger and despair, a large round glob dropped with a thud and spread angry sparks into the barrel. Mike's body became rigid as he saw the shears warp and bend under the weight and heat of the molten glass. He screamed for the operator to stop the flow. The operator leapt up the ladder and stopped the flow again. As he stepped off the ladder, Mike almost bowled him over with his shoulder. He grabbed the twelve-foot ladder and hurled it to the steel lattice floor. The sound was like a car crash. He turned and kicked the half-full barrel, knocking it over and scattering viscous glass across the floor. He suddenly stopped, frozen with his feet apart, and stared at the shears. He started to swear and curse, using every profane and blasphemous expression lodged in his mind. The expressions in both English and Ukrainian flowed like some eruptive river of lava. He stood like that for two full minutes, his neck arteries exposed like rubber tubing, spittle arching from his mouth. The operator and assistant operator just watched, unconsciously shuffling backwards.

Slowly, Mike's vehemence burned itself out. He wearily turned to the operator and made the shears gesture. The operator leapt to get a new unit from the machine shop, happy to be doing something out of Mike's range. The assistant operators rushed to sweep up the glass, empty the barrels, and recede into the machinery. Mike slowly lifted the steel ladder and set it up again. Now he was tired. He had drained himself physically and emotionally. His eyes were red. He shivered in his sweat-soaked clothes in the 110-degree heat. He felt a lassitude that was new to him. For the first time, he realized he was sixty years old. If he had been rational in this moment, he would have understood that he was dangerously dehydrated. He always cautioned his shift to drink lots of salt-infused lemonade made by the factory nurse, but he hadn't drunk anything for five hours. Rational introspection would also reveal his unrelenting preoccupation with the strike vote and the wedding.

When the operator returned with the new shears, he knew the storm was over. The pocket of turbulence and rage in the front end had been replaced by calm and quietude. Mike was moving economically and deliberately. There was no longer an uncontrollable agitation animating his features and movements. There was a sense of acceptance and intelligence. The mechanical beast could not be bettered by rage alone. Mike's weariness made him better. He climbed the ladder, installed the unit, and had it working perfectly within half an hour. Pristine Coke bottles appeared on the conveyor belt twenty minutes later. The machine had been down for over three hours. Mike didn't stay to correct the first ill-formed ware. He left that to the operator, who looked very tired and sallow.

Mike had to take a tea break. He walked along behind the machines like a man plowing along a beach in a foot of water, observing minnows fleeing in front of him. He kept his head down. Operators were surprised to see he didn't look at their machines with his usual sharp perception. The man of inexhaustible energy looked beaten and frail. Mike was thinking about what he had said about God and Jesus during his outbursts. He wasn't a religious man, but his childhood lessons from a severe Catholic priest inculcated a permanent fear of and respect for an interventionist God. Ever since Mike joined the Greek Orthodox Church, he stopped referring to himself as a Galician or a Ruthenian. Now, he was simply a Ukrainian.

He was deep in contemplation and full of genuine sorrow when a cheerful young man in spotless short-sleeved shirt and cotton slacks suddenly appeared before him. It was a university student from the test room. The jam jars on eighteen were under capacity as usual. Mike signed the test results on the clipboard without saying anything and just yelled, "Operator!" to the young man. The young man handed Mike his carbon copy of the results. Mike handed the sheet back to him, said "operator" again, and walked away. The young man accepted Mike's breach of procedure. The foreman was to keep all reports from quality control and attach them to a clipboard in the foreman's office. As a foreman began his shift, he would check the reports to see possible problems. The young man wouldn't dare challenge him. Having Mike's signature was good enough anyway. Mike was reminded again that his future son-in-law did this job on the following shift.

Mike opened the door to the foreman's office behind machine twenty-eight. He sat down on the oil-sodden office chair that was resting on coasters, some reject from the drafting department, too old for shirt and tie bottle designers. He noticed he had missed two changes while he worked on number twenty-two. Usually two or three times a shift, a machine would be changed from one ware to another. Sometimes start-ups could be difficult. This time, both changes had been done by the operators without Mike's supervision or interference. He was too tired to check the machines. He forced himself to believe that all went well. He had to have a drink of tea and some rest. He opened up his lunch bucket and took out his usual tea snack—two slices of buttered bread and a large piece of old cheddar cheese. Betta always packed the same lunch—four buttered slices of bread, cheese, kielbasa, two tea bags, a small jar of milk, and a small jar of sugar. Mike always tried to get two fifteen-minute tea breaks, although the times were unpredictable during an eight-hour shift. On a bad day, he didn't eat at all. On bad days, he would order assistant operators to bring him a jar of tea as he worked on a machine. Mike knew what it meant to be too tired to eat and too tired to rest. The body became irritable, pushing away the succor of food and sleep like a two-year-old crying and screwing up its face and fighting the things that would bring it peace—food and sleep. The body at war with the brain.

Mike pushed his chair away from the desk until it glided to a stop against the wall. He looked down at his oil-soaked boots; his work pants stained with oil, grease, and sweat—black, grey, and white landscapes—his shirt still damp with sweat lying limply across his stomach; and his black and greasy hands, gnarled and strong. He could feel the dry salt on his eyelids, stinging his raw eyes; salty-sweat stung the soft flesh below his chin and around his Adam's apple. He took off his hat and held it loosely on his stomach with his left hand. He ran his right hand through his hair and felt the stiffness of salt. At one time, his flat stomach indicated the muscular body of a man constantly moving and working. Now the flatness indicated a man without physical reserves, the look of an old man who looks thin and enfeebled rather than fat and robust.

For a full ten minutes, Mike sat perfectly still. He didn't even daydream. Body and mind had shut down. Then he slowly got up, feeling the pain of his tiredness and stiffness. He took a tea bag from his lunch bucket and began the slow walk back along the machines. Again, he passed machines without inspecting either the ware or the operators. On number twenty-two, he picked up a sixteen-ounce pickle jar and threw his tea bag in. He walked between eleven and twenty and down the stairs to the cafeteria level. It seemed very quiet down here. He walked slowly, with his head down, into the cafeteria. The hot water urn was against the side wall. The cafeteria was segregated by how much oil workers were covered in. Those who worked in jobs where clothes became soaked in oil, like the front end or the mould room, sat on oil-stained chairs. Those who worked in clean jobs, like the drafting department or the packing house, sat on oil-free chairs at oil-free tables. No hard feelings. Mike was so tired he either didn't see or chose to ignore the plant manager in discussion with the production supervisor at one of the nice tables. Both were drinking tea from large jars. It was Dominion Glass's form of democracy. Neither man enjoyed talking to Mike. He was too blunt and too right. He caught them up on minor, and sometimes major, incompetencies. They were happy to ignore him; he was happy to ignore them.

Mike carried his jar of tea by the rim with a folded glove. The operators watched Mike slowly trudge back to his office. Their sense of relief over his lack of supervision was beginning to be replaced by a sense of concern. They had seen other men at the front-end falter under the stress. A few of the ancient operators had begun work as young as fourteen. (One had begun at twelve.) They had worked for forty years with time off to fight a war. They remembered a more relaxed and leisurely pace at the factory. Modern methods and modern men kept pushing production and stress higher. A retirement at sixty-five after fifty years of toil was not a goal everyone achieved. Many simply could not make it. Today was ominous for Mike.

Mike was seated again in his office. The jar of tea sat on the crumpled green blotter that blotted everything but ink. The green pad had water stains, tea stains, lemonade stains, and a chaotic lacework of rings left by containers of various circumferences. There were three other foremen who used this same desk and they had one thing in common—the habit of eating while they did their paperwork. And so added to the liquid designs on the blotter were food stains—grease from meat, oil from cheese, jam smears, fish oil residue, and more. All the various detritus of lunch buckets; the debris of Ukrainian, English, Irish, and Italian lunches.

Each shift had a foreman from a different nationality. This situation existed for two years before someone finally noticed this interesting arrangement. It wasn't a management plan. Management didn't even notice it. Front end foremen were picked by ability. The reality of production targets couldn't be hidden at the front end. The machines either made ware to specifications or they didn't. The machines either ran or they didn't. The best operators became foremen after a long apprenticeship and nobody gave a damn about their nationality. Within this melting pot and meritocracy, Mike sometimes forgot his ethnicity because it was irrelevant. Now, he sat writing out his daily report very slowly. He stopped frequently to sip his tea or eat some bread with cheese or kielbasa on it. He was slowly regaining his strength and equilibrium.

Mike was almost finished his report when John McNeil opened the door and let in a quick burst of heat and noise. Mike exhaled slowly and announced that it was a hell of a day. John shrugged and quietly asked about specific problems. The foremen tried to overlap for at least half an hour to prepare each other for the next shift. They genuinely tried not to leave a mess for the next shift, although operators sometimes skedaddled with problems still a-boil. As Mike talked, John noticed how weary he was. During the shift summary, Mike was always clinically precise in his report. He was frequently angry and vehement. Never was he weary. John looked at him carefully. John had served in the Canadian Merchant Marines on the North Atlantic run. He knew men under stress. Mike was obviously under stress.

"Okay. We can handle it. Leave early today, Mike." Any display of sympathy between men had to be masked in brusqueness. Normally, Mike would have stiffened and refused the offer. This time, he nodded his head, wrote a few more lines on the report, and began to clear away his lunch. Without saying a word, he walked out of the office with his lunch bucket under his arm. John watched him from the office window until he passed the bend around the furnace.

John was a foreman because he was a brilliant machinist. Because he had seen sudden death and immeasurable pain in war, he wouldn't sell his soul to the company. Management knew they could push him only so far. A large part of him remained stubbornly inviolate. He didn't define himself through his job. He didn't need power over others to feel good about himself. If the company tried to strip away any of his sense of self, he would walk away from the foreman's job and let ambitious and obsequious men replace him, but he took pride in doing a good job and he took pride in working hard. He had no use for lazy men, ass-kissers, or subversive anti-company agitators. He believed in the old adage of a fair day's pay for a fair day's work. That put him in the middle between exploitative management and sit-on-your-ass-all-day unionists.

Unlike Mike, John was not anti-union. He knew workers had to be protected from unregulated capitalism. He preferred a model of labour similar to the ships he had served on in the war. There had been strong authority, yet a sense of teamwork and idealism. Perhaps he had been lucky, but on all the ships he was on, the officers treated one another well and respected one another. The fact that officers were better paid and had better accommodations did not cause hostility among the men. The officers sometimes drove the men hard to perform well, but when their ship carried out an operation with success, there was a sense of pride. It was true that the terror of German U-Boats and the hardship of the North Atlantic focused hatred outward from the ship. But John felt the struggle to turn molten glass into beautifully utilitarian objects could also unite men. He wouldn't say this to anyone, of course, but he saw his role as a foreman as very similar to a ship's captain or an infantry major. He would be competent, tough, and caring as he led his men into each eight-hour engagement. At the end of the war, he wanted to be known as a tough and good leader.

John was always struck by the similarity between the engine room of a ship and the front end. There was the same incessant noise: all the power of the industrial age manifested in steel machines of overwhelming power. All the finely engineered steel parts. Beauty in power. He understood why men fell in love with steam engines, car engines, power boats. The engine room of a ship had the same smell of oil. No machines could function without constant lubrication. The heat in the engine room was the same as the heat at the front end. In both cases, men were breathing in hot air infused with oil and asbestos. The men looked and smelled the same. They were covered in oil, sweat lines running across their shirts. And they stank. They stank to high heaven. John wondered how submarines could stand the smell of machines and men. He also wondered if the men in engine rooms on the North Atlantic run knew that on some convoy runs, eighty percent of the ships were sunk by U-Boats. He was sure they didn't. Governments waging war keep many secrets from their citizens.

John wasn't sure what motivated Mike to be a foreman. He suspected that Mike's arrival in Canada with about twenty words of English, eighty dollars, and a farm boy's education had driven him to strive with manic energy for success. Yet most men had come out of the Depression with no money, no education, poor health, and little hope. John did know that Mike was something of a loner. That great spirit of comradeship that affected many men in World War II had passed him by. He worked only for his family and the rewards work brought. John also felt that Mike respected only a few men on his shift—those who could match his energy. The others might expect his contempt. Yet, John felt empathy for Mike because he knew that leadership meant pain as much as power. Often it meant loneliness, hostility, and self-doubt. John and Mike shared much, and because of that, John felt Mike's sudden diminution as painfully as he would his own.

Meanwhile, Mike had made his way to the locker room. When he pushed the swinging door open, he felt the wave of hot humid air from the showers, then the usual but always shockingly offensive and fetid smell—oil, grease, sweat, body odour, and the stench of unwashed clothing. Some men wore the same clothes for five straight days. Their lockers hummed with the stench. Most men took daily showers, but a few never felt the need. Mike brought a change of clothes each day and Betta always had an extra set of work clothes washed and ironed, ready to go. Mike enjoyed a long shower with hot water and lots of soap. It was a luxury he never had in his youth.

He could relax in the shower, forget about battles, and plan his next duties as an owner and entrepreneur. When he entered the locker room, a wave of interrupted conversation flowed in front of him. Behind him, a backwash of altered conversation swirled around. His shift was startled to see him. Most men had never seen him in the locker room. They didn't even know he had a locker or used the room. One of the obsequious dolts who had been bad-mouthing him a few minutes ago with his doltish friends greeted him warmly. Most of the men simply nodded and ignored him. Conversation and horseplay was chilled. Mike was always here long after they had left. The transfer of information from foreman to foreman could be time-consuming, especially if there had been problems. Sometimes the meetings between foremen was complicated by the production supervisor's presence. A new and complicated job like the Gerber baby bottles could take hours. Sometimes the meetings dissolved into shouting matches.

Mike reached his locker and sat on the bench running the length of this section. One of the floor boys from the packing house was in front of the mirror shaping the waves in his hair. Mike stared at him for several seconds, his mind caught by the contradictory processes of removing oil from the body and depositing it in his hair. As he watched the young man, his eyes lost focus; although he stared in the boy's direction, he saw nothing. The young man turned to see Mike looking at him and his anger was immediately replaced by curiosity as he realized Mike's eyes were unfocused and unseeing. A shout one aisle over aroused Mike slowly from his revelry like a man fighting himself from sleep to consciousness. He turned again to look at his locker and its combination lock. He forced his mind to remember the most efficient way to shower and change. First open the locker. Take out the paper shopping bag with the clean street clothes. Hang the street clothes on the locker's hooks. Put the work clothes in the shopping bag. His mind had difficulty remembering. Mike bent down to untie his shoelaces. He had replaced the cloth shoelaces with leather laces that were gold-brown with recurrent oil-black patterns. His hands moved slowly: the task of untying the bows and pulling the laces through the holes to loosen the boots seemed very difficult, like a man taking off winter boots frozen and encrusted with ice. Once bent over, Mike straightened himself with difficulty. He paused between each function of undressing. Once, he stopped for several minutes as he pondered the oil in the young man's hair. He knew he never thought about the significance of actions, about the meaning of behaviour, about meanings at all. He knew that because he had willed himself never to think of meanings. As a young man, he had ventured into that quagmire—examining life. He quickly realized that self-examination and soul-searching led to inactivity, depression, lethargy, and pain. He had decided to be a man of action. In fact, he had become a man of activity, endless activity. Activity kept him from opening any of the gates to Hell that introspection demanded. In that respect, he became the prototypical North American, a person seeking refuge in endless activity, whether work or pleasure. Quiet moments of thought let the demons loose. Mike knew the demons from when the black-robed priests had created an atmosphere of religious mysticism. For a time, he had joined other young men at his church who had agonized over God. He had argued vehemently with this group around rough-hewn tables. And he had wrestled with God in his sweat-soaked bed.

Then when he was twenty, he had walked away from the agony of the mind. He had literally walked away. On a Sunday in May, instead of walking to church, he walked towards the horizon. He walked all day, thinking on all the old insoluble issues between man and God. He walked until it was dark. He slept on a bank near a creek; the last sight before he fell asleep was the sky pulsating with stars. In the morning, he woke with a strange rush of energy and well-being. He walked home with his head spinning with mundane ideas about his work, a marriage, and perhaps a departure from his home. In two days, he had not eaten and he had walked almost thirty miles. When his mother brought him his dinner late at night, she saw no difference in him physically, but she sensed a change. In fact, he had made the transformation that so many make; the change from speculation to action.

As Mike closed his locker and shuffled towards the shower room, he moved like an automaton. He willed his mind to be blank. The mind that he had trained must quell the mind that waited to be released when he was thoroughly exhausted. The rational mind must not let that irrational mind escape; the tiger with the burning red eyes must be kept in its chains. Mike could feel the tiger pacing back and forth and leaping at its chain. Each time the chain held and the tiger snapped back to the ground. But would the chain hold? Because the tiger would not stop.

Mike stepped inside the empty shower stall. Two of the shower heads still dripped water. The taps had not been turned tightly enough. Mike walked to each tap and turned each off completely. He had returned to action. He cursed the laziness of the men who had left the taps running. He had returned to the safety of mundane actions. He turned on his own shower and slowly made the water hotter and hotter. The physical pain, the scalding, allowed his rational mind, his comfortable mind, to re-assert itself. Mike was back in the haven of the every day. The black depths of contemplation were washed away by the scalding water; the tiger skulked back into its dark cave. Mike washed his hair with bar soap until a lather was raised. He washed his face several times and stood with his head lowered and let the water run over his body. He found strength and redemption in water. The physical world, the sensual world, was dominant again. He lathered his body with soap and rinsed it off. Again, and again, he lathered and rinsed. He meticulously and slowly washed and re-washed every part of his body. The process, he understood, was more than physical. He knew that his psychological balance was being restored. The last growl of the red-eyed tiger had been to remind him that his nude body enjoyed the sensual; yet the sexual part of his being was not aroused. Sexuality was another question that Mike banished to the tiger's cave.

Mike dried himself with a towel that had a rough texture from drying outside. The roughness across his back pleased him. The clean clothes that Betta had meticulously ironed felt pleasant to the touch. He combed his hair inattentively as he examined his face in the mirror. His skin looked quite pink. His eyes had liveliness and lustre again. When he realized he hadn't combed his hair properly, he smiled genuinely enough to reveal his teeth. He quickly re-combed his hair. He felt tired now, but it was the tiredness of physical labour—the happy tiredness that comes from hammering, or carrying, or sawing, or sanding, or painting. The fretful tiredness that comes from worry or strife was expunged. Mike knew that the one tiredness led to happy oblivion; the other meant fitful sleep and wakefulness. It was important now to keep his body and mind in a state of lassitude. He must not think about the issue that had dominated his thoughts and kept him from sleeping.

Mike grabbed his shopping bag and lunch pail and walked towards the locker room exit. Old Andy Newton was sweeping the locker room floor and picking up garbage. Andy had been a front-end man until he was sixty-five. One day, he asked the superintendent if he could become the new basement-level cleaner. Other workers were embarrassed for him. They thought being a cleaner was a menial job. Andy never even thought about that. He changed jobs without losing an iota of self-respect. The hierarchy of jobs so well defined for the majority of men never manifested itself to Andy. Either he thought all jobs were important or he considered all jobs slavery. Nobody questioned him about this. In any case, he was always polite and he always seemed happy. Now he smiled at Mike and wished him a good evening. He would have been shocked if Mike stopped to chat. They would have had nothing to say to each other.

Mike walked along the lower corridor towards the front entrance. Like everyone else at the plant, he had a punch card. It didn't mean anything for salaried employees, but the plant tradition was for everyone to punch in and out. Even the plant manager punched in and out. He was quite amused by the tradition. Occasionally, a salaried worker would feel offended by the protocol and point out that if he were paid on an hourly basis, he would . . . and so on. When the pay clerks came to calculate weekly wages, they just dropped the salaried workers' cards into a wastebasket. On Wednesdays, there was quite a stack of used time cards in the garbage. Sometimes the clerks were annoyed to see salaried workers who had put in seventy or eighty hours in a week. They just muttered, "Idiots!" Mike nodded at the two clerks behind the panes of glass. Both were speaking animatedly on the phone. The one was trying to persuade a floor boy to come into work to cover for a late sick call. The other was trying to persuade a young lady to meet him at the Grange bar at eleven. Both seemed to be losing their arguments.

Mike walked slowly to his car in the fenced-off parking lot. The parking spot was one of the few perks foremen got. Most cars were parked on nearby streets. More than half the work force walked to work, or rode bicycles, or took the bus. Mike's car was a serviceable 1958 Chev. He could afford a new car every year, but he liked to pretend that people didn't know he had money. And he was frugal. Besides, it was a concrete argument against the demands of his children.

On the day shift, Mike drove straight home to the meal Betta had prepared for him. Later in the evening, he would go to the pub to work a few hours. When he visited the pub, he always put on a rather theatrical scowl and spoke gruffly. He tried to look the very hard man. Tonight, however, for the first time in years, Mike drove east along Barton Street only as far as the Avon Tavern. He wanted to sit quietly by himself and drink beer. He parked the car on the east side of the tavern and entered off Barton Street. Going through the entrance, he glanced at the women's room—men and women gathered at tables drinking beer together. He wondered about those women. Betta would never go to a tavern. Luckily, there were no Dominion Glass men around. The one conversation at a table concerning a rolling mill meant steelworkers were here.

Mike was just going to sit down at an empty table when a loud "Mike!" erupted from a table of three men in the far corner. Mike's eyes hadn't adjusted to the darkness yet, and he wasn't sure who had called him. But he had no ready excuse for not moving towards them. As he got closer, he recognized members of the church. Igor Malvich worked at Stelco and John Muhkevich and Paul Miciski worked at Dofasco. Stelco and Dofasco were both steel manufacturing companies; Stelco was unionized, Dofasco wasn't. These men spent their beer-drinking time arguing about Ukrainian nationalism, unions, and World War II. Igor had two children who had been active in the church and had married Ukrainians. Paul had a daughter engaged to a Ukrainian. John's children were younger, but they spent all their spare time at the Chayka Dance Company. Mike had enjoyed some prestige with this group because David was a lawyer with largely Ukrainian clients and he had married a Ukrainian.

Mike knew when he sat down what would eventually come. Even as he sipped his beer, his throat became drier and more constricted. The conversation drifted from politics to the Tiger-Cats and their recent loss to the Toronto Argonauts. All Hamiltonians were expected to follow the Cats, to know their record, to name prominent players, to be elated at wins and fiercely angry at losses. Mike didn't give a shit about the Tiger-Cats, the Maple Leafs, the Yankees, or any other group of men running around in athletic uniforms. He had never had time to play or watch sports, and he had no time now. He would never pretend to be interested. He wouldn't learn anything or say anything or do anything to gain the acceptance of other men. He wasn't anti-social. He did like the company of men. But it had to be men he respected, doing something he liked. He could talk for hours with small business owners about zoning laws, taxes, health regulations. Never anything frivolous.

The men at this table flouted their nationalism. They were self-righteous. They were always looking for sinners. And Mike had become a sinner. The conversation drifted after the mandatory display of spleen against the Tiger-Cats coach and quarterback. There were desultory comments about the weather, the beer, Diefenbaker. Finally, Igor Malvich ventured forward. He was a steelworker and a unionist. He was therefore tough, blunt, fearless, outspoken—all the stupid self-congratulatory qualities steelworkers liked to attribute to themselves. In reality, Igor was basically a dim-witted bigmouth with too much beer in his belly. The beer lit his courage and Mike's unusual passivity fed it. So, he began the questions to which he knew the answers.

"I heard Alina got engaged?" Igor said. Mike nodded.

"Oh, yeah?" said John "What's her boyfriend do?"

Mike waited. The hesitation reflected his growing anger.

"He's going to be a teacher." Igor paused to drink some more beer to indicate that this was just friendly interest, not sharp interrogation. But Mike's pursed lips indicated he was not fooled.

Igor asked the final question with a feigned off-handedness to suggest that he expected the correct answer and would be surprised if it wasn't.

"Is he Ukrainian?"

Mike let the question hang over the table, almost as palpable as the cigarette smoke. He knew the question would come and he expected a sudden surge of rage. But he found himself strangely detached. In fact, he was amused, because as the silence lengthened, he could feel the three men's bodies become taut. The blood began to drain from Igor's face. Mike knew they were afraid, and in his strange detachment, he knew he should display some anger. John broke the spell when the rigid muscles in his arms involuntarily pushed the table forward suddenly and beer bounced out of the glasses. At the same moment, Igor ducked his head and raised his right hand to protect his face because he thought the movement was Mike lunging at him.

In the same split second, Paul had jammed his heels into the floor and pushed his chair backward, wood squealing against wood.

Mike waited five seconds, which seemed like five minutes, as the three tried to retrieve their dignities. Then he said simply, "No, he's not Ukrainian."

The men received the answer with slight nods. There was another eon of ten seconds. Then, almost as if rehearsed, like some arthritic, syncopated dance trio, they mumbled excuses and danced around their chairs and out the door. The only vaudevillian trick missing in their exit was running into one another or throwing themselves against a locked door and bouncing backwards.

Mike smiled wryly. The opinion of these men didn't matter. The problem was that Mike shared their beliefs. Just as both the liberal and archconservative might support capital punishment, or a Quaker might join a psychopath in waging war, Mike shared his antagonists' views about preserving Ukrainian purity. He hated all the rubbish about racial and cultural distinctiveness. He hated the louts who spouted this vitriol. Yet he wanted Ukrainians to marry Ukrainians to preserve the language and culture. At times, he even thought that Ukrainians were different or special—or better. He knew these beliefs were illogical, but he also knew that men's strongest beliefs were irrational and could never pass a test of rational examination. After all, the strongest beliefs were irrational—religion, war, and love. These beliefs were fortified and entrenched by rational assaults. Most conflicts were caused by the clash between two equally irrational arguments. Mike knew that the concept of a master race destroyed millions of people. But he wanted nothing in the world right now as much as he wanted his daughter to marry a Ukrainian. And he was convinced that the Evanses wanted nothing as much as they wanted their son to marry one of his own kind—whatever that was.

Mike didn't drink as he thought about this. He waved the waiter away twice, the second time angrily. Then he finished the beer in one last gulp as he stood up. He moved quickly across the room and out the exit. It was still daylight. He got into his car and pulled into Barton Street. He drove without thinking; a growing anger restored his animation and vigor. This stupid, illogical, unreasonable, incomprehensible anger made him feel better. It burnt off his lethargy and restored his force of action. By the time he pulled into the parking lot of his apartment building, he was invigorated by dark energy. He grabbed his lunch pail and shopping bag and stormed up the steps to his building, ignoring the hello from Mrs. Elliot with her head stuck out her kitchen window. He strode to the door of his apartment and pushed the unlocked door open so violently, it banged on the doorstop like a shotgun blast. Betta and Alina, sitting in the living room, were startled but came towards Mike smiling affably. The affability froze on their faces when they saw Mike. Alina had planned to ask her father for some more money for the wedding. The process was always lengthy, but she always got what she wanted. However, she had found her father more and more irritable as the wedding day approached. She had been forced to hone her techniques of obsequiousness, charming, pleading, whining, and silent sobbing. At times, she felt she was running out of techniques and might have to get her mother's intervention. But this was a new daddy tonight. His eyes were large, his face was red, and his breathing was audible. He looked taller and wider, and although he was perfectly still, his tenseness suggested a mad creature ready to spring. Betta was stunned for a second, then instinctively reacted like a mother protecting her young. She moved between her daughter and her husband.

"What the fuck do you think you are doing?" Mike yelled.

Betta and Alina froze. Betta thought the attack was on her and cowered slightly, turning her head away. Alina knew it was for her. She took two steps back, but couldn't move beyond that.

"What are you doing?" Mike yelled again.

His anger filled the apartment. It was even more horrible because in the final crescendo of rage, there was the plaintive note of pain.

The shout reverberated around Betta and Alina like the vibrations of a steel rod hit with a hammer. Not until the last vibration had stopped and complete silence filled the apartment did they breathe again. They inhaled together like swimmers surfacing after staying underwater too long. Mike just stared as they both audibly gasped. Betta reacted first, turning from Mike, grasping Alina by the shoulders, and turning her towards her bedroom. For a split-second, Alina resisted because she had reached the age of resistance, but her fear overwhelmed her. This was not her daddy.

"Just what are you doing?"

They moved towards Alina's bedroom. He moved forward now. His mouth was open because he needed air. His movements were wooden; rage stiffened his body and locked his joints.

"You're not marrying that fucking Englishman!"

Betta closed the bedroom door deferentially, no sign of anger or defiance, just a mother's protective instinct—nothing to antagonize this strange maniac who had come into her home looking like her husband.

Betta and Alina sat frozen, rigid, on a tiny edge of the bed. Their breathing remained deep and long, sucking oxygen to regain some equilibrium. Slowly, they realized their hearts were beating fiercely. They had just jumped out of the way of a speeding train at the last second, or been thrown out as a car sped over a cliff with their friends inside, or avoided a lightning strike that struck their friends. They were in shock. They felt perspiration on their foreheads, then on their necks, then under their arms. They sat minute after minute until they felt cold. Betta then moved to get the comforter and asked Alina to lie down. Alina took the comforter, put it on her shoulders, and beckoned her mother to sit beside her, sharing it. They sat like that and listened, unsure if there would be another attack, and if there was, whether they would be acquiescent or belligerent. Yet each feared that this monster would smash both acquiescence and belligerence with equal indifference.

Mike had retreated to the kitchen. His body ached with the rigidity of rage. He sat at the table with his hands on his thighs, his head bowed forward. It was the posture of an acolyte caught somewhere between heaven and hell, unaware that immediate decisions could have irreparable and eternal reverberations for good or evil. Simply put, in his daughter's eyes, Mike could either become a saint or a monster forever.

* * *

Alina's upcoming wedding was almost a physical pain to Mike. It was like having an infected tooth or a constant migraine. He blamed himself for allowing her to give up her Ukrainian heritage for the most part. She had become very Canadian, and maybe somewhat Anglo. She was the beautiful child of his reunion with Betta. Because he had a cantankerous relationship with David, Alina's love was very important. He didn't want a permanent breach with her. He was surprised at how resolute she was to marry Roy. She wouldn't give in to him. He wasn't sleeping well. He was in a bad mood all day long. Men at Dominion Glass and at the pub stayed out of his way.

Five days before the wedding, Mike woke from a troubled sleep. He was working twelve to eight. He banged on Alina's bedroom door and was absolutely cold. He announced that he would not attend the wedding. She could find someone else to walk her down the aisle. He left for the pub without eating. Betta had to console her daughter again.

That night when Roy picked Alina up, she told him the wedding would have to be postponed. Roy remained calm. They drove around Hamilton, quietly talking. By the end of the evening, Alina had her resolution restored. If they had to, they would be married without Mike's presence.

The next day, Mike rose from his bed as miserable as ever. He wouldn't be at his beloved daughter's wedding. He had dreamed of a beautiful wedding at St. Vladimir's Church, attended by all his Ukrainian friends from as far back as 1937. The fact that he seldom went to church didn't matter. Then there would be a wonderful Ukrainian dinner with bottles of whiskey laid out every few feet on the white-clothed tables. There would be dancing. There would be speeches in Ukrainian. He would embrace his Ukrainian son-in-law and his parents. There wouldn't be a word of English. He would pay for everything with magnanimous smiles. That dream was shattered.

Betta had his dinner waiting in the oven. He sat down at the table without saying a word. He hadn't had a conversation with Betta for weeks. She brought his dinner from the oven, held it two feet above his place, and dropped it. The plate shattered. Food shot across the table and into Mike's lap. As he sat there stunned, juice running off the table and onto his pants, Betta walked quietly and silently into the living room. She turned on the TV and began watching a soap opera she didn't understand. Mike didn't move for the longest time. Then he began to clean up the mess. He carefully put everything in the garbage container. He got a dish cloth and wiped off the table, then rinsed off the cloth several times and meticulously wiped the floor and chair. He was satisfied that everything was spotless again. Once that was done, he went to the bedroom and changed his shirt and pants. The shirt would be washed and the pants would go to the dry cleaners.

He returned to the table. He had willed himself not to be introspective his whole life. Now he had to examine his behaviour and beliefs. He thought about David's marriage in 1949. David warned him that when he attended the wedding, he was not to mention the war. David told him that several times. The third time he told him, it was in an unnecessarily loud and stern voice. The war was a divisive time for the Ukrainian community in Canada. When the Germans invaded Ukraine, many Ukrainians welcomed them and thousands joined the German forces. After all, Stalin had killed as many as seven or eight million Ukrainians. But the Germans were so ruthless and brutal that the Ukrainians turned against them. It was a terrible choice of two psychopaths—Hitler and Stalin. Nikita Khrushcher was the dominant personality of Kyiv and played a part at Stalingrad. He was loyal to Stalin.

Mike was very intelligent. He read the *Spectator* every day and had a keen interest in international events. During the war, most people were anxious for news. Of course, Mike tried to find out about Galicia and Ukraine. He knew it was more than a war of nation states. It was also a war of ideology—communism against fascism. He knew that when Germany and its allies were defeated, people began to have amnesia and carefully altered their roles. The Germans denied membership in the Nazi Party. They had never heard of the death camps. Fascists in Britain, the United States, and Canada hung up their jackboots. Many had believed that only fascism could save the world from international communism. The Stock Market Crash and the Great Depression proved that capitalism and the free market didn't work. Holland had a love affair with Canada because Canadian troops liberated the Netherlands. In the last year of the war, the Nazis starved the country. Canada helped arrange a truce and participated in air drops of food. Audrey Hepburn, who came from a wealthy family, may have survived on tulip bulbs. Yet there were around thirty thousand Dutch men who joined the German Army. They had an SS Division and Heinrich Himmler presented their colours in an elaborate ceremony. France was a country divided. The Vichy French were very pro-German. The Free French fought outside the country under Charles de Gaulle. The Milice francaise were often more brutal than the SS in fighting the Resistance.

Somehow, suffused within this war of nation states and ideology, there was the constant, historical anti-Semitism. There wasn't a country in Eastern or Western Europe that didn't have anti-Semites. The United States and Canada turned away the Jewish refugee ship MS *St. Louis* containing nine hundred passengers. The ship was forced to return to Europe and many passengers ended up in the ovens of death camps.

Mike knew all these things. He didn't talk about the war. Mike had pushed the details of David's wedding into a dark recess of his mind. Now, as he sat almost limp at the table, he forced himself to remember all the details of the event.

* * *

David's Wedding 1949

Ella and David were to be married in Edmonton. David arranged plane tickets for his parents while Ella's father booked hotel rooms for them at the Hotel Macdonald. It was the historic jewel of downtown Edmonton, opening in 1915 as another great railway hotel in Canada. The railway at that time was the Grand Trunk Pacific Railway. There was no mention of the Sir John A. railroad scandals. In 1939, King George VI and Queen Elizabeth stayed there. They were on a tour of the United States and Canada to bolster support for Britain in the war everyone knew was coming. When the royals came, it caused a traffic jam in the city. The power of the monarchy. The railway spared no expense in building this hotel. It cost $2.25 million at that time and took four years to build. Mike thought his future in-law wanted to display his wealth. But he didn't want to be rude and turn the offer down.

Neither Betta nor Mike had ever been on a plane. Trans Canada Airlines had a new fleet of Canadair North Star planes. Staff at the airport in Toronto helped them get their seats on the spanking new plane. Mike was nervous and Betta was terrified. They had to adjust to sitting in seats so close together, stewardesses handing out food, and a tiny bathroom that rocked back and forth. But they were brave. They had done a great deal in their lives. After a time, Mike began to look out the porthole windows. The view of the fields of grain on the

Prairies was magnificent. David and Ella were waiting for them at the airport and got them booked into the hotel. Betta and Mike were uncomfortable with the luxury. At breakfast the next morning, they had trouble coping with the white linen tablecloth, shining cutlery, uniformed waiter, and five-page menu. One of David's ushers was going to pick them up at 11 a.m. for the wedding.

They arrived at the church very early. This was a new church for the Parish of St. Anthony's Ukrainian Orthodox Church. In 1918, a group of Ukrainian Catholics became disenchanted with the Ukrainian Catholic Church. They formed an organization that created the Ukrainian Orthodox Church. The churches followed the Greek Orthodox liturgy, but had no connection with Ukraine. They were a uniquely Canadian institution. Many Catholics from Galicia, like Mike, joined the Orthodox Church. Ella's parents met Betta and Mike in the foyer. They were very warm and polite. They all took their seats. Of course, all the seats on the bride's side filled up quickly, so the ushers had to direct the latecomers to the groom's side. The ceremony was beautiful but long. Betta and Mike were happy they had left Alina at home with their Ukrainian tenant-friend.

The same usher drove them to the reception. It was a huge banquet hall owned by a successful Ukrainian businessman. It was a sea of white and silver. The dishes gleamed and they had a traditional Ukrainian design around the rims. The parents were all seated at a table in front of the head table. The tables were round and seated eight. Ella's two brothers with their wives completed their table.

As the guests arrived, Mike realized Ella's family was well-off. Her grandparents or great-grandparents had been recruited to come to Canada to fill the empty spaces of the Prairies. The Slavs had been the second or third choice of Sir Wilfred Laurier and Interior Minister Clifford Sifton. Sifton wanted Northern and Western Europeans and white Protestant Americans. He did not want French speakers. Mennonites, Norwegians, and Jewish refugees from Russia came. The land was free or cheap. Sifton continued his recruiting campaign, reluctantly admitting Ukrainians, Slovaks, Serbs, Hungarians, Poles, Czechs, Croats, and Romanians. Now these Ukrainian descendants of the immigrants in sheepskin coats were part of the establishment in Edmonton. Their grandparents and great-grandparents may have been poor, and perhaps illiterate, but they were successful. From shacks and sod houses on the inhospitable prairies, the immigrants forged wealth. The people in the room were members of parliament, judges, lawyers, businessmen, doctors, and teachers. Ella's father was head of a prestigious law firm that had offices in several cities in Alberta. It was the Canadian version of the American dream. But Canadians didn't use the phrase Canadian dream. They were just as successful without the American bugle-blowing and back-slapping.

Betta and Mike were uncertain about the choice of cutlery as each course was presented. They tried to follow their hosts. As the meal went on, Ella's family began to talk freely. Every now and then, someone would try to include Betta and Mike in the conversation. Betta was very, very uncomfortable. She didn't understand all the English phrases. The dinner was nothing short of torture for her. She wanted to be back in her apartment in Hamilton. Once, one of Ella's brothers tried to show off by speaking to Mike in Ukrainian. It was the Ukrainian of Kyiv, traditional and classic, learned at Ukrainian language summer schools in Edmonton. When Mike answered in his Galician-Ukrainian, he thought he heard a snigger.

When the dinner was finished, the speeches began. David's friends were clever and they made humorous speeches. When it was David's turn to speak, he had a long list of people to thank. He praised Ella's parents to the sky, but didn't mention his own parents. As tables were being cleared and moved for the dance, Mike took Betta by the arm and led her to the entrance. He asked one of the managers to order a taxi for them. They returned to the hotel and left the next morning for the trip home. On the plane home, Mike didn't look out the window. He thought about the wedding and his new in-laws. Betta had been born a peasant. His parents owned some land. The in-laws were well-educated and successful. But in his time in Canada, Mike had become a foreman at Dominion Glass. He owned an apartment. He owned a share of a pub. He was proud of his accomplishments. He had the roughness of an immigrant new to English, but he was not going to be put down by snotty-nosed young people of inherited wealth. They could chew and choke on their condescension.

When the wedding was over, Ella agreed to make their home in Hamilton. David joined a law firm specializing in real estate. All six lawyers were Ukrainian.

* * *

Mike was very, very still. He sat with his fingers intertwined on the table. Then he made a decision. He went to Alina's bedroom and knocked gently on the door. Alina opened the door slowly, wary and apprehensive. He said he would be happy to walk his beautiful daughter down the aisle on Saturday. He handed her an envelope with two thousand dollars in it and said he would pay for anything else she needed. He stepped forward and hugged his daughter. Alina was almost overcome with emotion because her father had never shown her any outward affection. She sat in the chair at her desk when he left. This time, there were tears of relief and happiness.

Mike didn't have time to go to the pub before work this night. As he got ready for work, Betta brought him his lunch pail. She handed it to him and kissed him on the cheek. She hadn't kissed him in a long, long time.

As he drove to work, Mike was surprised at how happy he was. The muscles in his neck and shoulders that had been taut for so long were now relaxed. He remembered a crazy campfire song that the workers used to sing when he worked in the lumber camp in Algonquin Park. He belted it out loudly and laughed when other drivers looked over. His crew in the front end were surprised to see

Mike smiling. He hadn't smiled in months. In fact, he almost looked drunk. Partway through the shift, he walked down between two lehrs to greet Peter. He extended one hand and put his other hand on Peter's shoulder. He joked that Peter better have a nice suit for Saturday because he was getting a new one. Then he walked casually, of all things, back to the front end. Peter almost had a heart attack. When he saw Mike walking towards him, he expected Mike's hands on his throat. The women in the packing house who saw this incident buzzed with amazement.

Chapter Twenty-Two

Ontario 1964

Betta Dubinsky was very, very nervous. She was a very shy person, comfortable only with a small circle of acquaintances. Now she was being coaxed and dragged to that most English of traditions: the wedding shower. She was never completely comfortable speaking English. Although she had been in Canada for over twenty-five years, she clung to her own language. She and Mike spoke Ukrainian in the home, and as she got older, she ventured out of their apartment less and less. When she, Mike, and David had run their variety store, she had to speak English more frequently. Now she spoke only to her tenants, and even then, as seldom as possible. She liked to walk a block to the new supermarket and buy groceries every day, but a few words to the cashier sufficed. She spent her days alone in her basement apartment most of the time and that suited her. As the years passed, she was content to become a recluse. She had seen so much conflict and lived through so many changes, she simply wanted to rest. She had no desire to live an active life and she had no desire to run her children's lives. In fact, most things her children did surprised her, and sometimes even shocked her. Her children broke all the old Ukrainian traditions. Luckily, Canadian-born Ukrainians helped soften the Ukrainian community in Hamilton so the older generation was more understanding of Canadian culture. Not Mike, of course. He ranted and raved about his children's decisions and actions. In this, he was the same as most immigrant fathers in North America. Although they wanted new and better lives for themselves and their children, they thought they could preserve the Old Country in the United States or Canada. But if North America wasn't a melting pot, it was certainly a catalyst for change. Every old political, religious, linguistic, ethnic, and racial tradition was under constant assault. No amount of transported churches, cultural groups, ethnic halls, summer camps, yelling and screaming, or dictums and ultimatums could stop the next generation from being North Americans. And, worst of all, sometimes there was intermarriage.

Betta literally sat on the edge of her seat as she waited for the doorbell to ring. Her daughter-in-law, Ella, had gone to the dressmaker for new outfits for her mother-in-law, one for this shower and one for the wedding. Her dressmaker was Ukrainian, of course, and Betta always felt comfortable with her. Betta had never been a seamstress and she never had much interest in clothes and certainly no interest in fashion. In Galicia, women wore simple dresses with loose sweaters most of the time. That ubiquitous outfit was suitable for the home and acceptable for church. There was no money for fancy outfits and very little information about clothing or fashion. In her tiny village, some two hundred miles northwest of Kyiv, there was no film theatre, newspapers were rare, and magazines were unheard of. Women dressed almost as their mothers and grandmothers had. Even though the Dubinskys owned land, they were very similar to the peasants on the large estates. The twentieth century had shaken the political and economic system of her area, but women's fashions would have to wait for a more peaceful and affluent age.

Anna, the dressmaker, provided all the fashion Betta needed. Anna showed her pictures from pattern books, and since Anna catered to Ukrainian and Polish ladies over fifty, most of the dresses looked suitable to Betta. She invariably accepted Anna's suggestions and only demurred when Anna presented fabrics that were too ornate or expensive. Betta always felt that dressmaker-made dresses were too good for her and she tried to keep them as simple and inexpensive as possible. Anna accepted these limitations because most of her customers were like that. Most had come to Canada with one suitcase of possessions. Their frugality and hard work in Canada might have made them prosperous, but spending money did not come easily to this group of people.

Now, Betta sat expectantly in a simple two-piece outfit. It was a Jacqueline Kennedy-esque jacket and skirt with larger dimensions, a longer skirt, and moderately-priced fabric. Betta felt overdressed. She'd had her hair permed several days ago and had applied powder to her face, but no lipstick. For most women, the preparation for a social event brings confidence. A new dress, a new purse, bright dress shoes, and a new hairdo impart a sense of self-esteem. But dressing up stripped Betta of confidence. She simply felt uncomfortable in clothing that was not part of her experience. She was not foolish enough to think that all these preparations could make her beautiful. More than anything, she wished she could be in her normal clothes, alone in the apartment. Mike was working the four-to-twelve shift and she never stayed up for him.

When the doorbell rang, Betta was startled, not because she was daydreaming but because she had simply stopped thinking entirely. She had closed down her mind and had been to a state approaching suspended animation. Whether consciously or unconsciously, Betta moved to this state when under stress. Just as there are times when people rev up their awareness and sensitivity, there are times when the mind dulls the senses and thought processes for self-protection. Betta awoke as if she had been asleep and moved slowly towards the door. When she opened the door, she saw Ella in full regalia. She wore a real Jacqueline Kennedy outfit. The jacket and skirt were finely tailored by someone superior to Anna. The fabric was very expensive and just slightly flashier than Jackie would have chosen. Her hair was perfectly set, sprayed into brittle obedience, and topped with a compulsory pill-box hat. Her makeup was elaborate and only slightly obtrusive. After all, the wife of a businessman had to look the part. Ella waited in the door frame as Betta walked to the kitchen table to get her purse. Ella still found it uncomfortable to cross the threshold and really sit and relax in her in-laws' home. Ella genuinely liked her mother-in-law, but Ella wasn't the type to kick off her shoes, plunk down on the chesterfield, and start gabbing. Ella retained a certain formality at all times and, with the vicissitudes of her marriage, formality became more and more of a defense. Betta had just put her hand on the doorknob when she thought she should go to the bathroom one last time. She excused herself and Ella gave her a tired, indulgent smile. In the bathroom, Betta checked her appearance again, and again wished for some sort of deliverance from this ordeal. In her nervousness, she had peed four times in the last hour. There was nothing for it but to get going, however.

Ella graciously opened the door of her car for her mother-in-law. Betta got into the Oldsmobile with the deference of a peasant entering the estate manager's home. Traditionally, as Ella's mother-in-law, Betta had a position of authority over Ella. Betta could never forget how hard her own mother-in-law had been on her sometimes. But that was a long time ago in a different country. Ella was a new woman in a new country who came from a wealthy family. Betta had become deferential to everyone, even her daughter-in-law. As they drove west along Barton Street, Betta mused about her son and daughter-in-law each having his and her own car. Both cars were top of the line Oldsmobiles. David considered an Oldsmobile the mark of a successful businessman. Cadillacs were for old people with old money. Betta said nothing to Ella or David about their extravagances, even though she suffered when David came to his father belligerently begging for money when he couldn't pay his creditors. Mike scolded loudly and always forced his son to swallow his pride, but he always gave him the money. There was an inevitable bitter parting when the two men had one of these sessions, and sometimes Betta wept silently. She was no longer demonstrative with her joy, love, or grief. As they drove in silence, Betta speculated about Ella's knowledge of these affairs. Ella behaved as if she and David really did have money to throw around. Is it possible that Ella didn't know that David was always on the edge of a financial abyss? A big house, big cars, nice clothes, effusive smiles and greetings, and in the early hours of the morning, a gnawing ache in the stomach or, on bad days, a sense of terror.

Betta had long ago admitted to herself, as many parents do, that she didn't know her son. She had become so quiet and timid and he was the opposite. Now she was on the edge of another admission—a heartbreaking and momentous admission. She was losing her daughter. Alina was twenty-three, about to graduate from university, and getting married. Betta could no longer cook or clean for her, iron her clothes, or pick up after her and serve her absolutely. The dictatorship of the absolutely slavish mother would be lost. Betta had gained power through her subservience and, in the last year, through her bravery. She had stood as a buffer between Mike's rages about the marriage and Alina's determined defiance.

Betta never expected love when her marriage was arranged in 1923. She certainly didn't expect love when she was re-united with this stranger in 1937. Yet marriages were sacred and sex was an obligation that must be met. Mike had no warmth or affection, but he was a hard-working man who drank very little and was a good, if overbearing, provider. Luckily, his job and projects were a substitute for any sexual energy he might have had and he seldom demanded sex. Betta wasn't sure as the years went by whether she would have preferred more sex or less sex. When she began to watch afternoon soap operas to assuage her loneliness, she was quite taken by the concept of expressed and romantic love. She joined millions of women around the world watching romantic dramas on television with beautiful women and handsome men, and then at dinner, they were joined by incommunicative, lumpish, fat, ugly oafs who were their husbands. By the time Betta thought much about this, she was in her mid-fifties. From the time she was twenty-four until she was thirty-one, she hadn't seen her husband, and events in Galicia may have shriveled her heart forever. And yet, the feminine need for perfect romantic love lingered in the soul of this fifty-eight-year-old woman.

Ella drove very competently. She did most things competently. Because her father had insisted that she marry a Ukrainian, her choice of suitors at the University of Toronto was quite limited. U of T was an Anglo university. The old staid university had been shaken into the new Canada by war veterans showing up with their worldly confidence. Professors could not intimidate men who had faced death on the battlefield. Then post-war prosperity meant that those bright young women and men from the lower classes could afford the tuition. Worst of all, the descendants of the Family Compact began to see names that weren't Anglo-Saxon. Ukrainians were not common at U of T and Ella was often upset and angry to discover that many classmates had never heard of Ukraine or Ukrainians. Out west, Ukrainians were numerous and becoming more and more powerful. The migration to the west in the early years of the century had made Ukrainians the second-largest ethnic group in the three western provinces. The first generations were content to farm the land and establish their economic stability. They were hard-working and silent. They meekly accepted their subservience to the dominant Anglos. After all, they arrived in the country as peasants from a life of peasantry. They were simply part of a national policy to populate the west, make railroad companies rich, and prevent American expansion. Like young men used as cannon fodder in war, the Ukrainians were herded to the west to fulfill a national need. Of course, they couldn't be treated as real Canadians. Ella was the next generation, however, who would be businessmen, lawyers, doctors, teachers, and politicians. They would not be silent, and they would not be second-class citizens. Ukrainian-Canadian nationalism was a force that helped drive the new generation to both achievement and despair.

This generation was expected to achieve too much—both from their parents and from themselves. The results of this high expectation were both marvelous and tragic.

Ella made a left-hand turn on Kenilworth Avenue and then a right on Hope Street. The shower was being held at the home of an old friend of the Evanses, Jane Lockwood. Jane was part of the large British immigration after the war. She had been born and raised in Liverpool and married another Liverpudlian in 1930. They had both worked in the munitions industry during the war and done fairly well financially, but they wanted a different life and came to Canada in 1946. They bought a house across from Alice on Lottridge Street. Alice welcomed Jane as a newcomer to Canada and Jane supported Alice as a mother with no husband present. Later, the Lockwoods moved further east to a bigger home. This home was a large bungalow with three bedrooms and a full basement. Now the parents and their two children could each have a bedroom of their own. The front room looked onto a small lawn and the dining room was separated only by a change of wallpaper. The front room and dining room were blended today by the placement of their four kitchen chairs along one wall and four borrowed kitchen chairs along the other. Their best tablecloth (white linen) was on the dining room table. It was the decade when women collected tea cups and saucers in different patterns, and the table had twenty various sets arranged in four rows. There were two teapots—one family, one borrowed. Coffee hadn't yet become part of the British tradition. The sofa and chair had had their protective doilies removed and revealed only a slight pattern of lighter material where they had been. The area carpet had been recently vacuumed (Mrs. Lockwood would say hoovered) and the border of hardwood shone with new wax. The coffee table was decorated with a centerpiece of various coloured bows and ribbons. Mrs. Lockwood had spent a great deal of time and effort getting ready for this event and she was voluble with nervous energy. Friends and neighbours from Hope Street and Lottridge Street were assembled and making small talk. The ladies had on their Sunday dresses and felt a little restricted but happy to be dressed up.

They were anxious to meet the mother of the bride. A few had already met Alina on her visits to the Evans family home, and those who had met her were immediately impressed by her warmth and friendliness. Without exception, the Evanses' acquaintances were British. The Ukrainian was a rare bird. The ladies were not intolerant towards Ukrainians because most of them didn't know where Ukraine was and they simply lumped all Central Europeans together as foreigners. Those in the neighbourhood who were intolerant called anyone who didn't speak English a DP—a Displaced Person. This generation had lived through World War II and their attitudes to different nationalities were shaped by the experience. They had hated the Germans, Italians, and Japanese. They had been cajoled to hate, then love, then hate the Russians. They knew they had to hate one group of Frenchmen but love another group, although they couldn't always keep the two groups distinct. They were told they must love the Jews because of the Holocaust, but dealing with local Jews always aroused an ambiguous response. One thing the ladies knew for sure was that those from the British Isles were an especially wonderful people, certainly superior to people from other places in the world.

When Ella knocked on the door, all the conversation quieted and heads were re-aligned to be able to see the front door. Ella had rapped on the wooden door with just the right amount of force. She had not knocked timidly as if obsequious, but she knew a forceful knock would indicate a certain peasant crudeness. She had to let the ladies know that she, not they, could put on an air of condescension if any social tension arose. After all, her home and her car were much more expensive than any of theirs.

Jane greeted Betta and Ella with such warmth that Ella immediately relaxed and the rigidity of her face and body softened. Betta was very apprehensive. She peered around Ella to see twelve faces silently looking at her, which almost impeded her ability to talk or walk. When Jane indicated the chairs that had been saved for them, Ella and Betta moved towards them, smiling at these expectant strangers. Once seated, Ella introduced herself and introduced Betta. Betta whispered hellos in an almost inaudible voice, frequently looking at the coffee table to avoid eye contact. The ladies were determined to be kind. They took pride in being more tolerant and flexible than their parents had been. Of course, they wouldn't want their own children to marry a Ukrainian or Pole or Czech or whatever these other groups were in Hamilton's East End, but they were remarkably equitable about what their friends' children did. It was the same unexpressed smugness that allowed these ladies to be very kind to friends' daughters who became pregnant but turned them into irrational screaming witches at the thought of their own daughters falling from grace.

When Betta saw the cups and saucers lined up on the dining room table, she became even more apprehensive. She had difficulty with these little objects and if she had to balance a tiny plate on her lap, she knew she would spill something. On top of that, she had to go pee again. But she could hardly ask to go to the bathroom in a stranger's home. She knew that polite ladies never went to the bathroom. Often, she herself waited until she and Mike got home from some rare social event to go to the bathroom, even though she might have been in pain for hours. As a girl working on the farm, she had often just slipped behind a tree or bush to relieve herself. But in polite company, normal bodily functions had become shameful. Ella had begun a three-way conversation with two ladies on her left and Betta pretended to be listening intently so that she wouldn't have to make conversation with the lady on her right. Betta didn't understand everything the ladies said to Ella, but she understood they were talking about a new supermarket on Parkdale Avenue. They were comparing Loblaws and Dominion. Each woman had her own preference for meat and fresh produce. Large supermarkets were quickly replacing the family grocery stores, meat stores, and fruit stores. Most people had cars now, although the Evans family did not.

Betta was wondering which of these ladies was Mrs. Evans. She really hadn't heard any of the introductions because of her nervousness. Actually, Alice Evans was out in the kitchen helping with the final preparations. Like Betta, Alice was extremely shy. She had been a farm girl, too, but in Saskatchewan and Wales. Betta's timidity was due in part to her inability to speak or understand English easily. Alice was timid and lacked self-confidence because of her family background and her own perceived shortcomings. Both would have preferred to be at home working in the kitchen or watching television. They could have survived this social tradition if they had been there simply as guests, but both knew they were going to be the centre of attention at some point.

Finally, Alice emerged from the kitchen with an heirloom tray of quarter-cut sandwiches covered with waxed paper. The sandwiches were the traditional mix of minced ham mixed with pickles, roast beef, salmon with mayonnaise, and tuna with mayonnaise. The crusts had been cut off the bread and Jane had put them aside in a brown paper bag for later use in a bread pudding or poultry stuffing. Ladies who were on rations during the war didn't throw anything away. The birds could fend for themselves. Strangely enough, Betta Dubinsky and Alice Evans had not met until this moment, although their children had been courting for two years. Neither family ever entertained friends for dinner, and they certainly wouldn't invite strangers for a social evening. None of the four parents was unfriendly or pathologically reclusive, but the essential routine of their lives did not include dinner parties or evenings of cards or dancing. Perhaps the fact that both men were shift workers and that all four were raised outside of Hamilton had much to do with their complete lack of social lives. For the most part, their social interaction involved the immediate family and fellow church-goers.

After she put the tray down, Alice moved tentatively to join the circle of women. There was an awkward moment when nobody moved spontaneously to introduce the mothers of the betrothed. Within seconds, however, Ella, who was quite socially adept and confident, made the formal introductions. The two mothers whispered hellos to each other and Alice opened the conversation by asking if Betta and Ella had any trouble finding Jane's house. When Ella stated they had not, and Betta nodded her agreement, the spontaneous conversation had reached its end. Everything after that would be tortuously slow, like worrying answers from an adolescent about activities. The artificiality of this situation put both women under a great deal of strain. Both knew that others were observing them with an unusual amount of curiosity. This mixed marriage was still uncommon in the various and variegated communities that made up Hamilton. Yet Alice and Betta were determined to be friendly to each other—certainly their intrinsic decency would not allow them to be rude to others. The ladies, however, were becoming a little restless. The bride-to-be, trailed by her groom-to-be, should have shown up by now. No food or drink had been served, and if custom had allowed some wine, mixed drinks, or cocktails to be offered, there might have been a more patient and lugubrious air. After all, kitchen chairs become a little hard after a while if the mind cannot be diverted by some interesting human interaction. The unexpressed sentiment, "She should have been here by now," became expressed. Although the ladies were becoming impatient with Alina, they offered excuses for her tardiness to hide their own growing exasperation.

Finally, the front door swung open and the honoured guest began the obligatory expression of surprise. Alina was a thin young lady with blonde hair and green eyes—typical Nordic Ukraine. She had a wonderful smile, and as she was introduced to each stranger, she exuded a genuine warmth. She was, in short, attractive and charming with a practiced vulnerable innocence. Roy Evans never left the three-by-three entryway. He wasn't expected to stay, of course—it was a ladies' night. But he made the minimum polite appearance acceptable. The ladies laughed at his reticence and made comments about the general ineffectiveness of men in social gatherings. They whispered comparisons with their own doltish sons and husbands. Roy was happy to escape after ten minutes of greetings expressed with tentative smiles, nods, and waves. Unlike Alina, he wasn't sure he was enjoying the attention that engaged couples got. His retreat down the front steps was hardly noticed as the ladies got down to the rituals at hand.

Alina was led to a chair decorated with blue and pink ribbons that had been moved towards the centre of the front room. As she sat down, Betta whispered to Ella in Ukraine. Ella answered in English that she should relax, nothing bad was happening to her daughter. Alina picked up the exchange and told her mother not to worry. The ladies looked benevolently and with amusement at Betta. Jane had prepared several cute little quizzes that Alina had to answer to predict when her first child would be born and what sex it would be and how many would follow. The cute little quiz to determine if Alina was a virgin or not was omitted for fear of offending the Ukrainians. During the quizzes, the ladies laughed and giggled and nudged one another, just as they had done during the same quizzes a score of times. But the party had finally begun and inhibitions were beginning to drop. The ladies loved the dance of the marriage ritual—the showers, the gifts, the new dresses, the strangers, the speculations, the conflicts, the nuggets of family secrets. The marriage of a friend or neighbour added a certain zest to their lives. This one was even more interesting because the bride and her parents were different and there was a rumour that the bride's father was not happy and may, in fact, be in a rage. It was important, then, that during the shower, all possible information be gleaned. Every answer or statement that Alina, Betta, or Ella made would be carefully remembered and scrupulously analyzed by the ladies in the days ahead. If there was conflict, it would be wonderful. Conflict in somebody else's family was always wonderful. One's own family problems had to be swept under the carpet. It was the days of fiercely guarded family privacy. The time had not yet come when people revealed everything about themselves whenever and wherever they could. The social psychologists were still finishing their PhDs at the newly funded universities.

After Alina's quizzes were over, Jane introduced three little word games to amuse the ladies and allow them to offer their favourite little witticisms. By the time they had finished the last game, which used paper and stubs of pencils, the ladies were laughing and talking noisily. The games had solicited a series of responses from the ladies similar to the responses a patient under psychoanalysis makes to words listed by his analyst. Some ladies responded with enigmatic warnings about financial difficulties, some about dietary problems, some about laziness, some about drinking, and even most subtle of all, about sexual conflicts. Each lady had her own little anecdote, or several, about marriage. Sometimes the veneer of good humour about these problems peeled at the corners. In a way, these ladies were importing their wisdom to the bride. Alina was so caught up in being the centre of attention that she heard very little of what the ladies were saying. The important thing was to smile and look attractive. As the ladies handed their paper and pencils to a volunteer, Jane pulled a large cardboard box decorated with pink tissue paper and large pink bows across the carpet. The opening of gifts was about to begin.

Finding the right shower gift was a dilemma that had preoccupied some of these ladies for as long as two weeks. The shower was designated as a "linen shower"—that meant tablecloths, towels, napkins, dish towels, bedsheets, and pillowcases. Shower gifts were generally inexpensive, often quite frivolous. The main gift was the wedding present. But some ladies were invited to the wedding and some were not. If they weren't invited to the wedding, the ladies might give a bigger shower present because that was the end of their expenses. On the other hand, they might give a smaller present because they felt slighted. The immediate family was expected to give more expensive shower gifts. The hostess could consider her duties as part of the gift. Neighbours didn't like being outdone by each other, but a gift that was too expensive was obviously in bad taste. Some gifts looked more expensive than others. The same ostensible gift, like bedsheets, could have a very wide range of quality and price. The calculations were complex and nerve-wracking. To make matters worse, the gifts were opened in front of everyone and immediate reaction was elicited. Usually, the gifts were passed around for even closer inspection. These warriors of sales knew the products very well and judgment would be indicated by a raised eyebrow or a tongue jutting the lower lip forward. It was not exactly a bazaar, but the skills were very similar. The recipient, of course, had to be grateful and effusive over every gift, no matter how much she disliked it. As she opened each gift, Alina thanked the donor profusely and the lady whose eyes had been modestly averted looked up smiling to receive her thanks and the general approval of the crowd. This is the formal part. Later, the gifts would be more critically examined by the recipient and the other guests.

Ella, who knew all about the Anglo culture, had taken Betta over to Sears to buy a lovely set of sheets. They were the best quality available. Ella knew the Dubinskys had lots of money; the trick was for Betta to wrestle it from her sullen husband. Mike was becoming more and more opposed to the marriage as each of the ceremonies took place. Alina's demand for the money to buy a wedding dress began a series of bitter battles.

Ella wanted to impress the Evans family and their friends with her financial success. Ella bought a bedspread that was even more expensive than Betta's sheets. Mothers generally think their sons' wives are too extravagant, but Betta was much too perceptive for that. Betta knew that David expected Ella to be extravagant; he needed the window-dressing. And so the gifts were beautifully wrapped by the salesclerk. Ella didn't do wrapping. When Alina opened the gifts, the ladies were impressed. But Alice paid for the social success of Betta and Ella. Alice's set of towels and facecloths were obviously not as expensive as the sheets and bedspread. Alice accepted the gracious thanks of Alina and the outward approval of the ladies, but she couldn't suppress the redness in her cheeks that revealed her embarrassment.

Once all the gifts had been opened, Alina made a hesitant little speech thanking the ladies and especially Mrs. Lockwood for their kindness. Again, she was such a pleasant combination of warmth, shyness, good humour, and vulnerability that the ladies were quite taken. Luckily, they thought, she doesn't have the obvious self-confidence, intelligence, and assertiveness of her sister-in-law. For some strange reason, the ladies preferred women like Betta and Alice, perhaps because their model of womanhood had been based on timidity and self-effacement. They were going to be in for a shock when their daughters and granddaughters came of age. After the little speech and general good wishes from all, Jane announced that the tea and food was ready. Jane and some conspirators had made their way to the kitchen for final preparations as the gifts were being opened and exclaimed over. Now the ladies had to exclaim over the desserts. Ella took Betta's hand and guided her to the table. Betta avoided the tea and took two quarter sandwiches for her plate, then hurriedly resumed sitting in her chair. Ella was effusive in her praise of the table. She took a cup of tea and four quarter sandwiches, vowing to return for dessert. Alina hadn't been able to join the ladies at the table. Mrs. Collingwood had ignored all the social niceties, as she always did, and was asking Alina some very specific questions about where she would live, how much Roy would be paid as a teacher, if they were planning on having a family immediately, and so forth. Alina, as usual, was very cooperative and forthcoming and Mrs. Collingwood thought she had hit pay dirt on the search for golden gossip.

The initial analysis of the gifts had ended and now critical attention was directed towards the dining room table. Because most of the ladies had been in Jane's house in the past, they needed only a superficial examination of the furniture and wall decorations. Some had not seen Jane's collection of cups and saucers before, so there was a little bit of leaning over the table to examine the full contingent arranged with military precision. Some immediately noted the heirlooms from Britain and were properly appreciative. At that time, China had to be made in Britain to be considered acceptable. China from China or Nippon was not acceptable, never mind the political consideration. Certainly, china from Japan had to be left on the shelf at Woolworth's. The ladies real critical powers, however, were aimed at the various desserts. Jane had asked each lady to bring her favourite dessert. As with the gifts, each lady wanted her dessert to be noted for its uniqueness, for that something special that indicated its creator was a culinary genius, no matter if the ingredients were inexpensive. The desserts were certainly wide-ranging pies, cakes, tarts, custards, tortes, and cookies. It was as if each lady wanted to control a particular category of dessert. Certainly, those in the know (and if they weren't in the know, they were told) did not intrude upon Mrs. Gates' control of the cheesecake category. Mrs. Gates had a marvelous recipe for this delicacy and at every social gathering, she made it clear that her recipe was nonpareil. Since she extracted support for this position every time she brought forth her platter, nobody else attempted a cheesecake. After all, would you sing a chorus of *White Cliffs of Dover* with Vera Lynn in the room? Other categories had not been as well established. Some ladies even brought different desserts from time to time. Cakes were always a problem because the height of the cake seemed definitive. A clarification of the recipe might have to be pronounced if a cake were too flat. Sometimes there was conflict between high-cake and low-cake advocates. Pies were another problem in objective analyses. This time, the exact shade of brown of the crust was in dispute. Here there were the white-brown adherents versus the brown-brown adherents. Luckily, the fat end of the egg and the small end of the egg disciples were not present at this gathering. The male will never understand the personal disgrace, however, of having a dessert, or casserole, or box lunch returned to him completely untouched. In these cases, the ladies simply leave their food behind rather than be seen carrying a full container home again. Those who were successful in getting other ladies to eat their desserts loudly announced that they would get the recipe for them.

The ladies were a little annoyed with Betta because she just nibbled at two small cookies made by the same person. Betta was too shy to utter the usual compliments. She simply ate slowly hoping that this ordeal would soon be over. In truth, she found some of the desserts strange and unappealing. The meals that she prepared for Mike and Alina were quite simple; she had no experience in dessert-making. Yet in her youth in Galicia, she had known elaborate feasts and been part of their preparation. The events of the 1930s burned and abraded the good times from her memory; she was left with only the basics, a simple life and a simple diet. Anything else seemed either ostentatious or dangerous. Certainly, it seemed as if all those who ate well in Galicia in the 1920s were either killed or deported in the 1930s. Better to eat simply and be quiet.

The ladies had all visited the tea and dessert table now and were chatting volubly in small groups. Alice had seen Betta sitting alone and ventured to sit beside her. Betta's normal protectors, Alina and Ella, were involved in two different animated discussions—one concerned carpet cleaning and the other, bridesmaid dresses. Betta and Alice offered each other little crumbs of opening dialogue like two uncomfortable passengers in a stuck elevator. In truth, the situation was not dissimilar. They both seemed to be saying with word and gesture, "Look, we're in an awkward situation, but let's try to get through it with the least amount of conflict and pain." Both Alice and Betta hated scenes. They scurried away from confrontation. Both had accepted the fact that their children would not be guided by them. They hated many of the decisions their children had made, but they realized that their youths and the youths of their children were vastly different. The world had turned upside down several times in their lifetimes. The almost sixty years of their lives had seen catastrophic changes in the world.

Strangely enough, both women looked at their days of hardship with more affection and understanding than these new days of vulgar affluence. Perhaps most people believe the places and ages in which they spent their youths are better than any other ages and places. And so, Alice and Betta had an affinity—they were both old women with merely acceptable husbands and their children had made decisions that made them uncomfortable. Within minutes, each understood that the other was uneasy. This led to the beginning of affection. They actually began to talk about things that were more than mere civilities. As with all people their age, they voiced concerns about the financial well-being of the betrothed. Betta knew that the Evans family had little money. Mike had fumed about this. But since both Peter and Roy were uncommunicative at home, Alice had scarcely heard of the Dubinsky family. She didn't know that the Dubinskys owned a small apartment building and a one-sixth share in a pub. Although they believed they shared the same middle-class life, one was the wife of a nascent manager-capitalist and one was the wife of a labourer. The income was significantly different and the outlook enormously different. This was a matter beyond the women, however; something only of significance to sociologists and micro-economists. The women were merely beginning to like each other.

The ladies were now beginning the ritual of departure. It was a Thursday night and *The Perry Como Show* began at 10 p.m. They had already given up *The Donna Reid Show* at nine o'clock for the shower. They weren't prepared to give up too much. Besides, there was an organic length to these events. Usually, from beginning to end, the shower took no more than three hours. The ladies first of all offered to help clean up. Jane politely refused all offers. Then the ladies praised the organization of the games and presentation of presents. Jane modestly accepted all praise—enthusiastic or not. Then the ladies awkwardly told Betta and Ella how much they had enjoyed meeting them (cross-cultural interaction is always difficult). Then the ladies warmly wished Alina all the best and offered humorous little bromides like, "Learn to cook his favourite meals," "Don't be a doormat," "Keep your own bank account," and so forth. Many humorous wishes reflected their own problems, but they good-naturally skated over them. Finally, they made arrangements with their own personal best friends to meet at such-and-such a place at such-and-such a time.

Only Jane, Alice, Betta, Ella, and Alina remained. The evening was a success because these women got along. They got along without any painful alterations of personality or repression of true character. They had been prepared to be nice even if it killed them, but that force of will was not necessary. In fact, they were all relaxed, even Betta. Betta was so at ease that she asked to use the bathroom without the slightest embarrassment. Alice thought that Alina had made a favourable impression on the ladies and that relieved her worries. Jane knew she had run a successful event. Ella realized that the ladies were aware of her expensive clothing and jewellery, and once she had even picked up a fragment of conversation alluding to her successful businessman husband. The tones of the ladies indicated the appropriate respect. Alina had basked in her fame. All the usual manifestations of the bride as the centre of the universe had been displayed. Alina loved these moments of glory. She had more attention and compliments than she had ever received in her life. Her parents were not demonstrative and did not grant praise easily. She hadn't accomplished either academic or athletic feats that would garner celebrity. But now she was the brightest little star in her small galaxy. Having a wedding day arranged certainly set in motion all kinds of very pleasant events.

The women sat for another thirty minutes discussing and finalizing the minutia of a wedding. They talked about who would drive, who would ride in what cars, how long the marriage ceremony might be, who would be on the receiving line, and so on and so on. Ella understood that most of the ceremony would be English and she accepted that. As a matter of fact, that made her own elaborate Ukrainian ceremony seem all the more wonderful and important. Not only that, she knew it would infuriate her father-in-law and that pleased her also. Betta didn't know much about weddings in Canada. She had already accepted the fact that it would not be a Ukrainian wedding and all she wanted now was a happy and uneventful day. But she knew that her husband's brooding was not good.

Chapter Twenty-Three

Ontario 1964

Tom was in a sweat. He was caught in commuter traffic on the Queen Elizabeth Way at 4:15 p.m. His old Ford Fairlane seemed to be labouring under the strain of the day—highway driving, then stop and go highway driving and ninety-degree heat. He was in a foul mood as he thought about the situation. As Roy's best man, it was his responsibility to run a stag. Well, he'd been surprised to be chosen as the best man in the first place since he hadn't seen much of Roy for several months. But they'd been very close during soccer season. They'd had drinking bouts at Paddy Greene's, done the bed push together, and even double-dated once. He'd been flattered, however, and set to work planning the event. He had been to a number of stags by now and knew the general pattern for those evenings. First of all, he decided that any of the weekdays before Saturday, June 21, the wedding day, would be fine. Then he had to find a suitable hall. Roy didn't have a great number of friends. His high school pals had scattered over the five years. Roy had left Delta Secondary School. He had lived at home to go to McMaster so he hadn't made any residence friends. He'd acquired a liberal arts degree in English and History and had no close friends in the same specialized course. People in religious studies, engineering, nursing, geography, and so forth usually formed a pretty close-knit group resulting in life-long friendships. Roy had played varsity soccer and intramural football and basketball, but it wouldn't be easy to contact these people. The result was that Tom contacted as many people as possible and then told Roy he would have to invite everyone who might come. Tom felt a disaster coming on. He had rented the hall but what if only fifteen or twenty men showed up? His potential loss of money would only hurt him slightly more than Roy's painful loss of face.

Things were not looking good the day of the stag. Tom had phoned the Mount Hope Air Force Social Club at ten to confirm that everything was ready. The club had kitchen facilities and the manager would make a midnight snack for thirty men at $2.50 per head. The meal would be rolls, cold meat, cheese, potato salad, pickles and coffee—the usual stag meal. The hall rental was fifty dollars and the tickets were five dollars each. Tom thought that with a little luck, he could break even. During the brief discussion with the manager, however, a sudden Laurel and Hardy storm broke. The manager asked Tom if he had the liquor license. Tom said he assumed the hall got the liquor license. No, the manager, answered, hardly keeping her voice under control. The person renting the hall had to get the license. She announced in a voice that was becoming higher and sharper that if Tom didn't have a license to present at seven o'clock, the event was off. Moreover, she wouldn't begin to make the meal. She then hung up abruptly. Tom sat stunned and angry for several moments, frozen both physically and mentally. He suddenly started and realized he had to do something. The event couldn't be called off. He phoned the manager—Mrs. Metcalf—back. He had originally hoped to have so little to do with her that he wouldn't need to recall her name. But it seemed that would not be the case.

"Mrs. Metcalf," Tom asked, perhaps more meekly than he needed to, "how do I get a liquor license today?"

"Well, if you had got the license two weeks ago as most men do," there was a long pause so Tom could realize how inept he was, "you could have got it in Hamilton. Now you'll have to drive to Toronto."

"What? Toronto? Couldn't I just phone?"

"No. You'll have to drive over to Front Street."

This time, Tom paused, frozen by an acidic combination of anger and resentment.

"Do you know the number on Front Street?"

"Yes. One-forty Front Street West."

"Thank you, Mrs. Metcalf. I'll drive over this morning."

Tom hung up the phone gently, a marvelous act of self-restraint—and then exploded. He screamed so loud his mother came in from the garden to ask what had happened. He told her he would have to drive to Toronto immediately. She clucked her tongue and said that was too bad and really meant it. Of course, she didn't know why he was driving to Toronto or why he was so upset. She did know it wouldn't be worthwhile asking him. He measured his independence by the paucity of information he gave his parents. She knew further questions would just annoy him so she simply told him to drive carefully and returned to weeding her vegetable garden.

Tom checked his wallet for the identification that would prove he was over twenty-one, then he went to his bedroom to get another forty dollars from the cache hidden in his sock drawer. He counted the twenty-dollar bills left, which added up to $140. He might make it to another payday. He hurried out of the house, climbed into his car, backed carefully down the shrub-lined driveway, did a half-turn on the road, and headed for the Kenilworth Access. He didn't bother telling his mother he wouldn't be home for supper.

As Tom drove along the Queen Elizabeth heading east, he fumed about Ontario's antiquated liquor laws. In an age of liberalism, Ontario was determined to curb the immorality of its citizens. There seemed to be a feeling that all sin stemmed from alcohol. Certainly, all the experiments with liquor control in North America in the last fifty years suggested that the New Jerusalem could be reached if fermentation of fruit and grain could be halted. Tom calmed down as he listened to a series of love ballads on the radio. Elvis, Frank Sinatra, and Perry Como seemed to be in an especially loving mood this afternoon. It was, after all, a beautiful June day, and he didn't have to return to the three-to-eleven shift at Stelco until tomorrow. He had become so quiescent, he was driving only 55 on a sixty-mile-per-hour highway.

Tom turned onto Lakeshore Drive and slowed even more to admire the sailboats on Toronto's lakefront. Obviously, not everyone spent every day working for a living. This is what he thought about as he saw the crowded courts at the Toronto Tennis Club and admired the white figures in sailboats. He might be there someday. He wasn't sure if he hated or envied the rich. He certainly wasn't driven by an unquenchable thirst to join or emulate them. Like most lower-middle-class young men who went off to University, Tom was quite happy to be himself. "Pleased with himself" might be the phrase. The school system had shown him that he was a fairly bright boy, and although Tom didn't give it that much thought, his prevalent role models were self-made men—athletes, pilots, politicians, and musicians. All the literature that Tom had studied and all the films and TV shows he had watched denigrated those who had inherited wealth rather than earned it. But the rich are never loved in any age.

This was not a time for philosophical musings, however. Tom had to get a liquor license and get back to Hamilton. He still had to pick up the condiments of a party—paper plates, peanuts, potato chips, pretzels, paper serviettes, playing cards, and a roll of draw tickets. Two friends from work who had met Roy at a couple of parties had agreed to help Tom with the stag. They weren't exactly altruistic; they wanted an excuse to go to a party, but they were genuinely helpful. Jim had volunteered to be the bartender. That would save the five-dollar-per-hour fee for the club bartender. Rob seemed almost anxious to bring his stag films and 16 mm projector. Like a man who volunteers his boat and motor for a fishing trip, or a man who insists you take his new car to the baseball game, Rob wanted approval from others. He also enjoyed watching his own films and watching the reaction of others to them. There might have been a slight bit of sexual perversion there but nothing that would make anyone uncomfortable. Certainly not after four or five beers.

Tom made a left on Spadina and then a right on Front. The parking lots had exorbitant prices of fifty cents an hour, but Tom didn't have time to look for a spot on a side street. He pulled into a lot, paid his money to an attendant, stuffed the receipt in his pocket, and marched briskly east along Front. He came to a large red-brick building that had accumulated a patina of dark soot. The building had housed any number of bureaucracies since its initial bureaucracy in 1928—the Internal Tariffs Board. As each bureaucracy grew or mutated, it found a bigger and better place. This building was now used for bureaucracies of mid-size, either on the way up or on the way down, depending on the political whims of the time. The sign in large block white letters said, "The Liquor Control Board of Ontario." A no-nonsense sign for a no-nonsense Bureaucracy.

Square and straight letters for a square and straight agency. Calligraphy of the utilitarian. Tom entered the second door on the right. On the left was a series of counters with attendants and large double doors leading to a very long single room with desks and chairs lined up in rows. The attendants in each chair looked through glass openings like a ticket dispenser at a theatre. People went randomly to any window that was either open or had a short line. Each person who spoke to an attendant received one of the two things: verbal or hand instructions to go somewhere else or a form to fill out. In dispensing either travel directions or paper, the attendants seemed angry, almost belligerent. They expected strangers to their bureaucracy to know exactly what to do and where to go. Ignorance got them very upset. Unfortunately, Tom was one of the ignorant ones. All he wanted was a liquor license for tonight, but he had no idea where in this vast building they might be dispensed. When Tom told his problem to the lady at the glass wicket, he received the travel directions. She told him curtly that occasional liquor licenses were issued on the third floor and implied by the tone of her voice that any nincompoop knew that. Tom clenched his teeth and stomped away. He knew he must not lose his temper. Bureaucrats love people who lose their temper and begin to scream and shout. It justifies the terrible treatment they receive. Of course, those who are polite and silent receive the same terrible treatment. In fact, bureaucrats treat people poorly because that's what bureaucrats do. They don't need any rationale for that.

Tom now walked in the typical fashion of men trying to keep their temper in check. The bad-tempered stomp was blended with a philosophical stroll, resulting in the disjointed, loose-limbed, wooden-hinged, air flapping march of a wooden puppet. Tom was trying to stay loose, but his body knew he was unconsciously piling coal into the furnace of his rage.

By the time Tom reached the third floor, he had uncomfortable beads of sweat running down and across his body. Thousands of glistening droplets stood like tiny globes of light across his forehead, temples, and upper lip. Slick lines of sweat gathered behind his ears and moved down his neck across his pulsating arteries. He could feel another line of sweat march down his spinal column and into the small of his back. He saw a white porcelain drinking fountain reaching out from the wall about thirty feet from the elevator. Water was probably the drink of choice at the Liquor Control Board. Unfortunately, the fountain wasn't working. The government buildings maintenance bureaucracy couldn't fix the fountain at the liquor control bureaucracy because the proper paperwork had not been properly filled out. The bureaucrats at the liquor control bureaucracy didn't understand the forms given to them by the maintenance bureaucracy. By the time a new washer, worth twelve cents, was put in the fountain, it would cost eight thousand dollars and take three months. Yet both bureaucracies were very proud of their competency and efficiency, and every six months or so, remarkable improvements were made by ambitious new managers on their way up.

Tom entered the door marked, "Occasional Liquor Licenses," thirsty and shining with sweat. It was the wrong kind of sweat, too. It was the rank, sulfur-laden sweat that leaks from the pores of a body, tense with anger and frustration. It was a nasty alkaline sweat that yellows clothing and leaves a persistent residue on chairs and hangs malevolently in the air. Yet Tom knew he must be calm. He must pay whatever price the clerk demanded. He must choke his anger and outrage and be subservient to these new masters of the bureaucratic age. On the elevator to the third floor, Tom had considered a number of personas: the hopelessly inept, loose-ended idiot hoping for mercy to overcome his debilitating incompetence; the out-of-control bully ready to smash anyone with his fists who stood in his way; the unctuous friend of politicians who could advance the career of anyone helpful. Tom decided to be the cheerful, this-is-only-a-minor-problem, smiling, carefree, good-natured citizen just popping in to quickly clear up an insignificant problem and an oh-so-grateful-for-your-help tax-payer.

When Tom looked to his left, he saw all these personas and more sitting on chairs, waiting to be received. He took a plastic number from a wooden dispensary box. Ninety-two. He knew there weren't ninety-one people in front of him. Did it mean ninety-two people this afternoon? Today? This week? This month? Would it be better if the bureaucrats saw a lot of people or a few people? Would it be better if they dealt with a lot of screw-ups or just a few screw-ups? If they dealt with a lot of screw-ups, would they just wave people through quickly? Or would a lot of screw-ups make them angry and vindictive? Would they happily accept ten screw-ups per day and then flail every screw-up from eleven on? What if ninety-two meant ninety-two this month? Then the bureaucrats wouldn't be as angry with the people they are paid to serve and who pay their salaries. A few screw-ups could be tolerated and the miscreants gently treated with honeyed condescension because they affirmed the intelligence of the bureaucrats. But a few screw-ups meant that each case could be dealt with more fully, be granted that commodity which bureaucrats had in abundance—time. Questioning an uncomfortable petitioner was always more fun than emptying an inbox of the same four items that had been there for over three months, re-reading them, deciding again to postpone action, and returning them to the inbox as if the matters had been dealt with. Harassing citizens was always more enjoyable than doing productive work—especially on afternoons in the summer when everyone else was leaving work early, but they were imprisoned by the new punch clock system. The manager who innovated that idea was moving up through the bureaucracy very quickly because he was smart enough to exclude middle and senior management from the system. Their parking spaces were always empty by 3 p.m. on weekdays and by 2 p.m. on Fridays.

Tom was beginning to stick to the wooden chair. His alkaline sweat and the varnish on the chair were melding into polyurethane glue. He had to periodically raise a cheek to free himself, each time emitting a heavy soughing sound like two hippopotamuses parting after a French kiss. Lips parsed, eyes narrowed, and heads raised a half inch disdainfully, suggesting that those sitting on adjoining seats thought he was farting—wet ones. Well, a clerk had just called number ninety. Tom thought he might have to lean to the left and then to the right only two more times. The two-month-old Maclean's magazine wasn't taking Tom's mind off his seating problem.

When the next clerk called ninety-one, no one responded. The clerk raised his voice for ninety-one again. A third call for ninety-one got no response. The clerk walked to the wooden dispensary. Ninety-one was not there. Ninety-one must have left the building with his plastic ninety-one. This was not good. Now every time a clerk in this office called ninety-one, there would be no response. Already there was no response for sixteen, thirty-two, and forty-seven. There were four numbers missing and no way of replacing them, no hope of getting a new set of plastic numbers. Any replacement would be slipshod. If all the numbers weren't exactly the same, it would grate on the nerves of the bureaucrats. People who spent four hours a day straightening the top of their desks couldn't stand numbers that didn't match. The clerk wasn't happy. In fact, he was fuming. He wanted to tell his friend Mabel what had happened and how angry he was. But Mabel was on her coffee break. Since her fifteen-minute coffee break had started only thirty minutes ago, she wouldn't be back for some time. Because Allen spoke only to Mabel in the office of twenty-five employees, his frustration was manifest.

Allen (his last name was Simpson) called angrily for number ninety-two, daring that number to be absent. Tom began rising from his seat. There was a split second of panic when Tom's chair began rising with him. The glue would not give up its hold. The chair lifted a full six inches off the floor before weight and motion asserted their full physical properties. The chair landed with a sharp crack on the terrazzo floor. Allen's angry frown grew even deeper as he tried to figure out what had happened. Tom smiled and tried to appear nonchalant as he furtively patted down the seat of his pants to make sure no part of the chair was stuck there. As he approached Allen's window, Tom smiled even more broadly, well into his persona, if a little disconcerted by the bang of the chair and the anger lines on Mr. Simpson's forehead.

"How can I help you?"

Tom knew he didn't want to help.

"Oh. Hi. Well. I've got a little problem."

Mr. Simpson compressed his lips to indicate there were no little problems at the Liquor Control Board. He remained silent. When a petitioner is uncomfortable, say nothing. Let them talk so that they become almost incoherent in their wretchedness.

"You see, there was a mix-up between me and the rental hall about a liquor license. They thought I would get it and I assumed they already had it."

Tom tried to smile broadly and chuckle quietly at the same time. The chuckle caught in his throat as his lips parted in a smile and there was a sharp gurgling sound like a death rattle. The thick, acidic saliva at the back of his throat caused a sudden spasmodic coughing spell.

Mr. Simpson was beginning to enjoy this.

Tom's persona was slipping away. He tried desperately to get back into character. Another smile. This smile had no elasticity. It stayed fixed like the smiles on billboard ads.

"The manager of the hall said I could just drive over here, y'know, and pay the twenty-five dollars, y'know, and get the license— y'know."

Tom had spent three years training himself to drop "y'know."

"When is this event?" The cool objective servant of the people said.

"Tonight. In Hamilton." Tom had added, "In Hamilton," thinking that the judge might forgive the dolts of Steeltown their lack of Toronto sophistication.

"Tonight! And you want the license this afternoon?" There was a jarring clash between real time and bureaucratic time. Mr. Simpson felt as if cymbals had met just behind his forehead.

"What is this important event?" Half anger, half sarcasm.

Tom's frozen smile began to melt at the corners. It became an untrustworthy slush, shaped by its own irresolution. Tom was neither man nor persona. He gripped the counter as the last firm place in the universe.

"Well, you see. I'm a best man, eh, and my friend's getting married on Saturday, eh. So, we want to have a stag, eh. And everything's arranged, eh. And the hall's rented, eh. And . . ." Gibberish with a Canadian "eh" added. Tom had successfully dropped his eh five years ago.

"Stag! You say stag? We don't allow liquor licenses for stags in Ontario!"

"Stag? No, no. No Stag. Wedding party. Just some friends. Like to sing. Watch the baseball game. Maybe one beer each. Not everyone drinks. Everyone's over twenty-one. No loud noise. Out in country . . ."

Tom's grip on the counter was becoming as tenuous as his grip on his mind.

Allen suddenly realized he was in trouble. Within the last two months, he had pushed two taxpayers over the edge. One was all right. He had simply started to sob. Large shoulder-lifting sobs that raised his whole body but didn't produce tears. He simply lifted and let go his shoulders as he cried the silent cry of a wounded animal or a discarded lover. His eyes had stared at Allen unfocused for perhaps a full minute before he turned, his shoulders still heaving, and made for the door. He braced his right hand then his left hand on the door frame before he had the strength to leave. Other petitioners gaped and then swallowed almost in unison. No problem. But the next taxpayer whom Allen interviewed snapped. Not a little raised voice, obscenity-laced snap. Not a banging-the-counter snap. All in a happy bureaucratic day. No. A colossal snap. A climbing-over-the-glass-partition snap. A grab-the-chained-pen-as-a-knife snap. A smash-the-wastebasket snap. A chase-around-the-office snap. A punch-in-the-face-of-a-bystander-clerk snap. A hide-in-the-locked-washroom-and-wait-for-police snap. More seriously, a wake-up-the-office-manager snap.

No. Allen couldn't cause another one of those scenes. The previous petitioner had the same smile on his face as this guy before he screamed like a wounded animal and began to climb over the counter, frothing at the mouth. Allen thought it best to end the interrogation. He remembered the district manager's warning. The manager explained slowly, if somewhat irritably, that although it was their job to make sure that Ontario was never ruled by the sin of alcohol, they must accept the fact that Ontario now had many citizens who were not teetotalling Protestants. (He omitted his speeches about Catholics and the federal immigration policy, luckily.) Even though they disapproved of these new liberal liquor laws, they must obey them. It was sufficient to indicate moral disapproval when acquiescing to certain lawful requests.

Allen casually took a form from a drawer in front of him. He avoided Tom's eyes as he asked a series of questions: date, time, place of event, number of guests, approximate alcohol consumption. On the line, "Type of Occasion," Allen filled in "Pre-Wedding Party" without looking up. Allen passed the completed form to Tom for his signature, adding that he should press hard enough for the carbon copy. Allen then signed the form himself, banged the paper with a metal stamp with the Ontario coat of arms and gave the original copy to Tom. Allen requested the fee and Tom handed over a damp twenty-dollar bill with a white and palsied hand. Allen recoiled slightly when he touched the damp bill. He looked at Tom and then at the bill and then at Tom again.

He pushed the bill to the side of the counter and said, "Thank you. Have a good evening." He had forgotten to ask for proof of age or write "paid" on the form. As Tom walked from the room, Allen noticed that his pants and shirt were clinging to him like wet, wrinkled wallpaper. Allen realized that his own shirt was damp with sweat.

Tom scarcely remembered his drive back to Hamilton. He showered, changed his clothes (leaving his sweat-soaked clothes on the bedroom floor for his mother to deal with), loaded the car with the snack food, and headed for Mount Hope. He was in the parking lot outside the social club at 6:50. *Luckily*, he thought as he struggled to open the door with his left foot while balancing the snacks on his outstretched arms, *nobody ever shows up on time.* After wedging the door open about six inches with his foot, he got his right elbow on the inside of the door and did a clever pivot-push to get inside.

This maneuver spun three bags of potato chips onto the floor, but he could get them later. Mrs. Metcalf stepped out from the kitchen. There were no preliminaries.

"Did you get the license?"

"Yes, I did!" He said much more sharply than he had intended. Tom was wearing down.

Mrs. Metcalf did an immediate about-face and marched back into the kitchen. She didn't ask him to show the license. She respected truculence. If Tom learned from today's experiences that a little belligerence and the hint of irrational behaviour can intimidate people, it would be a good lesson. Tom had become too unbalanced, however, to rationally analyze his behaviour and the response of other people. He thumped the snacks down on the nearest table as his arms involuntarily gave way. He moved them up and down several times to restore circulation, then walked over to retrieve the fallen bags. As he turned to walk back to the table, he noticed for the first time a man sitting at a table to his right. The man had his hands knit together and his elbows rested on the edge of the table. His back was very straight and he was seated on the forward part of the chair. His legs formed a perfect ninety-degree angle from hip to knee to ankle. He had a dark suit, white shirt, and very wide tie. Ties were very narrow these days. The man looked as if he had just buried a close family friend and had gone directly to this hall for the funeral reception. Tom thought he should help the man, who was about fifty, to his proper destination.

"Hello. You know I'm just getting ready for a party here."

". . . Peter Evans."

Tom heard a strange sing-song cadence of words strung together with about every third or fourth syllable highly stressed. He didn't understand a word until the end of the sentence when he deciphered the name "Peter Evans."

"Pardon?"

The man spoke louder. ". . . an old . . . neighbour of Peter Evans?"

"Pardon?"

Almost shouting this time but not losing his sing-song cadence, the man said, "I'm an old family friend and neighbour of Peter Evans."

"Oh! Oh!" Tom remembered. "Are you from Wales?"

". . . am."

"Pardon?"

"I actually am," the man said louder once again.

"Oh. Oh. Well." Tom couldn't keep talking to this man. He would go crazy.

"You see the party won't start for a while and I have some things to do."

"Good."

Tom understood that word but what did he mean? The man suddenly sprang out of his chair and extended his hand.

". . . Gan."

"Pardon?"

"Dai Morgan," he said louder, keeping a solid grip on Tom's hand. Tom shook his hand up and down to indicate a pattern before breaking contact. But instead of letting go, the man held tighter.

Holding Tom firmly by hand and making eye contact like the Ancient Mariner, Mr. Morgan said, "I will help you."

Tom understood that, and when he nodded at Mr. Morgan to indicate that he had, Mr. Morgan released his hand. Tom said they must put bowls of peanuts, chips, and pretzels on the tables. Mr. Morgan nodded his full approval. Tom walked to the kitchen door with Mr. Morgan at his elbow. Tom knocked. Mrs. Metcalf, frowning, opened the door. Tom asked if he could have bowls for snacks. Mrs. Metcalf nodded yes while examining Mr. Morgan, who was also nodding. As a matter of fact, Tom noticed that Mr. Morgan had been nodding constantly since he had said he would help. Mrs. Metcalf retrieved about twenty bowls, all containing small chips or cracks.

"These will do," she said.

Mr. Morgan nodded.

Tom carried the bowls to the food table. He ripped open a package of pretzels and dumped them into a bowl. He had to nudge Mr. Morgan slightly to get room to pour. Mr. Morgan nodded as the pretzels filled the bowl.

Tom suggested that Mr. Morgan start filling bowls with potato chips and pointed to the bags of chips and bowls to suggest the task. Mr. Morgan nodded but didn't move. He had returned to his elbow-to-elbow position beside Tom. Tom didn't know what to do. He didn't want to ask a man his father's age to do the job again. He thought that if he continued doing the job, Mr. Morgan would begin work himself. But he didn't.

A bizarre ritual began. Tom opened the packages. He poured peanuts, chips, or pretzels into a bowl. He nudged Mr. Morgan back six inches to move the bowl. Mr. Morgan then moved back again six inches. They were two men joined at hip and elbow who parted every two or three minutes like a gate opening and closing at a subway station. All the while, Mr. Morgan sang loudly into Tom's ear. At first Tom said "Pardon?" but that just meant the singer sang louder into his ear. Tom realized it was better just to nod, sometimes slightly, sometimes vigorously. Every now and again, he picked out words: "hay," "farm," "hilly," "slope," "ducks." There was a pattern. It had something to do with Mr. Morgan's and Mr. Evans' lives in Wales. Obviously, they both came from farms. What Tom couldn't comprehend were the other words strung together that were obviously hard-won words of wisdom.

If Tom didn't get the bowls filled quickly, he knew Mr. Morgan would begin sharing his adventures in Canada. He seemed to be becoming more emotional. At one point when Tom was simply holding a bowl, Mr. Morgan gripped his forearm as if the fierce restraint would clarify his words. Tom was reaching another breaking point. Luckily, there were three packages of peanuts left and no bowls. He nudged Mr. Morgan aside as he filled the last bowl and, hoping to catch the Welshman unaware, he dashed for the kitchen door almost screaming.

"More bowls! More bowls."

When Mrs. Metcalf saw Tom's face, she leapt to get the bowls. When she handed them over, she saw Mr. Morgan nodding at the table. This time, Tom circled the table and kept the table between them.

He shouted to Mr. Morgan, "Please put the bowls out!" pointing to the bowls and tables three or four times like a wind-up toy gone berserk.

Mr. Morgan understood. He took one bowl at a time to each table. Then he looked as if he might carry two bowls at once, but his forehead clouded as if a storm was approaching. He continued his untroubled way with one bowl.

It was now 7:20 p.m. and Tom was sweating again. Finally, at 7:22 p.m. (every painful second hung like a reluctant drop at the end of an eavestrough), three guests came bursting into the room together. Tom could have cried with happiness. He didn't know these three young men, but he would have held them there against their wills if they were in the wrong place and tried to get out.

"Hi! Hi! Hi! I'm Tom. Roy's stag. Oh good. Good. Good . . . Just sit down. Beer? Beer?"

The guests looked at Tom. He had picked up that strange verbal cadence that had been shouted into his ear for an eternity. Then he stopped and began again slowly. Sanity returned. He spoke without singing. He was understood. He had come back from the edge. Yes, they would have beers. Oh wonderful. Things are returning to normal. He went to the bar. He would serve drinks until Jim Lock showed up. He slammed and locked the door to the bar in case Dai Morgan tried to re-attach himself at elbow and hip. For the first few minutes, it felt odd turning and moving without another body attached and without pulsating declamations in his ear. He opened and served the first beers. He had broken the law, he knew.

Bartenders couldn't accept money, only tickets. Luckily Mrs. Metcalf hadn't seen the incident. He imagined the flashing lights of an Ontario Provincial Police cruiser pulling up at the front door, being handcuffed, and being carried out between two seven-foot officers without his feet touching the ground. He quickly talked to one of the three new arrivals into setting up a table and selling beer and alcohol tickets. The volunteer looked very concerned for Tom. Was his appearance that bad, he wondered?

The next two through the door were Jim Lock and Rob Duncan. The bartender and the porno film man were here. Tom had no interest in porn. In fact, he was disgusted by it. Nevertheless, the tradition, for some reason, persisted. And the owners of porn films were always anxious to show them. Let the party begin. Tom poured himself a beer and then relinquished the job. Jim was eager to get behind the bar; he actually had a sense of self-importance. *Good,* thought Tom, *a willing slave, chained to his oar and happy in his work.* Sometimes a rotten job has novelty for the first week, or day, or hour. For most people, their job is fine for the first ten years; it's the last twenty-five that are hell. Tom opened the door to the bar holding his beer in his right hand. He stayed low, using the ticket seller as a shield. Dai Morgan had only one more bowl to deliver. Then he would be scanning the room for his conjoined twin. Tom couldn't take any more of that. He stayed low to the ground and scuttled towards the washroom. He thought about heading to the women's washroom since there would be only men here tonight, but if Mrs. Metcalf came in, the Ontario Provincial Police really would drag him away. No, he would hide in a cubicle while he sorted out his next steps. He undid his belt and unzipped his fly with his left hand while holding the beer at eye level. He carefully wiggled his pants and underwear down to his ankles and sat on the toilet. Not a drop of beer spilled. He began to drink slowly as he sorted out his jobs: 1. Avoid Dai Morgan, 2. Check on things in the kitchen with

Mrs. Metcalf, 3. Relieve the ticket seller before he becomes pissed off, 4. Avoid Dai Morgan.

As the beer began to fill the cavities in his body and he became more drenched in sweat, Tom began to feel an overwhelming sense of lassitude. He almost dozed off sitting upright with a beer in his hand. His head had dropped slowly to his chest, but snapped right back up again like a hand touching a hot stove. That quick snap of his neck caused a sharp pain at the base of his skull and along the ridges that run vertically from shoulders to ears. The pain goaded Tom to get back to work. He spilled the rest of the beer on his pants and placed the empty glass between his toes. He pulled up his shorts and pants, retrieved the glass, and opened the cubicle. As he washed his hands, he studied the face in the mirror. He didn't look as young as he had yesterday. His eyes lacked sparkle, his skin looked red and blotchy, his hair was limp, and his mouth was a harsh straight line. Tom knew he needed sleep, maybe a month of sleep.

When Tom opened the washroom door, he was elated to see ten or twelve new participants. Things might go well after all. Another ten and the stag could be considered a success. It was now a few minutes to eight. He had been there for about an hour. He scanned the room for familiar faces. Suddenly, his heart leapt. There was Peter Evans, and lo and behold, attached to Mr. Evans' elbow and hip was Dai Morgan. The two men born and raised in Wales were nodding and shaking their heads in unison. Tom imagined musical chords dancing above their heads as they moved in some choreographed syncopation based on the vernal rituals of the Druids. He visualized their lips forming "sheep," "hay," "wool," "chickens."

Tom snapped his head and blinked his eyes several times when he realized he was moving his own head in time with the Welshmen. He must see Mrs. Metcalf. When he pushed the door to the kitchen open, he saw her with pencil in hand labouring over some document. Tom assumed it was the bill. She kept glancing at the food arranged on trays on the counter as if counting each slice of bread, each pickle, and each napkin. She had that strange archaic habit of licking the pencil lead before she made each entry. Tom wondered if there was a time when pencil lead had to be licked to work properly. He imagined hordes of little children in schoolyards sticking black tongues out at each other. Did good scholars have really black tongues? Did scholars get lead poisoning? No, that was gangsters. Tom realized again that he had to get a grip on himself. What did that mean? A grip was a small travel bag. Get a small travel bag on himself. Get control by putting himself in a small travel bag? That can't be right.

He was sweating heavily again. Mrs. Metcalf had stopped mid-task to stare at him. The pencil was frozen on her tongue like a tongue in winter frozen to an iron fence. That meant a tongue could be a sticker or a stickee. He shook his head again. Mrs. Metcalf shook her head.

Tom said, "Hello, Mrs. Metcalf. Any problems?" She shook her head very positively, lowering it at the same time so that she wouldn't have to look at his face. Now she saw his pants. As Tom hurriedly left the kitchen, he saw a woman whose nose was four inches from the paper with her left hand in a rigid fist and her right hand vigorously stabbing her tongue with a pencil. Maybe what he had was contagious.

He walked over to the ticket seller who was looking pissed off. His friends were busy telling stories at a table and he was left out. Tom thanked him profusely, told him to rip off two or three bar tickets for himself, and happily sat down in the vacated chair. Tom looked in the cashbox. Lots of dollar-bills, five-dollar bills, and ten-dollar bills. Thank God. The evening might even run a profit. He would wait until the evening was over to count all the money.

A sudden memory jolted Tom to his feet. The drying beer on his pants might bond with this chair. He imagined himself saying good-night to everyone with a chair stuck to his ass. Tom began to sell tickets with one foot on the floor and the other on the chair. That way he could take some weight off his legs, dry his underwear and pants, and yet still project the authority of a man in charge of taking the money. He wondered if monarchs ever stood with a foot on the throne. One foot on divinely-granted power and one foot on earth. Heaven and earth perfectly bonded, something man always sought. Of course, sometimes man had too much foot on the divine; sometimes too much on the profane. Didn't Lawrence Olivier as Richard III stand with one foot on the throne, his hunch-backed form thrusting forward towards the assembled lackeys? Didn't Lyndon Johnson have only one foot resting gently on the Camelot Throne of Kennedy? Or the Kennedy Throne of Camelot? Tom shook his head and blinked rapidly. This technique didn't seem to be bringing him back to earth any more. Perhaps if he took a cigarette and burned the inside of his wrists. Somebody did that in a novel or film once.

Two more guests had entered. Tom saw two five-dollar bills walking towards him with two two-dollar bills peeking over their shoulders. No worse than the playing cards in *Alice in Wonderland.* Would the bills talk? The men bought their tickets, staring at Tom as Mrs. Metcalf had stared at him. Then they hurried away talking rapidly and glancing back at him. Tom mused about oneself being mirrored in the eyes of others. He wondered about trying a pack of cigarettes.

At 8:15, Roy Evans pushed the door to the hall open. He was all smiles. Tom was speculating about cigarette burns bearing permanent scars. Roy did all the right things. He moved from group to group shaking hands, smiling, patting backs, rolling his eyes, shaking his head, laughing loudly. Tom realized that bridegrooms and politicians behave exactly the same way. He tried to avoid the analogy of patterned behaviour designed to legally screw people. He knew that Roy was basically a decent person basking in unusual limelight. It was a role that most people get to play only once or twice in their lives. Surprisingly enough, most people make good brides and grooms—gracious, effervescent, humble, self-confident.

They're aided by family and friends who want them to have this moment. The inexperienced look forward to their own brief moment in the sun; the experienced wish them well because they understand the immediate fall to oblivion. Roy shook Tom's hand lustily and thanked him with genuine feeling. Roy tried to look Tom straight in the eye to reinforce his manly and honest sentiments, but Tom's eyes couldn't hold a gaze. They flared up like a sudden blaze one instant and died like a snuffed candle the next. There was something frightening about those manic-depressive eyes and Roy turned away still vowing his thanks. He wondered if Tom had drunk too much. He called over another of his friends, introduced him to Tom, and asked him to take over the ticket table. He put his arms around Tom and he noticed as they shuffled forward that Tom had his legs splayed out. He also noticed that his shirt was wringing wet, and the muscles in his back jitterbugged with electrical pulsations. Perhaps he was ill. Roy said that Tom should meet his father since they'd both be important people on June 21. As Roy led him gently towards his father, however, Tom suddenly planted his splayed feet and the muscles in his back began to jump spasmodically. Tom had seen Dai Morgan look up and smile at him. He excused himself quickly, got out of Roy's grasp, spun like a running back, and made for the kitchen. Mrs. Metcalf might be all right after all.

With or without Tom's presence, the stag would evolve in its own organic way. The fruition would be dictated by a combination of evolutionary patterns and dominant personalities. The metamorphosis based on social interaction would produce an early and dull stag, or a late and boisterous one. There was no God of stags shaping the procedures and outcome. There was only random selection. This evening, the unpredictable evolutionary forces produced a successful social organism. By now, there were twenty-eight men in the hall, young and old. In one corner sat five members of the Canadian Legion playing cribbage; friends of Peter Evans. At the next table were some Dominion Glass boys playing euchre. There were always three or four men leaning on the bar talking among themselves or to Jim Lock. At several tables, groups of anywhere from two to five men sat talking with frequent bursts of loud laughter. The most boisterous table was the poker table. It had a strange mix of tipsy, intuitive players and serious betters. Roy Evans moved from group to group with increasing charm and ease, a giant step on the never-ending journey to manhood. Tom was sitting in the kitchen playing two-handed rummy with Mrs. Metcalf, who had decided to mother rather than bully him. Even that tough old manager of the social hall realized that Tom couldn't take any more of life's adversities. Tom had stopped looking at her mouth to see if her tongue was black and now watched the cards with little, pink, squinty eyes.

The Royal Canadian Legion cribbage table was going full blast. Obviously, this was a tradition. One of the group carried cards and a cribbage table wherever he went. Once four members showed up at an event, they found a table and started to play. Funerals were usually, but not always, excluded from this custom. Neighbourhood parties, fishing trips, bus trips, union meetings, protest marches, commemorative parades, all merged with cribbage games. The wives had learned to put up with this. All of them were past the stage where they thought a happy marriage depended upon husbands and wives doing things together. They had learned that a long marriage depended on doing few things together.

The poker table had attracted the biggest group with eight players and six onlookers presently, the numbers changing every half hour or so. This was a spontaneous grouping. That meant there was quite a mixture of poker games, skills, betting, bumping, and hundreds of other conventions. The present eight players included the following (the mix remained fairly constant throughout the evening): three very serious players who belonged to clubs and played for high stakes several times a year; two or three semi-serious players who knew the game but didn't play that often; two or three players who were either almost totally ignorant of the game or who were drunk. The serious players were happy to make a little money from the amateurs, but they were angered by their ignorance and their children's poker games (wild card games made them impatient). The semi-serious players were pleased to play a random game of chance without winning or losing too much. The ignorant and drunk players were dangerous and volatile. They misread their cards, betting wildly on weak hands and folding on strong hands. They tried to introduce games that couldn't work. They asked to join the game and leave the game at random. All in all, it was a devil's punchbowl of a game and getting worse every minute as beer consumption increased.

The spectators magnified the problem. They were men with nothing to do but watch. As they drank more, they became more and more intrusive. They wanted to see players' cards. Sometimes they wanted to see three different players' cards, actually walking around the table to do this. The amateurs gladly showed the spectators their hands, but the serious players held their cards very close to their chests and glowered. Sometimes the spectators even offered advice during the game. Being told by the serious players to shut up only shut them up for a hand or two. The spectators also came and went rapidly, sometimes making gratuitous comments as they did so.

It should have been the normal boisterous, chaotic, basically good-natured poker game. Everyone understands the difference between playing pick-up basketball and basketball with referees. Everyone makes allowances for the difference between recreational and competitive sport. This was supposed to be a recreational poker game at small stakes. Unfortunately, by eleven o'clock, Paul Henshaw, a serious player, had lost more money than he wanted in the chaotic game. His knowledge and skill were offset by the illogical pattern of play. He had also had about three more beers than he normally drank. Meanwhile, the drunken Ivan Bucci was winning hand after hand by a combination of unusual luck and preposterous bluffing. To make matters worse, Ivan was spilling beer on the cards, dropping them on the floor through drunken fingers, flashing cards to spectators with elaborate facial expressions, and making loud wolf calls when he won, pointing triumphantly at the losers. In other words, beer had made Ivan an obnoxious, loud-mouthed asshole. Even the spectators, obnoxious as they were from time to time, began to realize that Ivan was going too far. They could read the growing anger in other players. They quietly cautioned Ivan to calm down, slow down, and stop it. He was beyond advice.

Finally, the dam burst. There were three players left in a seven-card draw poker game. The players had two cards down, had received four cards up, and were now going to bet on a final down card. The betting and bumping had been a little reckless. Most players had stayed in for at least five or six cards. The result was a very large pot. The bet was at Ivan because he had two kings showing. Paul had two jacks showing and the third player had three hearts showing. Ivan bet one dollar on his pair. Paul bumped another dollar. The third player thought for a while and then folded. Ivan laughed, showed his down cards to the spectators behind him, and bumped Paul another dollar. Paul responded with the final bump of one dollar. The dealer dealt the final cards down, first to Ivan, then to Paul.

Ivan yelled, "Goddam it!" and with a drunken sweep of his hand, reached across the table and turned over Paul's card, laughing as he did so. Paul exploded. Screaming, he smashed his fist down on Ivan's hand, then grabbed his beer and threw it in Ivan's face. Like a grenade going off, the table exploded. Beer glasses, ashtrays, cigarettes, cigars, and cards flew everywhere. One player moved his chair back so quickly, he fell straight back over it. Another lost his balance sliding sideways out of his chair and slid to the floor. Paul had started around the table but two players grabbed him in time. Ivan had put his injured hand in the opposite armpit and was gazing around rather placidly wondering why his hand hurt and why people and objects were flying all around. Players and spectators were making soothing sounds and urging peace and restraint. Paul's temper subsided as quickly as it had exploded. He was immediately regretful and sat down again with his chin on his chest. Ivan continued to gaze serenely with his right hand in his left armpit. With a series of quick consensual statements, the players awarded the last pot to Paul and started to pick objects up. Players put their money in their wallets, indicating that the game was over. The onlookers who had rushed to the scene drifted away again. Players moved to the bar to get a drink and to proclaim non-involvement. The poker table was left with Paul, Ivan, and two other players slowly and silently sipping their beers.

Finally, Paul muttered, "Sorry."

Ivan replied, "My fault."

One of the players offered his opinion of the Tiger Cats. Hesitant conversation began and Ivan fell asleep with his injured hand in his armpit. Everyone left his money on the table in front of him.

When Mrs. Metcalf heard the noise of the poker table explosion, she ran to the kitchen door and understood immediately what had happened. *So common at stags*, she thought to herself. She shook her head again over the everlasting stupidity of men. The phrase, "Why don't men ever grow up?" and a hundred other similar phrases moved to the unloading ramp of her brain, ready for verbal expression. If her husband had been there, he would have received this shipment of female wisdom dumped right into his ear. She filled her lungs for her peroration, but poor Tom looked so beaten, she let the air whistle gently through her teeth. Female wisdom would be withheld until she got home. She stalwartly walked over to Tom and suggested that this would be a good time to serve the food. Tom nodded in agreement, a little spark of animation returning to his eyes. His brain turned over enough to realize that serving food meant the final stages of the stag were approaching. Thank God, his brain exulted, without Tom's conscious verbalization.

If Tom's brain had been on a hospital scanner, it would have been a flat line with a feeble burp every two or three seconds. Tom got up from the table slowly. His shirt was glued to his back by sweat. His sweat- and beer-covered pants were stuck to his ass and crotch. His clothing had become a malevolent opponent drawing sick humour to, rather than away from, his body. The chair he had been sitting in did not stick to his pants; the vinyl simply made a sound like a wet bathing suit being peeled off. Tom shook his body several times, like a dog shaking off water, to free it from the clothing. As the clothing broke away, Tom felt air on his body for the first time in several hours, and he shivered violently. He brushed his sweat-stiffened hair away from his forehead. His shirt had white sweat marks running in concentric circles with his armpits as the epicentres. The fabric of his pants was gathered in a washboard design around his crotch and patterns ran from his fly like high water marks in spring run-offs. Tom no longer knew or cared what he looked like. He must muster his last reserves of strength to finish his job.

"Okay. Okay. OKAY. Gentleman! We have a lunch for you. But before the food, a few words."

About half the gentlemen stopped talking and arguing. Five or six headed for the washroom.

"Thank you for coming tonight. I know Roy really appreciates it. Roy and I are old friends so there are lots of things I could tell you about him, but since his father is here, I better not."

The mandatory laughter filled the room.

"I'll just say his bride will be in for some surprises!"

More mandatory laughter erupted.

Tom realized that more men were heading for the washroom and only the men at the two immediate tables were listening.

"But seriously, Roy is a great person and a great friend. I'm sure he would like to say a few words."

Tom waved feebly to Roy and folded heavily into a chair.

"Thank you all for coming tonight; I really appreciate it. I know you don't want a speech when food is coming so I'll just say how much I appreciate Tom running this stag, and how much I appreciate my father's friends being here. I know some of you missed a baseball game and I appreciate it. Thank you all again."

Roy could have gone on appreciating things, but nobody was listening, not even his father and certainly not Tom, who was almost comatose. The awkwardness of ending the speeches was saved by Mrs. Metcalf who pushed open the kitchen door with the edge of a huge tray loaded with sandwiches. Roy stepped aside and yelled, "Food!" The ceremony appeared seamless. Now things could wind down to a happy desultory ending, with each person deciding how much to eat, how much more to drink, and when to leave.

Men streamed back from the washroom to gather at the bar and the food table. Right up at the rail were Paul Henshaw and Ivan Bucci. Paul had his arm around Ivan as they talked about union problems at Stelco. Dai Morgan had finally deserted Peter Evans to load up on food. Peter was trying to figure out a place to sit where Dai couldn't find him. Roy stepped behind the bar to help Jim and allow him to take a leak and then get some food. Jim wanted to hurry back in case something else interesting happened between Paul Henshaw and Ivan Bucci. Tom had gone back to the kitchen, helping Mrs. Metcalf set out cups and saucers for coffee. He looked like a medicated patient at a psychiatric hospital, happily working in a flower garden on the grounds. Mrs. Metcalf was the orderly; half-soothing, half-vigilant, the air heavy with unpredictability.

After all the cups and saucers had been put out, Tom walked slowly to the bar and waved to Roy. He curled and uncurled his index finger in the universal signal to come. As he held his finger extended, curling and uncurling, Tom seemed to have become hypnotized by his own finger. His eyes were focused on the finger and nothing else. His head tilted slightly left then slightly right as his eyes focused on the fixed point. His hand was extended and his finger moved without volition. When Roy came up, he had to wrap his hand around Tom's finger to break the spell. He thought Tom was drunk.

Shaken from the spell, Tom mumbled, "You'll have to clean up." He thrusted handfuls of bills at Roy, dredged up from various pockets, some of the bills quite damp. Roy accepted the bills silently. Tom turned his back and walked towards the door with that splayed-toe walk he had developed that day. Roy thought he looked like an animated bag of dirty laundry moving towards the next scene in a film. There he would join a box of detergent with legs, and a washer with legs, and the dirty clothes would be sparkling in seconds. Now Roy was anxious for the evening to end.

Tom got to his car and drove home safely. He was on automatic. He slept twenty-two of the next twenty-four hours. He missed his next shift at Stelco. It took a full ten days for his total humanity to return. He had been to the edge. One foot had hit a soft spot and started sliding down. Luckily, without knowing it, Mrs. Metcalf had stopped the full, rolly-polly, wide-eyed, screaming descent to the bottom. Her calm authority had stopped the avalanche. Circumstances had forced Tom to attempt what no person should. He had done battle with a bureaucracy and run a social event on the same day. Any encounter with a bureaucracy leaves one's nerves howling, immune system stopped, auditory and tactile senses cross-wired, and digestive and respiratory system dysfunctional. Only a three-day rest can bring some recovery. But Tom had gone directly from one nerve factory to another. For the next ten years, Tom would have a gentle eye tick whenever he heard the words Liquor Control Board of Ontario or Stag.

Chapter Twenty-Four

Ontario 1964

For Alina, May was the happiest and unhappiest time of her life. She and Roy had had wonderful graduation ceremonies at McMaster. Roy's had been in the old drill hall and Alina and her classmates had theirs in the Alumni Memorial Hall, known colloquially as the buttery. She and her classmates looked wonderful in their nurses' uniforms. It was a very intimate affair because there were only seven graduates. Alina's professors were beaming. Roy was there, being very circumspect with his future-in-laws. Betta, Mike, Ella, and David were also there. Betta was very quiet. Mike and David were polite but cold to Roy. Ella was warm and cordial as usual. It was ironic that the ceremony was upstairs in the buttery. Downstairs was the cafeteria where Roy wasted hours playing cards. Old life; new life.

Alina was very happy choosing her wedding dress. She got the bridesmaids together to choose their dresses. The four of them were full of laughter and giggles. One of her nursing bridesmaids was also getting married. She and Roy drove around taking care of the myriad of details. Betta supplied extra wedding money from her secret cache.

Saturday, June 21, 1964, was a beautiful day. All sun and blue skies, Alina was driven to the church by David. When she stepped out of the car, she had the transcendent beauty that brides have. She had chosen a beautiful wedding gown. Her bridesmaids joined her, and they, too, looked lustrous in their gowns. The nervous groom, as all grooms are, was sitting with his groomsmen in the minister's office. He was a little uncomfortable with his former minister from Laidlaw United Church. Perhaps the minister thought he could win him back. Perhaps he saw himself performing a humanitarian and kind act. He probably didn't need the honorarium.

True to his word, Mike escorted Alina up the aisle. He had a forced smile—but it was a smile. There were no glitches in the ceremony. Most guests thought it was unusually short. Roy speculated later that the minister showed his disapproval of him by cutting down the ritual. Perhaps the minister thought, in a very unchristian way, give me my money and I'm out of here. The ceremony was simple. It was a typical dull-as-dishwater Protestant event.

If Alina had been married at the Ukrainian Orthodox Cathedral of St. Vladimir on Barton Street, she would have had the usual magnificent pageant. The priest would have had strikingly ornate robes. As the ceremony proceeded, full of ritual and liturgy, the guests could have looked up at the striking ceiling with sunlight pouring in. The church was a beautiful example of art and architecture to serve God. At St. Vladimir's, the bride and groom would have walked around the table and had crowns held above their heads. There would have been a Svashky—a woman's chair. The ritual was long and arduous. Getting married this way really meant you were married. The Baptists weren't into any of that.

After the ceremony and the signing of the marriage document, Alina and Roy came out of the church to confetti and well-wishes. The wedding photographer took all the usual photos. After the photo of the bride, bridesmaids, groom, and groomsmen, the parents were asked to pose with the wedding couple. There they were framed by the arch of the McMaster Baptist Chapel.

The parents of the bridal couple were still young, but they had seen and experienced most of the turbulence of the twentieth century. When Mike was eight years old, he had gone to see Emperor Franz Joseph. The spectacular and chaotic Austro-Hungarian Empire was a few years from its demise. Perhaps it showed that a nation state that had so many ethnic groups could never function. When he was twelve, Mike saw the horror of war. Soldiers weren't clothed in glory: their dead bodies were clothed in blood and mud. Alice had enjoyed the prosperous twenties in Moose Jaw. There was confidence that things would always get better. Nothing could stop this economic improvement. When Alice was in Wales, her brother Henry described the Dust Bowl in Southern Saskatchewan and the unemployed in bread lines. In Galicia, Betta saw all the horrors of the Holodomor. The wholesale extermination of seven or eight million Ukrainians was hard to grasp. World War II seemed inevitable in the aftermath of World War I and the Depression. The idea of a Master Race could fuel the fires of bigotry. Peter joined the Royal Air Force when the concept of a just war was prevalent. The Democracies' victory in 1945 seemed an obvious victory of good over evil. Then all the details of the Holocaust became known and individuals and countries had to accept their moral responsibility. World War II caused fifty million deaths and fifty million refugees. Europe, east and west, had to rebuild from rubble. Canada was spared all that. As in World War I, Canada had brave warriors who were killed in many countries far away. Once again, Canada opened its doors to refugees and immigrants.

As Alina and Roy grew up, there was a new conflict—the battle between East and West, Communism and Democracy. As adolescents, they were drilled in school about what to do when the Russian atomic bombs were dropped. Their fear was justified by the two atomic bombs that had been dropped on Japan. It was the Cold War—the age of fear, the age of total annihilation. The Cuban Missile Crisis meant they were going to die. The assassination of President Kennedy again showed man's infinite attraction to violence.

History moves from conflict to conflict. Alina and Roy would witness many, many more. Their marriage itself was an example of the never-ending tension between ethnic, racial, and religious purity, and borderless assimilation.

CPSIA information can be obtained
at www.ICGtesting.com
Printed in the USA
BVHW042014131122
651869BV00006B/30

9 781039 138803